Thank you Laura, for your love, su

Thank you to the people that helped, suppor
writing and production of this book. Your patience, understanding and
talents are amazing. You know who you are.

This book is dedicated to my Mum, and all the people I have lost along
the way. You are always in my thoughts.

Colossians 3:6

Put to death, therefore, whatever belongs to your earthly nature: sexual immorality, impurity, lust, evil desires and greed, which is idolatry.

Because of these the wrath of God is coming.

Prologue

The baby's cries filled the air as the innocent new-born child was swaddled and dumped into its mother's arms. The pain that the mother felt only a minute before had subsided, and she was now filled with a huge wave of love, joy and relief. This labour had been much harder than the previous one, five years before. It had started sixteen hours ago, and she had been having painful contractions for at least 12 hours. The pain that the mother had gone through was, at times, unbearable and she had passed out three times. The doctors had taken control and managed her through it until, eventually, the baby was pulled from her.

It had been extremely hot in the last few weeks and showed no sign of relenting. The air-conditioning was broken, and so three fans in various corners of the maternity room, buzzed and drifted from left to right; but they were only really blowing warm air around. The mothers sweat drenched her, hair stuck to her face and forehead as she looked on at her newest addition.

Screams of pain from other laboured mothers, and the cries of new-born babies, could be heard from other busy maternity rooms nearby. All of the windows were wide open, and the gentle hum of traffic and horns could just be heard from the streets below.

An expectant and excited man, who was now a father for a second time, waited just a short way away from the maternity room with his own mother and father. They were also with a young girl of five years old - the new-born's sister - who was sound asleep on her father's lap. He had been removed from the maternity room the last time the mother had passed out, when the medical staff knew there were serious complications. But he had since been informed that the complications were now resolved, and it was just a matter of time. As he sat, awaiting his new child, the sweat coated his back and he was desperate to get his wife and family home to the air conditioning, cold water and clean, cool beds. Soon after, the man was ushered into the maternity room, where he met his son for the first time. The son he had always dreamed of. His family was now complete.

Along the corridor, towards the exit and out of sight, was another man. A man with no family requiring his love and support. A man with dark intent. He had also been waiting in the hospital for the last sixteen hours. The sweat clung to him and he was tired, thirsty and hungry, but he was also focused, and nothing would deter him from his orders.

3

For he was also expectantly waiting the birth of the same child. But not because of love and affection, nor for the contentment of completing a family. His orders were to make the necessary contact with the new-born's mother. The mother, who with a heavy heart knew that, at some point, he would be arriving.

The man intently watched the father excitedly hurry into the maternity room and so he knew it was time. From his pocket he removed a small black box and opened it to reveal a tiny scroll. On one side a number in tiny script was printed '294574'. He turned the scroll over and wrote the date in black pen, carefully rolled it up and slid it back into the box.

Chapter 1

09:54am, 17ᵗʰ August 2016

It was a bright, clear day over Evanston. The sky was still hazy from the early mist, but the sun was slowly burning it away, and there was a soft, warm breeze blowing in from Lake Michigan. The smell of freshly cut grass and the sound of hiss-hissing from sprinkler systems filled the air. People had started to go about their business and the odd person or vehicle drifted past Tom and Jenna's large Georgian style house, set back amidst a well-groomed garden in the pretty and manicured, Sheridan Place.

Tom was finishing his first coffee of the day in the large, modern open plan kitchen. On TV in the background Fox had switched to local news. He wasn't paying much attention to the newsreader informing viewers that a light aircraft had made an emergency landing in a farmers' field over in Kendall. No one was hurt apparently. Not that Tom was worried either way.

He didn't take much notice of anything other than work these days. His mind was always racing with priorities, deadlines and too many other things to do. And, of course, there were the 'strange' happenings.

Tom had hated Evanston at first. It was a safe, high class and beautiful place but he just hated it. The move was purely business and it was basically too good an offer to refuse. His company had offered him the new position 3 months ago to the day and when he had first read the contract, he thought he was dreaming. That was the first time he realised how much his company thought of him. No one had told him before. But that was the way it was. You did your job to a high standard, were reliable, worked hard and got results. You didn't expect praise or a pat on the back because praise or a pat on the back never came, and everyone knew it.

The organisations philosophy was that they paid well. Very well. And that was reward enough. If you wanted the money, then you knew the score. Make money and tow the line. If you didn't like the hard work and long hours, then get out. There will be plenty of other talented and hungry people happy to do it. And one thing you certainly didn't do was rock the boat. Ever.

Tom had seen some bad stuff down the years. Illegal business practices which had been cleverly covered up using financial loopholes and business law knowledge. He'd also witnessed some very immoral behaviour towards clients and other employees. Total bully boy tactics. He had seen people treated so badly he wanted to get up and walk away. But he stayed put, kept his head down and delivered the results the organisation wanted. And eventually he got his reward.

A contract with basic salary of $350k, with potential bonus of $75k depending on investment success and company share value which, up to now, had been achieved easily. Some major corporate mergers by invested companies and some solid trading had seen to that.

A company car, brand new Mercedes S Class. Membership to Evanston Golf club, membership to an exclusive spa resort. Full medical and dental care plus some other perks including discounts from some of the major stores.

His value to be company had then been suddenly clear to him. If they could afford to employ him under that contract, then his hard work must be making them 'A god damn king's ransom' as Tom's father would call it.

Tom had known he would hate Evanston. His house was a beautiful property worth around $1m in a very desirable location close to the shores of the lake, and a short 12 miles commute to the new company downtown Chicago HQ. It was the corporate, capitalist American dream to many, but to Tom it was a fake, soul-less, hypocritical stage set. The huge, luxurious pretty houses and manicured gardens simply hiding people's problems. Those flower-strewn, wooden porches with beautifully adorned front doors hid adultery, troubled marriages, financial troubles, alcoholism and recreational drug use.

The 'American Nightmare' painted over by a rose-tinted view of the good ol' US of A. Tom knew people had these problems everywhere but he hated the way everyone here acted so perfectly and pretended they lived in a fantasy world.

Downtown Chicago was ok though. They had spent quite a lot of time there at first. They had found some good restaurants and bars, but they soon got boring. Downtown was the most genuine place around, and he did actually like the true Chicagoans. They were honest, tough and brash. But they weren't New Yorkers. They were different. Tom and Jenna soon stopped going there as often.

Plus, at the start of the transfer things were pretty smooth with work. They let people get settled in and then all of a sudden it was made clear that anyone working less than 50 - 60 hours per week was seen as 'not committed'. Word went around that the organisation was watching. Closely.

They had invested a huge amount of money into the new HQ and moving employee's, so Tom appreciated they had a right to monitor them. But things had got a little 'Big Brother' and now the employees were falling over themselves to work all the hours god sent just to appear 'committed'. Tom included. So, by the time he had worked 50 - 60 hours a week he neither had the time nor the energy to go out and socialise. This suited Jenna who had become a regular 'Desperate Housewife' but for Tom, he still had a little pang for that bachelor life he had in New York City.

Tom had been born to a modest but comfortable home in Montclair, New Jersey. His parents were native New Yorkers who had moved out of the city when his father's successful haulage business expanded. He enjoyed a typical New Jersey childhood, up's and down's but mostly good memories. He was a popular kid, stayed out of trouble, well, for the most part. He had his moments, but it was all teenage pranks and nothing that the FBI would be interested in.

He competed to a high standard in College athletics, 400 and 800 metres were his events. He still had the medals and trophies tucked away somewhere. He was also a very decent basketball player and, like most, dreamed of the NBA but as he got a little older the realisation dawned that he was way, way off the required level. He remembers back as a 17-year-old thinking he would make it. Now when he looked at the huge, power-house athletes playing pro in the modern NBA today he knew he never had a chance.

Just as he left high school his father's haulage business was doing so well, he was offered a deal to sell up as part of a merger into a huge multi-national haulage company. After short deliberation with family and his financial advisor his father sold.

Tom's father had worked so hard all his life he deserved it. With the money from the sale his family were set up for life. His parents purchased a property in Franklin Lakes which was beautiful, and it was Tom's first taste of living a life in and around the high society.
His father felt guilty at first about moving out of the neighbourhood in Montclair. And it took Tom's mum a while to make his dad realise he deserved it, and this was what they had been working towards. All those hours, hard graft, problems and money invested. This was the ambition achieved. His father had said he never really had any ambition except to

make life as comfortable for his family as possible. Then the penny dropped. He had done exactly that, so why not now enjoy it.

His dad was a modest man. He wasn't a New Jersey socialite. But eventually he became more comfortable with his new status and begun to move in different circles; the golf club, the Masons, the health spa, the shooting club and, one of his favourite places, the yacht club over at Avalon. After a while he became good friends with some very well off and powerful people.

It was such a shame that his father wasn't around long enough to really enjoy it. Almost three years to the day after the business was sold, Tom had begged his dad to take him to a Yankee's game. But his father had got into sailing in a big way. It had become his obsession and he didn't want to miss the charity Regatta he had been invited to at Lake Carnegie on the same day. All his friends would be there, and he had been so excited leading up to it. But that was the fateful day that his father was killed in the boating accident. Tom always found it hard to believe he was gone, and he struggled to cope. But he had a lot of support from friends and family and was almost shielded from the major grief it caused within his close and extended family. Eventually, time healed, and he had no choice but to accept it and move on with his life.

Later in life, Tom had sailed through college and eventually attended Princeton where he studied business law and Economics. He got his passion for this field from his father who had regularly taken him to his office. When he was younger he sat in trucks and played in the office. But as he got older his father started to show him the more serious side to the business, including the finances.

He graduated from Princeton with top marks and Tom never forgot one of the professors, Alan Carlisle, who took him under his wing and spent so much time with him through College, just to make sure he kept out of trouble and stayed focussed. Professor Carlisle became almost obsessed with ensuring Tom got the grades he needed and, as Tom could recall, became the father figure he lacked during these years. Tom recalled some problems he had with two kids who bullied him. It went on for a few months and almost became a ritual for them. Tom couldn't go to his dad as he wasn't around but one day Mr Carlisle had asked him if he was alright and Tom had opened up to him and told him everything. Mr Carlisle told him "I will deal with it". Tom, nor anybody else for that matter, saw those two kids again, and nobody ever bullied Tom again.

Eventually, through a connection of Professor Carlisle, Tom moved to Manhattan and got a job at a private investment bank in Hanover Street, near Wall Street. Tom soon realised that he was very good at his job and the organisation needed people like him. He was earning good money almost immediately and had a dream life for a bachelor.

He had everything. He was part of the fabric of Manhattans young social scene and nothing was beyond him. He had a swanky little apartment, a Porsche Carrera. Everything he wanted. And he loved his life. He frequented the best bars, clubs and restaurants either with friends or with company clients. Regular corporate tickets to Yankees, Knicks and Rangers games and the company offered employees the opportunity to take short breaks at luxury cabins upstate in Catskills.

Born into New Jersey and adopted by New York City he felt part of something special. Something real and organic.

After a few flings and one long term relationships he eventually met Jenna, fell in love and this one lasted. His life changed but Manhattan still offered successful professional couples like them all they wanted. Exclusive bars, high-end restaurants. The champagnes, fine wines, best seafood and steaks in town. It was wonderful. And the uptown accommodation was perfect. They moved into an exclusive Upper East Side apartment overlooking Park Avenue. Life was good.

Jenna was a tough NYC girl who had pulled him into line. She had tamed him she always said Tom couldn't deny it. She had lived in New York City all her life. Her mother was a successful artist and her father was a Marine Biologist. She had a very colourful and well-travelled childhood and had plenty of great stories from travelling through Italy with her mum or being out at sea in a Caribbean storm with her father. The tales were endless. During high school her parents continued working but settled and worked more locally to the North-East.

After a short career as a tennis junior she had reluctantly followed her father into Marine Biology and worked with him on many projects along and around the US coast. After she had finished her education her father would take on work further afield and she spent time working on projects off the coast of Brazil and Scandinavia. She grew to love it.

They had first met at the gym they both went to. Tom had noticed her before they had spoken and had been immediately attracted to her. But it was Jenna that had first approached him and introduced herself. They spoke several times on a friendly basis and Tom could recall that he felt like he was the one being chased; which he loved. And eventually it was Jenna that pushed it to a more romantic level by asking Tom out on their first date.

They dated for a few months and had so much in common and both sets of their friends like each of them respectively. It blossomed very quickly and soon they were in a very deep, loving relationship. Early on Tom loved to get the keys to one of the company cabins at Catskills and take Jenna there for the weekend. One of the most memorable visits was the first time they went, after a Saturday night out clubbing with friends. Tom remembered he still had the keys from a previous weekend at his apartment, so he grabbed Jenna, took her outside and called one of the company chauffeurs. It arrived and he told the driver to take them to his apartment to get the key and then on to Catskills.

This wasn't really allowed but a $300 payment to the driver, who luckily Tom knew anyway, saw that it would be alright. They arrived at 4am, went in and Tom lit the fire. They made love until the sun came up and then sat, huddled in furs, watching the sun rise above the pines and mountains. It was the moment they truly fell in love.

They had a great relationship in those first few years. It was so exciting, and they lived the high life. Jenna had made some good money from her work, plus, her parents were pretty much set up and she had a decent allowance from them each month. Tom was also earning very good money so they could pretty much what they wanted. They travelled and had amazing holidays. They did so much together.

He knew he wanted to spend the rest of his life with her and she felt the same. So on a visit to Las Vegas one month they got very drunk and ended up outside a drive-thru church. They had kissed and both had the same idea. Tom proposed and without hesitation Jenna accepted. It wasn't the most romantic proposal, but it was the proposal which suited them. Direct and no messing.

The next day when they woke they were both shocked at what they had done. But after a long chat they decided that neither of them regretted it and it was exactly what they wanted. That day had been one of the best of Tom's life. His first day as a married man. He always remembered how proud he was. On their return they told their families who weren't so impressed at first, but Tom and Jenna promised they would do the traditional thing and arrange it all and get married 'properly'. Jenna did all the organising and it was a wonderful, glamourous and happy day for everyone.

After they had married 'properly' they continued to live their exciting life and Tom couldn't have been happier. He often pinched himself at how quick Jenna had come into his life and how much of a whirlwind it was. He often thought it was almost too perfect to be true.

But Jenna had grown quickly and lost the 'work hard, play hard' philosophy before Tom. She now chased that American dream, so he knew when the transfer to Chicago was offered she would demand he it. But he wanted to make his own mind up. He realised he would miss Manhattan so much he contemplated refusing. He was earning more than enough anyway and why he would he give up the great life they had. So he had not told Jenna about the job offer at first.

But there was another problem. Phil Carter. He was the boyfriend of Jenna's best friend, Carly. Tom thought he was a prick. But they had been forced together through Jenna and Carly's friendship, and he had had to endure many a double date with them. He was a typical rich boy, born into serious money. He was loved by all who were also born into money and in that scene. Phil was like a poster boy for the upper-class socialites of New York. He had worked at the same investment bank as Tom for a while. It had taken time for Jenna to realise that Tom worked with Carly's boyfriend and from that moment it was hell.
They spent many evenings and weekends together and Tom started to hate Phil so much he even feigned illness a few times to avoid dates.

Jenna had even talked him into taking Phil out one night for drinks with his own friends. Tom's friends were great guys, but loud and brash. Phil turned up and it was a disaster. Tom's friends had made fun of him, but Tom didn't intervene. In fact, he had done the opposite, Tom had drunk too much and had got personal with him. At one point even Tom's friends had told him to ease up. The next day it had got back to Jenna and she really tore into him. Tom had been surprised how angry Jenna was, but had understood. He was way out of line and had to apologise to Phil. It was a tough thing to do but Phil had taken it well and was good about it. It had made Tom change his opinion of him a little.

But the real problem was that Phil also got an offer to move to Illinois, and so Tom knew it would get back to Jenna. Tom and Phil had spoken about the offer and Phil had even told him how much he was being offered in his new contract. Tom was surprised that it was nowhere near his offer; but he never said anything.

However, Jenna asked Tom one day if he had an offer. He had said he hadn't, just to give himself more time but somehow something told Tom that Jenna knew straight away he was lying. The question she asked were quite direct and Tom felt she knew. She must've already spoken to Carly. So he knew he had limited time.

After a week or so after getting offered the contract Tom was called to a meeting with the company Director, Alan Shields. As he walked in he also saw sitting next to Shields was James Rutherford, company Chairman and board member. Tom respected them from a business perspective but from the perspective of a New Jersey born kid they were stiffs.

They had asked why he was yet to accept the offer. They had expected him, like the other employees, to come in straight away and offer his thanks and accept with gratitude. They questioned if they had made the right decision with the offer to him and thought there may be someone 'more committed' to the new position. Tom had quickly moved into 'tow the part line' mode.

He explained that he was extremely thankful for the offer and felt honoured that the company felt he was worth it. He said he loved working with the company and getting them the results. It was what he lived for. They lapped it up.

He then said he was having some 'personal difficulties' with his current relationship and his mind had been 'a bit wayward' with trying to deal with this. Also, his mother had recently been ill and, with his dad not around, he had also been attending to her and assisting her to hospital frequently.

Both bullshit stories but Tom was now in the zone and putting on a show. It came naturally. He asked for advice and said to them, for the first time in his life he felt like things were not quite in his control, and without his father about he had no one to turn to.

Shields and Rutherford loved it. They loved nothing more than thinking of all their employees saw them as father figures and so they fell for it. Tom then dropped the bomb. He asked them if they could advise him on what to do. He saw the relish in their eyes as they went into father mode. At the end of it he felt numb. They advised him on every part of his life and what 'they would do'. But, more importantly they gave him another week to sort things out and then think about the offer. Shields loved this. He knew what Tom meant, he was old school and always said to the guys, 'Do not show weakness….Ever'. Tom knew that, which was exactly why he said it. He knew how to play them.

However, just as Tom got up to leave Rutherford called him back. He then dropped his own bomb with the famous words, "You won't let us down will you, Tom?" Then gave his smug, patronising smile that Tom hated. That was it. Tom knew what that meant. He had seen guys hounded out within a week because they did not do what the organisation wanted. Careers ripped apart at the seams for 'rocking the boat'. Tom had seen it and did not want to be part of it. He then knew what decision he had to make, but at least he had a week before he had to do it.

During that week Tom swayed one way and the other. He had tried to play down how great it was living in Manhattan and the life he and Jenna had. He heard his father every day in his head with that broad New Jersey accent.
"All good things come to an end".
"Life moves on".
"Don't look a gift horse in the mouth".
"Take opportunities. They don't come around often".

All were true, of course. His father selling the haulage business was proof of that. Tom was over-thinking it. Soon his friends would be older and moving on anyway. Marriages and kids were already being discussed in very brief, awkward conversations at the sports bar. It was inevitable. But, regardless of all that, Rutherford had made it clear. Tom knew he either took it or he was gone.

With that in mind the organisation had guaranteed they get what they want. They always did. Why was he fighting it? Next day he told Jenna and as he had already anticipated she was over-joyed. She said she saw this as a major step in the natural evolution of their life. Their life was going perfectly, and Tom now had to go with it. He was fully committed.

He told the company the day after and officially accepted the offer. There was not much in return from them apart from a "You made the right decision" comment. It could be taken two way's, but Tom knew exactly what way to take it.

Arrangements were made. Apartment put up for sale. Car sold. Family advised of decision. Lots of tears and hugs from his mum, his sister, Claire, and her husband Paul. Their two sons, Jake and Paulie, who Tom loved dearly, and hadn't realised actually how much he loved them until the 'farewell' dinner.

A last night on the town with his friends which was also very emotional. And ended being a seriously heavy drinking session which took in at least seven Manhattan bars and two clubs that Tom could remember. There had been more, but the latter part of the night was a blank.

His friends had originally planned a weekend in Atlantic City, but Tom wanted to do it in New York. Plus, Jenna wasn't too keen on the idea after the last visit to Atlantic City. Tom had somehow ended up asleep on the back of a cattle truck heading towards Baltimore. Luckily, he woke at Abingdon and eventually got the drivers attention. That was a long story. Suffice to say Jenna had a long drive to pick him up.

Tom had got bored with the amount times he had reminded family, friends and work colleagues about keeping in touch through e-mail, Facebook, Skype "There is no reason not to talk each day" he would say. But he knew full well as time goes by everyone gets too busy to do it too often.

Then it was all a haze. The rest was just a blur. The goodbyes, the loading of the removal truck, the flight down, moving in and his first day at the new office. That was all now a few months ago, and so here he was. Saturday morning in Evanston, Illinois. A warm, calm and serene, ordinary Saturday.

But as Tom sipped his coffee and watched the news he wasn't aware of the black Sedan that slowly cruised past his house, of which the occupants knew everything about him.

Chapter 2

Tom put his coffee mug in the dishwasher, picked up the remote and switched the channel to Bloomberg. He sat back down at the large breakfast bar. His attention was caught by two financial experts discussing a merger of two pharmaceutical companies and he instinctively wondered what affect this would have on their shares and trading. He made a mental note to do some research on this Monday.

But, like many times these days, his mind snapped back to thinking about the 'strange' happenings. One of which had been around two weeks before his transfer to Chicago, when Tom had been at work:

It had been a Wednesday around 6:30pm and about the time when all the traders wanted to go home but daren't until they knew it was safe to. Once the floor director gave the nod you knew that management were happy for the day. However, you could still be asked to stay on to finish something urgent, attend an emergency trade meeting or do some stock analysis. Tonight was one of those nights. Tom had hoped to get out for drinks with the guys, but his luck was out. As he got up to leave there were still several of the guys working. He heard a door nearby open and he looked up. Harrison Conway emerged and looked directly at him. Conway looked a little uncomfortable and Tom knew why.

Harrison Conway had been Tom's Floor Director for about a year or so. Tom had always thought he was brash, a little odd and two-faced. He was a broad, moustached New Yorker who made a fortune in the 80's boom. And he subsequently seemed to avoid any financial damage in the crashes thereafter. He was an old school trader and frowned upon the new breed. He was an old dog who had no interest in learning new tricks, especially from the 'green boys' as he called them.

One night, a couple of months prior, Tom was working late preparing an agenda for a corporate trade meeting the next day which he was leading. As far as he knew at the time he was the only trader left on the floor; the only others were Conway and one of the young secretaries.

Tom was meeting Jenna later for a meal and a show at Broadway. Realising that time was now short Tom had closed his PC, got up, gave Conway a nod, which got no response, and left. The secretary, who Tom only knew by face, had disappeared. He got out into the cool Manhattan air. Being a little late he headed uptown and quickly walked towards Wall Street to hail a cab. He then checked his phone as he walked and noticed a text from Jenna, which she had sent half an hour ago. He opened it:

"Hey you, C U @ 7. Don't forget tickets! X"

Tom had forgotten the tickets were in his top drawer. He swore and turned around and jogged then bounced up the building steps three at a time and went through the large glass entrance doors. The night-guard, Billy, saw him and Tom made a face as if to imply he was forgetful and uttered, "Tickets!!". Billy smiled, tutted and raised his eyes to the ceiling, then carried on his rounds. Tom leapt out of the elevator on his floor and jogged down the hall, through the reception and into the main floor.

It was very quiet. He walked briskly to his desk and as he got to his desk he heard a shriek. He stopped and listened again. It was a female voice. He heard some shuffling and then mumbling followed by a louder groan. Then his heart stopped as he clearly heard an audible "No!" from the same female voice. He stood still; eyes wide.

He then heard some more in-audible mumbling. It was coming from the direction of the meeting room area around the corner from the main floor. Tom then heard what he realised was Conway's voice, "You slut!". Tom decided to go and look so moved quickly through the desks to the corner. He noticed a meeting door open with a low light emanating from the entrance. He walked slowly to the door and peered inside and saw the secretary lying on the desk with one of her legs upright and her foot around Conway's head. He was gripping her ankle tightly with one hand. Her other leg was one the desk spread wide and being held open by Conway's other hand which was holding her thigh down with what looked to be excessive force.

Her face showed what appeared to be a combination of fear and sexual pleasure. Conway was almost barging her off the desk he was fucking her so hard and she whimpered and groaned with each thrust. Her blouse had been pulled apart and one of her breasts was out of its bra cup and bouncing with each slam from Conway.

Suddenly the secretary turned and saw Tom. She froze. Conway noticed her eyes and he then looked round. "Oh fuck," he exclaimed as he pulled out and quickly tried to pull his pants up. The girl got off and moved to the other side of the desk and cowered down as she adjusted her clothing.

Tom froze. All had been able to say was, "Sorry to bother you….". He wanted to leave but something told him the girl was not entirely at ease. For some reason, instinctively he had asked her if she was OK. Conway had gone mad, "What the fuck are you on about!?" he had shouted. He asked Tom what he had meant but Tom hadn't answered. He had then asked Tom what he was implying by, "is she ok?" Conway walked from the room and closed the door leaving the girl inside.

He had walked straight up to Tom and went nose to nose and Tom had moved back. "Well?" he had asked. Tom said he had not known what to say as was so surprised. He had apologised. Conway was still angry and asked him again what he had meant. Tom explained he had heard the girl say, "No," and just thought it odd for someone to do that if they are having sex.

Conway told him she was into all that sort of thing. It was a game. She had pretended to be here alone and wanted him to jump out on her. Like a role play type thing. It had been her idea and she had initiated it. She had begged Conway for weeks until he agreed.

By the time Conway had explained, Tom could sense a climb down in his aggression. He probably realised now that Tom had something on him. Conway also knew that Tom had met his wife at a company function. She was a lovely lady and Tom had always wondered how she ended up marrying such an arsehole.

Tom assured Conway he wouldn't say anything and to him it was no big deal. Conway finally seemed to have fully calmed down and had walked with Tom to the elevator where they had said an awkward goodbye. Conway stared at Tom just as the elevators closed. Once closed Tom put his hands on his head and just stood frozen with his eyes wide. He couldn't believe what he had just seen. Had he done the right thing? Should he make sure she was ok? He wondered what type of conversation they would have when Conway went back in. Or would they just get back at it?

But Tom had been very uncomfortable. His instinct had told him the secretary definitely had a look of fear in her eyes and if he didn't know any better she was being over-powered. Was it rape? He had told himself he was being stupid and over-reacting. It had been a sex game. Some girls like to be dominated. Although he had known he had not been truly convinced.

The rest of the night had been strange one for Tom. All he could see was the fear in the girl's eyes. He had not told Jenna. He feared she may have told him off for walking away. Plus it would have put a dampener on the night. Tom thought he could've just said he caught them having sex which would have made a great conversation piece. Jenna loved a bit of gossip, but he just felt uncomfortable about it so hadn't mentioned it.

Jenna seemed to have a great time without realising Tom had spent most of the night re-running in his head what he had witnessed, constantly asking himself if he had done the right thing. Jenna had mentioned that Tom had been quiet while they ate but he said he was fine, just a little tired. He had seen "Les Mis" before so he wasn't too bothered about missing most of the show.

The next day at work Conway was nowhere to be seen. Neither was the secretary. Tom had got a call from Rutherford who asked him to come to the office. Tom had been told that the secretary had been sacked for gross misconduct. Allegedly the organisation had evidence that she had been providing confidential investor accounts to competitors, 'Bullshit' Tom had thought. Rutherford had gone on to explain Conway had been given 'special leave' to work with investigators as he was the one that caught her and blew the whistle, 'more bullshit'.

Tom then had one of his sudden rebellious urges and asked why Rutherford was specifically telling him. Rutherford got up and looked out of his panoramic window across the city. He had said to Tom that he believed he may have seen something unusual and he would hate for anything of that nature to get around. He added that Mrs Harrison was a very upstanding, fine lady and he would hate for anything to upset her. He had explained that the company's foundations are built on good reputation and dignity.

Tom got the message, "Keep your mouth shut or else". Tom knew the secretary had been paid off and told to keep quiet and Conway was suspended and on a warning.

So, Conway had every reason to be uncomfortable when dealing with Tom. He had eventually returned to work and had been ok with Tom, but it often made things awkward. Tom was one of what Conway called the 'new breed' who he treated with contempt, but now Tom had a major hold on him. Conway knew that. Therefore, his behaviour towards him made Tom think the organisation had told Conway to keep him sweet and don't do anything to jeopardise the situation. Conway definitely treated Tom differently. With more respect. It had been noticed by the other traders, but Tom just said they were paranoid and said no more than that.

After Tom's meeting with Rutherford, Conway came from the door and approached Tom. He had asked if he was ok. He had then explained some major investors were flying in first thing and they needed a full stock trend report for the last quarter. He told Tom if it really wasn't important he wouldn't ask and even said he was tied up in a trade meeting, otherwise he would do it. Tom had almost felt sorry him, even though he was a potential rapist. Tom had agreed and Conway was grateful. But deep-down Tom knew Conway hated him as much as the others did.

Tom had got a coffee and text Jenna to let her know he would be late. He then started working on the report. The report itself was pretty easy but time consuming as he had to extract data from so many different sources. Just after he started he heard a door and looked round to see 'H' emerge from the archive room. Tom smiled. H was a good friend and colleague, "Just me and you kid," H had said.

Harold Tweddle was a company legend. Known by all who knew him as "H" he had been at the company right from the start. In his younger days he had been one of the most prolific traders in the Wall Street Stock Exchange. He had then been head-hunted by the organisation. He was a well-known and respected person within the Manhattan financial district. As he had got older he moved more into client liaison and over his later years had become an industry expert in stock trends, market conditions, asset resilience, financial advice. Basically providing the people with the money the information they needed to hand it over to the bank. For the company he was the go-to guy in these areas. A prime asset.

Now H left the major trading to the younger, energetic guys. He could've retired years ago but he loved his job, he loved Wall Street and he especially loved the people he worked with.

Tom worked hard on the report and unfortunately had little time to talk to H. The night flew by. Tom looked at the clock which told him it was almost midnight. He had gathered all the data and prepared a very detailed stock analysis report which could make or break a deal with the Japanese investors. Tom was confident it would be a 'make'. H had then told Tom he was done but he would wait for him.

Tom finished and asked H if we would scan his report. H smiled and came over. Tom was pleased with the nodding and positive comments H offered as he looked over it, "You may be a trader, but you'll do me out of a job you keep turning out stuff like this," he finally said. Tom saved the report and then e-mailed it to Conway, "Eat that," Tom shouted as he pressed send. H laughed. They both felt the same about Conway.

They went down to the ground floor and said goodnight to Billy as they passed. He stood and saluted them with a smile. They both laughed. The company laid on chauffer driven cars for staff working past 11pm so H turned and signalled a V sign to Billy, "Two cars please, my man". Billy had sent back a thumbs up and got on the phone.

Outside they sat on the steps of the building. It was a cool night and the sound of horns and sirens could be heard filling the air. H offered Tom a cigarette and he accepted. He wasn't a real smoker anymore but liked the odd one when he felt he deserved it. As he lit it H had offered him a hip flask, "Nightcap?" he asked. Tom had smiled, took a big slug and it felt good.

He had got home just after 12:30pm, the house was dark, but Jenna had left the kitchen light on above the island as she always did if he was late. He took off his jacket and sat on a stall at the island. The slug from H's hipflask had given him a taste and he thought about a shot of Jack. But just as he thought better of it he suddenly felt a cold shudder shoot through his body, like he had been submerged in water. It shocked him and he couldn't move a muscle. The icy cold flowed through his body and held him in a body lock which, as it drained from his feet made him he shiver and then he had slowly felt his temperature return to normal.

But it was followed by a heavy, deep feeling of dread. His stomach knotted and he now suddenly felt hot. His stomach turned and twisted, and he suddenly felt fear beyond anything he had known. Frightened he stood up quickly and the stall fell on the floor, crashing as it landed. Tom then suddenly felt presences all around him and hands reaching to grab him, he looked around to see who or where it was but saw nothing; and then suddenly the fear faded. As quick as it had come, it had gone.

19

Tom picked the stall up and sat down. His mind raced with fear. He felt his hands and they were sweating. "Tom…Is that you?" shouted Jenna from upstairs. Tom had left the kitchen to go to the stairs to confirmed it was him and that he just bumped into the stall. Jenna asked if he had been drinking. He hadn't answered but just said he would be up soon. He sat back down. What had happened to him? What was that feeling? Stress? Working too hard? Maybe he needed a holiday? He would look into a nice break for the two of them. They both needed it.

The next morning Tom had gotten off the subway at Broad Street. He had walked down to Hanover via Beaver Street. This was so he could grab a coffee from Manon's which did the best Cappuccino in the financial district. There was the normal buzz about the place that he loved. But this morning it was extra special. The Knicks had beaten the Supersonics at the Garden last night putting them 4-2 up in the Playoff's. New York City was buzzing.

As Tom walked towards his building he sipped his coffee his phone rang. He stopped and looked at it to see "Conway Mob". His shoulders sank. He took a deep breath and thought he must make his answer sound positive, "Hey, Conway...Wassup?"

"Wassup? I will tell you wassup" Conway had blurted, "The Jap's are here in fifteen and I don't have that fucking report!"

Tom had replied that he had done it, saved it and mailed it direct to him the night before. Conway had confirmed he had checked both his in-box and the stock analysis files. There was no e-mail and in the analysis files there was a folder titled, "Japanese Invest014-Conway" but it had been empty.

Tom decided that talking on the phone was not solving anything, so he had ditched his coffee and ran to his building and up to the trading floor. A handful of people were in and Tom knew straight away that they knew because as he jogged in their heads went down and towards their VDU's. He knew Conway had been openly talking about him.

As Tom walked to his desk Conway looked up and did the same.
"Right, I definitely did it" Tom had said loudly so they could all hear.
"Well it ain't fucking there, Tom," Conway had replied.

Tom opened and re-opened the file that had been created for the report, but it was empty. He had then started opening other files around it to see if he had saved it to them by mistake. Conway had not been amused and had said to him if he was going to do that then he "will be all fucking day" as there were thousands of files, but, Tom knew he had mailed it to him, so he went to his sent files and the last e-mail sent was titled, "Existing merger accounts – FAO James Rutherford". Tom looked at the sent date and time "18:09 – Wed 24th Jun".

He had remembered sending that e-mail to Rutherford yesterday. It contained some brief data on the accounts from two small companies they invested in who had recently merged. But he had sent it way before the last mail he sent to Conway later that night.

Tom felt himself getting hot. Conway's huffing and sighing had been like a knife stabbing at his back. Tom looked up and into Shield's office. Rutherford had obviously been in there too and they were both staring back at him. This Japanese company were big fish so management had a right to know but Tom had wondered why Conway couldn't just keep this between them. But as Tom had known, he was two faced.

Tom got Conway to check, double check and triple check his in-box just in case it had been undeliverable for any reason. But if it was, he would have had a message to say it had not been delivered.

They both decided to go down to IT to check the e-mail account history. Conway did not talk in the elevator. He had just stared at the changing digital numbers......06.....05.......04. Tom had interrupted, "Look, Conway, I definitely did it. I was here till midnight doing it," Conway did not speak or look at him. The doors had opened, and they briskly walked to the IT department.

They buzzed and a young guy with long hair came to the door and opened it. Conway just walked through "Hey!" said the young guy angrily. Tom had apologised to him and explained it was an emergency. As he jogged to catch up with Conway the young guy shouted, "Yoshi is here....He will sort it". Yoshimoto was the IT genius that everyone went to, "Thank fuck," Tom had thought.

Yoshi, was as usual, staring at a VDU with what looked like some very complicated stuff showing on screen. As usual he was twiddling a pencil through his fingers. He had spun to see what the commotion was and after they had explained he had simply said, "No problem". But Tom had known he was in trouble after a few minutes, as Yoshi put the pencil down and leaned towards his screen. He started to work faster, and the cursor was zipping about the screen like an angry fly.

Yoshi sighed. And to Tom's despair and Conway's disgust, after several e-mail account checks they could find no sign of an e-mail sent to Conway with the right folder name around the exact time. Tom's last e-mail sent was to Rutherford at 18:09. Yoshi had checked all recycling archives, data storage files and server back-ups. He did a full system search for the file name and all it brought up was the empty folder. He did a system sweep to analyse in and out logs, deletions, amendments on all folders currently on the server. Basically, if a user logged in just for a millisecond it would be traced and shown. But he had found nothing. Tom had known he was screwed.

Conway was seriously angry and quickly left the IT room. Tom knew the Japanese would be here by now and with no report the meeting would be short. And possibly a failure.

Before Tom had gone back up he asked Yoshimoto to run the system sweep again to look at his user log. What was confusing was that it showed that Tom had sent the e-mail to Rutherford then logged out at 18:19. His user account then showed a re-log dated for that day at 07:43 when he had come up this morning after Conway rung him. So where was his account usage from last night up to just before midnight when he logged off? Tom had paced up and down. He told Yoshimoto the system was faulty, or the sweep didn't work. Yoshimoto had given him that look. Tom knew what it meant, and Yoshi said, "I feel for ya, Bud, but this system is not faulty". Yoshimoto was an IT genius and they both knew it. The system wasn't faulty, Tom was.

He had got back in the elevator and suddenly it hit him. H was with him! He had checked the report and given it full marks! He had seen Tom send it to Conway! Tom had jumped up and down the elevator, "Come on, come on…" He slipped sideways though the opening doors and jogged through reception to the main floor. He looked for H at his desk, but it was empty. He then noticed Conway in Shield's office. The Japanese consortium was also already there.

He sat down at his desk and watched. All seemed quite civil. Shields spoke and the Japanese laughed. Conway and Rutherford laughed too but Tom knew it was fake. Shields then put his arm around one of the other Japanese men. Rutherford laughed again. Tom thought that perhaps it would be ok, and the organisation would sort it.

He had wondered how can he tell them about H? But then wondered if it had mattered anyway though? The file wasn't there, Yoshi had looked. But H was respected and at least he could vouch for Tom. It may soften the blow; however, it had now got to 8:35am so where the was H? He was always in at 7:50am. Coffee and donut. Then he kicked off work at 8am. Like clockwork.

Conway came out with a smile which disappeared as soon as he shut the door. He came over to Tom and leant over his desk. He told him he had been a lucky son of a bitch and the Japanese had asked to go breakfast and see some sights before the get down to business. Obviously the organisation had obliged, and no doubt would show them the best breakfast ever known to man. They would drag it out till lunchtime until, as Conway had put it, "That fucking report will be on Shield's desk". Tom said to Conway he will get on to it straight away but then had taken the opportunity to bring up H and told Conway about H being with him the night before and that he had checked it and seen Tom e-mail it.

Conway's face had suddenly dropped. His demeanour quickly changed, "Oh look, er…come with me". Tom had been confused. Conway lead him towards one of the meeting rooms. He had walked towards the meeting room where Tom had seen him with the secretary and so diverted at the last second. Obviously trying to avoid old ground, thought Tom, as he pretended not to notice the diversion. They had gone into another room.

Tom had asked if everything was ok. Conway said it wasn't and had explained to Tom that Rutherford had got a call in the early hours from H's wife. H had died. She remembered he had got in about 12:45pm and she heard him pour a drink. He usually sat on the settee to wind down, but she thought something was wrong so went downstairs about 2am and found him dead on the settee.

Tom had been shocked. Stunned.

Conway added that they hadn't officially told anyone yet as the morning had been hectic, what with the Japanese and the missing report. They were going to wait till everyone was in and then inform them then. The post-mortem was taking place that morning, but initial diagnosis is major heart attack. Conway had tried to make the situation a bit lighter and said he had always told H those donuts would catch up with him one day. Tom also knew that H smoked and that in the last 6 months had started drinking heavily too, but he hadn't told Conway.

Conway had then consoled Tom with a hand on his shoulder, "Look, I know you two were close. I.....well, I'm sorry," he had said with a slightly embarrassed manner and had then left, leaving Tom standing alone in the silence. Then Tom had heard a knock and Conway opened the door and poked his head in. "Report?" he said.

It had been a long, tough and draining day for Tom. He had been devastated by news of H's death, but he had to get on with the report. That was why they paid the money. You got the job done. Regardless.

It had all worked out OK. The Japanese consortium had got back to the office about 2:30pm after the best breakfast - and lunch - known to man. Conway, Shields and Rutherford all came in with them and the air soon stank of expensive scotch and cigars. Conway had looked at Tom and Tom simply nodded. He had put the report in a leather file and left it neatly on Shields' desk and saved it sixteen times whilst working on it. He then printed it before he saved and closed it for a final time. He then e-mailed it to Conway. He had checked several times afterwards that the electronic file still contained the report. It had. He then checked eight times that it was in his sent files to Conway. It was.

During that afternoon Tom had been sat at his desk when he felt a hand on his shoulder. He looked round and Conway lent forward and whispered to him, "Don't worry. I squared it with Shields. I saved your scrawny little arse," and he had smiled *and walked away. What did that mean? Tom had thought. How had he saved him? What had he done?*

Later, after work on the train home, Tom puzzled over it. What had happened? How could that file have just disappeared with no trace? Why hadn't his network usage showed for that night before? It was as if he wasn't there. He had sighed heavily, and he closed his eyes. His mind had now slowed to the confusion of it all and he was coming back to reality. As he had sat on the crowded subway train his head bumped from side to side and his thoughts had turned to H and to his wife and family.

H had always spoke fondly of Marjorie, his wife, and when Tom and Jenna had finally met her, she was everything H had said she was. Beautiful, stylish, cool. And she had a wicked sense of humour. Tom thought about what she must be going through. He had witnessed first-hand how hard it was for a person to lose a lifelong loved one with his own mum when Tom's father had died. It had taken her months to become a functioning human again. But he hoped Marjorie would be strong. He also hoped that their family were all together with her now, comforting her.

Jenna had loved H and Marjorie too, so she would be devastated. Then he realised that in n the madness of the day he had forgotten to tell Jenna. That evening would be tough he had thought. And he had been right. Jenna had never coped well with death and that night had been no exception.

Chapter 3

Tom got up from the breakfast bar and as he slowly walked across the kitchen his eyes scanned an update scrolling across the bottom of the screen "....market conditions continue to be negatively influenced by slow growth in the US manufacturing sector..."

He had known this for a while, but it wasn't his area of expertise. He recalled how H had informed him about it. He smiled as remembered H's work ethic, and that there wasn't anything he didn't know. H was always one step ahead of the game. Shields had spoken at H's funeral and had said, "As a man, husband, father and company asset, he was irreplaceable". They were genuinely touching words, and very true.

As Tom went out into the main, spacious lobby he picked up the New York Times and Chicago Tribune from a study table. He walked through the foyer of the house, through the expansive, stylishly decorated lounge and into the garden. It was still early as he hadn't been sleeping well since the transfer. No matter how hard he worked and how tired he felt he couldn't switch his mind off. So every Saturday he got up early, had his coffee and read the papers. He had decided to sit in the garden as it was such a beautiful day.

He scanned the financials but saw nothing of note so turned to sports. He noted the Cubs were on a winning streak of 5 and 0 and their next game was at Wrigley Field against the Yankee's. Tom smiled. That was definitely one he would watch indoors without any Cubs fans to spoil it.

He settled into the detail of the Cub's story when his mind, as usual, leapt back to the missing file at his old office in New York. He had been doing this a lot since it happened. He just couldn't get the incident out of his mind. He felt guilty some days as he thought about that more than H's death.

Had someone at work got it in for him? If they did it would have to be someone who had the access to his electronic files. Security was tight and you had a username which only worked with a security pass.

Could it have been someone in the organisation's management? They could get access to files, but they would need to go through the IT network. Someone would've had to ask IT to do this. That wasn't beyond the realms of imagination. They did what they wanted. There were strict IT policies around security, but the organisation could sidestep those.

Basically, they would say to someone, "You want to keep your very highly paid IT job? Then go into Tom's network and delete the file".

It could be kept hush-hush. But Yoshi had shown Tom the complete network history. It would show up on an audit trail and the last thing that showed on Tom's account was the e-mail to Rutherford. If anyone had been in and deleted it that would show.
But could a trace of a deletion be deleted? Surely Yoshi could find a way to do this if he was asked to. But Yoshi had said this was a solid audit trail and can't be tampered with.

He decided he would ask Yoshi again on Monday. He was friends with him, and Tom hoped that he would tell him if anyone had been snooping around.

But, then again, it had all worked out. The report had been done again and all was good. If it was the organisation who wanted to make Tom look incompetent why would they allow him to do the report again and get the Japanese out the picture for the morning? The report got done, the Japanese re-invested millions through the bank and Tom's reputation at the company withstood the mess. In fact, Tom had even got a wry smile from Shields as he had left on that day which was unheard of.

However, more worryingly, Tom had been unable to let Conway's comment about saving him rest. It had played on his mind and he never slept a wink the night before. If Conway had squared it with the management what did he say? And why had he squared it? That was obvious Tom thought; he had the night he caught him with the secretary. Conway owed him for his silence and Tom had not told a soul.

Or was Conway lying and taking the opportunity to demonstrate to Tom a bit of a payback for his silence. You scratch my back and I will scratch yours. Although Tom wasn't sure how much scratching Conway has actually done.

But Tom hadn't been called in, disciplined, spoke to and not even given a gentle reminder not to mess up again; so Conway must be telling the truth. Tom thought that if anyone else would have done this he would expect them to be toast. An employee says they worked till midnight doing a report which the next day is missing and there is no trace of them even being logged in. No way would the organisation accept that.

Tom had been unable to let it rest and a few days later had asked Conway what he had told Shields and Rutherford. Conway had looked at him puzzled. He then replied to Tom, "not worry," and to, "just be thankful". And as Conway had walked away he had turned and said to Tom, "Put it this way, Rutherford likes you."

Tom hadn't pushed it further. He suddenly accepted that Conway may have been telling the truth. Or, of course, he may have got one over on him. It may well have been fine without any intervention from Conway, but very unlikely, so Tom just never really knew. But it was nice to know Rutherford liked him. And, honestly, there was no reason for Conway to lie. Why take such a risk? If there was someone high up the organisation trying to make Tom look incompetent then they would know Conway was lying. It was too risky for him. But nothing else had happened at work to Tom, so was his conspiracy theory just paranoia?

Conway wasn't just a fresh-faced trainee coming on the scene that see's every secretary as a sexual conquest to brag about. He had a reputation, a family, a pension, and huge investments. He had far too much to lose. So, having sex with a secretary in the office was a major deal to Conway if he got caught. Or had Tom seen something else? Something else that would make Conway take more of a risk to ensure Tom's silence. Something like raping a secretary in the office.

They hadn't spoke about that night, so it had never been confirmed as a consensual sex game. That was just Conway's version. But Conway had never asked Tom what he thought actually happened. He didn't know whether Tom had believed his story or not.

He tried to snap his mind out of it but was drawn into more thoughts about Jenna. As usual, she had not been too interested in Tom's disappearing report. She had been upset for a few days about H's death and he had heard her weeping gently twice when she thought he couldn't hear. Her eyes had been red and puffy even when she seemed OK in herself.

He had heard her on the phone to Marjorie one evening telling her to be strong and that her and Tom are there for her. He had heard Jenna taking funeral details and then making further plans later on to spend a weekend with Marjorie at her house. H and Marjorie lived in Armonk in a modernised French Country-style mansion. They had spent a few weekends there in the past and it was these weekends that Tom had realised how special H was. H had told Tom on the last visit that he saw him as 'the son he never had'. They had a subtle relationship, but it was very special.

Once the upset of H's death had settled, Tom had raised the missing report with Jenna again. Jenna had wondered why he was making such a fuss. She told him that computers did silly things, "You can't live with them can't live without them," she had said. Tom hadn't pushed it too far as a lot of what she was saying was true. Computers did do silly things.

As she cooked dinner one evening, he had tried to explain the cold, unsettling feeling that it had given him and how he still, at the time, felt an anxious feeling about it. In fact, he had said, it wasn't just unsettling, it was frightening. She was listening, sort of, in between chopping peppers and stirring sauce. She simply said he had probably been working too hard. He had got confused. Forgot to save the file or done something wrong. Or the system was at fault. Who knows? Who cares? "What was done was done. No harm caused, get over it, Tom" she had ended with.

And Jenna had been right. Although Tom was still frustrated at her. If it had been something to do with the house, or a social event, it would have had her full attention. But it wasn't and so it didn't. Then again, what could she say? A disappearing file. It wasn't exactly news story of the year. But it had affected Tom strangely and he had still wanted Jenna to understand that.

But it was all a while ago now and Tom had much more going on and thought that he should really stop wasting energy trying to work out what happened. It was done. As his dad would say in his broad NJ accent, "Forget about it."

Chapter 4

Tom finished scanning the papers. He had heard Jenna moving around upstairs so knew she was awake and up. He put some fresh coffee on as he knew she would want a mug when she came down. Tom noticed how nice the weather was and thought that he would have a swim later. He poured himself a fresh cup of coffee and went into the lounge and sat down. His mind was a little fuzzy and he wanted to try and even out some thoughts he had.

He felt he needed to make sense of things. His mind raced constantly. He got up and went out into the garden and sat on a lounger, it had been warmed by the sun. A soft breeze brushed over his body and he squinted his eyes from the glare flashing through the trees. He felt his body relax, but his mind didn't.

Despite Jenna's view, Tom was still been struggling to understand the death of H and the feelings of dread that he experienced and scared him. He had tried to follow Jenna's advice and forget it. And he had forgotten about it as best he could until the night that really troubled him after he had recently spent a great weekend with, Davy, an old friend from New Jersey:

Around the same time Tom's family had moved to Franklin Lakes, Davy's family had moved to Minneapolis. Before that they had been very close buddies. Davy's family had lived three houses down from Tom's and their parents were also friendly. They had been so close as kids that their parents joked they were 'The Siamese Twins'.

They had stayed in touch as pen pals for about a year after Davy moved but the letters soon became less frequent and then stopped altogether. Life moved on and both Tom and Davy had very busy, full lives. They never forgot each other but had simply became fond childhood memories in each other's minds.

It had been late one evening, while tom was relaxing in his apartment in Upper East Side he picked up Jenna's I-Pad and she had left her Facebook account open. Nosily he had browsed her page and looked what her friends were up to. Nothing of note, so he decided to check his own account. He wasn't a regular Facebook user and couldn't understand why people would want to tell other people what they had for dinner or what TV show they were watching. He hadn't been on there for ages but just thought he would check.

There were a few requests to be friends with people he didn't know too well, but he then noticed a message. It was from a Davy Hayden who had sent a message asking if this was the Tom Callaghan that knew Davy Hayden and lived in Montclair around mid-

80's. Of course, Tom knew exactly who it was so replied excitedly. He was hoping for a reply that night and constantly checked his messages while watching The Knicks at Portland.

He was so excited. His old friend Davy Hayden. What was he up to? How had his life turned out? Was he OK? But it wasn't until the next day that Davy responded. And from that moment they had sent messages back and forwards intermittently for the next few weeks.

Davy explained he had flown back to Jersey to attend a funeral of an old Auntie. It was Aunt Bess who Tom could vaguely remember from his childhood. She lived a few streets away from their houses in Montclair. Davy had said that one day, whilst there, he had taken a walk down the old neighborhood and it had got him reminiscing. So, when he had got home he had tried to trace some of his old friends. Tom had been the first to respond which Davy was pleased about as he was hoping out of all of them it would be him.

They updated each other on their lives so far. Davy had enjoyed his life in Minneapolis. His latter teen years were good although he admitted had probably not been as exciting as they may have been had he stayed in New Jersey. He had dropped out of University and ended up getting a job at his dad's car workshop. He eventually started his own recovery and repair business which was doing well but had faltered during the recession and it went bust. He now worked as a mechanic for a garage in the area. He lived in Shoreview, Minneapolis. Rented a 2-bed apartment, he had a wife and two young children and from the content and upbeat tone of his messages, Tom assumed he was happy with his lot.

Tom had played down the financial success of his life as it was obvious Davy was not in the same position, but Davy had caught on that Tom had done very well for himself and, as always, was very happy for him. One thing that Tom loved about Davy was that he was very modest and never, ever showed any hint of jealousy. He was the same as a kid. Tom's family was better off than Davy's and Tom had got some cool presents on birthdays and Christmas, Davy received more modest gifts. But he was always happy and never made it an issue. That was why they were so close. They were just very compatible, and Tom knew that it was probably more down to Davy's accepting and laid-back nature than anything he did.

So, eventually Davy had invited Tom and Jenna to visit. He said it would be wonderful to meet up and they would be welcome to stay with him and his wife, Julia and the kids, or they could stay in a hotel. Davy never pushed any situation and always gave people options to do what they wanted.

Tom had to put him off in the short term. Work had been very busy at that time and the organisation had put a sanction on any leave until things calmed down. The previous quarter had been slow. The markets had been influenced negatively due to industry wide litigation matters, increased penalties and further regulatory restrictions on banks from the Government. With this period now settling the bank wanted to re-coup lost profits. All employees were required to deliver.

All this had occurred just prior to news of Tom's transfer to Chicago. So during this period Tom had lost contact with Davy as his life was in limbo with the decision he had to make. When he had finally decided to accept the offer one of the first thing's he did was to contact Davy and tell him. Moving to Chicago meant a much closer journey to Minneapolis, and so they could set something up. Davy had appeared absolutely delighted.

After the move to Chicago and the settling in period Davy had contacted Tom about visiting again. He had an idea that Tom and Jenna could come up on the Friday and they could all spend the night downtown for a meal and drinks to really catch up. Then on Saturday he would arrange a fishing trip for just the two of them. Davy suggested the ladies could spend some time together shopping, eating out…whatever.

This had thrown Tom. By now Jenna had really settled into Evanston life. He hadn't been sure she would want to spend a weekend with someone she didn't know. Jenna wasn't shy or retiring and made friends with anyone she met but Tom just felt spending a weekend in a 2-bed apartment in Minneapolis with a stranger was not Jenna's idea of fun. It may have been once, but not now.

He had also been concerned about Davy's kids. Since the move to Chicago this had been an issue brewing with Jenna. She had first started to make fun comments about them starting a family which Tom playfully dismissed. Then it had become a little full on. They had spent an afternoon at a company barbecue on the shore of the lake. It had been a great day. Tom had thought to himself several times that day that maybe Chicago and Evanston wasn't so bad. They drank, played party games, ate great food and it was really the first time Tom had felt settled and part of the place.

He had even started to get on better with Phil Carter, who he had noticed had changed for the better. He seemed to have dropped his 'poster boy' character and had become a normal person. They had spoken in depth several times since the move, during meals, a bowling night and then again at the barbecue and Phil actually seemed OK. Tom had thought maybe he was all along, but the distraction of New York had made Tom selfish and ignore Phil's good side. He wasn't sure. But Tom had not just noticed a real change in Phil socially, but also at work. He had started to ask Tom if he was ok and made a comment one day after a seriously stressful day that, "We are in this together, it's best to have each other's backs". And at a beach barbecue one day, Phil and Tom found themselves alone on a boat as others had jumped in for a swim. Phil had opened up to Tom and told him that Carly was pregnant. Tom was congratulatory but Phil then told him he wasn't sure if he was ready. Tom gave the best advice he could but *knew it was very limited and he advised Phil it was probably best to speak to someone with experience in this area of life.*

Phil had said he had tried to speak to his father, but he was a straight down the line, upstanding Conservative and he never wanted Phil to show weakness. Phil was expected to do his bit for the reputation of the family and bearing children was what every man did, "Continue the line, my boy," Phil's father would say to him in esteemed company. Tom felt for Phil. For the first time he had showed his human, sensitive side to Tom.

But, that was Phil's problem for now, Tom had his own. Carly had told Jenna which had doubled the pressure from Jenna to start a family. He had managed to divert it away but what he actually wanted to say was, he didn't want to have kids. He had known this would come one day but he was surprised at how aggressive and forthright Jenna was about the whole thing.

Her new Evanston friends were either already parents, currently pregnant or, at the very least, currently trying. It seemed to be the current trend. Tom had argued with himself that it was a natural, fundamental human instinct to continue its race and not just something that was fashionable in Evanston. But he felt the way he did and that was it.

He had put it off and always avoided any lengthy conversation with Jenna but, in reality, nothing was stopping them. Jenna would be a great mother. They were settled, financially sound and had a huge property in a safe, exclusive area. They had the foundations to bring up a good, healthy family. Schools in the area were of a very high standard too as Jenna had told Tom along with showing him various brochures she had got on them. He was at an age now where this was the next natural step.

They had argued about it and one night and Tom told her he wasn't ready and then wished he hadn't. Jenna had stormed out and they hadn't spoke about that night. Ever. Tom wanted to erase it from his mind. Needless to say, he also wished not to go there again so he had been avoiding any sexual contact with Jenna. They used to be very sexually active in New York before the move. Sex was a pleasure and naturally instinctive.

So, Tom had made a decision. He had never told her that Davy had invited them both. Tom thought it was a perfect opportunity to get away from the intense, suffocating pressure that Jenna had created. It didn't help that another of her friends had invited her to a baby shower in a few weeks. A lavish, over the top affair, no doubt. And Tom heard Jenna speak of nothing else over the last few nights on the phone planning and discussing the details.

He had felt angry with himself. He was putting up a brick wall in Jenna's life, but he couldn't help it. He argued with himself as to whether he was being selfish or being sensible. On top of the missing file and H's death he needed to get away from it all for a few days.

So Tom had made arrangements with Davy and the visit was scheduled. Tom couldn't wait. Jenna had seen how excited Tom was and wished him well. She had initially questioned why Tom hadn't flown but Tom said by the time he gets to O'Hare, sits around, boards the flight, flies to St. Paul, gets off and gets a cab to Davy's it will roughly be the same. It wouldn't really have been, in fact, it would be a lot less, but Tom exaggerated. He had booked the Friday off work and had decided to drive up, leaving about 10am to arrive for mid to late afternoon.

But Jenna was dead right. In normal circumstances he would fly but the believed the drive would give him some time. Time to sit, relax and think about things. His mind had been a little messy around that time and he wanted some time to think about the things that were bugging him, and he wanted to get his head straight.

So with a hug and a kiss, he had set off. He skipped across town and jumped on the Interstate 94. He had, at last, got on his way to Minneapolis but, as he had hit the freeway, he had not noticed the black Sedan following him, which had been doing so since he left his street. Tom had changed lanes a few times before relaxing and soon after the Sedan had done the same, but just held back and followed, with Tom, oblivious to its presence and intent.

Chapter 5

As Tom lay peacefully on the sun lounger, the Saturday morning sun coated his face and body with light and warmth. He closed his eyes and took a deep, relaxing breath and felt himself sink into the lounger cushion.

Jenna had asked him to get the maintenance guy to paint the picket fence as it looked drab and her parents were coming for dinner the next day, "Roll out the red carpet," thought Tom. They were nice people as far as in-law's go. A little too 'aloof' for Tom, but they were decent people and they loved Jenna and, despite some embarrassing moments in the past, they loved Tom too.

It was a big deal for Jenna as this was their first visit the new house in Evanston and she wanted it to be perfect, which was understandable. She was doing everything, planning, shopping, cleaning and doing the cooking; but she had asked Tom to just get the fence done. He had assured her he would do it, but she told him to ring the guy, but he insisted. He knew he needed to get out and start acting like he wasn't just a lodger.

It would only take a few hours he had thought. He had all the paint and brushes. After lunch would be good. He settled into the lounger when his mind darted back to his trip to Minneapolis and the most recent "happening" he couldn't explain that had further unsettled him:

It had been a pretty easy, straight forward drive to Minneapolis. Davy lived in the suburbs in Shoreview. Tom had headed towards downtown and then on the outskirts had picked up the freeway north around Maplewood. He had Sat-Nav but rarely used it. He preferred the old -fashioned way of using road signs, but he had a rough idea anyway.

The drive had been great. It was a true American route. Great highways slipping through wonderfully diverse and beautiful landscapes all teaming with wildlife. Tom headed up through Black State Forest and saw two deer at the side of the road that then bucked and pranced back into the bushes as he approached. He was glad he had driven. After a long but relaxing drive, he approached downtown and spotted the route north indicating Shore View and came off on the 94. Soon he arrived in Shore View and turned his Sat-Nav on to give him the exact route to Davy's street, Midland Terrace. He arrived around 4pm and had done a lot of thinking so he had been physically and mentally drained.

His first meeting with Davy was emotional. All the nostalgic feelings and good memories from the past came out and, at one point, they both had tears in their eyes.

This wasn't just a meeting, it was a full-on return to their childhood and reliving those happy, innocent times.

Davy's apartment was modest. Tom had immediately banished any thoughts of how small it was. Davy seemed so happy for Tom to be there and did not, in any way, seem concerned about their apparent differences in status. His wife Julia was a very pretty lady with Latino features and the kids were a little boisterous but polite and fun.

Tom and Davy had sat in the kitchen diner drinking bottles of Coors Light and talked for hours. They had planned to go downtown around 6pm but were still sitting there talking at 6:30pm. They had talked about girls, school, sports, other friends, teachers, pranks, their parents. Endless memories flooding out and Tom had felt as happy as he had for a long, long time. Eventually they had gotten ready and hit downtown. Tom had insisted he pay for a taxi, but Davy would have none of it. He said they used to travel by train before so they should do it again. Tom agreed. And it was good fun.

Davy had taken Tom to a homely and inviting place and his favourite Italian restaurant. Tom was surprised at how good the Lasagne was but still insisted it was not anywhere near as good as the Lasagne at Carmine's back in Jersey. Davy had to agree on that one. Tom commented that he had not found anywhere in New York as good as Carmine's.

They had talked and talked about the past, moved onto current lives, back to the past and then back again. Tom updated Davy on everything in his world. Davy was listening intently. He seemed genuinely happy for Tom, and Tom started to remember how much he liked Davy. He had always been so engaging and interested in other people. Tom had thought a couple of times to mention the strange feelings but then decided not to spoil the mood.

They had then hit the bars and spoke and drank until late. Davy had gotten a little too drunk and by 10pm he was slurring and cuddling Tom at every opportunity. He eventually half passed out in a bar that Tom had to ask someone the name of and he hailed a cab, helped Davy in and got them home. He couldn't believe he found himself throwing Davy on the sofa. He settled onto the camp bed they had put up on the floor for him. Julia did not appear, and Tom assumed she was in bed and he had hoped they had not been too loud and woke the kids. That was his last thought as he drifted into a very heavy alcohol induced sleep.

The next day Davy said that he had decided they would not go fishing at nearby Lake Ossowa, which was local and Davy's usual spot. But he wanted to make it more of an expedition so had decided to go White Bear Lake. Plus, this time of year the Bass were jumping, and they were a good size. It wasn't too much further on out of town, but it was more rugged and would seem much more like an expedition.

Although a little hung-over Davy had gotten up early and cooked them breakfast whilst stepping around and over Tom's camp bed in the kitchen / diner. Tom slumbered but didn't get up from under his blankets. He was hung-over too and had regrets that it may spoil their trip.

Davy had already loaded his truck with the fishing equipment, tent, more than enough beer, huge pastrami and gherkin subs, chips, soft drinks and cans of soup. He had also told Tom to pack some warm, overnight clothes and he had loaded the bags in too. After bacon and eggs, they said goodbye to Davy's family and set off on the short drive out of town and into the wilderness. They eventually found a great spot and set up camp.

Once all set Tom stood at the side of the lake and took in a huge, slow inhalation of the crisp clear air. His hangover started to slowly fade to a mild fuzz and soon the beer and conversation were flowing again. They had tucked into the subs and all was good. Davy caught a few average sized Bass which were tough fighters. Tom was not a fisherman and couldn't believe how strong they were when Davy handed him the rod while landing one of the larger ones.

As the sun set over the pine covered hills Tom eventually caught a small pike. He was ecstatic. Davy helped him land it and the feeling of achievement was bursting from him. They put the pike and the two smaller Bass back but kept the largest one for their evening meal. Davy then cooked over a fire that evening and they devoured it with cold beer. The mosquitoes ate them alive and the temperature dropped to a ridiculous low, but Tom didn't want to be anywhere else. His body buzzed from being tired and drinking on top of the morning's hangover. But he was content. For the first time in a long time he felt genuinely happy. Davy's life had opened Tom's eyes. Davy had next to nothing materially, but he had so much more emotional wealth than Tom.

Davy didn't earn good money and had very little but that meant nothing to him. When he had previously told Tom about his business going bust he mentioned he still had some legal fees to pay. But they could basically go and screw and would get what he can afford. But he told Tom with such carefree abandon. Tom was never in debt and the thought of debt scared him; but why? He had lived in a bubble and Davy had shown him real life for the first time in ages.

Davy had also shown Tom lots of photos on his phone of him and his family. At this place and that place. And this was Joe's birthday at McDonalds…And his first day of soccer practice…They went on. And he spoke with such love and passion. Tom had denied himself these feelings. His non-stop world had prevented him from pushing out of his bubble and actually experiencing real life. He had the material but not the emotional.

He would stop worrying. Stop over-thinking. Go with the flow of life. And he would start by telling Jenna he was ready to start a family as soon as he got back. The thought of it had excited him. A new start. A new chapter. He stretched and felt a wave of comfort sweep over him and soon fell asleep.

As the early sun had risen, Tom awoke to Davy snoring next to him. Tom had slept very well and decided to get up out of his sleeping bag. He went outside and the crisp early chill woke him up and so too did the view, which was breath-taking. A mountain loomed over the landscape engulfed in a mango sky. He took in another huge gulp of air and he recalled last night's thoughts. His head was clear despite all the alcohol he had drunk in the last two days and he was happy his thoughts still felt right. Had his life finally slipped into place? He was sure it had. An eagle screeched high up and it echoed across the hills. The sun, now rising higher, appeared above the horizon with a yellow glow and glistened off the shimmering blue lake, which lit up a whole mountain side, turning the trees from a dark grey to a stunning emerald green. Tom suddenly felt lucky.

By the time they had got themselves together it was almost mid-morning. They packed up and hit the road and were back at Davy's apartment by lunchtime. They relaxed and Davy put on the TV and they chatted while watching basketball. Davy was a Nets fan and as big a sports fan as Tom. He jokingly ridiculed Tom how he had switched allegiances to the Knicks. Tom assured Davy he will always be a Nets fan deep down.

Tom had then realised he had a long drive back so said that he would get going but Julia joined them, and they just sat at talked more. The kids played around them and Julia had asked Tom to stay for dinner before he got going. He declined at first and had said he didn't want to be any trouble. They had insisted and Julia said she would get dinner on early, so he doesn't leave too late. Tom accepted. He sent Jenna a text and told her what a great time he had had and would be leaving a little later and she should probably expect him late, maybe around midnight.

Julia had cooked meatloaf which was something Tom hadn't eaten since he was a kid. It was a hearty and tasty meal and a lot of fun. It gave Tom a glimpse of what his life could be like in the future.

But soon Tom's thoughts had turned to work. His mind started pacing and he started to get focused. It was hard. After this weekend he was having trouble getting his work priorities set. Plus, he had a long drive home. He had wished he had flown. If he had known how he would've felt after this weekend he would have wanted to get back as soon as he could. He missed Jenna. But he had driven and that was it.

After an emotional farewell with Davy and his family he had suddenly found himself outside by his Mercedes with Davy's family all standing nearby, huddled together waiting to wave him off. They looked perfect together Tom had thought.

Tom had invited them all down to Evanston for the weekend. He would get them the flights and pick them up at the other end. It would be his treat. Davy said they would come but Tom would not be paying for flights. Tom had insisted and would not have it any other way. Tom looked at Davy and gave him that look from their childhood. Davy knew it meant "It's done, don't argue". Once Tom had said he was doing something it would happen. That look had gotten them into trouble as kids, but Davy just laughed. Tom got in, started the engine, and reversed out the space. As he slowly drove out of the parking lot he beeped the horn and waved and watched them all waving his rear-view mirror.

His phoned had beeped and it was a text from Jenna:

"Drive careful. Missed U. C U Later! X".

Tom had then settled into the drive and as the sun started to set he noticed dark clouds building up way off in the distance in the direction he was heading. He was low on fuel so would have to stop soon to fill up. As he drove he noticed signs for Eau Clair but would have to get on freeway 12. He could fill up and then pick the 94 back up at Black River.

After eventually finding a fuel station in Eau Clair and filling up he had set off again, left Eau Clair and headed down freeway 12 toward Black Forest. As the night blanketed the road the drizzle got heavier, and he had to put his wipers on. He had been going along well when he had noticed a sign for Mill Bluff Park. Just as he passed he was surprised by a flash of light filling up the car. He jumped and his stomach turned over. His body flushed with heat and tingled with the shock.

Then another flash of light but this time longer, blue and red and then a quick burst of a siren. He looked and saw a single headlight and realised he was being stopped by Highway Patrol. He hadn't been speeding and had been driving carefully.

He had slowly pulled into the shoulder and the officer stopped behind him, got off and came to the window, Tom had opened the window and asked if there was a problem. The officer appeared to be a decent guy and had told Tom he noticed a brake light out back up prior to Mill Bluff. Tom had got out and the officer invited him to go around the back then had sat in the front and pressed brake pedal to show him. Tom's driver side brake light was out. Again, Tom wished he had flown.

The officer had made it clear he wasn't going to take action. The rain had got heavier, and Tom thought he didn't want to hang around writing a ticket. He had then kindly suggested to Tom he get it repaired as soon as he can and directed him to 'Red's Garage' just past Augusta and then head to Camp Douglas. Tom had been very appreciative and said he would head there straight away.

As Tom had come off the slip road at Camp Douglas he followed the directions in his mind and eventually saw, on the left, a large premises with a neon light "Red's Garag". The 'e' was out. As he drove off the main road and onto the garage access an intense flash of lightning directly overheard made Tom jump. Almost immediately after the flash, a deep, growling roll of thunder filled the atmosphere. The rain started to fall harder, and Tom had to increase the wiper speed to see the garage. He pulled in and stopped in one the parking bays, looked around and realised he was the only person there. He had then noticed a small light coming from the main premises where a shutter was fitted into the window. He saw a shadow move behind and hoped it was the owner. He pulled up as close as he could get and waited. Nothing else had happened so reluctantly he got out.

It was an eerie place and the wind had picked up. As it did the rain lashed across Tom's face. He put his hand up as protection and walked across the forecourt and, just as he approached, a blind was pulled aside at the shutter and a face appeared. Tom had just been able to make out what looked like an older man with a beard. Tom waved, the blind went back, and Tom saw a main light turn on at the front door. It had opened and the old man appeared at the door.

Tom had shouted so he could be heard over the storm, "I got a brake light out!! Highway Patrol said you could help?"

The old man had shouted back to Tom this was fine and to get over to the sheltered bay and pointed round the side of the premises. Tom ran back to the car, reversed and then quickly drove it to the bay he had been instructed, as he did the old man jogged to the same bay.

Under the safety of the shelter the old man had introduced himself as Red and told Tom it wasn't a good night to be driving. Tom had agreed and explained what had happened. Red had said he can have him back on the road soon and went off to get a brake lamp. Upon his return he had told Tom to go wait in the dry, but Tom said he would wait outside. Tom watched intently with his arms crossed, he shivered a few times and just wanted to get back on the road. Red efficiently removed the whole light fitting unit, took out the faulty lamp and fitted the new. He then re-fitted the light unit. As he did he made a comment that he liked the German cars, "They make things nice and easy......Not like those French mother fuckers."

Red turned to Tom, rubbed the dirt and dust off his hands, "All done, you look while I test her," Red got inside and turned on the engine. Within a second Tom saw both brake lights beam bright red, "All good," he shouted and showed a thumbs-up not sure *if Red could see it or not. Red said they should settle up and he tilted his head towards the door he had come out of.*

Inside Red had asked for ten bucks just to cover parts and labour. Tom gave him a twenty and told Red to keep the change; Tom noted Red's response was genuinely grateful and sincere. He then asked Tom which way he was heading, and he confirmed to Tom that following the 12 to Black Forest and then skipping onto the 95 was the best route. As Tom had walked back to the car, he noticed the rain getting heavier. He was concerned how late he would be, and, with a busy day tomorrow, that thought of flying flashed across his mind again.

He had set off again but could only manage 40mph at most due to the heavy rain. He was concentrating so had no music on and sat more upright. There was very little traffic though. A couple of cars overtook him, and he saw headlights heading in the other direction but not much more than that. Just as he thought he must be coming to the 94 he noticed a sign for Augusta and also advising of the 94, "not much further," he had thought. And once on there he can open up a bit and hopefully drive away from this storm.

He had been driving for about fifteen minutes when a fork of lighting spiked down in the distance in front of him and a rumble of thunder rolled across the sky. Then, suddenly, he felt very, very cold and his hands started to ache, with the icy feeling. His whole body shivered. Slowly the cold passed, but a feeling of utter dread and despair raised up through his feet and coiled into his stomach like a bolt. The fear and anxiety rose, and he felt arms closing over his shoulders and round his neck. It caused him to brake sharply and stop. He turned in his seat and looked, scared and panicking. Then nothing.

What was he doing? What or who was it? He eventually felt fine and he realised he had stopped dead on a main freeway. He quickly got into gear and moved away. He looked in his rear-view mirror and he could see several headlights had caught up with him.

Then he had seen another flash…But blue and red again. He heard a siren and looked in his rear-view mirror and could make out a headlight again. At first he thought it was a mistake and they were trying to get by, but after travelling a little further Tom realised it was him they wanted. Tom had no choice but to pull over again, "Jesus fucking Christ! What now!?" he had shouted as he stopped.

The officer walked to his car. Tom noticed that the rain had eased considerably and was again just a drizzle. As the officer approached he wound the window down. It was the same officer as before. And he did not look happy.

"Now I thought we had an understanding, son. I thought we had a bit of rapport," the officer said. Tom was confused but kept calm. He put on a confused face and hoped it was genuine.

The officer had then said, "Now I had already told you back up at Mill Bluff to get that brake light fixed. You told me that was what you were going to do," Tom was now panicking but smiled nervously.

"Look, officer, it is fixed. I've just been to Red's, where you said. I've only been driving ten minutes or so. Red fixed it." Tom went to get out. The officer went for his gun and stood back and pointed it at Tom. "Whoa! Sonny!" he shouted, "Do not move".

Tom held his hands up, "Look officer, I swear, I just got it fixed. Back at Red's…Do you mind if I look?" he asked the officer.

"You calling me a liar, son?" the officer had replied as he slowly re-holstered his gun.

Tom was trying to concentrate on the conversation but his mind kept racing back to what happened just before. He felt 'De ja vous' like he had never experienced. It hit him and he couldn't recollect the feeling he had just had but he knew it was the same feelings he had felt before.

The officer had been very angry. Tom had told him several times he had been to Red's and got it done. He had been there fifteen minutes ago. He then explained to the officer what the place looked like and gave a description of Red. The officer had responded by saying that it didn't mean he had got his light fixed and Tom realised that he had a point. The officer had then proceeded to write a ticket, "I thought we had an understanding, son. I am bitterly disappointed".

At least he had holstered the gun, thought Tom.

Tom tried his best to explain and must have been believable because when Tom asked the officer to go back to Red's to ask him, the officer thought about it. He stopped writing and looked up at Tom for a few seconds. "Look, I can't be dallying back and forth up and down the road all night, son". But Tom pleaded. It was only a short drive back. "Please," he had begged.

Eventually the officer took a deep breath, exhaled and shook his head. Without looking at Tom he gave his location over the radio and said he was heading to Red's to clarify a situation. He then turned to Tom and said, "You try anything funny I will shoot you. You try running out on me and I will catch you and shoot you, ok?" Tom nodded. That was clear enough, he had thought.

Driving back slow enough so the officer didn't think he was jumping Tom thought he didn't even know if the light was out. The officer hadn't shown him, and he wasn't going to sit in the car and test the brakes while Tom looked on. For all he knew Tom could've walked round and shot him. Tom just had to take his word. Plus, it appeared the officer was quite keen on shooting people, so Tom just went with it.

41

After almost fifteen-minute drive Tom had seen the sign for Mill Bluff and Camp Douglas so he took the off ramp. He circled around and down the ramp with the beaming single headlight right behind him. As they came to the access road Tom had noticed what he thought were red flashing lights in the direction Red's garage.

Tom had cruised slowly across the crossroad and took the road that lead up to Red's. As he had approached the bays he saw an ambulance with its red lights flashing. He then noticed the officer behind speed up and pass him and then stop the bike in front of him, forcing Tom to stop. Then the officer got off and ran to Tom's window.
"You wait here, OK? Do not move. You drive away and I will put an APB out and you will be picked up and I will not be happy." As he finished talking he was already jogging backwards slowly towards the ambulance.

Tom had watched the officer approach. There was a body on the ground of the garage forecourt and two paramedics appeared to be doing CPR. A young girl stood ten yards away with her hands to her face and she looked like she was in some distress. The officer knelt down next to the paramedics for a short time then got up and approached the girl. He put his arm around her and tried to lead her into the premises, but she tried to get away and go back to the body on the ground. The officer then grabbed her, pulled her into his body and slowly walked her back into the garage.

Tom was hot. The heaters had been on since he last left Red's as he was frozen from the rain. He turned it off and got out into the now cold night air. The damp wetness immediately clung to him. His curiosity had got the better of him and he took a few steps closer to the paramedics who were now stabilising the person and looking to get them ready for the ambulance. One of the medics put the stretcher up and they put the person on a board and lifted them on. The person had an oxygen mask and from what Tom could see did not look in good shape.

Just then the officer came out of the garage door and jogged to the paramedics, "I'll give you an escort," he had shouted to them and pointed over across to the main road. Tom looked and saw more blue and red lights flashing over the tops of the trees. Then the officer jogged to the direction of Tom.
"Right, it's your lucky night. Looks like poor Red has had a heart attack, so I can't ask him about your light. And I need to get this ambulance escorted to ER," Tom froze...he hadn't heard anything the officer had said after 'heart attack'.
"Now you listen to me. You get that light fi..."
"Is it definitely Red?" Tom had asked. The officer stopped.
"Yeah...Why?"
Tom must've looked stunned as the officer had asked him if he was ok.
"Is he gone?" Tom had asked, ignoring the officer's question.
"Well, no, but don't look good."

As the officer had been speaking Tom had started to walk backwards to the car, "Get that light fixed, son," he heard the officer shout as he turned and walked towards the car. He got in and just sat.

A patrol car had then pulled up and two officers got out. Tom saw them have a brief conversation with the motorbike officer, he pointed to Tom and then pointed to the premises. The two officers both stared at Tom briefly and then walked towards the premises and went in. The ambulance and the motorbike officer then barrelled out of the forecourt and away. Tom could hear a siren for a short time and then silence. Total silence. Soon after Tom's senses had returned, and he could hear hundreds of drips and running water nearby caused by the deluge earlier.

Eventually he had started to drive back. Slowly. He felt like he had been hit by a truck. Another death. In just over three months he had been close to two deaths. Two heart attacks. His mind had set off.

Was it a coincidence? What else would it be? He had realised he was with H just before he died and now Red, the garage owner. Just coincidence, that's all. But as he had cruised along the freeway suddenly he had realised. That feeling. That awful, sick feeling of fear and despair. He had felt it the night H died. He had pulled over and stopped. He put his hand to his mouth and gasped. His breathing was heavy and erratic.

But at that point it was clearly obvious. The same feelings. It was too strong to deny. This was no coincidence. He had been with H and had got that feeling which must have been roughly around the time H had died. The same with Red. By the time he had spoken to the police officer and they had drove back to the garage the paramedics had been called and already got there.

Tom told himself to stay calm. It had been raining hard, there was a damp cold feeling in the air. It was dark and the roads were slippery, and he must have got the jitters. But then how to explain the same feelings at home the night H had died. Then Tom's mind calculated something that made him sit up straight with shock. H had witnessed Tom create the file which went missing. H was the only person who could've substantiated that fact, but he died before anyone could confirm.

Red was the only witness to Tom getting his brake light fixed but he died before he could confirm. Then Tom had snapped back at himself realising that Red hadn't died. He was in a bad way but hadn't died. He may be OK. Tom breathed a sigh of relief. He was now scaring himself.

Tom had shivered. This time it was the cold. He turned the heaters back on and tried to get his mind clear. It was getting late and he still had a three-hour drive from that point, and it had been almost midnight. He tried to get his head sorted and get going.

Brake light working or not he just wanted to get home. He had driven home in silence the rest of the way. And when he had eventually arrived home it was almost 3.30am.

Since that night Tom had not been able to sleep properly or stop thinking about Red's death. He had not also not been able to stop thinking about the feelings of dread and despair that hit him. He feared it. And he did not know when it would hit him again.

Chapter 6

Tom cleared his mind of all of the negative thoughts about driving home from Davy's. The sun on his face was getting hot and he got up and moved into the shade. He was determined to paint the picket fence that surrounded their front lawn, but he felt tired. As he had been unable to relax with the papers, and it was already too hot to sit in the sun, he decided to have a swim.

He went to the outside changing area, put on his trunks, walked across the decking section and slipped into the pool. The coolness woke his body and he felt a sudden surge of energy. He slowly eased into his breaststroke and begun his lengths. He would definitely paint the fence after lunch he thought.

He hadn't done much in the way of 'home maintenance' since they had been in Evanston. He hadn't really had to. The house was immaculate and the gardens, front and rear, even more so. They had a gardener attend weekly and any minor and major maintenance or DIY they could arrange through a local firm. It was another little perk as the bill for such work would was always picked up by the company.

Tom could quite easily have picked up the phone and got them in to do the fence, but he was determined. He had thought that if he did it would take his mind off things but, more importantly, make him feel a bit more settled and part of the community. He often saw neighbours out doing their gardens, potting plants, fixing stuff on the driveways. They would talk in the street or wave to each other. But he felt a little isolated and he hadn't really got into the community spirit.

Jenna, on the other hand, was hugely into the community aspect of their life. Coffee mornings, baking mornings, afternoon tea at this house or that house. Ladies lunches, days at the Grove sitting round the pool. Spa days, picnics on the lake. He was happy for her. But he hadn't really done much socially that didn't involve his company, so he was going to try to put this right. Get out there and start doing things that didn't have a connection to work. And tonight was the start.

They were attending a charity benefit at City Hall, downtown. Jenna's friend, Marie, was married to a local congressman who did a huge amount of work for AIDS foundations and children's community projects. All very worthy stuff. Jenna had been invited purely because of her friendship with Marie and Tom found this refreshing. It was not work connected and it was genuine. He actually found himself looking forward to it.

Jenna had woken and he had noticed her sitting on a lounger in her dressing gown watching him swim. In between strokes he had managed to offer her a wave. She pressed her hand against her lips and blew him a kiss. He realised he loved her. He had always loved her. But he was surprised she still loved him. He was even more surprised she was still living in the same house as him after everything that had happened recently. She had every reason to have packed her stuff and left.

He had been acting strangely and his mind had been running and re-running the events of the past three months constantly. H's death, Red's death, the cold feelings, the fear and dread, the missing file, the brake light. Were they linked or not? Tom had been playing situations, scenario's, explanations over and over in his head since that drive back from Davy's and ever since.

He hadn't been able to concentrate at work and he was tired. He had managed to cover his tracks at work by mentioning some personal problems and an illness that appeared to have bought him some discretion, but it had been noticed. He was there early one day recently, because as usual he was unable to sleep, and he went up onto the floor and overheard some voices from Shields' office. He heard Shields' voice "….This is the big league. When you play at this level you don't do illness…Jesus, get him fucking sorted!". Tom knew they had meant him and was about to leave to avoid embarrassment when Conway and Rutherford came out the office.

It had been an awkward moment between him and Conway. As were most of their moments but they brushed it aside and both pretended Tom hadn't heard. But neither Conway nor Rutherford were yet to say anything. Tom supposed Conway was hoping he would soon be back on fire again and it would avoid the dreaded moment for Conway when Tom turned around and told him to 'go fuck himself' or he would spill the beans on his little secretary story. Tom would never do that; but Conway didn't know. He had expected Rutherford to do the pep talk, but nothing was said.

But Tom was struggling. Work was busy and his mind was just not in the game. Jenna was creating a huge social network for them and Tom couldn't keep up. Jenna had plans for the house which she went over in detail with Tom but soon after they had disappeared from his mind and this caused arguments and she accused him of not caring. He argued back that he did but, she was right, he didn't care.

She had also mentioned a nursery. Tom had not bulked or given anything away and acted comfortable with Jenna describing how it would look. But it had led to the obvious. To have a baby you must have sex. But as soon as he thought about having sex to make a baby the pressure hit, and he couldn't cope.

He had recollected his moment of clarification at the lake. The moment he decided that everything was in place for him. He was set. He was ready for the next chapter of his life. He had been so clear about it until that moment. The moment he felt that fear again and Red had the heart attack. It set him back. The vivid clarity of his decision had been overwhelmed by thoughts that Tom hated and couldn't understand. The jumbled mess of theories and explanations swallowing up his once clear thought of the next step with Jenna. He felt so sorry for her. All she wanted was the final piece of the jigsaw in her life. He could picture the pride in her face when she told her parents that she was pregnant. It gave him a warm, fuzzy feeling which was then ripped from his mind by the recollection of the deep fear he felt on those two occasions.

It had been a tough time and he felt he needed clarification. He needed something or someone to confirm to him his theories that the two deaths were somehow linked were rubbish. The evidence in Tom's mind was overwhelming but there had to be an explanation.

He had thought about Red a lot. Tom had not actually known if Red was even dead. If Red had survived Tom may have been worrying over nothing. He had needed to know. If he didn't find out then how could he get over it all? But could he accept it if Red had died? Especially of a cardio related death? There had only been one way to find out and he eventually realised that he needed back to Red's garage and find out. And he had needed to go back as soon as possible. The urge to go had been over-whelming. So much so that Tom had made the trip:

It had been difficult. Tom's main issue had been how could get away again so soon? Jenna had been so understanding and he had realised that he just couldn't drop another bomb on her. He had thought about telling her it was business but knew she wouldn't have believed him. Plus, involving work would have been too risky because of Phil.

Work had also been too busy to go in the week. It was a three-hour drive and they were not sanctioning leave at that time. He had thought he could go after work but that would have meant leaving at 7pm getting there around 10pm, and he didn't know how long he would be there for. He may not get back until early hours and Jenna would ask questions.

He had decided he would go on a Saturday. It would give him time to think of a reason. But Jenna had known something was up through that week. Tom had been quiet, and tense and she had been asking him if he was OK. He had tried to act normal, but she knew. Tom cracked and at dinner on the Thursday he had blurted out, "Look I need to go somewhere Saturday". Jenna had looked confused. In his mind he had realised what he had done and what his appetite for clarification had made him do. He had no cover story.

So he had to think on his feet. Jenna's head tilted and she turned her hands upwards as if to say, "Well, where?".

Without even thinking Tom had told her he had to go back to Davy's house. And, again, without thinking, Tom had created a scenario that sickened him. He had said Davy had asked him to go back to support him as he had split with his wife, Louise. They had not been right for a long time and Davy knew it was coming but had not had the guts to say. Tom's recent visit had been a last chance for them. Davy had suggested getting out of Louise's hair for a weekend and see how she would feel. They had gone downtown and then fishing and as soon as Tom had left she had told Davy it was over. She had left with the kids.

"Tom. Stop," he had told himself. But he had continued and told Jenna Davy had rung him and sounded suicidal. Tom had said he was concerned about him. He had to go back. Davy had said Tom was the only person he can turn to. He hated himself.

Soon after Jenna had raised some very apt questions and suggestions.
"Why go so soon, he can sort it out with Louise better if you aren't there"
"Why can't he come here?"
"Why can't you fly out next week?"

Tom knew he had to drive as Camp Douglas was halfway so flying would be pointless, but as far as Jenna was concerned he was going to Shore View. So he had told Jenna that Davy had moved away from Minneapolis to stay with a friend, and he would have to hire a car when he got to the other end so he may just as well drive. Tom somehow had answers for all of her questions. He had to go. The urge had been too great.

He had said Davy had wanted him to go back the next day but because of work he waited all week. He had left it as long as possible. Davy was in a bad way. He had said to Jenna that Davy couldn't come to them as he had no money for an airfare, and she had taken the car so couldn't drive. Tom had said he offered to pay for his air fare but Davy hates flying. That would make him worse.

As he had spoken, he felt even more sickened with the lies. It had all sounded plausible, but Tom knew it also sounded very crooked. It just didn't add up but what was he to do?

Jenna had finally cried when she reminded him that Saturday was Helen's engagement and they had been invited to her Summer ball - everyone would be there. It was the perfect chance for Tom to meet all her friends. She had been looking forward to it for ages. Tom argued his friend's condition was more important than some engagement ball. Jenna had cried even more, and Tom had walked out. As he did Jenna had screamed, "I don't even know you anymore!!"

Tom noted the shout was more of a wail and it sounded full of despair. It stabbed Tom hard, but he didn't turn. He just kept walking. He had known if he went back she would talk him out of it, but he had made his move. He was going.

He had gone into the lounge and sat in silence. He absolutely hated himself. He kept thinking what he had got himself into but the pressure to know about Red was too strong it overwhelmed him. The week passed very slowly, and all Tom could concentrate on was the drive back to Camp Douglas. He had tried to tell himself it hadn't been noticed at work, but he knew it had.

On the Friday Tom was thrown into disarray when he had been asked to go into the office on the Saturday. His mind had raced. They hadn't worked a Saturday since he transferred from New York. They had been asked to attend a strategy meeting to discuss some recent prevailing market conditions. Tom had agreed to work but had made up a story that his mother was ill, and he was flying back to Jersey to see her. So he had to leave a couple of hours early. More lies.

He knew Phil may get hold of this information and it may get back to Jenna but what the hell was he supposed to do? As he had put his jacket on and went to leave, Rutherford was walking onto the main floor from the reception foyer. As he passed he said to Tom that he had hoped his mother was OK. Tom had thanked him but as he walked out he couldn't help feeling Rutherford knew he was lying and was testing him to see if he would lie more. Tom had felt Rutherford was just reeling him in, laying down bait and then 'Boom'. He would strike and catch him out. Tom hated his paranoia.

He shook his head as he got into the lift and cursed himself for being so paranoid. But the organisation knew a lot of things about people. Rutherford may know the truth. When he had got home the house was quiet. Jenna had obviously been out. Probably on purpose as she was still angry with him. He had taken a quick shower and put on some comfortable clothes. He went into the kitchen and grabbed an apple from the fruit bowl adorning the island and he saw a note. He picked it up:

'Hope Davy is ok. Drive careful. Love you. J xx'

She was still on his side. He shook his head and had realised what an idiot he was being. But he picked up his keys, went to the car and set off anyway. He had hoped the drive would be around 3 hours. It was mid-afternoon so once he got out of the suburbs the roads were pretty clear. He stopped once just inside Wisconsin, had a drink and a toilet break and set back off. As he drove his mind had been going over the past, present and future.

Was H's heart attack and red's heart attack just a coincidence? Surely. But were they linked? The two people had been the only people who had known he had done something when straight after it appeared that he hadn't done it. His only witnesses. Surely it was coincidence. They weren't big deals...Just a missing file and a brake light. But, then again, he could've got into deep trouble in both scenarios.

But it was the feelings of dread that linked them. Tom had felt the same both times. Did he just feel that way out of coincidence? Anyhow, Red may not even be dead. He had hoped more than ever to see him at the garage. He knew it was unlikely as if he had survived, he wouldn't be back at work already would he? But Tom just hoped he would.

He had also thought how disappointed he was that he hadn't been able to return from Davy's last time and tell Jenna he wanted to have children with her. It had all been so clear at that time. If only his brake light hadn't been broken, he would never have gone to Red's and could've got on with his life. But had it been fate he had ended up there? He didn't know and wanted the answers.

After just over three hours he had started to see the signs for Camp Douglas. The scenery and landscape were, as usual, stunning, but the place had filled him a sense of foreboding and he was anxious when he had arrived. Anxious that he was going to be told what he didn't want to hear. He had still been still hoping to see Red but recalled how bad he looked just six days ago and would be surprised if he did. The sky was grey and for all its natural beauty the place had made Tom felt very unwelcome.

He had taken the slip road off and followed the signs and there, past the trees was Red's Garage. As he approached, he had noticed several cars around, and a few people dotted about. One of the cars had its hood up with two people looking in. He pulled over the crossroad and onto the large forecourt. As he did a child ran from the garage with a small Stars & Stripes flag, waving it in the air. Tom looked over and the child's parents were laughing.

Tom had suddenly stopped. What was he doing? What was he going to say? He had driven for almost three and a half hours and he hadn't thought this through. Whoever was here will just look strangely at him. He had shaken his head and got out. As he did, he had noticed in the garage at the counter was the young girl who had been so upset on that night. Who was she? Just someone who worked there or closer, maybe a relation? Tom had been relieved anyway as at least there was someone here who was linked and who would know what he was on about.

50

He had taken a deep breath and gone inside. It was a standard garage shop with the usual array of items most garages would sell. Magazines, books, car accessories, sandwiches, snacks, maps, camping accessories, that type of thing. Country music playing quietly through a speaker in the corner above the counter. The girl had been serving a customer, so Tom stopped at a post card display and begun looking at the various postcards on sale. As he spun the display, he kept checking on the girl.

Eventually the customer left, and Tom started to approach. As he got nearer the girl looked at him and smiled and then someone said from the other side of the shop "Excuse me Miss, how much are the foot-pumps here?" The girl looked at Tom and he had indicated that she should go and serve the other customer. She said thank you and left the counter. Tom looked at the various maps and charts behind the counter and could hear them discussing the foot-pump in the background. As the girl had returned to the counter, she had looked at Tom and asked if she could help him. Tom stepped back and gestured to the large, lumberjack looking man with the foot-pump to go ahead. As the girl served him Tom looked anxiously outside hoping not to see anyone else coming in. The forecourt was empty.

What seemed like an age passed as the girl finally bagged up the foot-pump and the man had left the shop. The girl had then taken a deep breath, smiled and asked Tom what she could do for him.

Tom faltered for a split second. He lost his track. But had eventually explained to the girl he was at the garage on Sunday and he had witnessed Red's heart attack. The girls face had dropped. Tom had quickly continued that he had come back just to see if he was OK. With this the girl had left the counter and shouted through a back door. She explained they had better go outside and just then a young man came out from the door to cover the counter.

When they had got outside the girl lit a cigarette. She had told Tom she was Charlie's niece. Confused by this, Tom had questioned the name and the girl had explained Red's name was actually Charlie Redmond but had been known as 'Red' since he was a little boy.

She had asked Tom if he knew Red personally. Tom had confirmed he hadn't and was just concerned for his welfare. She had then told Tom what he didn't want to hear. Red had died later on in the night of a heart attack. He had suffered major cardio trauma and they just couldn't get him back. Tom had been stunned. He must have shown it too as the girl had asked if he was OK.

Tom had gathered his thoughts and tried to sort the jumble in his head. As he did the girl had asked if he was local and Tom said he had come from Evanston in Illinois. The girl had looked shocked.
"You drove all that way just to find out about a stranger?"

Tom was embarrassed. He nodded and the girl looked at him strangely then said, "That's nice. But you could've just called".

Tom shook his head and smiled. He could've called. Why didn't he? He couldn't explain but he had felt somehow drawn back to the place. It was almost as if he needed to be here to accept what he knew he was going to be told.

The girl explained they had been at the ER for half an hour when he was pronounced dead around 11pm. She went into explaining how the drinking and lack of exercise hadn't helped but Tom wasn't listening. This was a part of the jigsaw he hoped he wouldn't find. Why couldn't he have just seen Red alive and well?

The girl had offered Tom a cigarette which he accepted. She told him she had to get back and thanked him again for coming up. Tom stood there and smoked the cigarette not being able to think straight. After standing in the forecourt trying to take the information in, he had walked back to his car. He felt sick but had eventually set off again and drove slowly back. He wasn't in a rush so had driven calmly and just let the thoughts roll across his mind until he became numb to them. He had planned to eat on the drive back but had lost his appetite.

He had arrived home about 10pm and had gone indoors. Jenna was at her friend's engagement party and he suddenly wished he was there with her. He had been alone too long. He had gone in and walked through to the reception lounge and sat down. Then he had heard a sob. He had jumped, startled. He then heard another sob but this time louder, 'What the hell?' he had thought. He went to the bottom of the stairway and could then hear crying more clearly.

He had shouted, "Jenna, is that you?". But got no answer although he had still heard sobbing. He had repeated his original question but this time louder. Soon after he had seen a dark figure approach the top of the stairs. It was hard to see properly but he was sure he could make it out to be Jenna.

"How was Davy?" Jenna said in a bland, monotone type way. The direct line of questioning surprised Tom.
"Er, yeah, he is ok....Look, are you ok?" Tom had replied.

As he spoke Jenna had started to walk down the large staircase and as she did her face had become clearer with each step. As she had drawn closer Tom could now see her face was red and puffy and her eyes were black with mascara.
"Jesus, Jenna..." Tom went to step up to reach out to her and as he did she launched herself into him. Her weight had forced Tom back and they both fell to the floor. As soon as they did Jenna launched an onslaught of blows to his head, neck and chest. Tom felt a wave of heat through his body due to the shock and ferociousness of the

attack. He had tried to hold her hands but couldn't quite grasp them and several more hits reigned onto him.

Jenna was screaming and crying in despair and was surprisingly strong, but Tom suddenly managed to get a grip of her wrists and used his strength to twist her onto her back and hold her arms down and out of range. As he did he felt the strength ebb from her and she lay, crying loudly underneath him. Saliva was strewn across her cheek and her hair was knotted and messy.
"Jenna!" Tom shouted but she looked away.
"Jenna!" Tom shouted again and she turned to face him
"What!!" she shouted at the top of her voice.
"What the fuck is wrong with you?"
"Who is she? Who the fuck is she?" she shouted
Tom pushed her hands down and lifted himself away and stood up at Jenna's feet who just laid in the same position.
"Who?" Tom enquired
"The fucking bitch…What's her fucking name?" she had said spitefully

Tom had been shocked. He had denied seeing another woman and had desperately tried to find out why she was saying these things. Eventually Jenna had calmed down enough to explain and had told Tom she had been getting ready when the phone rang. She had answered it and the guy had explained his name was Davy, Tom's friend from Minneapolis. He had said it was a shame she couldn't come when Tom visited last and he was wondering when Tom was going to visit again, and when they could come there. Jenna had said he seemed very nice.

Tom admitted defeat. The game was up. He couldn't talk his way out of this. He could try but it would just end up even messier. Jenna had then sarcastically told him Davy sounded very well. And she had asked how the family were and he had said all very well and looking to all meet up, adding that Davy didn't sound like a man on the brink of suicide as his wife had left him. In fact, the wife had called to him that dinner was ready as he was on the phone. All very happy families it seemed.

Tom had got the urge to lie again and try to come up with something. He had thought about suggesting that obviously Davy was putting on a show for Jenna and was just trying to find out where Tom was. He was hiding his pain. But Tom had realised it was over and he had known he now had to tell her the truth.
"So where the fuck was you?" Jenna had growled through gritted teeth.
"Look, we need to talk," said Tom quietly. Jenna gasped and begun crying uncontrollably expectant of news of Tom's affair. Tom had tried to calm her and promised it was nothing to do with anything like that. Eventually Tom had made coffee and they sat in the lounge.

He then went on to explain everything. About the brake light and the police officer. Going to Red's and then getting pulled over again. Going back to Red's. The cold feelings. The deep fear and panic that came and then passed. Red's heart attack. The urge to go back to find out the truth. Then finding the truth. The link to H's death. The same feelings. The same cold, despair that fills him with the ultimate dread. The fear he had now. What was it? Did he sense death? Is he a danger to people? A danger to Jenna? How scared he now was.

It had all come out. Tom had told her everything. And at the end he started to tell Jenna how good he had felt before he left Davy's. How clear his thoughts had been. That he had wished to return to start a family. And with that tears had rolled down his face and he slipped to floor and started sobbing uncontrollably. Jenna had just held him and rocked until he had eventually stopped.

Chapter 7

After finishing his swim he dried himself and made another coffee Tom
went back outside to relax on a lounger in the shade, although, he kept his
feet in the sun, as they were the only part of him that hadn't warmed after
his swim.

He had an unusually positive feeling about the weekend and was
determined to try to keep the memories of the last few months at bay. He
had thought it all over enough for today and he looked up at the clear
blue sky, took a deep breath and closed his eyes.

The visit to find out the truth about Red and the consequent night of
confession to Jenna was now one week ago. After all the tears and truths,
they had eventually gone to bed at around 4am. They had slept in until
around 3pm the next afternoon. It had been so physically and emotionally
draining for them both.

The three weeks that had past had been strange. Tom felt uncomfortable
at first but as time had gone by things had slowly returned to normal and
it was almost as if they had found a new sense of loving for each other.
They started to have fun again and talked more. Jenna seemed happy that
at least Tom was not having an affair. It had seemed to have invigorated
her and she seemed more like that excitable, fun loving girl Tom had
fallen in love with.

Tom had taken his car to a local garage and got the brake light fixed.
Which he found difficult as it brought his confusion to the forefront of
his mind again. Although as the days passed and a week went by he had
started to feel more relaxed and the thoughts about the two deaths had
become a little faded and foggy. Perhaps the crying he had done that night
had been what he needed to release the tension of the last few months.
Maybe it was that tension that was playing tricks on his mind. The
questions had lessened, and his conspiracy theories had been reduced to
flashing thoughts rather than long drawn out intense personal
interrogation.

Work had also been unusual for Tom. He still had those thoughts about
the missing file and H's death and he still couldn't quite work out why he
had not been hung out to dry. However, the company was doing well and
some solid financial performance figures for the first quarter were being
celebrated and touted as proof the transfer was a success. But
management and shareholders only saw success in monitory value. Tom

knew that some of the staff were still not particularly happy with the transfer and had still not fully settled; especially him.

Rutherford had been really good with Tom in the last few weeks, and Tom had felt a little less pressure to maintain the high standards expected. Rutherford had, on two occasions, asked if Tom was OK and how his family were. And one night when Tom was the only one on the floor, Rutherford had asked him if he fancied heading downtown for a drink. Tom had reluctantly accepted as he knew it was going to be the pep talk, or worse, the grilling. But it hadn't been either, and Rutherford had actually been good company, but it was so unusual and out of character for Rutherford. He had a reputation for being aloof and detached from the worker ants.

Even so, Tom had still been expecting a meeting after hearing Shields' concerns about his sickness and personal problems, but he actually got the opposite. No heat. Tom wondered if Shields had even been speaking about him. Tom thought that he must have been. But nothing came his way.

And Tom sensed Rutherford's sudden attraction to him upset Conway. Tom knew Conway was getting a little frustrated at this new trend. He hadn't seen Rutherford extending the same warmth to others. and Tom noticed Conway had suddenly become edgy. Tom thought that Conway felt isolated and wondered why he was receiving Rutherford's advances. Rutherford hated Conway anyway; everybody knew it, even Conway and Rutherford themselves. But Rutherford accepted Conway because he got the job done.

Tom had also been in touch with his sister, Claire. She had phoned him a week or so ago. At first Tom was a little embarrassed and felt guilty. Things had taken their toll not only on him mentally and physically but also detached him from his family. The months had flown by and Tom had not even thought about them. They spoke and he knew his sister could sense this but as ever she was the ultimate diplomat and eased him with her ability to cope with awkwardness. She filled him in with life back in New Jersey and how the boys were getting on in school and sports.

Tom tried to return the favour but, as he had to leave all the weirdness and strange stuff of the last few months out, he didn't really have much to say. They arranged for Tom and Jenna to visit them all in the next few weeks. Claire also told him their mum had been ill recently and so Tom had called his mum immediately after the conversation with his sister.

They caught up and he told her about the visit he had arranged with Claire.

He had asked how she was and as usual she was coy. "It's nothing" she had said. But it turned out to be stomach pain, tiredness and a loss of appetite. He played the caring son and told her to visit her GP, which she had already done. And also to take it easy, which she was already doing. "Your sister has got it all under control," she said.
Tom felt a pang of jealousy as he usually did, but he was glad his sister was there for her.

As he slumbered, he could feel the world around him drifting away and he was soon in a deep sleep. The next thing he knew he was woken by a gentle nudge. He still jumped a little and opened his eyes to see Jenna standing above him with a smile. He smiled back and rubbed his eyes. "You'd fallen asleep Mr Lazy," she said
"I know, just too relaxed I suppose," Tom replied.
Jenna looked at him and smiled again, "That's good" she said with a nod, "Look, I am going shopping for a few hours. I have to get groceries for my parent's dinner tomorrow. Are you going to do the fence?" she asked politely.
"Yes, definitely. Just gonna have a bit of lunch and then will get to it."
"Please, make sure you do as it's now too late to call the maintenance company."
"I know, I know, I know," Tom interjected
"Ok, just saying." Jenna tailed off as she started to walk back indoors. As she went inside she shouted, "Will be a few hours," and then she was gone.

After the short nap he had had, Tom really didn't want to do the fence anymore, but was now committed. He went inside and made himself a pastrami sub and a coffee and she sat at the breakfast bar and ate it, eventually tearing himself away from the TV. He went to the garage and got the paint and brushes and then went out front to get in with the fence. When he got there, he felt odd. Like people were watching and wondering who this stranger was.

As Tom got going a few odd cars drove by. Tom looked up at the drivers and didn't recognise any of them. He was sure he had seen one of them walking past at some point, but he didn't wave. He felt frustrated and wondered why he felt so awkward being neighbourly. He smiled as he thought it was probably the New Yorker in him.
The light cloud that had drifted over had now and it was hot. The sun was beating down and Tom was sweating. It wasn't much time before he had

worked his way through about a third of the fence. He stepped back and looked at his handy work and was impressed as to how much better the fence looked. He felt he was quite enjoying it now.

He got back to it and a little while later Tom heard a voice.
"You're doing a good job there, young man." He turned to see very smart and elderly lady walking past with a Chihuahua.
"Thank you." Tom replied a little tentatively.
She stopped, "I've not seen much of you out and about."
"Oh no, been very busy with work since we arrived," he replied, which at that point he thought it best to get up and go over to her.
"Hello, I'm Eva McGeedy. I've met Jenna a few times but it's nice to finally meet you too."
Tom offered his hand and then realised it was covered in white paint, so retracted it and offered her his other hand which she shook.
"Good to meet you. I'm Tom Callaghan"
"I have heard a lot about you," Mrs McGeedy said with a wry smile, and they both laughed.
"Oh dear," Tom replied with a smile, "Doesn't sound too good."
"No, no, no….On the contrary, don't be too hard on yourself," and just as the conversation tailed off Mrs McGeedy saved it from becoming awkward, "Well, you are busy, so I will let you get on…….Hope to see you out and about more," and she started to walk away giving the dog a tug away from where it was sniffing.
"I hope so too," replied Tom with a wave, "Just busy at work. Goodbye", Tom turned and walked back to the fence.

He thought that the conversation was nice, and it made him smile to himself. It was the first time he had any real proper contact with any of his neighbours other than just a wave or a nod.

He dipped the brush in the paint and carried on. Soon he was flying along and without even realising the time he soon only had a few more panels to paint. He took another step back and the fence looked great. A sense of pride washed over him. He was glad he had taken the effort to do it.

He was soon finished and took one last look, "Oh yes", he said under his breath. He looked at the time and it was almost 3pm. He thought he could go in, wash up and catch a couple of hours sports before they have to get ready to go out.

He went inside and washed his hands. Turned the TV on and flicked through the channels and a hockey match caught his eye. He was about to grab a drink when he realised he had left the paint tin and brush outside.

He went back out to retrieve them and just as he did he heard a car approach then looked up and it was Jenna. He stood and watched her pull onto the driveway but caught a strange look of frustration on her face.

As she got out she shook her head. "I knew it," she said and went to the back of the car and opened the boot.
"Huh?" said Tom confused.
"Why the hell do I listen to you, Tom? Why can't I trust you just to do anything? You think you will get that fence done before we go out!!"

Tom froze. He turned slowly to look and when he did what he saw almost knocked him down like a freight train. The fence was still in its original state with faded and cracked paint. Tom just stood and stared. He tried to speak but no sound would come out. His hand went up to his mouth and he slumped to his knees, "Tom? What are you doing?" said Jenna angrily looking up and down the street.

"Jesus Tom," she spat, "You are embarrassing us. Get up!" she commanded as she walked to the house with the shopping bags. She stopped at the door and turned, "Tom, get the hell up and get in."

Tom slowly stood. But he couldn't move. He couldn't think. His mind had gone blank. Then he came to. He looked down at his hands and they still had the odd specks of paint he couldn't get off. He looked at his sweatshirt. It had paint flicks on it and was sweaty under the arms and around the chest.

Tom felt sick and did not know what to do. Was he going mad? He did not know. His situation now took a serious twist. It was now clear there was either something very unusual happening to him or he was going mad. He laughed. He didn't know why but it just happened naturally. He was mad he thought.

"Tom!!" he heard. He looked and Jenna was shouting from the front door. He looked down at the tin. The brush was covered in paint and the tin was almost empty. He stared. He rubbed his eyes and hoped he was having a bad dream. But he wasn't. He slowly walked up the front path, past the manicured and landscaped front garden and into the house. He took one look back at the faded and peeling fence and shut the door. He walked into the lounge and sat down. Jenna stormed into the room.

"Tom, what the fuck do you think you are doing? You don't do what I ask and then you are on your knees like a fucking zombie in the

street…Are you being serious? I thought we was over all this weird shit."
Tom just sat and stared at the floor.

"Tom!" shouted Jenna "I ask you to do one thing and you promise to do it. Then you just go all weird. What the fuck is wrong with you, Tom? Why can't you just be…Normal."
"I painted the fence," said Tom quietly.

"No Tom, you didn't paint the fucking fence. Go look, it's still how it was…Jesus! This is ridiculous. You are like a stranger, Tom. You are freaking me out, as well as completely fucking me off. My parents come tomorrow, and I wanted it perfect. You've just wasted the whole day…", with that she walked back out the room.
"I painted the fence," said Tom again.
From the kitchen Jenna shouted "And thanks very much, Tom. You may not give a shit about us and this house, but I do…Why did you just not let me call the maintenance guy? Why do I even listen to you?"
"I painted the fucking fence!" shouted Tom. Jenna stormed back into the lounge, "Don't you dare!! Don't you dare shout at me, you arsehole! How dare you!" She got close up to Tom and he thought she was going to launch into another tirade of punches. He stepped back and raised his hands to his chest.
"Tom. Go and look. The fence is not done. Are you telling me you painted it, but now by some miracle it's not done?"
"Yes" Tom said sharply.
"Oh my god. Oh my god!" shouted Jenna, "This is sick. This is sick. No, this is beyond sick….You are out of control. You are fucked. You need help…You need professional help," her hand now on her forehead, which she did when she was angry.
"It would help if you started talking to me," Tom said sarcastically.
Jenna stopped, shocked, "Sorry? What did you say? Just repeat it Tom as I am not sure I heard that right. Or if I did I am not sure I believe what you just said."
Tom shook his head.
Jenna continued "The shit you have put me through since we moved here. All this weird shit. It is so unfair for you to blame me…"
"I'm not blam…" Tom tried to interject but Jenna countered him.
"You complete arsehole, Tom. You somehow blame me for not listening? You sat crying on the floor while I hugged you and listened to your story about the file at work, the cold feelings, the weird people grabbing at you……..Some fucking guy you don't even know that you drove into another state to see if he was alright. The fucking brake light you supposedly got fixed that never happened…Jesus!" Jenna's hand again now on her forehead,"2 hours I sat and listened to your bullshit…No

more. You need help. We have a life here. I have a life. And you are doing your best to ruin it."

Tom cut in, "Well. I am sorry an over-worked, under-sexed nut-job is ruining your perfect life."

Jenna stared at him. It was the look. Tom had gotten this look once before only. And it was when they almost split up after he admitted he had kissed another girl in a drunken moment of stupidity. That time she said to him that he had one more chance. Tom suddenly wished he hadn't said it, but it had come out, and that was it. As she stared at him a tear rolled down her face. Tom knew it was him that was avoiding sex. Jenna was too angry to even respond. She walked out the room and he heard her go upstairs and slam the bedroom door.

Tom just sat. Head in hands. A perfect weekend. A charity ball; then dinner the next day with the in-laws. How the fuck did it get to this he thought. The fence. The fucking fence. Why did he get involved? His mind was a scrambled mess. What was going on? He looked outside and confirmed the fence was as it was before, faded and cracking. He sighed and just stared. A tear rolled down his face.

Outside a black SUV slowly cruised past the house but Tom was completely unaware. The driver spotted Jenna upstairs at the window. She also noticed the vehicle and just as she and the driver made eye contact it sped away.

Chapter 8

As the third large whisky slipped down, Tom started to wonder why he had started to drink. He couldn't recall actually thinking about it and making a rational decision to get the whisky out. But by the time he had realised he was already three down. He wasn't feeling any better yet though, just slightly warmer.

He hadn't heard anything from Jenna for an hour or so. Not even footsteps in the bedroom or across the landing. It was a large, well-made house so people walking above didn't make too much noise. But when the house was quiet you could normally just about hear movement. He realised she was probably just laying on the bed sobbing.

He thought what a prick he had been. Why did he have to make the comment about being 'under-sexed'? He knew the impact it would have. But just like the whisky he hadn't thought. It just happened.

He had wondered a few times if he should go up and check on her. Or maybe find out if they were still going to the ball tonight. But then thought better of it. A charity ball is probably the last thing Jenna was concerned about, especially when she was living with a spiteful freak. She was probably laying up there wondering how she got involved in all of this. He just sat and stared at the marble breakfast bar as his thoughts raced.

At one point he had even got halfway up the stairs and then just stopped and turned back. He knew Jenna too well. He knew it would be pointless and make things worse. He always said she was like a wild animal. When she was up against it or had her back against the wall she went into the zone. Survival. And when she was in that zone you just could not communicate or negotiate with her. He had seen it several times. And it was one of her traits that allowed to rise quickly through the junior tennis ranks when she was younger. After they got together, she showed him some old tapes of her matches. She was an aggressive player who zoned out on the court. He always said it was like she was in a trance.

There was one particular match where she had been thrashed in the first set 1-6 so was one set down, then four games down in the second set and she came back to win the game. You could see something in her eyes change at the start of her comeback and the girl she played never won another game. Hardly even another point. It was brutal. She turned everything up to maximum. She ran faster, hit harder, jumped higher and each time she hit the ball it was like the last time she was ever going to hit a ball. The power and accuracy were frightening. Tom found himself feeling sorry for her opponent. A young girl from Seattle. She was like a hurt boxer on the ropes clinging on for dear life.

At the end of the game Jenna walked up to the net, shook her hand and walked away. The girl was close to tears, but Jenna didn't even speak to her. Tom mentioned at the time that he felt this was a little harsh after what she had done to her, but Jenna said she didn't remember it. She didn't remember hitting one ball during her comeback and didn't remember walking up to the net.

Tom was amazed. At the end of the match she sat down, and the camera catches her look up and then she just snaps out of it. She waves to her parents in the small crowd and smiles that wide, cute smile. It was like Jenna had returned from that place she had been to.

And it was that place that she went to. That intensity that she could muster up that made people believe she could be a champion. It made Jenna believe she could be a champion. But after the injury disappointment that intensity and focus stayed inside her. She didn't really have anywhere to let it out. The tennis court was where she did for a long time, but that was cruelly taken away.

So when they argued, and Tom upset her, she went to that place. In the past he had tried to smooth things over after an argument but soon realised he was wasting his time. She just needed to go there, and she would come back when she was ready. He folded his arms and rested them on the worktop. He laid his head onto his arms. It felt nice. His body relaxed and his racing mind slowed. He took a deep breath and closed his eyes and drifted slowly away.

The first claw came from behind. Tom turned and looked into the darkness but there was nobody there, although he could feel a presence. There was also no indication where he was. Just a vast blackness with no focus points. Suddenly out of nowhere another claw swiped at him and this time he saw where it came from. He tried to block it, but it went through and connected. He reacted expecting a cutting pain, but he felt none.

He then saw the assailant. Thin, bright eyes of yellow, firstly right in front of him, then suddenly to the left and then darting to the right. A wet cold claw tried to grab him, but he dodged backward. He felt an abyss below him, but he knew he had to step backward to escape the assailant, but he couldn't force himself to. He froze.

Now the eyes. again central to him, came closer. A feeling of enclosure wrapped him, and the claws reached for him. He had no choice. It was coming now to finish him. He made the move and stepped back. The feeling of falling overwhelmed him. His stomach turned and he tried to see where he would land but it was just darkness. Open and vast. As he fell he could feel claws trying to grab him and with each grab he flinched and juddered with fear. His stomach turned and turned and turned.

Tom woke with a start. His eyes wide. The clatter of something close to him. He looked around and saw Jenna at the sink pouring herself a water. He noticed how wonderful she looked. She had a black evening gown on and high heels. He then realised the clatter was the heels on the tiled floor. She finished her drink and put the glass in the sink. The air was filled with perfume and it didn't help Tom's groggy feeling. Jenna turned and walked across the kitchen.

"You think that will help?" she said pointing at the whisky bottle. Tom was about to answer but Jenna continued, "And before you ask, I am going to the ball. I do not want you there to ruin my night. I am staying with a friend," the last part tailed off as she was walking whilst talking and had already got out in the hallway towards the door.

"Wait......Jenna!" Tom shouted but he then heard the front door slam shut.
His head was thumping, and he suddenly felt sick. He stopped and went to the sink to throw up what he felt was coming out. Then it subsided. He took a deep breath went out into the dark hallway and to the front door. He opened it but Jenna was already reversing at speed off the driveway. The car bumped off the driveway into the road and was away before Tom could even get halfway down the driveway.
"Shit!" he uttered under his breath.

He stood and took a deep breath. The surge from his stomach came quickly and he vomited onto the driveway. Luckily it was more liquid than lumps, he looked around to make sure no one was watching. He then scraped the liquid with his foot hoping it would disappear. It didn't.
It was just after dusk and he realised what a nice evening it was. And how nicer it would be if he was dressed up driving to the ball with Jenna. What a complete fuck up this all was. He looked back at the unpainted fence adorning their front garden and he shook his head. What was happening to him?

He walked back to the house and retrieved the whisky bottle then went back outside and to the far end of the front veranda. He had never used the furniture Jenna had put in the corner overlooking the front garden, so he thought this is a good as time as any. It was peaceful and quiet. The sound of crickets filled the air and Tom found it very relaxing.

He took a swig from the bottle and started to think. What was happening to him? First it was the computer file at work. He had done that, and it had disappeared. The brake light he had got fixed and then it was like it had not been done. Now the fence. He had spent two hours working his balls off to get that done and now it was like he had never even touched it. But he had done it and he knew had had. He had had the paint on him and his clothes to prove it. The sweat. How could he prove to himself and Jenna he had done it?

Then his mind switched to the deaths. With the file at work H was the only person who could say he had done it. He thought about this and wondered if H had not died what he had been able to say anyway. He would've been in work and told Conway, Rutherford and Shields and every other person, that he saw Tom complete the file, read it and watched him mail it to Rutherford. But then all people would've said in response to that would've simply been, "Fine. But where is it?"

It wouldn't really have solved the problem. And Tom knew that behind closed doors they would've been saying the two of them were close. They were friends. H was not likely to drop Tom in it anyway. It was weird. Was it just coincidence that H was there and witnessed Tom do something but wasn't around to clarify? It possibly was but it was it a coincidence that the same thing happened with Red and the brake light. He was the only person who could clarify to the cop that Tom had been in and got the brake light done. But he then was no longer able to clarify.

It was a long shot, but these could've been coincidences. But what alarmed Tom most was the feelings. The cold, despairing feelings that frightened him so much. He had thought over and over about the times of these feelings and he was sure they would've been around the same time of the deaths. He shook his head. Were these coincidences? Or more to the point, what where these feelings?

And now the fence. Tom stared. He looked at the fence. Why? He took another swig. He realised he was starting to feel drunk and thought it may be best to lay off the whisky, but he took another swig regardless.

He thought about his and Jenna's lives. And how it was so planned out. And how it had all gone so wrong. He felt like his life was unravelling. Work was getting too much, and he wasn't focused. It had been noted and he knew that at any time he would surely be called in. His marriage was slipping away. He felt isolated from his mum and sister. And his friends, even if he still had any? This whole thing seemed to be eating him up.

He took a deep breath and looked across the street at the house opposite. It was a beautiful Italian Renaissance style mansion. Owned by a couple by the name of Harrison. Jenna had spoken to them a few times and told Tom they were lovely. She had told Tom he should try and go over to meet them. Apparently, he would get on well with the husband, Frank.

He was a real man's man. Ex-military, Ex-CIA, a real American hero and genuinely nice with it. He had put Jenna's mind at rest and said to her he was always on the look-out. Always ensured everyone's properties were ok. Some were gated but most weren't, and he said he does the rounds when he takes the dog out for a walk. "This is a lovely place, but you can't be too careful. Bad people with nothing are drawn to good people with everything" was what he had said. Apparently, they had asked Tom and Jenna to go over for drinks in the summer house, but they hadn't yet found time.

Tom thought. He wondered if Frank had seen him doing the fence. Then he realised how stupid he was being. That would be a great introduction wouldn't it? "Hi, I'm Tom. Did you see me paint the fence today?"
"Er, no son. Sorry. Why is that?"
"Oh, it's just that I think I am going mad and just wanted you to confirm it" Tom would say.
"Oh, well OK sonny, you are mad. Fancy a drink in the summer house" Frank would ask.
Tom laughed to himself and took another swig.

Then Tom noticed something. The Harrison's property was gated. And on the top of the security gate was a small camera. Tom stood up. Focused. He noted the trajectory of the camera. It appeared to swivel slowly from side to side but looked as though it was facing so that it covered the area in front of the gate but also a lot of what was beyond.

He put down the bottle and quickly walked down the driveway and then stopped to get a closer look. He needed to get up closer to see the trajectory it was covering. If it covered the whole road and footpath opposite the street it would show Tom's fence. He was suddenly excited "Take it easy partner," he thought. He realised that you can't just go and walk straight up to a neighbour's CCTV camera. That would get people quizzing.

He decided to go for a walk. Tom left the driveway and turned left on his and Jenna's side of the street. He took a quick look opposite at the camera but couldn't work it out. He walked further up, kept going past three, four, five and six properties. Then he stopped, crossed the street and started to walk back down. If anyone saw him, he would say he had a headache and was just trying to clear his head. Then he realised what an idiot he must've looked. But who would ask? It's not illegal to walk up and down a street. Just looks a little odd, he thought.

He kept walking and as he started to approach the Harrison's he looked down at his foot. He instinctively did this and surprised himself and how he was acting. As he approached, he looked down again without thinking and then just as he got to the gate he bent down and pretended to tie his trainer.

He actually undone the lace, and then did it back up, but whilst he did he took what he thought to be an innocent look up around and at the camera. He got a good look. He saw it swivel clearly and when he looked at the trajectory, he was sure it was looking out to the whole road and would cover the other side and the fence. He was sure of it.

He stood up. Straightened his sweater and took another look. He was sure.

He carried on walking further up and eventually when he thought it didn't look too obvious he crossed back over and walked back to his house. As he walked up the driveway he realised how stupid he must've looked, but it seemed quiet and he didn't think anyone would've seen him. Then he thought of his neighbours looking out their windows at him walking up and down the street.
"Fuck 'em," he said under his breath.

He picked the bottle up off the veranda, took a big swig and smiled. He went inside and closed the door. Tomorrow he would go over and ask to see the footage. How he was going to do this he was yet to work out. But he would think of something. He always did.

Chapter 9

The darkness engulfed Tom, and he had no idea where he was; although his senses told him he wasn't alone. Each time a cold, clawed hand reached for him he flinched and dodged, but he knew he couldn't avoid its evil contact much longer. Then suddenly another claw and then another, all from different angles, reached out and swiped at him. Then more, too many now to avoid. But each time Tom expected contact and pain there was nothing, like they were passing through his body.

He screamed out for someone to help. But he knew deep down there was no one who could hear him. The pressure was now building as the claws multiplied. Grabbing and swiping from all directions. But then two claws came at him from directly in front and grabbed him around the neck. It was then finally that he sensed contact and suddenly it became much more vivid. Almost real.

He tried to pull the claws away, but his arms would not work. He could feel the momentum of his arms swing up but then no feeling at the vital moment of attempting to grab his assailants. The claws got tighter, and Tom started now to struggle for breath. He attempted to scream but nothing came out. Then he saw the eyes. The evil, foreboding eyes that looked directly at him. As the claws tightened the eyes thinned. Tom knew his time was up.

The eyes then glowed brighter and the glare stronger. Tom was now unable to look directly at them as it was too bright. He tried to take one last breath, but he failed. His lungs and throat now burning, he knew this was the end. The feeling of despair made his stomach roll and the last of whatever oxygen he had dissipated, and he was gone.

Tom jumped up and screamed. He was sat in his bed. Sweat poured off him. He tried to look around, but it was too bright. He noticed the curtains wide open and the sun beaming directly in and onto him. He shielded his eyes but then felt his stomach turn. He leant over and vomited down the side of the bed and onto the carpet. As he leant over the last remnants of sick dripped from his mouth. Sweat dripped from his upper lip and amalgamated with the mucus dripping out of his nose. He retched with a low growl from his stomach but nothing else came up.

When he knew the worst had passed, he lifted himself up and lay back, shielding his eyes again. His head throbbed with pulsating pain and he lay there until he thought it best to close the curtains to protect himself from the heat and glare. Eventually he swung his body around and sat up but inadvertently stepped in the vomit on the carpet.

"Fuck!" he whispered.

He stood up and as he did everything spun and he thought he was going to vomit again so he bent over, hands on knees, ready to relieve another stomach full. But, again, he just retched and then had a coughing fit. His mouth now full of phlegm made him feel worse and so he just spat it out onto the carpet knowing he was going to have to clean it anyway.

He made his way across the room to the en-suite bathroom and as he entered felt the relief of its cool interior. He sat at the toilet for 15 minutes with his eyes shut. The floor was hard, but cold, and so quite inviting and the banging in his head subsided slightly. Eventually he felt well enough to take sips of water from the tap to help his parched throat. It felt good but at the same time a little nauseating as his body was still in protection mode and automatically trying to reject anything by mouth.

He took a deep breath and wiped the sweat from his brow. He ran the tap and splashed water on his face and round the back of his neck. It felt refreshing. He dried himself and the left the bathroom but as he did, he noticed the trail of vomit footprints across the carpet. "Fuck" he whispered again. Jenna had picked the carpet and it had been delivered by courier from Saks in New York City, both at great cost. He had to get this sorted.

He went back into the bathroom and washed his feet in the bidet. He dried them and went back into the bedroom avoiding any vomit. Suddenly the smell of the sick engulfed him and made him gag. He opened the window and leant out, taking in a huge gulp of fresh air. The coolness that drifted in was pleasant and helped him relax.

He sat on the end of the bed trying to get his thoughts in order. He recalled the nightmare he had just had and realised the similarity of it to the dream he had had the night before. He wondered if it was the drink. They were very vivid, and he shuddered at the thought of them. They were similar to nightmares he had as a child which, at the time he recalls as involving creatures with claws and also being very vivid. He remembered his mum getting in bed with him and comforting him after such a nightmare. He would slowly fall back to sleep in her arms as she comforted him, "My special boy," she would whisper as she stroked his forehead.

Then, in a flash, the events the day before and last night started to slowly come back to him. As he remembered the argument with Jenna his heart sank. He held his head "Fuck" he whispered to himself. Then his memory became more vivid and he realised what a mess it all was. He turned and looked at the bed wishing Jenna was sleeping next to him and he shook his head.

Tom went downstairs and as he did, he reluctantly called Jenna's name, half of him hoping she would answer and the other half hoping she would not. He called again when he got to the bottom of the stairs and walked into the lounger. He went into the kitchen and diner and looked out through the expansive sliding doors. He couldn't see her. He finally went to the front reception room and looked out onto the drive, but her car wasn't there. She wasn't home.

It was then he recalled her saying she was staying at a friends' house. Tom went back to the kitchen and made himself a glass of ice-cold water and downed it in one go. He gagged. Even the water tasted sickly, but he knew he had to rehydrate. He sat at the breakfast bar and cupped his chin into his hands. He needed to think and get himself straight.

He looked at the time and it was 9.49am. The first thing he needed to do was get the carpet sorted and that he had to try clear up the worst of the mess he had made in the bedroom, so he went outside to the garage to get a bucket and sponge. The heat of the day hit him, and he hoped none of his neighbors would see him in this state. He went in and back upstairs and before anything else he got into the shower and set it to cold. The cold water made him shiver but woke him up some more. He slowly adjusted it to warmer to take the edge off and then got out. Feeling slightly better.

He dried and dressed and then attempted to clean the mess in the bedroom. He made the best of it and got rid of the lumps, but it still looked bad but would need to be left to the professionals. He grabbed his iPad from the drawer and turned it on. He typed 'Carpet Cleaners Evanston' into the search engine. Several came up and he rang the top one which went to answer phone. He then amended his search to '24/7 Carpet Cleaners Evanston'. He rang the next on the list, A1 Cleaners and eventually got through to a young lady who made the arrangements to get someone there around 2pm. He told her they would get a big tip if it could be sooner and she said she would see what she could do.
He then needed to try and find out when Jenna would be home. He took a deep breath and dialed her number but cancelled it before it rang. "Fuck," he whispered.

He then realised how stupid he was being and so took another deep breath and called her again. This time it rang but then went to answer phone. He terminated the call without leaving a message.

He headed back downstairs and recalled his reconnaissance mission to check out Harrisons camera on the front gate. At first, he cringed with embarrassment at the thought of a drunken guy walking around the street trying to look casual. But then he thought more of it. He recalled how big the urge was to see the footage; how nobody would've stopped him. It reminded him of the same urge he felt to go back to check on Red's wellbeing.

He went into the lounge and laid on the settee. As he relaxed a wave of relief and comfort washed over him and he thought it wouldn't hurt to stay there for a while. Before he knew it, he had dozed off and it was only a truck driving by that stirred him. He lay there with his eyes closed but he knew he was awake. He took a deep breath and sat up. His head spun but not as much as before. He looked out of the window and the sun was now a lot higher and he realised he may have slept longer than he had wanted.

Tom went into the kitchen and checked the time on the cooker clock, 11.06am. He calculated he had slept for about 40 minutes. He opened the fridge and noticed a large bowl of leftover pasta bake. The thought of eating it didn't repulse him, but he knew was still too hungover to eat but at least he knew he was slowly recovering.

He then wondered if there was a way that he would be able to get to check the CCTV footage at Frank Harrisons'. He grabbed milk and set about making a coffee, nice and strong. While he did, he ran scenarios through his head about speaking to Frank and turning the subject to his CCTV system. Maybe he could go over and ask Frank to suggest a system as he was thinking of investing. It wouldn't seem to strange to go over and ask. Maybe if he was lucky, he could get Frank to show him the screens. If he was as nice as Jenna says, then it wouldn't be a problem. He thought he would have his coffee and go over.

Tom ran the scenario through his head a dozen times while drinking his coffee. It would be fine. No need to worry. He would see the footage, somehow show it to Jenna. That would prove he was right and that he wasn't going mad. But then he had a strange thought; would it be safe to show it to Jenna? He needed to be careful how she got involved. What if it caused her harm? He thought that she needed to be kept clear of seeing it, but then quickly realised that she should be fine. She was the one he had to prove it to, not the one that could clarify he painted the fence.

He sat and thought some more. The computer file at work went missing and H was the one that knew he had done it, but the organization was the one he needed to prove it to. The brake light had been repaired and Red was the one that knew, but the cop was the one he had to prove it to. Jenna was safe, she could see it and would be fine.
"Fuck!" Tom suddenly shouted.

What was he thinking? He was scaring himself. This thing was eating him alive and consuming him. He was falling deeper and deeper into a state of paranoia and conspiracy. He threw the empty coffee mug into the sink and lent forward onto the side.
"Get a grip," he whispered to himself.
Normally his Sunday would be relaxing with Jenna, or at golf, or the gym and spa. But now his mind is racing with all these scenarios and theories. Why was he worried if Jenna watched some CCTV footage? He needed to snap out of this. He then wondered if he did need professional help. Or that that he may just need to get away completely for a couple of weeks.

His mind soon diverted itself back to the CCTV footage scenario and Tom wondered if Frank would even be in. He may even tell Tom to go away. Tom laughed out loud when he realised that Frank may not even have any footage. It was such a long shot. Tom sat down again and then wondered if it was that much of a long shot? Cameras hold footage for long periods. He would just ask. It wouldn't hurt. But then he thought the camera may not even go across the street as far as their fence. But, then again, if it didn't, then it didn't. And that would be it. The end of it. So, what harm could be done in checking?

And with that Tom jumped up, grabbed his keys from the side and went out the front door. He walked quickly across the driveway heading for the street knowing if he stopped, he would never do it. But Tom couldn't help asking himself in his head,
"What are you doing?"

He knew deep down it was right to try and confirm if he was on film painting the fence but there was something stopping him. A small desire not to see it. He tried to work out why and then he realised. It was because he feared what he may see.

If he saw the footage of him painting the fence, then he will know he was right. But how will he cope with it not showing him painting the fence?

He knew it would mean something very unusual was happening or, of course, he was going mad. Tom felt a wave of dread flow through him and suddenly felt hot. He wiped beads of sweat from his lip, took a deep breath and carried on. If he did get to see the footage; whatever he does see, he will just have to deal with it as best he could.

Chapter 10

As Tom crossed the road he noticed what a clear, fresh and beautiful day it was, and the thought crossed his mind that he should really be doing something a lot less stressful. As he got to the other side he looked up at the Harrison's house and noticed a couple of the upstairs windows open. A feeling of dread and excitement went through his stomach as he approached the large, ornate front gate. He held his breath and then pressed the buzzer. After a short time he heard a voice.

"Howdy neighbour, what can I do for you?" came a deep and confident voice from the speaker.

"Hi, is that Mr Harrison?" asked Tom, cringing to himself at how fake it sounded.

"Affirmative. And it's Frank to you, son"

Tom smiled, "OK, I'm Tom, Jenna's husband, we live across the street. It's nothing urgent but I just thought it may be a good time to introduce myself," Tom paused, "I mean, only if it's convenient for you?"

There was a pause and then the speaker burst to life again.

"About time, son. Come up to the house," and with the gate clicked, buzzed and slowly swung open.

Tom stepped through and set off up to the house. As he did he noticed how well kept the garden was. It was immaculate. There were rockery's and water features all set within intricate landscaping work. As he approached the large oak front door it swung open and short, well-built man stood there with a huge smile. He had silver hair with a slight natural curl and a tan that had been obtained through lots of hours of sun.

"Well, at last, good morning neighbour, I'm Frank. Come in, come in". Frank gestured to Tom with an open arm and he smiled and ascended the steps to the door. As he did Frank held out a stocky hand and as Tom took it he noticed how it dwarfed his own.

The house was a similar layout to Tom and Jenna's and although it was luxurious and spacious, Tom noted the décor was a little old fashioned. He also noted immediately that Frank obviously had a large family as almost every wall was adorned with framed photos of young people on the beach, at Prom's, graduations, barbecues, boats and a whole array of scenarios and environments. Tom also noticed more formal family photographs of which Frank and an older lady were present with what looked like two or maybe three generations of family.

"Big family, I see," mentioned Tom, breaking the silence.

"Oh yeah, 3 of my own children, all grown up now, and they kindly supplied me with 9 grand kids, just to keep me and my good lady busy," Frank chucked as he finished talking.

"Is your wife around?" asked Tom, not sure why he had asked it.

"Pammy? Nope, she has gone to the mall. One of her favourite hobbies. Spending all of my hard-earned cash," again he chuckled at the end of his sentence and Tom laughed out of politeness.

"Drink?" asked Frank as he pointed to what looked like the kitchen. They both walked through, and Frank gestured to Tom to sit at a stool beside the island. The kitchen was expansive and had an old country feel, or old fashioned as Tom thought, "Just a water for me," replied Tom.

"Oh? Anything stronger?" Frank replied with a wry smile.

"Oh, no thanks...I had a few last ni....."

"Got a cold Bud with your name on it, neighbour," Frank had opened the fridge and raised his eyebrows to Tom.

"It's a little early for me tha..." Tom tried to reply.

"Never too early!" Frank's voice boomed and startled Tom. Frank continued, "Look, this is our first meet. Time is just a set of numbers. I always say do not be constrained by time if it stops you doing what you want!" his voice boomed again, followed by the inevitable chuckle.

By this time he had already opened two Bud's and handed one of them to Tom who now realised refusal was not an option. He thought to himself that Frank appeared to be a man that usually got his way, but he did it in good nature and without being too offensive. Tom sipped the beer and appreciated how good it tasted and felt.

"See, I told you, a nice crisp beer before lunch doesn't hurt nobody. Dean Martin once said, 'I feel sorry for people who do not drink, because when they wake up that's as good as they will feel all day.' But this time what followed wasn't a chuckle but a booming laugh that, again, startled Tom. However, Tom did find it funny and genuinely laughed. He took another swig and started to relax. As he felt the cold lager slip down he knew he had done the right thing in coming over.

Frank enquired about Tom's work and Tom gave him the pretty standard response he always gave with little detail as possible. But, the way things were, he didn't want to talk about work anyway. Tom made the same enquiry back, and Frank explained he had been a military man all his life. Left school for the military as he just knew it was what he wanted to do. His father had been a WW2 veteran and had seen action on the beaches. Took part in the Omaha landings and then through Europe onto Berlin. So Frank said he felt it was in his DNA.

Frank continued and spoke how he was first sent to Indonesia with the Engineer Corp and then as a young man went to Vietnam. Said it was crazy and out of control. Explained he was put in charge of men that saw some heavy-duty action in Da Nang and some other areas. Eventually got injured and was pulled out, but later got some medals. After his recovery he went back and was promoted to Lieutenant Colonel and saw serious action in Na Trang and Saigon. Came home with more medals. As Frank spoke Tom realised he didn't do the 'little detail' thing.

After Nam Frank joined Special Forces and was stationed at Alaska, Hawaii and Germany. Also served as a CO in Granada. His final action was as a regional CO in the Gulf War. Ended up at the Pentagon as a military advisor for the CIA. He ended by saying it had been 'colourful'. Tom had sat and listened intently and soon realised that Frank was what you could call a true American hero. Whilst his own parents were always anti-war and had objective views of what they termed 'war-mongers' it was difficult for Tom to not respect someone like Frank.

Frank soon stopped and took a gulp of beer. Tom felt the silence engulf him and felt the urge to break it.
"So, you see some bad stuff in your time?" but then immediately regretted it and knew how immature it sounded and so tried to intervene, "I mean, obviously you did, but I didn't mean…" but before he could finish Frank looked into his eyes and nodded.
"Shit that still keeps me awake at night".

Tom felt frustrated. He knew it was obvious and he was ashamed for not following 'the code' and trying to discuss details. "I'm sorry, I wasn't after details…."
"No!" interjected Frank, "It's nice you show an interest. Its good your generation understand. I am just glad you don't have to see the same."
Tom felt ashamed and suddenly felt like he was a million times less of a man than Frank.

Before Tom could realise, Frank had already got up and retrieved another two Bud's. Tom's was already opened and in front of him before he could even say anything. But he had enjoyed the first so was not going to refuse anyway.
"You have a nice home, Frank"
"Thanks, kid. So do you. I know what that house was valued at. My friend was interested but got outbid. You must earn well keeping the world's financial system rolling along," Frank chuckled again.
"Well, to be honest, I didn't pay for it, it was part of the package my company set up for my transfer."

"Wow!" shouted Frank, "Money talks!"

Tom smiled, "Yeah, we earn them a lot of it."

Frank asked where Tom transferred from and he explained about New York and he offered up some details that led up the transfer. Frank asked Tom how he liked Evanston and he lied and told him he really like it. Although he did comment that it was no New York City. Tom also obviously left out the details about how his life had spiralled out of control since his arrival. Not the time nor the place.

Just as Tom felt the courage to bring up the security system, Frank intervened. Said he was looking to invest some shares and started to quiz Tom and seek advice. Tom had to go along and try to look interested. Frank obviously had money, but Tom was too polite to tell him that the sort of money he was discussing was a drop in the ocean at his company. Tom gave his best performance to politely put Frank off, all made the easier by another Bud and then when Tom got the chance, he jumped in. "Look Frank, on another issue, I noticed you had a camera out front. I assume you have a security system,? I'm in the market."

Frank's face came to life with a huge smile.

"Oh yeah! One of the best on the market. I had a bit of experience from my CIA days. Knew exactly what I wanted. It's got door and window sensors, direct link to the police, cameras. There's not a foot of my property I can't see. Also got it all linked up to my phone so I can check it when I'm out too…Look!"

Frank got up and grabbed his phone from the other side of the kitchen and came back. Tom could sense excitement from him as he logged in and showed several camera views of his property. Then when Tom sensed Frank coming to the end of his demo he took to the opportunity to move things on.

"So, where is all this linked to? Is there a main system?"

Frank smiled again and raised his eyebrows, "Wanna see it?"

Tom sensed he had hit the jackpot.

The next thing Frank new he was on his way upstairs. As they ascended Tom saw more family photos on the wall up the stair way. They went along the hallway and Tom noticed Frank started to breathe a little heavier. They reached a door and Frank turned to Tom, smiled and took a key from his pocket, "Boys only," he then chuckled and opened the door. He stood aside and gestured for Tom to go in.

Inside was a large room decorated quite plainly. On the wall was a mass of picture frames containing photos of a young Frank in various situations.

One of him in formal standard military pose. Several others not so official and showed groups of soldiers in various places, one on tank, one with Frank and another soldier sitting on the edge of a Huey chopper. All in exotic and exciting locations. The photos raised conversation about how old Frank was in various photos which Frank then offered a back story to. Tom could feel the pride glowing from him as he spoke.

After a while Tom was concerned they were getting too entrenched in military talk and so felt he had to move things forward again so politely pointed to a computer on a desk and asked if that was the system. It worked and Frank immediately led him over to the desk which hosted the screen. Frank turned it on, and Tom noticed behind it was a bookshelf which contained books about the Civil War, Native Americans, Classic US cars but the majority were military books about Korea, Vietnam, The Cold War and The Gulf.
"Here we go," said Frank as the screen burst to life.

Tom started to run through his head ways that he could get Frank to get the footage from the day before at the time he was painting the fence. He knew it was done around 2 to 3pm because he can remember checking the time when Jenna left. As thoughts started racing around his mind a banging sound came from downstairs. The both looked at one another and Frank put his finger in the air to suggest they 'hold on'. Frank got up and went over to the door and opened it.
"That you, dear? he shouted.
"Yes, darling,' came the response from downstairs in a female voice.
"We got a visitor," Frank continued, "Young Tom from over the road. Just showing him the CCTV system."
There was a pause and then a reply, "Ok. Hi Tom, has Frank offered you a drink?"
Tom smiled, "Yes, I got him a drink," said Frank rolling his eyes and smiling.

While this was happening Tom noticed the system had loaded. Frank came back and went to enter a password but before he did he looked up at Tom "Don't look". Tom laughed and pretended to avert his gaze while Frank chuckled. Noises started to come from downstairs like items being put down in cupboards closing. Then the sound of the music clicked on and started to make its way upstairs.

What appeared was basically the screen split into twelve sections. Each section had a number, time and date in the bottom left corner. Frank then explained that each section was a camera and they are all working 24/7 and footage kept for 3 months. Tom scoured them as closely as he could without making it obvious he was searching for one specific camera.

To his astonishment he noticed one of them was a view that looked outwards onto the road and across. He then felt a sense of excitement and fear as he saw the fence that run along the line of his property.

His mind switched into over-drive and he suddenly realised the impact that the next minute or so may have on his life. A wave of dread washed over him as it started to sink in that he may now find out if he was going mad or some other strange force was at work.

Frank moved the cursor to one of the sections and double clicked. That specific image then opened up as the whole screen and Frank explained you can see the individual camera view in more detail. The image of his rear garden came up and then he started to move the camera using zoom and pan from the computer.

Tom was not interested at all but sensed he needed to show some appreciation.
"Amazing," he said, realising how fake it sounded and so continued, "So this is real time, but can you see historical footage?"
Tom was aware that he had to be careful not to allow Frank to believe he was leading him.
"Easy," Frank replied, "Look," and he moved the cursor to the bottom of the screen to a calendar and he double clicked. It opened up on the screen, "It goes back three months….So let's go back to last week, say".

He changed the date on the calendar and then a clock appeared, and Frank entered a time. Within seconds a new image had appeared which was the same view, but the weather had changed, and it looked a little different.
"This system is amazing" Frank said excitedly, "Cost me an arm and a leg though, but I don't think you can put a price on security."
"I agree," replied Tom, knowing that he had never actually even thought about it.
"May I?" Tom asked, gesturing to Frank if he could sit down.
"Be my guest, son."

Frank got up and Tom sat down. He knew this was it. He minimised the whole screen view of the garden and returned back to the twelve sections. He noted the front gate camera and he double clicked on it trying to make it look like he was just perusing it and his actions were random. He spoke as if trying to intimate he was remembering what Frank had done.

"And so, just for example, if I double click this one…"
The view suddenly appeared of the whole screen and Tom was amazed how clear it was.

Tom continued to try and make his actions random.
"Oh, is that my fence?" he asked.
Frank leaned in, "Oh yes, I hope you don't mind, you can see we don't get a view of your house and that's a static so I can't zoom into your bathroom window," Frank then laughed out loud and it made Tom jump. Tom laughed too but his face was deadly serious.
Frank continued, "I just thought if I had such a good system I would give my fellow neighbours a bit of added security…I have two other statics which show small part of the Anderson's driveway and another to the rear of the Wrigley's, the other side of me. I've shown them and they are happy with it".

Tom then realised Frank may need some reassurance.
"Oh, no, I think it's great, really good idea. Good of you to think of us."

By now Tom had got the calendar on the screen and as he typed he spoke.
"So….if for example I put, say yesterday's date in…And then say from 2pm, is that right?

Tom asked but knew exactly what he was doing,
"You got it, buddy" replied Frank unaware of Tom's intentions.

The screen popped up but there was nobody at the fence. Tom urgently moved the image along in time by selecting a red button on the bottom along a time bar. Nothing appeared and then suddenly he saw movement. He stopped and moved it back slightly and what he saw nearly made him fall off his seat.

The screen flickered and then, there, in full view, as clear as day itself was Tom, on his knees, across the road painting the fence. He suddenly felt sick. The beer started rising and he had to close his mouth tight. It stung his throat.

In the background Tom heard Frank laugh out loud and his voice boomed.
"Hey! Evidence of you working! Hold the front page!" Franks voice was like a dagger in the back of Tom's head. He tried to laugh to cover his emotions, but he knew it was a poor attempt,
"You see, it has its uses," continued Frank chuckling.

Tom felt a wave of heat rush through his body and wondered how this could be happening. More to the point, what was happening? But, now at least, he had evidence. He had it to show Jenna and she would believe him. This was what he needed. But how can he get her to see it? He realised that the three early Bud's had taken their toll and started to feel a little woozy.

'Keep calm," he told himself.

Frank then suddenly leaned in again,

"Look, you can move it on a little further," and as he did, he took control and the image sped up and then a figure quickly sped into view, so Frank stopped it. Then it became obvious it was Mrs McGeedy and she was talking to Tom. Frank immediately burst into laughter and Tom felt a sudden urge to punch him.

"Looks like Mrs McGeedy collared you for a chat. Between you and me she's s a nosy old girl and made a beeline for you.

As the conversation between Tom and Mrs McGeedy played out on the screen another thought burst into Tom's head like an arrow which scared him. Frank had now seen the footage. Did this have ramifications? Was Frank safe? Tom's mind raced and he tried to fit pieces together and go back over what had happened previously to H and red. His head was fuzzy, and he struggled to think straight. Was Frank now involved? Tom's head was buzzing with anxiety and a thought process that he couldn't comprehend.

Suddenly he was broken from his thoughts by Frank.

"You ok, kid?" Tom's sense of panic and frustration suddenly dissipated, and he looked round to see Frank put his hand on Tom's shoulder, "You look pasty" Frank continued.

"Wow…er…yeah, just got a bit hot, I'm ok."

Tom stood up. He had to get a grip on the situation. Frank walked over and opened the window and gestured to Tom to sit down on the sofa next to the desk.

"Sorry Frank, just had a few last drinks last night and it has caught up with me…"

Frank smiled, "No problem, son. It is stuffy in here You take your time. I'll log off"

As Tom sat down on the sofa he noticed the view showing him painting the fence disappear back to the one of the smaller twelve images. Frank closed the calendar and all the images switched back to real time. It was just then he noticed a white Audi pull up onto the drive and he realised

Jenna was home. Tom got a sudden fear that she would walk in and see the carpet and a surge of anxiety passed through him. He sensed sweat on his lip and wiped it off and then wiped his brow. He realised that Frank must now realise was acting weird. He took a deep breath and composed himself as best he could.

But more important than the carpet was now the urge that he felt to show Jenna the footage. He quickly felt it rise and start to eat away at him. It was exactly the same powerful urge he had to go back to see if Red was ok. It scared him. He took another deep breath and as he did Frank, now finished shutting of the PC, turned to face him. Tom stood up.
"Look, Frank, I really hope you don't mind, but, I really love this system and I have been trying for months to talk Jenna into investing the money," Tom laughed nervously, "She thinks we have more important things but…I think if she sees this she will be sold…Do you mi…"
"Go get her, boy," boomed Frank. Tom sensing how excited he was to be of assistance.
"You sure? It's just that as we are here we may asw…"
"I said go get her, didn't I?" Frank laughed out loud and Tom knew it wouldn't be too long before he had to get away from Frank and that laugh.

They went out to the hallway and down the stairs, as they approached the front door Frank shouted behind Tom, "Pammy, Tom's getting Jenna to see the camera system. They want one!"

There was no reply. Tom opened the door and as he went to leave Frank spoke.
"Hey! How about lunch? Once Jenna has seen it we can have lunch pout the back. I can show you my pond…Got some real huge Koi"
"Oh no…Really, Frank, it's not necessary"
"Oh come on. The good lady has been shopping, I can knock up some grilled chicken and…"
"No, honestly, Frank, we don't…"
"It's our pleasure!" boomed Frank, slapping a huge hand on Tom's shoulder.

As he did a petite and pretty older lady appeared from another room and walked into the reception area.
"What's all the fuss here?" she asked with a huge grin.
"Pam, meet Tom. This is Jenna's husband," confirmed Frank.

Pam came forward and gave Tom a hug,

"Oh its lovely to meet you at last," she said. Tom noted she looked good for her assumed age and whilst she seemed down to earth he thought she was obviously not shy of a bit of pampering.

They exchanged pleasantries and pam explained that she had already met Jenna and she had told her so much about him. Tom was as polite, and patient and he could be under the circumstances. He felt himself fidgeting and wave of anxiety him again. Then a sudden wish that his life was different. How this moment should have been a pleasure. He should be excited about grilled chicken and drinks in the neighbour's garden on a Saturday afternoon.

He suddenly thought about forgetting it all and going over to Jenna and just telling her they were going for lunch at the Harrisons. Forget the CCTV footage. Forget the weird feelings. Just fuck it all. They can eat and drink all afternoon, go home, have sex, make a baby and just have a happy life.

That was when he decided that was what he would do. Forget it. His mind was made up. But then another thought hit him. Things weren't right with Jenna. She was avoiding him; thought he was mad and wasn't even speaking to him right now. And exactly at that moment she was probably going ballistic at the state of the bedroom carpet. He started to sweat again and suddenly came around from his thoughts and noticed Pam was still talking. He noticed Frank laugh and raise his eyebrows to Tom and so Tom, completely unaware of why, just raised his eyebrows back and smiled.

Frank cut in.
"Pammy, by the time you finish it will be dinner time…" Frank and pam laughed out loud.

Pam apologised for what she called 'rattling on like an old dryer' and arrangements were quickly made for the afternoon. She would get the chicken from the fridge and prep a Greek salad; Frank would fire up the barbecue and get some Prosecco on ice. Tom's only directive was to go get Jenna.
Tom walked out and heard the door close behind him, his ears still ringing. The cool air washed across him and brought a relief from the sweating. He wished he could just disappear somewhere and sit with that breeze caressing him. But as he walked through the garden to the front gate it all suddenly started to dawn on him what a mess thing's were.

As the gate clicked, buzzed and slowly swung open he realised Frank was in danger. Just like H and Red, Frank had been the witness to Tom painting the fence. The only person on this earth that could prove he did it. His stomach churned. But then his eyes widened as another through flashed across his mind that Mrs McGeedy had also seen him.

She even stopped to talk and commented on it. So was she actually the one in danger and not Frank? Frank had seen it but after the actual event and not when it happened. He stopped as he got through the gate. He had to warn Mrs McGeedy and he had to warn Frank.

He then realised that he had subconsciously stopped and so carried on. He looked up towards the end of the street toward the way the road led to Mrs McGeedy's. But then he wondered what he would even say. What would he actually say to Frank? "You need to go to hospital and tell them you are going to have a heart attack". He realised how stupid it sounded, "Jesus" he whispered angrily. He shook his head and uttered to himself to get a grip.

He walked across the road towards his house and he noticed that the door was open and there was a holdall at the front door. This suddenly snapped him out of his thoughts, and he started to jog across and up towards the house. As he did he saw Jenna appear with another holdall and he then realised what she was doing "Jenna!" he shouted. She looked up and went back in without acknowledging him.

He got halfway up the drive when she came out again and closed the front door "Jenna, wait"'" he shouted again. She picked up the two holdalls but realised there was no way to avoid him. She put them back down and looked straight at him.
"What are you doing?" he asked frantically.
"Look, Tom, I don't want to fight… I ju…"
"What are you doing" Tom asked again pointing at the holdall's.
"Tom, I need some space. I am going to Lucy's"

Tom knew Lucy. He had her down as the biggest fake of all of Jenna's fake friends. And she probably put Jenna up to this. But Tom had no time to dwell on who and why. Right now he had to get Jenna over to the Harrisons.
"Look, Jenna, I know things have been fucked up lately. But right now I need to you be here for me and help me…"
"No Tom! No!" Jenna shouted and then realised where she was and looked around the street. She continued but in a hushed voice, "No. Do not even got there. That is not fair. I just need some time…"

"Jenna, I have evidence that can prove I am not going mad. I have been over at...."

"Tom! I do not want to do this right now. I need to go . I need to get away from you."

Tom shook his head and instinctively moved closer putting his hands around Jenna's arms.

"Jenna, listen carefully, just come over..."

"Oh my god" she suddenly interrupted smelling his breath, "You have been drinking! Have you been drinking?"

Tom tried to explain about an innocent beer with Frank, but Jenna wasn't hearing him.

"You are a drunk," she told him in a disgusted tone.

Tom held her arms tighter, "I am not a drunk," he answered back.

Jenna felt his hands squeeze tighter, "Tom , let me go right now," she raised her voice. She swung her rams up and out to try get his hands off, but his grip was too tight, and he withstood her attempt.

"Stop it, Jenna, fucking listen to me..."

"Tom, fuck off!" she shouted no longer concerned about the volume and scene being caused. She swung her arms up again now fighting to get free of his grasp but Tom, without thinking, released one arm and delivered a hard slap to her face. It knocked her head sharply to the side. She slowly raised her hand to her cheek and as her head turned back she looked at him in bewilderment and disbelief.

Tom now realised it was now or never. He could forget the CCTV and let her go or he could push on. But he realised that if he let her go now without explanation his marriage was over, so he took the initiative.

"Jenna, I am sorry. But I am not going mad. And I have evidence. I have been over at the Harrisons and I managed to get him to show me his camera system. I have just stood there with Frank watching yesterday and it shows me painting the fucking fence! Clear as the sky is blue. We both watched it. But I need you to see it, please tell me you will. I need you to do this for me or, I don't know...I just can't cope...I need to you to see it and to understand. I need you, now more than ever. Please..." he tailed off and his voice broke.

He noticed a tear rolling down Jenna's face and he realised how mad he must have sounded.

"Please Jenna, give me something. I am sorry for hitting you but I...We don't have much time. Frank may be in danger, just like H and red....You know? What I told you. About them having proof. Well, Frank may the next one, or Mrs McGeedy, she spoke to me too… It's on the footage…She could be in more danger…" Tom's voice was now fast and frantic.

"Ok," replied Jenna intensely.

Tom continued, "Please, just give me this one chance to prove it, I need you to give me one ch…"

"Ok" Jenna repeated louder. This time Tom stopped.

"You will?" he asked, and she never replied or changed her expression, "Thank you. Oh my god, I love you..." He leant forward and grabbed her into an embrace and held her with all his might.

"Get the fuck off me," she ordered as she shrugged him off.

She turned around and put her key back in the door and went back inside. She tried to shut the door behind her, and Tom had to quickly step into the door and stop it closing. He shook his head and went in behind her. He wondered if she had agreed to let him prove it out of fear. The realisation that he had slapped Jenna suddenly hit home. He wasn't sure how all of this was going to work out. He closed the door and went inside and saw Jenna turn to him and fold her arms.

"Well?" she asked sarcastically, "What do we do? Go over and say Trick or Treat?!"

Tom looked confused and shook his head not taking the hint that she was being sarcastic "No. No, no, no….Look, I said I was looking to buy a security system and wanted to show it to you before we spend it. He said for me to come and get you…"

Jenna thought it sounded plausible but still shook her head and sighed. "I was over there and I deliberately set the date for yesterday at the time I painted the fence and it showed me doing it, I swear on my father's grave."

Jenna had never heard him say that before and suddenly felt a sway towards his point of view. Although she still had her doubts.

"But Tom, what does it prove? I mean, what does it really prove? It shows you painting the fence, but so what?" as she spoke she wiped a tear track from her face.

Tom's eyes widened, "So what? Are you fucking serious? It proves I am not fucking going insane. It shows that the fence will be painted. It proves that something fucking weird is going on here. Jesus, Jenna!"

Tom started to feel angry but had to hold it together otherwise he could lose Jenna again.

"Ok, I see your point…" she replied

"But, as I came out they invited us to lunch…"

"No, Tom! Look at me, my mascara has run and…"
"Don't worry!" Tom jumped in, "You look fine, quickly, just freshen up…"

Jenna thought about arguing some more but she knew Tom was never going to give in. Tom had quickly already gone to toilet and grabbed some wet wipes. He handed them to her. She looked in the mirror and did her best to make herself look presentable.
"You look, fine Jenna. Please. Time is against us," he pleaded.

They walked out of the front door and past the holdalls. Jenna went to pick them up, but Tom grabbed her arm and ushered her past and off down the driveway. She tutted and glared at him. But just as they got to the road Tom was stopped in his tracks.

A cold icy feeling rushed through him. First in his feet and then slithering up his body. He shivered. Jenna, who had carried on, stopped and turned. She was confused. Tom's stomach suddenly knotted with a primal fear. The dread that he couldn't cope with or understand had hit him. He doubled over and put his hands across his stomach.
"Tom, are you ok?" asked Jenna, concerned.

Tom then felt the claws. Cold claws crawling us his back. He turned and tried to fend off whatever it was but found nothing here.
"Jesus Tom, what the hell?" shouted Jenna as she ran back to him.

She grabbed him and tried to lift him, but he was frozen. Then suddenly the warmth returned and, as it quickly as it had come, the cold deathly grip had passed. Jenna lent down, "Tom, please I am scared…"
"I am ok…I think" Tom whispered.

But then he panicked. It had dawned on him. He realised what it was. He suddenly grabbed Jenna's arm and ran towards the Harrisons house.
"Tom will you slow down!" she shrieked.

He grabbed her arm even tighter and ran even faster, "Just fucking move it," he ordered. Jenna tried to reliever herself of his grip, "Just keep moving," Tom snapped.

As they ran and stumbled across the road Tom noticed the front gate was open and, then beyond that, he noticed the front gate the front door also open. Tom was pleased as it meant easy access. They slowed at the gate, Jenna now becoming really angry with Tom's insistence on ordering her around. Tom stopped and turned to her "Just be polite and keep pleasantries to a minimum, we will get upstairs as quickly as possible..."

Then it came. The sound that was possibly the most horrifying that Tom had ever heard. And it came directly from the Harrisons house. It was a loud blood-curdling scream that seemed to go on forever. They both looked at the house and then back to each other, Jenna immediately noticed the fear on Tom's face. Then a second lower pitched, but more desperate scream came from the house. Tom and Jenna ran as fast as they could towards the house and up the stairs through the front door. The sight that greeted them from within shocked them both the core.

Lying face down in the lobby was Frank. He appeared to be convulsing. Desperately trying to help him was Pam who appeared to be in major shock and did not appear to know what to do. She tried to roll Frank's stocky body onto his back, but she never had the strength. She just looked up at them in sheer and utter desperation.

"Please!!!...Please help my Frank" she moaned helplessly to them, before letting off another sickening scream.

Chapter 11

"So, let me get this right. You'd come over to get your wife to go back for lunch and it must've been during that period it happened?" the young policeman was very matter of fact.

"Yes," replied Tom, trying not to get to agitated.

Jenna had tried desperately to revive Frank Harrison. She had learnt CPR from her marine biology days where she had been a first aider on board several ships. But her almost long forgotten training had no hope against what had happened to Frank. He had suffered a major heart attack and they wondered if all she had done was prolong the inevitable.

Whilst Jenna was carrying out CPR Tom had called the emergency services. He had then gone back inside to usher Pam away, but she had fought to stay by Frank's side. But Tom knew he had to get her away from the sickening and distressing scene, but she wouldn't give up. Her screams and wailing of 'Frank!' were still ringing in his ears and had affected him badly.

It had been at that point that another neighbour, who obviously knew the Harrison's and who later on Tom found out was Irene Anderson their next-door neighbour, appeared at the door with a look of shock. She had heard the screams, come running and had seen what was going on so and had taken the same initiative as Tom and joined in trying to usher Pam away. When Irene had grabbed Pam, Tom had felt Pam's body crumple completely and she gave up. Irene held her and slowly moved her away to another room trying to console her.

Tom had then tried to help Jenna but really had no clue what to do to help. Luckily, the ambulance crew turned up shortly after and took over. Jenna moved away and then fell to her knees in physical and mental exhaustion. Tom then picked her up and ushered her away. They had sat on the stairs away from view and Jenna had cried.

After a short time Tom went back to look and Frank had been put on a stretcher with an oxygen mask and a drip attached to his arm. He was not moving. A small crowd of neighbours had gathered at the front of the house and a couple of other people that Tom did not know had come into the house to help Irene with Pam who was still hysterical.

Eventually Frank had been taken away to hospital. Irene took Pam in the Anderson's car which followed the ambulance. Pam had wanted to go in the ambulance, but the crew had advised against it. Tom had assumed he knew why. Bill Anderson had locked the Harrisons house and a sense of calm and a quiet descended back onto the street; albeit with a dark and surreal feeling around the neighbourhood.

Tom had not yet had time to absorb what had happened. Shortly after the ambulance crew took over to help Frank a policeman had approached Tom and advised him that as he and Jenna had been confirmed as the first people on the scene he would need to come and speak to them once it settled down. Tom had been on the front veranda trying to make sense of what Frank's condition meant for him and his own situation when the policeman started to walk over. Jenna had already been indoors a short time and was still upset.

The policeman had asked Tom the standard questions. What was he doing at the time? What had he and Frank been doing before he left? Had Frank shown any signs of illness or distress prior to Tom leaving? Everything Tom had said, and all his answers made perfect sense and were all completely plausible. But it did not help the huge feeling of guilt that weighed down upon him. Tom wondered what the policeman's reaction would be if he told him the whole truth. That this was the third death Tom had been connected to lately.

"Ok, I think I have all I need," the policeman confirmed. Tom nodded. The policeman took one last sip of his coffee Tom had made and put the mug down on the side.
"Look" he said, "It's all routine, standard stuff. Don't worry. From what I gather your wife did a great job." Tom smiled and nodded and then thought it was the first time in the last half an hour the officer had shown any emotion or empathy. Just as the officer stood up the doorbell rang, "I'll be getting off. You have a visitor anyway."

As Tom followed him to the door, he wondered who it could be at the door and wondered if it was neighbor. As Tom opened the door a young guy was standing there in overalls holding a clipboard. The officer said goodbye and nodded to the visitor as he passed. Tom was confused.
"Can I help you?" he asked the young man.
"Oh yes, sorry Sir. I am from A1 Cleaning. Got an urgent job booked at this address?"

With all that had happened Tom had completely forgotten the carpet cleaner he had booked earlier that morning, "Oh…Er…Can you give me a minute?" Tom said in a defeated tone. The young man nodded and smiled. Tom closed the door and looked at the ceiling.
"Fuck," he whispered.

He went upstairs and made sure Jenna was OK. She was sitting in the bathroom. Tom had suggested he would send the guy away, but Jenna had insisted he get the job done now that he is here. She had given Tom a look of disgust, but he knew he had gotten away with it, for now.

Jenna dried her eyes and had gone downstairs and into the garden and Tom showed the guy in and to the bedroom. The guy explained he may need to go in and out to his van, so Tom left the door open and let the guy get on with it. He went outside to the garden and sat next to Jenna on a lounger and they could both hear a loud vacuuming noise from the open window to the bedroom.

They just sat and didn't speak. Neither know what to say. Each time Tom thought of somewhere to start it didn't feel right, so he just waited for Jenna to speak. Soon the silence had dragged on long enough and Tom was about to speak when Jenna stopped him.
"So., where do we go from here?" she asked.
"I don't know, Jenna. I just don't know," he replied and let out a huge sigh.
"Tom," Jenna cut in, "The way you acted today, just...well, y' know, before what happened with Frank. It scared me. It wasn't you."
"I know, I know. I scare myself. All of this scares me. I feel helpless. I had a way to prove it to you. A way for you to see how confusing all of this is."

Jenna moved around to face Tom.
"Look, Tom, whatever is happening I think we need to look at it rationally and with the facts," she paused and then continued, "The fact is you didn't pain the fence..."
"I did!" shouted Tom, frustrated again at her failure to admit how weird this all was.
"No!" Jenna shouted back, and Tom sat back in shock, "No! No!, you didn't, Tom! It's not done. You think you did but you didn't. End of story!"
"So, am I going mad?" he asked.
"Yes," Jenna replied indignantly, "If that's what it takes to make you see sense then, yes, you are going mad, and you need to see someone urgently. Someone who can help you cope with your feelings...."
Tom shook his head, "Jenna, if there as some way I could show you that CCTV it would prove I am not mad. At first, I was worried it may endanger you, but it won't. You see, the connection is the person that can prove I did it. You were the one I had to prove it to; not the person that could prove I did it," Jenna shook her head and looked at the floor, Tom continued.

91

"Just like H. He could prove I did the report. Red could prove I had my tail-light fixed. Frank could prove I painted the fence. H could prove it to my company…. Red could prove it to the traffic cop and Frank could prove it to you," Tom leant forward and touched Jenna's knee's, his voice becoming excited and faster.

He paused hoping that it was sinking in and then a thought crossed his mind, "But there is one last chance…Mrs McGeedy. She spoke to me," Tom stood up, held his hand up with his finger in the air, "She spoke to me while I was doing the fence!" his eyes widened and he suddenly felt intense pressure to speak to Mrs McGeedy, "She can prove it to you, Jenna!"

Jenna sighed.
"Tom, people are dying. And all you can worry about is your little game. It's sick. You are unstable. I can't deal with this…" Jenna went to get up and Tom pushed her shoulder back down, she glared up at him as he stood over her. Tom faced her down and tried to demonstrate to her he was serious.
"Jenna, it's not a game."

Tom looked upstairs to the window where the sound of vacuuming was still coming from, and then turned to face Jenna angrily and whispered. "You already admitted to me it was strange. Three people I know had heart attacks in the last few months and all three of those people knew something about me. It's unexplainable. And Frank won't survive either," as spoke did, he pointed in the direction of Frank's house, "Jesus, he was dead when you were doing CPR, you were wasting your time…"

Jenna just shook her head and Tom immediately knew he had said the wrong thing. It obviously hadn't meant to sound that trying to save someone's life was a waste of time. Tom went to explain but Jenna shot up and barged him out of the way, then jogged back into the house. Tom sat back down and blew a deep breath out and put his head in his hands.

He realised he was suddenly desperate for a drink. He went inside, poured himself a large whisky and went back outside the lounger. The afternoon had cooled due to cloud and as he sipped his drink felt it smoothen out his muscles and relax him. He put the drink on a side table, sat back and closed his eyes. He wasn't aware of when he had dozed off but was awoken by talking in the background. He sat up and looked around, then got up and moved to an angle he could see through the house and noticed Jenna showing the carpet cleaner to the front door. He then walked back to his lounger, picked up the whisky and down it in one.

He sat back down, and a pang of hunger hit him. He realised he hadn't eaten all day. He then wondered if Jenna was going to stay or follow through with her earlier decision to go to stay with a friend. He then remembered the pasta bake in the fridge and so got up and went inside to retrieve it. As he did, he noticed Jenna walking back through the kitchen heading for the garden. She stared straight at him. Just then the phone rang and so she turned and walked away, Tom assumed to get the phone.

He went to the fridge and picked up the pasta back and could hear Jenna's muffled words. But then heard more clearly, "Oh my god. Oh no..."

There were a few more pauses and inaudible words and then he heard, "Ok, thanks for calling."

He had a fork and took three huge mouthfuls of pasta bake and waited. He knew what was coming. Jenna walked into the kitchen and sat down. A tear rolled down her face.
"He's dead, isn't he?" asked Tom pragmatically.
Jenna just nodded.

Although he was expecting the answer she gave, it didn't stop a feeling of numbness drift over his body. He couldn't summon any emotion but just asked.
"Who was it?".
Jenna replied, "Mr. Anderson. Irene phoned him from the hospital."
"Jesus," Tom whispered. Jenna just got up and left the kitchen and went upstairs. Tom didn't feel any need to go after her.

Having had a few mouthfuls of pasta bake, Tom's hunger had subsided, but his thirst for another drink hadn't. He poured himself another whisky and went out in the garden and sat on a lounger. He took two huge gulps and started to feel the alcohol kicking in, which he liked. He sat back down and finished the whisky in one. It felt so good. He laid back on the lounger and shut his eyes. He started to relax but then a wave of tension washed over him as he realised it was Monday the next day and he was due in work at 7am.

He was supposed to have prepared an agenda for the weekly briefing but had done nothing. He knew his work was slipping, and he felt like it was only a matter of time before he was spoken to. He was used to juggling his personal life around work; that was one of the expectancies for such a good salary and lifestyle. But with everything that had happened his work was spiraling out of control. Along with his personal life.

He couldn't go in tomorrow. Even though it was only late afternoon and he had time to eat, sleep and get his head straight, he just couldn't face it. He had nothing prepared anyway. Going sick was better than going unprepared for a meeting and he had never really taken any sick. He calculated probably just a small handful of days over the years. No matter how brutal a company was they can't sack you for taking some time off sick. He got up and went inside to get his phone. He sat down and typed a text to Conway:

'Hi Mr Conway. It's Jenna (Tom's wife). I am really sorry, but Tom won't be able to work tomorrow. He has picked up a bug and has been really rough all day. He got no sleep last night. Its's quite serious and doctor has said its contagious. He said he is really sorry about the briefing. We will keep you updated. Jenna.'

As Tom sent it, he thought it may buy him some time. Bugs normally take a day or two to clear, and when he got back to work, he could just drink water and eat dry crackers. Just to set the scene and clear up any doubts that he was lying, which he knew there would be. Anyone off sick was always scrutinised, often unfairly. The immediate instinct was it was fake. But it usually was.

Tom went back out to the lounger and sat down. He laughed to himself as he thought his only real comfort now was a sun lounger. He laid back and relaxed and as he did his phone bleeped. He looked and saw a text from Conway, which he opened and read:

'Hello Jenny. Tell Tom I will cancel the briefing and will re-schedule for Tuesday when he returns. Alan.'

Tom shook his head and laughed out loud. What an arsehole, he thought. No, 'get well soon' or 'give him my regards'. And just blankly assuming Tom would be back the next day. He couldn't even get Jenna's name right.
"What a cunt," he whispered to himself.

He smiled and wondered how Conway had made it this far without being beaten to a pulp, stabbed or even shot by anyone. He wished at that point that something would happen where Conway was the only person in the world that could prove Tom had done something It would be the first time Tom would be happy to see someone have a heart attack.

He smiled. He felt a little drunk. And soon enough without knowing he was in a deep sleep. Sometime later he suddenly felt a presence. He wanted to wake up but was in such a deep sleep he couldn't pull himself out. The presence was soon stronger, and he fought to open his eyes. His head felt fuzzy and when he eventually opened his eyes, he saw Jenna sitting at the end of the lounger in her dressing gown. He must have looked a little startled.

"Sorry," she said quietly, "I didn't mean to scare you," as she put her hand on his leg and gently rubbed it.

"It's fine," Tom replied. His mouth was dry, and a headache quickly started. His stomach was so empty he felt hunger pains.

"It's nearly 11," Jenna informed him, "I have warmed up the pasta bake for you."

"Shit," cursed Tom, rubbing his head, "I must have slept for hours"

"You obviously needed it," replied Jenna in a comforting tone.

Tom could smell the cheesy aroma from the kitchen and his mouth filled with saliva. Jenna took his hand and led him indoors and he sat and devoured the whole bowl of pasta. It felt good. He looked up at Jenna who had sat and watching him, and he hadn't even noticed.

"So," she said, "You say Mrs McGeedy also saw you paint the fence?"
Tom felt a sudden alertness and focus and nodded intently.
Jenna continued, "Right, OK, tomorrow we need to warn her. Even if it sounds ridiculous to her, we need to at least warn her. Then we need to find out a way to get to see that footage. How I don't know? But we need to try".

Tom smiled. He felt a wave of relief.
"Now, come to bed," and Jenna held out her hand.

Tom rose from the kitchen stool and took her hand but instead of walking towards the stairs she turned to him smiled.
"And, I swear to god, if you ever hit me again, I will slit your throat while you sleep. Do you understand?"

Tom nodded and smiled back, and she led him upstairs to bed.

Chapter 12

The next day had started well enough. For the first time in a long time Tom had woken and felt like he had slept properly. He and Jenna had had sex before going to sleep and it felt like the best sex they had ever had. Jenna had been different and had done things with Tom she had never done before. He had also surprised himself at his stamina and the things he had also done.

He wondered if it had just been a huge release. This thing had pushed them apart and they had almost been living separate lives. He had felt Jenna was slipping away from him and last night was perhaps a re-connection.

Tom had hoped that Jenna had slowly come to see his perspective, which was the reason why she suggested they go and see Mrs McGeedy today. This acceptance had made Tom feel like they were united again.

Tom had woken first. He sat up and looked at Jenna as she lay naked. Her breasts were full and laying down to one side and her body was resting in such a way that Tom thought about cuddling up and quite easily sliding into her, but then thought better of it. She looked so peaceful and he didn't want to wake her. Even if he had a desperate urge to do so.

He had gone downstairs and had a good, strong coffee. He sat and watched TV for while then Jenna had come down. She had smiled and her dressing gown was open and showed off her cleavage. They had cuddled and they ended up having sex in the lounge. She had then made bacon, eggs and pancakes. It was a great feeling. A Monday that felt more like a Sunday. The weather was fine, and they had sat on the sun loungers to relax after their breakfast.

But it was while Jenna was upstairs that Tom felt the sudden cold feeling of despair. He had been in the kitchen filling the dishwasher when it came. It hit him hard. He'd felt sick with anxiety and his cold hands hurt. Then something grabbing at him from different directions. He didn't panic. He just closed his eyes, took a deep breath and held on. Hoping that it would soon pass. Then it had gone as quick as it came. The primal fear slowly lifting from his body. The weight releasing. He never told Jenna. He didn't want to spoil the day and start the tension off again.

Slightly later it was Tom who had raised the issue of Mrs McGeedy and he was disappointed at Jenna's reaction when she seemed a bit distant on the subject. They had argued a little about how to go and warn her and what exactly they would say. Tom had criticised her for now not seeming to be concerned about it, and that for all the idea's Tom put up she shot them down.

Tom had ended up suggesting they just need to go down there and be honest. Jenna had suggested they don't do anything. Tom had argued with her about her change of attitude and she said she had thought about it and it no longer seemed reasonable to go and scare someone. Tom had walked away. The 'thing' had got between them once again.

He paced back and forth in the bedroom thinking that Jenna had not really believed him. She had only said it to relax him and make him feel like she cared. She never gave a shit. She just thought he was mad and was just trying to placate him for an easy life.

Eventually he had taken a shower and it was when he was in the bathroom drying himself, he had heard the door-bell ring. He then heard the door open and talking to which he couldn't quite hear and just heard the odd word here and there.
He carried on drying himself and as the talk from downstairs continued, he became agitated as to who it could be and what was being discussed. He went to the bathroom door and opened it; he heard Jenna say "Ok, thanks for telling us. I'll let Tom know". He heard goodbyes and then the front door close. He closed the bathroom door and went back to drying himself expecting to hear Jenna coming up the stairs. But he heard nothing.

He got dressed into a polo shirt and lounging shorts and went downstairs. As he was descending, he wondered whether to ask who it was or just wait for Jenna to inform him of whatever it was. He opted for the latter. He went into the kitchen and turned the TV on. He normally opted for finance or news channel but just left it on Fox Sports and an interview with a young hockey player he didn't recognise. He poured himself a cold water and started to think about his briefing at work tomorrow. He was normally so efficient at stuff like this, but he just couldn't get his mind focussed when it came to work lately.

"Hey," Tom turned, and Jenna was standing in kitchen doorway. Tom thought that last night and the majority of that morning had been the best between them for a while and wanted it to continue so he started to apologise.
"Look Jenna, about things…"
"No, Tom. Listen," Jenna interrupted, "That was Jean Anderson."
"Oh?" replied Tom.

"She said funeral arrangements for Frank are being made. Probably going to be next week. Mrs Harrison wants all the neighbours to go…"

Jenna broke off but Tom sensed she hadn't finished just from the look on her face. He stared at her, but she never said anymore.

"And?"

"Tom…Don't flip out."

"Jenna?" he replied becoming frustrated.

"Look," she went on, "There's been some other bad news. She said Mrs McGeedy is away visiting relatives in Florida. But…Well…Mrs McGeedy's daughter called her, as Jean is watering her flowers while she is away…"

"Jenna. What the fuck is going on?" Tom interrupted, now very concerned.

"Look, Tom, Mrs McGeedy has been taken ill…"

Tom closed his eyes and rubbed his forehead. He knew what had happened and what Jenna was trying to say.

"Jesus Christ" he said, and he started to walk away.

"No, Tom, wait," exclaimed Jenna, "Tom, she's not dead. She's been taken ill…"

"With heart problems?" interrupted Tom. Stopping at the glass sliding doors that lead to the garden.

Jenna sat at on the stools at the breakfast bar, "Look Tom, you…"

"Was it fucking heart problems?!" he shouted.

Jenna jumped at the ferocity of his voice and couldn't speak for a few seconds. She looked at him, again wondering where this anger was coming from. She raised her finger to him but before she could speak Tom interrupted.

"Don't raise your fucking finger to me. Just tell me. Was it heart problems?"

"Yes," she said quietly, "Yes, it was a heart attack. She's in intensive care," Jenna looked down at the floor. They were both silent for a minute at least.

Eventually Tom spoke, "Ok, so do you want to ring Jean, get her to call McGeedy's daughter and tell her to start making funeral arrangements?"

"Don't be a prick, Tom," Jenna said still looking at the floor.

"Well, we may as well do some good from all of this!" Tom shouted, "We may as well prepare them for the fucking worst because she is on the way out, Jenna!"

"Tom, you don't know that!"

Tom laughed hysterically, "I don't know that? I don't know that?" he walked towards Jenna pointing at himself.

"I am a fucking freak. I make people have heart attacks and I know they die from it……I mean, I've got a great fucking track record, Jenna. H,

98

Red, Frank Harrison and now McGeedy! Jesus. I'll put up an advert. You got some cunt in your life causing you grief? Come to Tom, he'll give them a good send off!!"

"Tom...You..."

"No. Jenna. No! Do not fucking start. You lied to me. You didn't think this was going to happen, did you? Last night even when you said about warning McGeedy you were just brushing me off. I'm not stupid! Now, look at you. Looking at the floor...Not knowing what to do now. That you may actually now realise all the shit that's been happening to me could be real!" Tom had raised his voice and was shouting again.

"Tom, keep your voice down," Jenna said as she looked up, "I admit it's a bit odd..."

"Oh my god! Oh my god!" Tom shouted frantically, pacing up and down, "A bit odd?"

"Tom, just calm down. You just need to stay calm."

Tom shook his head and turned to face the garden.

Jenna continued, "What you are suggesting is ridiculous. That you can cause people to die from a heart attack. It's just absolutely ridiculous," Tom looked down at the floor, "You know don't you, Tom"

Tom turned again to face her, "But then explain it, Jenna. The facts. All the people linked to me by knowing I have done something have died...."

"McGeedy isn't dead!" Jenna interrupted

"She's as good as Jenna and you know it!" he snapped.

"No, we don't, not yet. Look Tom, we need to look at this rationally. You are getting yourself in a state and, well, it's just hard for me too. I mean, you are saying these things have happened but... Well, how do I really know?"

Tom signed and looked down and Jenna noticed him physically slump. He turned and walked out to the garden.

"Tom," called Jenna and followed him out to the garden to find him sitting on the edge of a lounger. She shook her head and walked towards him speaking as she approached.

"Tom, you must see how difficult this is for me. I am not sure what to do."

"Nor do I," replied Tom solemnly.

"Tom, just relax. Go back to work tomorrow and get back into it. Then I can make some calls and get you booked in to see a therapist. You can explain it all and see if they can make sense of it. You need some professional help just to get yourself back on an even keel," Tom just stared at the pool that was shimmering dramatically in the sun.

Jenna continued, "The drink isn't helping either. You've been excessive recently, Tom. Stay off it for a while. Get your head clear."

"I had those feelings again earlier this morning," Tom said, "The same feelings when we were going to Frank's, and I stopped, and you asked me what was wrong. It was that fear. The feeling of cold and despair. Just before Frank died"

"Tom, it could be anything….."

"I have had it each time. It is linked. I know it is linked. I had it this morning! It must've been when McGeedy…"

Jenna interrupted to try and stop Tom over analysing things, "Ok, but a therapist can help you with that. They specialise in these feelings and can give you advice on what it is and how to deal with it"

"But Jenna, I don't want to know how to deal with it! I want to know what it is!"

Jenna sighed, "Does it have to be anything in particular?"

Tom looked at her confused, then she continued.

"I mean, it could be stress, it could be anxiety…Look, Tom, it could be depression…I know you don't want hear that, but depression can…"

"Jenna!" interrupted Tom, "I am not depressed. There is something wrong with me and I need to know what. But it's not depression…."

"How do you know, Tom? Have you been depressed before? Been stressed before? How the fuck do you know how these things manifest themselves?"

Tom shook his head.

"Look Tom. It won't hurt to see a therapist, OK? I will look into it".

Tom just stared at the swimming pool.

The rest of the day had been a blur. Tom had watched some sports on TV and Jenna had gone to a friends. The house seemed cold and distant and Tom couldn't relax. He went from the house to the garden and back several times. Jenna had called to say she was staying out a little later due to her visit to a friend turning into a few friends visiting the same friend and it had now turned into a bit of a get together. She had said she wouldn't be too late.

Tom had reluctantly started work on his briefing for work. He had been mailed all the relevant data and documents and after about an hour or so he thought he had put enough together to get by. He still had the evening to tidy it up, but the main body was there. Tom hoped others would step in and make contributions but feared he would be met with blank, cold faces.

He was frustrated. Weekly finance briefings were his bread and butter. Normally he would be able to breeze in, speak for as long as needed and impress everybody there. But everything that had happened had shook him. His confidence was shot, and he wasn't himself. He felt lost and alone.

He put his work away and went to the kitchen and suddenly the urge hit him and was too great. He grabbed a bottle of Jim Beam and cracked it open. He took a big slug. It felt like golden syrup and he felt an immediate wave of comfort. He put the lid back on and put it away. He was going to have an early night. But before he went up, he grabbed the bottle again, opened it and took four huge glugs.

The whisky dribbled down his chin. It felt so good. He felt calm. Over the next half an hour he finished the bottle and hid it at the bottom of the trash bin. With that he stumbled up to bed and fell asleep immediately.

Chapter 13

Tom arrived home from work. They day had been very hard, and he was totally drained. Work was very busy as usual, and Tom was doing all he could to maintain a level of standard to keep himself off the radar, but he knew he was faltering, and his standards were dropping. But worse than that, he was sure he was being watched anyway.

He had noticed Shields around and about the trading floor a lot more and Tom was certain he was watching him closely and testing him. He believed it may have been due to a lacklustre performance in his briefing which Tom felt went well enough under the circumstances but knew it wasn't up to required standard. Add to that the fact that Tom had already shown signs of poor performance lately anyway.

Shields and Tom had never really had a close working relationship, in fact, no relationship at all. Shields was known for being aloof and kept his distance from all of the traders, so Tom knew it wasn't personal. But today he had asked Tom a few questions and had requested verbal updates and reports. Tom knew it was a test although, for now, he was confident that he had done enough to convince him that he was still on the ball.

However, another thing that Tom did notice was that whenever Shields was near him or speaking to him, Rutherford was also close by. Listening and monitoring. Tom sensed an air of frustration from Rutherford; which he put down to him feeling undermined, as monitoring the traders was his job, not Shields'.

Tom drove up onto the driveway and immediately noticed a light on upstairs; although the whole of the downstairs appeared completely dark.

He was exhausted and put his hands around his waist and realised that his usually trim and flat stomach was started to grow a paunch. He hadn't been to the gym for a long time and immediately thought that he must start attending again. Then his mind pushed that thought out of his head as he realised that his current mental and physical state was not conducive to a good workout.

His drinking had got out of hand and he felt lethargic most of the time. A sense of frustration washed over him as he recalled how, before all of this, his life was in order, he was in control of his time and always managed to find time for the gym. Now he felt completely out of control of everything and all he did currently was just manage to get through each day.

He slumped, rested his head on the back of the head rest and closed his eyes. He inhaled and then let out a huge sigh. It felt nice and he felt like he could fall asleep right there and then. The thought actually crossed his mind to do just that, but he decided against it and summoned up the energy to get out and go indoors.

As he opened the front door, he got the feeling the house was empty. It seemed vacant and lacked life. But he noted the light upstairs and wondered if Jenna had gone out and left it on. He was about to shout out to Jenna when he heard the sound of a conversation. It was inaudible but he felt it sounded heated. He stopped at the bottom of the stairs and listened intently. Then, all of a sudden, he heard Jenna say loudly, what he gathered to be, "Well you need to make a decision as I can't keep this up much longer!".

Tom felt he could have been mistaken but he was almost certain he had heard her correctly. He stayed at the bottom of the stairs but subconsciously took a step up and listened more intently; almost leaning his head and body toward the sound.
"No! I have done my part… This is not fair. You need to step in…"

Jenna's voice suddenly became louder and Tom realised she had moved and so he stepped down and prepared to move out of sight, but her voice then tailed off and became inaudible again. Tom moved back up the stairs, but this time walked up to the third stair and listened again, "Ok, but don't leave it too long this time…"

Jenna spoke sternly as her voice faded quickly back in louder and Tom realised she was moving to the top of the stairs. He turned to the front door and quietly but quickly moved towards it, opened it and slipped through to the outside, slowly closing it behind him. He stood outside next to the door. He wondered if he should get back into this car. Then he wondered why the hell he was running away. He realised he was just being foolish and paranoid again.

He turned back to face the door and took a deep breath. He put his key back in the door and opened it but this time he immediately shouted.
"Hey Jenna, you home?"
There as a short silence and then he heard her shout from upstairs.
"Hi Tom, yes, upstairs".

He waited at the door, put his briefcase down and started to slip off his shoes. As he did Jenna appeared at the top of the stairs holding her mobile phone. He felt that she looked a little flustered, but he never commented.

"Hey, how are you?" he asked.

"Hey, I'm fine, honey," she replied as he started to walk down the stairs.

She walked up to Tom and gave him a hug and then walked to the kitchen.

"I will get dinner on. Meatballs OK?" she asked as she walked into the kitchen. Tom noted that she put her mobile phone next to the fruit bowl on the island in the kitchen.

"Yeah, I am starving" Tom shouted.

The evening passed without event and it had been nice and relaxed. Considering the events over the last few days Tom was surprised at how relaxed he actually felt. He had desperately wanted some red wine with his dinner, but Jenna had, quite rightly, said to him that it was not a good idea. She said that he needed to keep his head clear and look after himself some more. He had argued it would just be one glass but, as they both knew, that was not going to be the case. Tom knew she was right, but he was also a little concerned at how strong the urge was.

They had gone into the lounge and laid together on the sofa channel hopping. They had eventually settled on a wildlife show following a pride of lions. Tom could feel his eyes getting heavy and has his mind settled he started to drift off to sleep. Then Jenna's phone rang and startled him out of his slumber.

Jenna got up and walked to the kitchen. Tom took a deep breath and stretched. He heard her answer the phone and then a few seconds later saw her head pop round the door.

"It's a friend, I need to take this".

She had a look on her face as if to intimate worry and concern which Tom gathered that she meant it was a crisis which needed managing. A crisis in terms of a female friend crisis which was almost certainly a relationship or costume malfunction.

He heard her go upstairs and continued to watch the wildlife show but suddenly got an urge to try and listen into Jenna's conversation. He didn't think she was lying but, because of his paranoia earlier, it was too much to bear and he could not fight it. He slowly got up and went to the bottom of the stairs. Like earlier he could hear Jenna talking but it was too muffled to hear exactly. He then hard a door close and could no longer hear her voice at all.

He crept upstairs without thinking but realised that if Jenna saw him she would wonder what he was doing. He quickly thought that he would say he was getting some papers from upstairs. As he got to the top of the stairs, he noticed that the bathroom door, study door and one of the other bedroom doors were open. But his and Jenna bedroom door was shut and so he knew where she was. He slowly and quietly walked up to it and listed through the door, again realising that if he got caught it would cause huge problems. He tried to listen in, but her voice was muffled, although not completely and he filtered was he could.

He realised that Jenna was speaking deliberately quiet and in between her muffled voice he made out various extracts from sentences.
"…No, that's not the point…"
"…Ok, but don't wait too long…"
"…I am trying but it's difficult…"

Tom suddenly realised he had been there a minute or so and felt is safer to go back down the stairs but then he had the sudden urge to be brazen and before he could think it through, his body had taken over. He then he backed away from the door and then walked back towards it trying to be as loud as he could humming a song. He walked straight up to the door and opened it and walked in.

Jenna was on the bed and looked up in complete shock. She immediately shook her head and mouthed the word, "No," without speaking and waved him out. He walked across the room and moved around the bed and whispered.
"Sorry, need a report for tomorrow," and walked around to his bedside table.

He sat down on the bed and opened his draws looking for something he knew wasn't there. Jenna spoke behind him, "…Oh baby, I am sure things will work out. Just be strong, OK".

There was silence as Tom ruffled though his drawers. He got up and looked at Jenna, shaking his head as if to demonstrate frustration at not being able to find the report. Jenna was angry.
"Hold on," she said down the phone and then held it to her chest, "Seriously, Tom? Some privacy please".
"OK, OK" Tom whispered, "Just need that report".

He shrugged his shoulders and said sorry then made his way to the door and left the room. He closed it slowly and looked behind him as he did and saw Jenna shaking her head at him as the door closed.

He made his way downstairs feeling that something wasn't right. What was Jenna up to he wondered. The things he had heard did not correlate to a relationship crisis, but he couldn't be sure, and then he realised they may have been. It could've been innocent. At the bottom of the stairs his paranoia got the better of him again, so he turned and went back up. He had already worked out that if Jenna came out and saw him, he would say he was going to look in the study for his report.

He slowly slipped across the hallway to the door and listened intently again. He could hear her muffled voice but then he heard her say something very clearly and sternly "Ok, but don't ever call me like this again. Keep it pre-planned like we agreed, OK"

His stomach turned and his chest became hot. It was a statement that confirmed to Tom all was not what it should be. But he realised it also sounded like it was the end of the conversation. So he quietly but quickly moved across the hallway and down the stairs. The lush carpet and well-made staircase made moving up and down the stairs almost silent. Then quickly thinking he grabbed his car keys from his jacket pocket and went outside to the car.

He pressed the bleeper and opened the boot and pretended to look around and move items. He kept an eye on the doorway and, sure enough, as he had thought, Jenna's head popped round.
"What are you doing?" she asked.
Tom looked round from the rear of the car, "Looking for that damn report," he replied.

Jenna shook her head and went inside. Tom was confident he had covered his tracks sufficiently. Luckily, he remembered he had an old finance report from the last quarter in the glove box, which had been there a few weeks. He went around, grabbed it, smiled to himself and went back inside and closed the door.

He made his way to the lounge and Jenna was sitting on the sofa with a concerned look on her face. Tom waved the report as he walked in. "Got it!" he said enthusiastically and put it down on the coffee table directly in front of her with the intention of cementing his reason to walk into the bedroom as being valid.

Jenna never spoke and Tom sat down, "Who was that?" he asked.
"Tom, do not ever interrupt me like that again".
Tom looked shocked, "Whoa, what's the big deal? I am not spying on you."
"No, but I need some privacy sometimes," Tom noticed she was still holding her phone.
"Ok, I said sorry," he replied, "You don't need to worry, I am not interested in you counselling your friends".

Tom grabbed the TV control and sat back making himself comfortable again.
"Well OK" Jenna replied, still a little flustered, "Just be a little more courteous".

Tom slapped his wrist gently as if to demonstrate to Jenna he had told himself off and had learnt his lesson. He relaxed into the sofa and picked up the wildlife show which was still on and the pride of lions were now stalking a herd of wildebeest.
"So who was it anyway?" asked Tom still staring at the TV.
"I thought you said you wasn't interested!" Jenna said bluntly as she turned and faced him.

Tom laughed as he knew Jenna was not being deadly serious. The lions slowly got closer and set themselves in their designated positions, ready to pounce and start the chase, but before they did Jenna spoke.
"If you must know it was a friend. She is having a tough time with her boyfriend and thinks he may be seeing someone else".
"Oh OK, I gathered it was something like that," replied Tom a little sarcastically but he sensed that Jenna did not pick up on it.

The lions had pounced and were now bounding across the plains sending the wildebeest into a mass panic and running in all directions. A younger, smaller calf had been targeted and had been steered into the path of another lioness.
"Is she OK?" asked Tom still staring at the TV screen. Jenna looked at him again.
"Mr Nosey, tonight!" she stated with a fake level of amazement.
"Just making conversation, that's all. I am sure you gave her sound advice," Tom said slowly and surely.

The calf veered one way and then noticed the lioness careering towards from another angle off to its right. It quickly changed direction and the lioness suddenly found herself further away now having to make up more ground. But the trap had worked perfectly and within five seconds the lioness was now close and gaining with dust and sand being thrown high up behind her from her powerful rear legs.

"I did. She's fine," said Jenna also watching the TV, "I am meeting her tomorrow for lunch". Jenna paused and Tom sensed she was going to say more. She turned her body again to face him.

"Anyway," she finally continued, "enough of that. I have been thinking about you."

A huge cloud of dust blew up and the lioness took the young calf down and within seconds others had joined and the calf disappeared under a mass of the powerful beasts.

"Oh, have you?" replied Tom indignantly and he realised that Jenna had either ignored or failed to catch his tone.

"Well, yes, it's just all the things going on. I think you definitely need to see a professional. Someone who can help you understand the feelings you are having. A friend gave me details of a really good therapist that can help you."

Tom looked away from the savagery now unfolding on the TV and turned to Jenna but said nothing. She continued, "Someone who can make you see sense of it all. I think you are stressed. And that's causing you anxiety, which is causing you to imagine things and have silly thoughts. A therapist can help you process it all."

Tom stayed silent and Jenna expected him to reply; when he didn't, she felt it best to fill the silence, "You have had so much to cope with. The job, moving. It's just got too much".

Again Jenna had hoped for a response but did not get one. Tom simply put his head back on the couch and looked at the ceiling. Jenna shuffled her body towards Tom and continued, "And the drinking is not helping, Tom. You know that. You need to stop worrying, and I think the drink is making you anxious and paranoid. Whatever you are feeling you need to get help to manage it and get yourself back up straight and moving along with your life… Our life".

Tom just continued to stare at the ceiling and took a deep breath.

"What do you think?" Jenna asked caringly. Tom shrugged his shoulders. Jenna leaned closer and took his hand.

"Look, Tom, the feelings you get which you describe as dread and fear, and those cold feelings, well, I have been researching and it's all explainable. Its severe anxiety. I mean, all that stuff about causing people harm, well, it's…It's far-fetched. I don't want to dismiss or patronise you, Tom, but you have to start looking at things from a perspective of reality.

You need to stop. Think about things sensibly. This is real life, Tom. You need to pull yourself together and take positive steps to get your head straight, make sense of it all and manage it."

Jenna sat waiting for Tom to speak but he just sat silent.

"Tom?" she asked frustrated, demanding he respond.

"You are right" he suddenly said.

Jenna relaxed slightly knowing she may have got through.

"I know," she said quietly.

Growling and roaring could be heard from the TV as the lionesses were joined by a large male lion who scared them all off and sat over the dead calf, claiming it for himself.

"I will make an appointment for you. I know who to call."

Tom looked down from the ceiling at Jenna.

"Yes, I would like you to do that for me," he said with a smile.

Jenna smiled back and leaned over and cuddled him. Tom cuddled her back and they embraced for a short time. She then moved her head around to Tom's face. He felt her breath on his neck and became immediately aroused. She sensed this and kissed his neck. He turned his head and gently kissed her neck too. Jenna let out a quiet, soft moan. Tom moved his hand around from her neck and up to her breast which he cupped and realised she was not wearing a bra. He circled the tip of her nipple with his finger and she groaned quietly. He lifted her shirt to reveal her breast which he held and caressed gently, while he moved his tongue more quickly around on her neck. They both re-adjusted their seating positions to get more comfortable and closer into each other when the phone rang and startled them both.

Jenna jumped up and Tom sat up, "No, leave it," Tom pleaded.

"No!" said Jenna bluntly as she brushed her top down, "it may be important".

Jenna looked around for the phone as the holder was ringing but the phone wasn't on it. She walked out of the lounge and into the kitchen. Tom left frustrated and alone with his arousal.

Tom then heard her say, "Hi!" and then the sound of genuine and happy inaudible conversation. Suddenly Jenna came back into the room and mouthed, "It's your mom," to him.

He was surprised and immediately tried to clear his head. He had a lot of thoughts floating around in his mind and one of them was that he hadn't spoken to her in weeks. He realised what an arsehole he was and how a quick phone call before now would have sufficed.

After some more idle chit-chat Jenna suddenly said, "Here he is," and handed him the phone. As she did she pointed to the ceiling and mouthed to Tom she was going up. Tom nodded and put the phone to his ear. "Hi mom!" he said as enthusiastically as he could. It wasn't that he didn't want to speak to her. He desperately did but, for some reason, he felt awkward.
"Hi Tommy" she replied, "How's things?" she asked sounding genuinely excited to be speaking to him.
"I'm fine…We are fine. How are you?"
"Well, I am OK I suppose," she had said, Tom sensing that she was finding it difficult to hide that things weren't OK.

Tom queried her response and it had eventually led to a conversation about her wellbeing. She had explained to him that a couple of months ago she had started to get some pains in her stomach and had been to her GP. Her GP had been concerned and had sent her for some tests and she was waiting for the results. After further questioning from Tom he had managed to get out of her that she had coughed up blood once or twice. Tom was furious. His mum had kept saying, "It's fine," and, "Don't worry," through the conversation, but he had argued that it wasn't fine and how could he not worry.

She said he was busy work and the resettlement, and she didn't want to worry him. He had again argued that she shouldn't have to worry about this on her own, but she had replied that she had, Claire, Tom's sister. This made Tom even angrier and more frustrated.

Tom had always thought she was the first to know about everything. Always involved and always the mature one that family went to with issues and problems. Tom hated it. He loved Claire but deep down he thought she was a martyr and did it on purpose to maintain the status-quo. Tom's mum explained that Claire had taken her to the GP and accompanied her to the tests and said there was nothing to worry about. Tom's frustration boiled over.
"Oh, so Claire is now a fucking qualified physician now? Her skills are never ending"
"Tom, wash your mouth out" his mum demanded, "and do not talk about your sister that way, she has never done anything wrong. Ever"

Tom sighed. He sensed the genuine shock and anger from his mum. He knew his mum was right. Claire had never done anything wrong. She was mature and well balanced, just a really wonderful person. A great Mum, wife, sister, daughter and model citizen. Perhaps that was what annoyed Tom. That although he had had a successful career, he felt slightly detached from family life. Like he was just 'Good Ol' Tom' and not really a person that anyone in the family could genuinely lean on for support or guidance. That was Claire's area.

"I am sorry, mom…I just…Well, I just feel a bit weird at the moment. A bit stressed"

"Well, Tommy, there is something else I wanted to talk to you about….In relation to that"

Tom suddenly felt concerned, "Ok" he said, not sure what was going to be said.

She went on to explain that Jenna had called her a week or so ago and had been really concerned. At first she had said work had been stressful, plus the transfer and stuff. Maybe also some pressure to start a family. It had all got too much. She continued on to say that Jenna had said that Tom had been very anxious and not himself.

Jenna had eventually asked her to call him and discuss with him about seeing a therapist to help process everything. Tom felt suddenly shocked and was struggling to find anything to say in response. As he did he walked to the stairs to make sure Jenna had gone up. He then walked through the house to the rear doors, slid them open and went outside to the pool. He felt a cold as the night air hit him.

"Mom, things are fine. Look, she shouldn't have called…"

"No Tom," his mum interrupted, "I asked her some questions about it, and we got talking and, quite frankly, she told me your behaviour had been very odd and that you were also drinking more than you should," she paused but Tom, now angry, never spoke.

"Have you been having bad dreams again, Tom?" she suddenly asked. Tom was stunned into further silence, "Tom, are you still there?"

"Yes, still here," said Tom quietly as he sat down on one of the loungers.

"Look Tom, don't be angry. Jenna loves you and cares for you. None of this was to hurt you, just to help you. She did the right thing to reach out to me. You can't deal with this on your own"

"Deal with what?" asked Tom suddenly. There was a pause as she seemed inadvertently felt unable to speak. Tom heard a sigh, then she spoke. "Well, Jenna told me about you mentioning some strange things happening"

"What?!" Exclaimed Tom, "she had no right, what did she say?" Tom could feel the anger and frustration building up.

"Tom calm down. Please. Getting angry won't solve anything."

Tom was silenced through embarrassment but also anger. He couldn't help thinking how dare Jenna betray him and go behind his back. He didn't want his mum to know what had been going on. His mind raced. Had Jenna said anything about the deaths? The computer file. The brake light. The fence? Tom felt himself tense up.

"Tom, Jenna said some things to me in complete innocence. Like she was worried you are losing perspective and things are tipping over the edge. She wants you to get help."

A tear ran down Tom's face. He had never thought his dear mum would know or ever be involved. He was embarrassed and angry. But then what his mum told him next made him freeze.

"Tom, I can't say too much and I need to be careful. Jenna had mentioned some incidents that you feel you may be responsible for. But, Tom…" There was a pause and then she whispered, "You aren't going mad.".

"What?" he whispered in disbelief.

Again, she whispered, "You aren't insane. There is a connection. But don't be afraid. Put all of this to the back of your mind and live your life to the fullest."

She paused and then continued again but speaking at normal level again. "Tom, if certain things happen that confuse you then just let them happen and do not worry…I can't say anymore, I have probably said too much…"

"Mom you are confusing me, I need to come and see you…"

"Ok, that's fine. You and Jenna can come up when you are free…"

"No" interrupted Tom, "I am coming tonight…I need to know more about …"

"No!" she said sternly, "Just relax. Don't do that…Just work out a weekend when you are free and come up and see me. Look Tommy, don't be afraid. Everything is fine. When you come and see me I won't be able to say much more but just be assured there is nothing to worry about."

There was a pause as the information she had given him started to sink in.

"Mom, what did you mean, 'there is a connection'?"

"Oh, Tommy, it's not fair, I just want you to be happy," Tom heard his mum's voice breaking but she continued, "You are such a good boy and I am so proud of you"

Tom felt the urge to let it go but something inside him made him ask again, but this more directly, "Mom, what you did you mean?"

He heard her sigh and then there was a pause.

"Tommy, just be calm. Enjoy what you have. You have worked hard for it. You have Jenna and she loves you. If something unusual happens then ignore it and move on. You are going to be just fine."

She stopped speaking and expected a response, but Tom left her hanging. Then he asked again, "Please…"
"Tom I have to go. When you come up we can talk. I love you, son"
There was another pause and this time Tom gave up, "I love you too, Mom".

But just as Tom was about to say goodbye, his mum spoke again.
"Oh Tom, just one more thing. Don't tell Jenna what I told you. Just tell her I called to make sure you were OK and that I also think you should go see someone to help you. No more than that, OK?

Tom was now upset and unable to reply apart from mumbling, "I love you, Mom".

He heard the click which ended the call and then the dialling tone buzzing in his ear. He sat on the lounger. He could no longer feel the chill as he was numb. He never understood what his mum had actually told him, but he felt a little relieved that she appeared to understand him. He wasn't completely sure, but he felt he could rely on her for support.

He got up and walked back inside and closed the doors. As the warmth engulfed him he then realised how cold he was and shivered. He into the lounge, sat on the couch and started watching TV again. But it was all just movement and sound. His eyes never blinked and nothing on the screen registered. He snapped out of his trance and went to make himself comfortable then noticed Jenna's mobile phone on the coffee table.

The thought immediately crossed his mind that the last number that called would be on her received list. He paused for a few seconds, contemplating. Then he leant over and grabbed the phone. He knew her security number, punched it in and then quickly opened the call list.

He noted that the list was made up of contact names, all except the top number which he confirmed to be around the time when Jenna's friend had supposedly called about her alleged relationship crisis. He then scrolled down and noted that in between various names the same number appeared infrequently. Both tagged as calls to and from.

Jenna had accused him of having an affair but was she? His mind was frantic, and he wondered if he should just call it. He processed what would happen if he did. If a female answered and said, "Hi Jenna," then he would know it was the truth. And he would just terminate the call. But he wondered what to say if they just said "Hi" or "Hello" and he surmised that at least if it's a female voice it would almost certainly be OK.

He then wondered why if it was a friend were they not in the contact list. Maybe a new phone? Or Jenna may just have not got around to updating her contacts?

His thumb hovered over the green phone image to make a call. He suddenly felt very tense. But before his mind could elaborate further his thumb had pressed and the green 'Calling' message appeared. He put the phone to his ear and listened. The ring tone began and continued to four rings, then five, six and seven before Tom got the urge to terminate the call. But just as he was about to press end he heard a click and a deep male voice asked, "What now?"

Tom sat, frozen with fear and confusion suddenly wishing that he had not called the number.
"Jenna?" the voice asked.

Tom held his breath. No sound came from the other end. Tom realised that whoever it was at the other end maybe knew it was not Jenna. He then heard a click as the person terminated the call. He turned Jenna's phone off completely, so whoever it was couldn't call back, even if they wanted to. He put it down the coffee table and shivered again.

He then went around the house, locked up and turned off the lamps and lights. He slowly made his way upstairs and wondered if Jenna had slipped up by leaving her phone on the coffee table. The person at the other end may have been her friend's boyfriend and it could be innocent. But somehow it just didn't feel right. He got into the bedroom and slowly slid into bed. He noticed that Jenna was already asleep, or at least appeared to be. He couldn't sleep. He needed to see his mum. He felt that right now she was the only person in the world he could trust.

Chapter 14

Tom's head bobbed from side to side as the train rattled along into the city. He was hungover. He had driven to his local station and parked up and as he was walking to the station, he realised he must have been way over the limit. He put another piece of chewing gum in his mouth to try and mask the smell of whisky.

He had got up earlier than needed just to avoid Jenna. But he also knew he had the report to check. He opened his briefcase to but after reading it for a few minutes he felt motion sick and was now quietly heavy breathing to try to help quell the nausea.

The train was busy, and a man stood close to him reading a paper. Tom had noted how smart the man looked but was getting frustrated by the belt on the man's jacket flicking the side of his shoulder each time the train jolted from side to side. He watched the world pass by outside and noticed that watching the movement and the heavy, relaxed breathing was helping him feel better.

Soon enough, the skyline of the city came closer and details emerged within what Tom had, over the last few months, started to perceive as like Lego blocks. The Red CNA Plaza, John Hancock Centre and Sears Tower always drew his eye. But as the train trundled into the city all the buildings merged into one and loomed over the passengers like giants.

Eventually the train arrived and ground to a halt, and after the hustle and bustle of disembarking and joining the snake of people marching its way through the station, Tom was soon out into the street and was finally able to relax a little more.

He headed north towards West Washington Street to cross the bridge to his office in North LaSalle street, but he stopped and looked at his watch. He was early. With that he quickly turned to go back into the station to grab a newspaper from the vending machine and as he did, he felt a barge and realised that the smart man from the train had walked straight into him.
"Woah," exclaimed Tom, "Really sorry, man"
The man appeared shocked and taken aback then glared at Tom sternly who, noticing this, repeated, "I am sorry."

The man's face remained stern but he held his hands up to suggest it was not a problem and walked away quickly. Tom just stared at him as he did.

"Jesus, I said sorry," Tom said sarcastically, loud enough to pretend he had said it to the man, but quiet enough to hope the man didn't actually hear.

Tom picked up a copy of the Tribune, quickly checked the front page and then set off again towards his office. The footways were busy as usual, and walking too quickly was difficult, so in the end Tom gave up and just walked at a slower more casual pace. He stopped for a coffee and realised that water would be better but the thought of something warm and tasty appealed to him more than something cold and tasteless. The coffee house was busy, and Tom got in line. He looked at his paper and then at the menu deciding what to have. He looked around. He looked out of the shop just out of interest.

It was then that he noticed the man from the train that had accidentally barged into him. He was getting into a black 4x4 on the opposite side of the road. Something told Tom this was unusual, but he quickly dismissed it as completely normal. It was just coincidence that he had seen the man a few times already that day.
He looked around again and saw another smartly dressed man get out. This man had a shaven head and a goatee beard and looked like his suit was very expensive. Tom quickly looked back at his paper to hide his interest in them. But unable to resist the urge he looked again had noticed the 4x4 had driven away and the man was nowhere to be seen. Not unusual he thought.

He got his coffee and walked out of the shop. He took a sip. As he did he realised that his choice of coffee over water was a good one. He started off again cross the bridge heading towards North Wells Street but as he got across he stopped, looked at the sports pages and took another sip of his coffee. As he did he noticed across the street the man with the expensive suit looking into a jeweller's window.

He looked back down at the paper but wasn't reading it. His mind raced. Was this unusual, he wondered. Why would the man get out of a 4x4 that the other man had got into? Just to go and look at a jewellery shop? Something wasn't right but Tom looked left and right and then set off again.

As he did, he wondered if it was worth just dismissing all of this and making his way to work. But he knew he had time and decided to test his paranoia. So instead of continuing he turned right into North Franklin Street, knowing full well that at any time he was going to turn and go completely back in the opposite direction. But when was the right time to do it? Was he being paranoid?

He then realised that a throng of people had built up around him and so turning now wouldn't be noticed too much. He looked up and saw an expensive tobacco shop of which he had no interest, but the front window was packed with paraphernalia; expensive boxes of cigars, lighters, bottles of scotch, that type of thing. He stopped and looked at the window trying to look as if he was interested then, after 30 seconds, he headed back the way he had come. As he did he looked ahead, and he could see the man with the goatee beard heading towards him, amongst lots of other people all hustling to get to work.

As he got closer, he looked at the man and the man quickly made eye contact and then looked ahead and past Tom. They passed quickly and Tom realised that if something was happening then him and the man were the only people who knew it. He picked up speed and started to walk quickly. He daren't look back. He was still questioning himself, but he was concerned if he did look back and the man was following him again then he would alert the man that he knows this.

Tom's mind raced. He turned down right back onto West Washington and noticed a small book shop just ahead on the right. He looked back and calculated if the man was following him, he would not be close enough to see him go into the shop. Tom walked as fast as he could to the entrance and looking back he never saw the man. He quickly slipped through the door and into the shop.

The shop was dark and colourless, it smelt musty and there was only one other person in their browsing. The bell on the door had rung as he entered and a small old lady shuffled from a back door and asked Tom if she could help him. Tom made sure he got behind a bookcase in the middle which shielded him from view. As he did, he politely informed the lady that he was just browsing, and she told him if he wanted anything to call. Tom nodded and thanked her.

Tom picked up a book and pretended to read the back all the while watching the window. He was then shocked to see the man jog past the window. Tom moved slowly to the front of the shop and found a display which allowed him to stand behind but also see out and past the shop in the direction the man had headed. Tom could just see him. He was looking back and forth and up and down whilst trying to avoid people walking past. He looked edge and frustrated at something, what it was Tom didn't know.

Tom picked up another book and moved slightly closer to the window to keep an eye on the man, who had now moved further away. Tom then watched in horror as, on the opposite the side of the street, the black 4x4 appeared and stopped quickly. The smart man from the train got out and made a circling sign in the air to the other man. The other man then checked the road and ran across out in front of a taxi and it beeped it horn, then the two men had a short conversation and the 4x4 drove away.

The man jogged back across the road and then past the book shop, as he did Tom put his head behind the book and crouched slightly looking at the other customer to make sure his behaviour hadn't been noted. It hadn't. Tom waited a few minutes. He checked his watch noting he now had 20 minutes to get to work. He worked out the best route in his head and slowly left the shop. He checked each way to try and see if the 4x4 or the men were about. As far as he could see, they weren't.

Tom went headed up North Wells keeping an eye ahead and behind him as he went. Realising that he may looked nervous he tried to calm himself and look more natural. He turned into West Randolph Street and was happy to find it very busy with pedestrians and so he felt safer as he enveloped himself into the throng of bodies.

He quickly walked within the throng and realised he needed to cross the road to get over South LaSalle. He edged towards the kerb and suddenly felt isolated as the throng appeared to filter out. As he stood on the edge of the kerb, he suddenly spotted the 4x4 on the opposite side of the road. He froze. It appeared to slow. As it cruised past Tom noticed the man from the train staring directly at him. He felt as though his heart stopped. Then his instinct made him take action.

He turned and tried to get back into the crowd. Luckily, he spotted an alleyway through the buildings only ten yards away. He made a move for it bumping into two people as he went. He never apologised and one of them shouted. He never heard what was said as his mind focussed. He looked back and the 4x4 had now stopped and the car behind it was beeping its horn. Tom ran into the alleyway and instinctively started running faster without knowing his route or where he was actually heading. The alleyway was long and looked as though it had smaller alleyways branching from it at various points.

Hot steam came up through a grate and Tom put his hand up to clear it as he ran through it. As he got through it, he stopped and tried to work out a route. He could go straight ahead or take a left or right at what appeared to be the central point. He realised he was now frozen but needed to move, and so he kicked on and ran past some boxes and trash bins, but then what he saw ahead made him freeze.

The man with the goatee beard and expensive suit was walking very quickly towards him. Tom looked back and now the other man from the train was standing at the far end of the alleyway where he had come in. Tom now realised he was in serious trouble. His mind raced and he noticed the man with the beard had now started running. He quickly realised he had to make the central point before him so started running again, but now as fast as he could in a suit and brogues. The man sped up and Tom realised it was going to be close, but he then realised it was going to be too close and that the man was going to get there at the same time.

Tom stopped. Looked back and the man from the train was walking up the alleyway in his direction. Tom was about 20 yards from the central point, and he could now see the man clearly. He had shaved head and a ginger goatee beard, his face had sharp features, almost shark like. The man now almost at the central point stopped running and slowed to a light jog. Tom sensed that both men now knew they had him.

Tom looked back. The man from the train was still some way away and was walking more slowly. Tom turned and look back. The man with the beard was now 10 yards away and was now walking slowly. Tom put both his hands up to protest his innocence.
"Look, whatever this is you have the wrong person…I don't know anything…Please," Tom felt his voice crack and tail off; his throat was burning.

The man put his hand inside his jacket and then pulled out a handgun. Tom noticed the thickened end which appeared to be a silencer.

"No!" screamed Tom, "This is a mistake!" but Tom realised with the intent on the man's face that nothing he said was going to deter him. The man stopped. He lifted the gun and aimed. Tom felt his body crumple and he tried to protect himself with his arms. He looked at the man one last time waiting for the end.

Then suddenly from the left a figure appeared. A large, dark figure that was moving swiftly and with a swinging motion. Tom saw the split-second reaction by the man with the beard and as his head turn to see the figure, a large blunt instrument bludgeoned his forehead with a sickening,

119

dull thud. Tom froze as he saw the man's head fly back with such force it looked like his neck would break.

The man stepped back two or three paces and then slumped to the floor in a heap. The dark figure moved to the man. Lifted the rod-shaped instrument and brought it down with such force onto the man's head that Tom was certain he had seen his skull crush. The sound made Tom feel sick.

He looked back. The man from the train had gone. Tom assumed he had obviously seen the attack from the dark figure and was not up for the fight. Tom looked back. In the dark alleyway and the steam Tom had first thought the figure was almost super-hero like.
But he could now see the figure wasn't so. He realised that it was a man and his face had a black beard and dark skin wearing what appeared to be dark combat gear and a black wool hat.

The man stared at Tom. Tom was frozen with fear and said nothing. The man checked all directions of the alleyway. He then put the baton he had used to smash Tom's potential killer back into his jacket. The man straightened himself out and brushed himself down.
"You are in danger," he said with a deep voice that Tom noted had a slight southern drawl. Tom said nothing.
"If you keep calm and follow instructions you will be OK". Again, Tom said nothing.
"Are you ok?" the man asked.
"I think so" said Tom and after a pause asked, "Who are you?"
"No time for that," the man replied, "Just stay with people you can trust. And stay out in public with lots of people"
Tom nodded and the man continued, "And take this", as he did, he leant down and left what appeared to be an envelope on the floor and in a second he had gone the same way he had appeared.

Tom didn't move. He looked back. He suddenly felt very alone. He must get back to where there are people. He quickly got up from his crouched state and went and picked up the envelope. He looked down at the man and a large pool of blood had now built up around him and had started running down the alleyway. The man's head was completely caved in and his eyes were open with what looked like complete fear. Tom felt sick again, but he knew then he had to move.

He started to jog down the alleyway the same way the man that saved him had gone. He looked ahead but couldn't see. He looked back at the dead body, then looked forward again and then down at the envelope which had written on it:

FAO Tom - Private

He got towards the end of the alleyway and could start to hear traffic and hustling people again. He realised he must look terrible. He took a deep breath and brushed himself down. He edged towards the end of the alleyway. Looked left and right and then filtered into the throng of people. As he walked along taken with the flow of the people, he saw a coffee shop ahead on the left and headed towards it.

He went inside and saw a small table to the left. It was warm inside, and Tom immediately realised he was sweating profusely from the exertions. His head was throbbing. The shop was not too busy, as by now most people would have made their way into work. He sat down at an empty table for two. He tried to calm himself and his heart was beating hard.

As he composed himself, he felt a presence and looked up. A young lady who obviously worked there stood next to him, "Excuse me sir, you have to go up to order…" followed by a pretty smile. Tom thanked her and said he would order shortly. The girl smiled again and continued to clear tables.

Tom looked down at the envelope. He opened it. Inside was a folded note. He unfolded it and on it were the words scribbled:

Tom. We can help you. Text the word 'ODIN' to 07659422058 ASAP. Destroy this note.

Tom just stared at it. Then he put the note in his pocket. He realised he was now late for work and the briefing. His mind was frazzled. He suddenly realised his breathing was erratic and he was sweating. He looked up and the girl who had spoken to him glanced at him and he knew she thought something was odd.

How was he going to go to work now? After what had happened. He needed time to clear his mind. Was he even safe? If he left this coffee shop would the next potential killer come. Was it even linked to anything? Was it mistaken identity? Why had Tom had been given the envelope? He needed to calm down, take stock and try to think clearly.

Tom realised there was no way he could go into work. What could he do? He needed to get out of the city immediately. If anymore of those people were after him, they would be heading straight there soon. Whoever sent those people would now know Tom had been rescued. The man that had got away would surely send an update. Would they send more men? Or would they wait? Did they know where he lived? Tom was at least content that this had taken place away from home. It gave him some hope they never knew where he lived, but, then again, what difference would that make?

Tom wiped sweat from how brow. He was hot. He needed to cool down. He looked around and spotted the toilet sign. He got up and made is way over and the waitress glanced up at him again and he smiled trying not to look too unusual.

Inside he cupped water and doused his face several times. His heart was still beating. What should he do? He thought about going to the police. He had nearly been killed. Any right-thinking person would call the police and report it. A man had tried to shoot him. There was a dead body in the alleyway back there. Why would he not go to the police? It made sense, that's what he would do.

But what about work? He had to let them know. He then realised that he had been in the toilet a little longer than normal. He dried his hands and face and looked in the mirror. He was hot but looked pale. He straightened himself out and took a deep breath. He left the toilet and noted the shop was less busy. The waitress glanced up at him and he smiled again.

He hesitated and realised he had told her he would order. He went to leave. As he got up he felt her watching, "Are you ok, Sir?", she asked politely.

He turned and she was looking at him holding two mugs.
"Er…Yeah thanks" said Tom "Look, I just got into a bit of trouble, I need to call the police."
"Oh my god," the girl exclaimed in response and made her way over to him.
"Please, sit down, what happened?" she took his arm and slowly moved him to a nearby seat, "Do you want some water?" she asked, but before Tom could answer the girl had already called for cold water. Tom looked up and the counter staff were now looking on intently.
"What happened?" she repeated.
"I think someone tried to rob me?" Tom answered. He wasn't sure at first why he said it but then realised that it was what it could well have been.

Except the envelope made him realise it was more than that, but he couldn't explain.

"Oh no! Where?" the girl replied genuinely, passing him a glass of water that had been brought over.

"A few blocks back. I was cutting through an alley and a man came from nowhere and pointed a gun at me...But...Well, I don't know, another man came from out of nowhere and hit him...I think he's dead...I need to call the police...No I need to ring work first." Tom realised he was mumbling.

"Oh my god" replied the girl, sounding genuinely frightened, "Look. You sit here and take your time and call who you want, OK?"

"OK.... Thanks"

The girl smiled and walked away. Tom started to think and took a deep breath. He could hear the girl telling the counter staff what had gone on. Some it audible, some of it not. He did hear her say "This city is getting worse each day..... Just not safe anymore....."

Tom took out his mobile. He was going to ring work. He thought it best to just cut to the chase and ring Conway. He looked him up and pressed call. After a few rings Conway answered, "Where the fuck are you?" Tom was not surprised by the greeting.

"Look, Conway, I am really sorry, something had happened. I have been robbed at gunpoint on the way to work; I need to call the police and they will obviously want to take a statement. I am going to ri..."

"Whoa, there cowboy!" interrupted Conway, "Where the fuck has this happened?"

"In an alley way, not sure exactly where? Close to City Hall."

There was a pause "Ok, so what they take?"

"Look, that's not important, a man aimed a gun at me, and something happened, and I need to get a report to..."

"Ok, Ok. So, are you coming in?"

"Look I don't know? I need to ring the police, or I may even go down to the precinct. I just don't know. I need to ring them at least and then go from there"

"They won't do fuck all. It's just an attempted robbery," replied Conway condescendingly.

"No, you don't understand. There's a dead body...Someone stopped the robber...I think, I'm not sure..."

There was a pause and then Conway spoke again.

"You sure you ain't covering your tracks? Was it you who did the killing?" Tom heard a wheezy laugh follow. Conway could make light of anyone's misery. He had that knack.

"Look, Conway, please just tell them I'm sorry and if I can get in I will but I don't feel great and a bit freaked out. And I know it's the briefing but I...."

"I will tell them. Put the briefing off until tomorrow. Make sure you are in!"

"Right ok thanks," said Tom, relieved, "Look I'm sorry...I know I have been a bit flaky lately and I prom..." Click. Tom realised Conway had terminated the call.

Tom took another deep breath and took a sip of water. He looked up and the waitress and two other counter staff were chatting, and the waitress looked round and gave Tom a face that intimated she was concerned for him. Tom smiled back. He got his phone and was about to call 911 then realised he wasn't far from the precinct. He got up and turned to the shop staff.

"I think I will go straight to the precinct."

"Oh OK if you are sure?" asked the waitress and came over to him. She put her hand on his arm, "I hope you are ok and get all this sorted"

Tom nodded and smiled, "I will, thanks".

The waitress nodded. Tom stepped out. Then realised he may not be safe. He stopped at the doorway to the shop. He looked up and down both ways. He could not see the 4x4 or anyone that appeared to be watching him. He then thought it may be safer to just ring the police. Or should he call the number on the note given to him. Or was that just confusing matters. No, he decided he would walk. He looked up and down the street again and was just about to set off when he heard his phone beep.

He looked down to see a received text. He clicked in and noticed it was from an unknown number. He quickly checked it by opening the envelope symbol:

'Do not involve the police.'

Tom's stomach turned. He felt sick.

"Jesus!" he exclaimed under his breath. He looked around to see if anyone was watching him. He could not see anything obvious. Tom quickly thought he should just go to the police. Then he realised that could be dangerous. Who the fuck was this anyway? In a hasty moment of frustration and anger Tom called the number that had texted him. What was he going to say? He didn't know.

It never rung. Just a female voice advised, "The number you have dialled is not available right now. Please try again later"

Tom then opened it again and sent a text to the number:

'Who is this?'

But there was no immediate response. He tried to call again but got the same message. He realised he was sweating again. He wiped his brow. What the fuck was going on, he thought.

Tom decided it best not to go to the police. He had almost been killed and it was obvious something bigger than he could understand was happening. But why him? He thought of phoning Jenna but then just as he was about to dial he decided against it. He was confused. Why was his instinct telling him not to call her? She should be the first person to call. He felt alone and isolated. Then he remembered the note. He got it out of his jacket and read it again.

Tom opened up his text function on his phone. He entered the number and then compared it digit for digit to the note saying the numbers out loud as he did. He then entered the word 'Odin' and pressed send.

He looked up and down the street to check for the 4x4 and the other man but couldn't see neither or any other signs of danger. In his mind he thought of a plan to keep his head down and make his way carefully back to the station. He would take the most indirect route and keep his eye on the streets. He thought that he would go into various premises on the way to keep a check on if he was being followed. He would get out of the city and get home and then try to figure things out. As he was thinking he heard his phone buzz and he noted a received message. Tom opened it.

'Tom. Do not reply to this text and do not call the number. You are in danger. I can help you. Remain calm. Get to a safe place. We must meet soon. I will text again at 9pm tonight. Do not trust anybody. Odin'

Tom shuddered. This was now all getting too weird. He was obviously involved in something serious, but he didn't know what. He was desperate to ring the number and ask questions, but he followed the instructions. Tom slowly made his way back to the station following out the plan in his head. Stopping, going back on himself and looking in shops and checking the streets for anything suspicious.

He eventually got to the station and had an anxious fifteen-minute wait for his train. When it arrived, he felt a wave of relief and boarded and started to make his way home.

Chapter 15

Tom got home safely but he still felt very uneasy. Driving back from his local train station where he had left his car, he was trying to think of what to tell Jenna as to why he was not at work. He decided to say he felt ill and had been sent home. Again he kept wondering why his instinct was telling him not to involve her. But the 'Don't trust anybody' advice kept flashing around his mind. He realised how out of control this was all getting.

He had opened up to Jenna once before about what had been going on and something was telling him to do that again, but his instinct fought it. Luckily when he arrived home Jenna wasn't in, so he had time to compose himself and rack his brains for another reason why he was home if he eventually thought of one better than 'being ill'.

He also kept thinking of the advice to get to a safe place. He assumed that home was safe. But how could he be sure? He looked out of the window and by chance noticed Frank's wife letting two people into her house. They dressed smartly and one had folders and what looked like brochures. He realised they were probably organising the funeral.

Tom had been thinking about that briefly since Frank's death. He had been trying to think of a way of getting Jenna over to the house to see the footage. He had initially thought that he may get an opportunity at the wake but having known Frank such a short time he couldn't be sure if they would even be invited; but he assumed there was a good chance they would go, being neighbours. He had pictured him and Jenna slipping upstairs and him showing her the footage, but he had soon realised that with Frank gone he did not know the password to get into the system.

It had frustrated him knowing the footage was there of him painting the fence, but it could never be viewed. Although Tom also realised that ship may have sailed anyway as the last couple of days had proven that Jenna was definitely of the logic that this was all down to Tom's stress and depression. He realised that although recently she had acted as though she was on his side and believed him, deep down she never did and could not be persuaded.

Tom suddenly then realised that getting Jenna to see that footage was now really the least of his worries. Much bigger events were now occurring that needed his attention. Obviously, his attempted murder being one of them, but also his mum. He had to make plans to go and see her. He thought that he would try and go this weekend or next. His mum had said to go with Jenna and so he thought this may be a good idea. Getting away would do them both good he thought. Maybe they just need a change of scenery. He also thought that in view of what had happened that day he would prefer to be with someone.

He checked his diary and realised that this weekend would be better as work looked busy the week after. He needed to get this worked out. He searched for his mobile phone, eventually finding it in his jacket pocket. He phoned Jenna.

He explained that he was feeling ill and had been sent home, that he was getting stomach cramps and felt sick. Jenna has asked him if he had been drinking and he shouted down the phone at her and accused her of always getting at him. She put the phone down, so Tom called her back and apologised. He explained he was anxious and told her that he wanted to go and see his mum. At first Jenna appeared to be a bit taken aback which confused Tom, but then suddenly said to him it would be good and she will go with him. They agreed that they would go this weekend.

But Jenna then suddenly interjected.
"Oh Tom, but I had made an appointment for you Saturday to see a professional. You know what we discussed?" Tom never replied and so Jenna continued, "They were referred to me and they can counsel and guide you through the way you are feeling. But obviously I can re-arrange if you..."
"Yes, please re-arrange it" said Tom abruptly. There was a silence. Then Jenna continued, "Right...Ok that's fine. I will re-arrange for next weekend, if he is available, no problem"

They said goodbye and Jenna told him she was at the yacht club and would be home around 5pm. Tom was happy with this as he realised then that he had most of the day on his own to gather his thoughts. As he ended the call, he noticed that he had a missed call from 'his sister, Claire. He wondered what she could want. He wished that it was just natural for him to call and speak to her, but they spoke so infrequently these days the awkwardness had made it more difficult.

He took a deep breath and was just about to call the number when his phone rang again, and he saw it was Claire. He answered the call.
"Hi Tom, It's Claire"
"Oh wow. Hi...How are you?" Tom actually felt genuinely pleased to hear her voice and a thought flashed across his mind that his surprise greeting sounded believable.
"Erm...I'm fine. But...." Tom knew the pause was ominous.

"But?" he said, hoping it wouldn't be as bad as he had thought.

"Look, Tom...It's mom. Sorry to spring this on you but She's not doing too good...."

Tom cut in," I spoke to her last night, she was fine"

"Yeah...But look Tom, when mom spoke to you last night she should've been a bit clearer with you," Tom was silent waiting for her to continue. "Are you there?" she asked.

"What's going on?" Tom said sternly

"Tom, it's been a while since mom has been unwell. She's been in and out of hospital several times in last few months and had tests and...Well...She's got cancer. Pancreatic cancer and.... It's spread pretty bad. And now it's got into her bones. The doct..."

"Why the fuck did you not tell me?!" Tom interrupted angrily, "Why did she not tell me!" I spoke to her last night!" His raised voice shocked Claire.

"Look, please Tom. With the move, your new job and everything else, mom just felt you needn't be worried about it. She was originally told it would all be OK..."

"What gives you the right to hold that from me?" Tom asked abruptly

"Tom, it was her decision. I asked her a few times when she was going to tell you. But she just kept saying you had enough to worry about"

"Jesus!" Shouted Tom, "And it sounds like you went along merrily just so you can be the one who is there for her, the one that cares for her...Always the one leading things, and the person in the know..."

"What do you mean?" She asked suddenly.

Tom wasn't sure if by the sound of her voice she knew exactly what he meant and was saying it to cover or if she genuinely didn't know. But Tom wasn't waiting to find out.

"Oh, come on Claire; What do I mean? You have always been the same. Head girl. Mommy's girl. The family Martyr. Always on hand to be there to know everyone's business and be the one to help them. Always busy, busy, busy, being the head of the family. The one that holds it all together. While keeping me in the dark and making me look like I don't give a shit.....I mean, even when nan died, you were the one who stayed at mom's and helped with the funeral arrangements, phoned everyone. But you didn't involve me. Just told me a date and time to be at the funeral. Even on the day, there's you and mom together, whispering and you holding her. Well, where was my involvement? And did anyone think I had lost my nan? How was I? How the fuck was I doing?...."

Tom broke off. He'd said too much, and he knew it. There was silence from the other end. He was hoping she would respond but nothing came.

He was suddenly surprised by his own outburst. He obviously realised he had to get it off his chest. Then eventually Claire spoke in a broken whisper. Tom knew she was close to crying.

"Believe it or not Tom, life is not always about you." There was a silence. Tom didn't really know what to say. He thought he had been right but now wished he had spoken to his sister about it in a different way and at a different time but before he could rectify it she spoke again.
"Tom. You were young. You had your life. Career. Friends. That's fine. But if you had just once stopped and looked at your family, you'd have seen why I had to take the lead," Tom was about to cut in, but Claire continued.
"Mom was broken by dad's death. She never ever recovered. There's so much you don't know, but mom always, always said to me not to involve you in a lot of things. She always said you needed protecting from all the grief and aggravation. I never really knew why. While you were off enjoying your life, I had to hold this family together and you never even knew. I don't hate you for it because it was what I had to do. But please don't think it was ever anything personal..." She broke off and Tom heard her start to sob.

He felt his stomach turn. He had enjoyed his life. He had lived it to the fullest. Down the years, dad had died, Tom's uncle died, Tom's nan died. But these people were also his mum's husband, brother and mother and Claire's dad, uncle and nan. Tom then realised that all he ever really did was cut away from his life for a few days to attend a funeral and then get back to his normal life.

He felt a tear run down his face.
"I wanted to be involved," was all he could say. And even then, when he said it, he wasn't sure how much substance it held.
"I know." Claire replied quietly, "well, I suppose if you did want to you could've made more of an effort to...But Tom, you were busy. I know you're not selfish, it's just the way our lives turned out. I know you care."
"I'm sorry," Tom said.
Claire laughed, "What for?" she asked laughing again, "Why are you apologising? Your life went one way mine went another. I am very happy, Tom. With everything. And I have no regrets. Neither should you."
There was a pause. Tom composed himself.
"So? About mom. What's the situation?"
He heard Claire sniffle and clear her throat.
"Ok, here we go. It's not great news, Tom. Her test last week showed there was nothing much more they can do for her."

Tom felt sick. And a wave of emotion swept through him. He couldn't hold back his upset and he started to cry.

"Oh Tom, I know, I know. I just wish I could be there with you."

Claire started to cry again and neither of them spoke for a minute or so. Eventually she broke the silence.

"Tom. I think it's best if you come up as soon as you can. The doctors have said they have been surprised at how fast it has spread, and they aren't able to guarantee her long-term health. I asked her doctor what they actually meant, and he said he would be surprised if she lives until the end of the month."

Tom knew it was the 18th and felt sick. Claire went on, "But, he also said it could be any day."

There was a silence while Tom digested the information. He needed to get up there as soon as he could. He had things to sort out. Work would need to know.

"Oh god! I have to get there…" He said thinking out loud.

Claire cut in "Tom. Do not panic. Just take a breath and calm down. It will be fine. Just speak to Jenna. Then speak to work and let me know when you can come, and I will book your flight and e-mail you the details. Will Jenna come?"

"Oh, I don't know. Things are a bit strained."

Claire felt a bit taken aback by the comment and suddenly realised he had his own personal issues that she needed to help him with, but now unfortunately wasn't the time.

"Tom. Don't worry about anything else now. Just speak to Jenna. Speak to work. And then let me know when you can come and how many tickets to get. Ok?"

Tom let out a huge breath, "Ok. Thanks. I will get onto it straight away," Tom paused, "Look, Claire, I am sorry, I didn't mean what I said"

"I know. Don't worry. Ok? I love you, Tom. See you soon."

And Tom realised that this was the first time she had ever said that to him in his adult life.

"I love you too" he replied.

And it felt the most genuine thing he had ever said. He heard the phone click off the other end. He put the phone down. He started at the wall. His life went spinning through his mind. All the times, events and occasions when he could've and should've been more help to Claire but was too busy.

He thought then of his mum in pain and unable to be cured. It filled him with sadness and regret.

He sat down. He stared at the TV. He seemed to do a lot of staring at the TV lately without actually watching anything. And then suddenly it hit him. The ice cold sped from his feet up to the tip of his head. It was so fast and hard it made him rigid. He tried to move but was almost in a state of rigamortis. He started to shake and couldn't breathe, he panicked as he couldn't catch his breath, he panicked, suddenly feeling he was going to die. He didn't know how or why but the feeling was so strong it made him scream, but nothing came out. His arms, then shoulders, then neck became tight. Like a feeling of being slowly squeezed. He tried to scream again at the crushing feeling, and again nothing came out.

Then the crushing, icy feeling slowly subsided. He caught his breath. His arms felt able to move again and he brought them up to his neck to fight off what he thought was whatever was crushing him, but nothing was there. His heart rate slowed. His breathing returned to normal. He was sweating profusely and wiped his brow. He sat up slowly starting to breath normally again, but he was frightened. He had hoped, since the last time, he would've never felt this again since.

Questions buzzed around his head again. Was he ill? Was this mental or physical? What was happening? If this was the connection that he thought it was, then who the hell was this affecting? Had anyone died? He stood up and tried to calm himself. Stop questioning he thought. He sat back down. Closed his eyes and tried to shut down his mind. He eventually settled and got his breathing calm and back into a steady rhythm.
He went upstairs and got into bed. He curled up and eventually his fear subsided, and the upset cleared, and he fell into a deep sleep. As he slept, he had no idea of what was going on over at Frank's house. While one of the funeral representatives comforted Pam and spoke about the arrangements and costs. The other person was upstairs. They had managed to gain access to Frank's study after telling Pam they wanted to look at photographs of him which may be suitable for some presentation photos at his service. But, in reality, they were removing a disk from the CCTV system which was slipped inside a folder.

Chapter 16

Tom woke early as is mind was racing. He had to get in contact with work to tell them he was going to New Jersey to visit his mum. His other predicament was Jenna. Did he allow her to come or should he just go on his own? He wasn't completely sure if he wanted her there, as lately she always seemed to be trying to tell him what's best and direct him. He felt like he just needed to be free and able to go where and when he needed to go of his own accord.

Tom had heard her come in last night around 5.30pm. He knew that as he was in bed but had been awake. He had heard her come up and come into the room but, for some reason, he had pretended to be asleep. He felt her sit on the bed and then her hand start to stroke his forehead. He heard her say "You sleep" and then felt her get up and leave. He had stayed in bed for the rest of the evening and tried to think why he hadn't wanted to see her or speak to her. He had lied about being ill and thought that he was sick of lying, so best just not to speak to her. So he had not told her about his mum and that he had to get to her fast.

This made his mind jump to travel arrangements. He remembered his sister had said she would organise this but obviously she would need to know when he was coming but he only would know that when he had spoken to work. This was his first job.

He looked at this phone. It was 6.18am. He looked at Jenna and she appeared to be sleeping soundly. It was too early to call work, but he remembered that Rutherford had once said to him that he can call him "at any time, for any reason". He had never needed to do this before and realised that it may not go down too well. But then thought that Rutherford was always straight down the line and wouldn't have said it if he didn't mean it.

He dialled the number. He heard it ring once and then heard it pick up and Rutherford's deep voice.
"Good Morning, Tom. How can I help you today?"
Surprised, Tom hesitated for a few seconds.
"Are you ok, Tom?" Rutherford asked.
Tom suddenly sparked into life.
"Oh, Hi Mr Rutherford. Look I am so sorry…."
Rutherford cut in, "Tom, please don't be sorry. I am here to help you"
"Oh..er…OK, thank you. Look, I am sorry, but I am going to have to take some time off work. My mother is very ill, and I need to go to New Jersey."

"Oh, I am very sorry to hear that Tom," Rutherford replied with a lack of emotion.

Tom went on to explain that his sister had called and informed him that things had suddenly taken a turn for the worse and so having just only found out the extent of her illness he really needed to be there to see her before the inevitable.

"Tom, I am truly sorry. Please take all the time you need. Do not feel pressured. Forget work. As good as you are and as much as we need you, we support our people and allow them time to deal with personal matters. Family comes first Tom, you know that"

"I am very grateful Mr Rutherford, and I will try and get ba…"

"Tom," interrupted Rutherford, "No need to discuss now. Go be with your family. When do you intend to leave?"

Tom hesitated again, then answered, "It will probably be a flight this evening; maybe a red eye? Or first thing tomorrow? It depends what I can get booked at late notice."

Rutherford paused, "Leave it with me. I will get it all handled this end and the documentation will be e-mailed to you shortly. I assume you wish to fly into Newark?"

Tom was surprised and caught off-guard, "Oh, er, yeah, Newark, thanks. Look, I really apprecia…"

"No problem. Look Tom, before you go tonight I would like to come and see you. Will you be at home today?"

Again, another surprise, too many for such a short phone call, thought Tom.

"Oh, there's no need, I am fine…"

"Tom, I like personal communication. I want to speak to you face to face. Be in around 2pm. Thanks. See you then."

With that Tom heard a click and Rutherford had gone.

Tom was bemused. Why did Rutherford want to come to see him? Should he be worried? Tom thought about it and couldn't work out why he would be worried but couldn't help being so.

Then suddenly his heart skipped, and his stomach felt hot and sick. He remembered that the person called 'Odin' was going to text him at 9pm last night. He realised he must've have been asleep. He quickly walked to the door where his jacket hung to get his phone. He went through the pockets, but it wasn't there. He quietly went upstairs and into his bedroom where Jenna still appeared to be asleep. He looked over at his bedside cabinet and saw his phone so went around, grabbed it and started to walk out. As he did, he checked the phone and then heard Jenna.

"How are you feeling?" she asked in a sleepy voice. Tom stopped.
"Oh, fine now, I think I had a bug…. I seem OK".
"Ok good, fancy breakfast?" she asked.
"Oh, not so sure, may just have some dry toast," He was desperate to get out and check his phone.
"Ok I will be down soon," she replied.

Tom left the room and shut the door. He walked across the landing and as he descended the stairs, he looked at his messages and noticed an unread text and anxiously opened it:

'Tom. Do not reply to this text and do not try to call the number. I am organising a meeting. I will text you in three days. Do not trust anybody. Odin'

Tom read it and then read it again. It didn't tell him much more than he knew. He desperately wanted to reply. He was going to see his mum. He wondered what would happen if he couldn't meet as he was in New Jersey? Should he reply and say she was ill and he had to go there? He decided it best to reply. He hit reply and typed:

'Odin. My mother is very ill. I am leaving urgently to go to see her so I may not be able to meet you. Please advise. Tom'

As Tom pressed send he wondered how ridiculous things had got. Sending texts to people that he never even knew. He shook his head and tried to understand what was going on. As he did his phone bleeped and ne noted a new message. He opened it.

'Tom. You must not reply if I tell you not to reply. No unnecessary contact. I will text you in three days with details of our meet. Odin.'

Tom's stomach turned. Unnecessary contact? Tom shook his head. He now felt more out of control of his life than ever. He walked into the kitchen. He took a deep breath. He told himself to try and be calm and just let things flow. As he went over to make some coffee he heard Jenna coming down the stairs. She came into the kitchen dressed in her dressing gown.
"How's my little patient?"
"Oh, I am OK," replied Tom, trying not to show the tension that the texts to Odin had caused him., "I feel a bit washed out, but I will live."

Jenna told Tom to go relax and she will make coffee. Tom went into the lounge and he sat down. He was worried about telling Jenna, but he knew he had to do it. She came in with coffee and put his down next to him.

She was about to walk back into the kitchen when words just came out of Tom's mouth without him actually having time to think.

"Jenna, my sister phoned, and my mom is really ill. I have to go there immediately. She hasn't got long, and I must go so I am going to go tonight on my own and…"

As Tom spoke, he could see Jenna's face become confused.

"Woah, Tom, hold on, what the hell is going on? When did…"

Tom interrupted, "She rang yesterday. Mom has only a short time left…"

"Right," said Jenna, "Ok, look I will get dressed and then look at flights…"

"No," Tom interjected, "It's all sorted, my company have done it. I am going to go on my own, it's just easier."

"Why is it easier?" asked Jenna with a confused and frustrated look suddenly appearing on her face.

"Look, Jenna, please. I am going to pack a bag, wait for my travel doc's to be e-mailed and I am off. It's just easy…Anyway, I think my company have booked for me only…It was all done in a rush."

"Don't shut me out Tom. You need me right now. I want to see her as well. Why can't I go?. I want to be there for you…"

"No, look, Rutherford spoke to me this morning and said he would sort it all out and for me to go and take as much time as I need…"

"Rutherford?" asked Jenna, "Why would he be involved?" Tom noted a look of confusion on her face.

"He's my boss, Jenna. He told me he would help me and that its important I get all this sorted," Tom noticed Jenna's confused look continuing, "What's the problem with that?" he suddenly asked.

"No, nothing," she replied, "It's just that…Well, he's the top man, why would he be booking plane tickets?"

Tom shook his head, "Well, he will obviously get someone else to do it," replied Tom, "he seemed really concerned. He is coming here to see me later"

Jenna stopped and her look of confusion changed to what appeared to be concern.

"He's coming here?…Why?"

"I don't know, he said he wanted to see me personally."

"What time?" asked Jenna abruptly

"2pm, why?" Jenna walked out of the room and on the way she said rather flatly.

"Well, if you think you will be OK," then she stopped and turned, "I am really sorry about your mom."

She continued to walk into the kitchen.

"I thought you'd be happy that my company are looking after me?" said Tom loudly as she walked through into the hallway. She didn't respond.

The rest of the morning had been weird. Jenna had helped Tom pack and had seemed quite co-operative. She never pushed Tom again about going with him. She had been so insistent at first but then suddenly accepted it. Tom wondered if it was normal behaviour. But then thought he had also been quite insistent and so perhaps she just never wanted to upset him more than he already was. Tom never really knew anymore. He felt like he hardly knew her anyway. Happy one day, sad the next. Warm and loving one day, then cold the next. It was just so difficult to read her. Tom then thought that she probably thought the same of him. With all that had been going on he had been so up and down emotionally it was a surprise she hadn't already left him.

Tom thought to himself that as soon as he was back from seeing his mum he must find some time to sit with her and talk. Maybe she needed to know everything. He had told her a lot about his feelings. But now a lot more had happened. The attempt at his life. The texts. His most recent feeling of coldness and anxiety last night.

He sat down in the lounge and closed his eyes. He took a deep breath. He thought of his poor mum suffering and he just wanted to be there. Jenna had told him whilst they packed that she was seeing a friend for lunch and would be leaving at 1pm. He checked his watch and noted it was 12:45pm and realised she would be late as she was still in the shower.

Tom's phone then bleeped and he noted he had an e-mail from his company. He opened it and noted he had his travel documents from, Kelly, his team secretary. It confirmed a one-way ticket to Newark leaving Chicago at 21.05. It also confirmed a car would pick him up at 18.30 from his home and that he was to notify her of when he wanted to return so she could book his return flight.

He made a coffee. He felt more content. He was leaving tonight, on his own and could just get to his mum and get this part of his very complicated life out of the way.

He phoned his sister and updated her on his flight plans and when he would be getting in. She offered to collect him, but he insisted he would get a cab to her place and they could go to hospital in the morning. She updated him on their mum, said there was no change and she was still critically ill. His sister got upset on the phone and he assured her all would be ok and to be strong. Tom suddenly realised it was probably the first time he had assured her in his whole life. First time for everything.

His sister said that they may need to discuss him mum's personal affairs at some point but they both decided that could wait and they didn't go into much detail. As they spoke Jenna came down so Tom ended the call and said he would speak to Claire later.

Jenna looked nice, Tom thought. She had said they were going to a new restaurant that had opened downtown. They looked at each other. A tear rolled down Jenna's face.
"Woah, what's that for?" said Tom as he moved forward and hugged her.
"I am sorry about your mom, Tom."

Tom never spoke. They just hugged. Then Tom felt guilty that he hadn't allowed her to go. But he knew it was for the best. His paranoia about Jenna whether it be justified or not would get in the way and he needed to travel light and be alert. He didn't need passengers.
"Please just let me know how she is…And how you are? I wish I could come but I know it's easier. Just go. Be with your family but keep me informed, OK?"

Tom nodded and smiled. Jenna moved back and dried her eyes to stop the mascara running. They looked at each other again. Jenna then looked at her watch.
"Look, I've got to go…I love you."

She leant forward and kissed him and then quickly turned and was gone out of the door. Tom realised that she was upset, and she never liked to show weakness. He looked at his watch and he noted 1.16pm. His stomach sunk as he realised Rutherford would soon arrive. He wished he wasn't. During the day Tom had felt he had accepted a few things, got some ducks in a row and felt as good as he had felt for a while. He was hoping Rutherford would not pressure him about work.

Tom sat at the breakfast bar with a coffee. He was ready to go and just waiting for time to pass. Eventually he looked at the clock and it told him it was 1.54pm. He went to the front and looked outside. He immediately noticed a black limousine parked on the road outside. His stomach turned. He shook his head and cursed at himself. Why was he so nervous? His boss had visited to make sure he was OK. What was the big deal?

Tom stood and watched without being able to be seen. He wondered why Rutherford wasn't coming in. He went back and looked at the clock.

1.57pm. Rutherford was a man of immaculate timing. After a minute or so Tom noticed the driver get out and walk round to the side and open the door. Rutherford got out and started to walk up the driveway. He was impeccably dressed as usual.

For some reason Tom went back into the kitchen. As he did, he wondered why he hadn't just opened the door and realised subconsciously that he didn't want Rutherford to know he was looking out for him. Tom shook his head again and asked why he was always worried about what others thought.

He heard the doorbell. He waited. He took a deep breath and then jogged to the door and opened it trying desperately to look like he had been involved in something else prior to answering the door and not nervously waiting.

"Hello, Tom" said Rutherford confidently.
"Hi Mr Rutherford, please, come in"

As Rutherford came in Tom got the aroma of very expensive aftershave and cigars. It was a very seductive smell and Tom's mind immediately questioned if Rutherford had been a lady's man…Or, in fact, still was? They walked though and Tom asked Rutherford if he could take his jacket. Rutherford declined and simply said, "No, won't be long".

Tom lead him into the lounge and offered Rutherford a seat They both sat down; Tom acted nervously but politely. Rutherford didn't hesitate, "I must say I have been a bit worried about you lately, Tom. I suppose this confirms a few things to me. Why didn't you tell us your mother had been ill before today?"

Tom thought it best not to explain too much as to why he hadn't known and to bring up his family issues, "Oh, works a busy place…Everybody has their own problems…"
"Oh, but Tom. Our company is different. We are a family. We are *your* family. As a company we like to help our family members and we can't help if we don't know. You have to be honest and open up to us, Tom."
Tom played it cool, "Yes, you're right. I just thought I could handle it and well…It's OK. I am OK, thanks."
Rutherford came back in sharply, "I was also disappointed that you didn't show up for your briefing the other day. And to be told that you just hadn't showed up was disappointing too"

Tom was a little surprised and shocked, "What? No, I did ring…I spoke to Conway! I had an incident in the city…someone attempted to rob…At gunpoint…I think. Well, it shook me up and…"

Rutherford cut in, "Ok, don't worry. I never knew."

"Mr. Rutherford, I am so sorry. I rang Conway and told him. He said he would pass the message on. I had to report it to the police, and I was in state…I mean, it's not every day that happens…Please, ask Conway, he will…"

"Conway is ill. I am afraid to say that on his way home from work yesterday he was taken very ill and is in a bad way in hospital. Fighting for his life."

Tom's face must've dropped and the shock of what he had just heard obvious. Rutherford just stared at him. Tom's shock suddenly evolved into a sense that Rutherford was checking for his reaction. The silence was deafening. Rutherford appeared to hold his ground and never spoke and so Tom felt he had to speak.

"Oh, I am really sorry to hear that."

"Yes, he was a hard man. But a good man…Deep down."

"Was?" questioned Tom. "Isn't he still alive?"

Rutherford's face never changed. "Yes, but as I say, in a bad way and they say his chances are slim."

Tom started to sweat and wiped his head. He suddenly remembered the feelings of dread the night before. Was this another connection? Tom's mind went fuzzy, he then realised how it must be looking to Rutherford and tried to compose himself.

"Oh OK," said Tom, "But, even so, he has a chance, doesn't he?"

"I don't know?" Rutherford paused, "The world moves fast, Tom. Things change instantly. That's why it's important to stay focused and achieve our goals. Life goes on. Time waits for no man."

Tom thought better off not to ask but before he could stop himself, "What happened to him?"

Rutherford stared at Tom. Tom felt like his eyes piercing into his mind. Then after a long pause Rutherford spoke, "A heart attack, Tom."

The silence again was deafening. Tom felt his chest tighten and his breathing had become a little erratic, but he did his best not to show Rutherford.

"But look, Tom, why I am here. You see, it's like this. You are one of, if not, *the* companies star performers. You have a huge future. You've been shaped and molded, and you are one of our main asset's, and, as a company, we care for and nurture our asset's, and, if they start to underperform, we need to know why. If we don't know why then we can't make them better."

Tom felt sick, Rutherford continued, "Tom, the industry we are in we have to be ahead of the game. We have to forecast and take action to make sure we don't get caught out. Unfortunately, your performance over the last few weeks has raised some questions. Your ability to do the job to the standard we expect has been brought up several times..."

Tom felt isolated. He felt pressured. Why was Rutherford telling him this now? Was this an appraisal?
"I don't like being kept in the dark, Tom." There was a long tense pause. Rutherford got up and walked over to the sliding doors.
"How's Jenna?" he asked directly whilst staring into Tom's garden. Tom was taken aback by the question and was confused as to its relevance.
"Er, she's fine...Look, what has this got..."
"How are you and Jenna? You know, as a couple," Rutherford interrupted
"Well, we are ok I supp...."
"Look Tom. We need to be honest with each other. Things are not fine, are they? I mean, it's obvious. Your punctuality has been poor. Your appearance a little off kilter. As I said, your performance questionable. It's obvious your home life is suffering. I've seen it before. I just wish you'd come to me for advice."

Tom was completely shocked and unable to speak. He didn't know what to say.

Rutherford walked back over to the settee and squeezed Tom's shoulder as he past.
"Tom, I want to be honest with you. I like you. In fact, I care for you greatly. You transferring to Chicago was not chance. There was a reason you came here. You are one of the best and I needed you here to make the Chicago base a success. But there was more to it," he paused for a few seconds, "Do you believe in fate, Tom?"
Tom thought for a few seconds, "Fate?"
"Yes. Fate. You know? Fate. Situations or developments outside of a person's control. An event destined to happen. An event or occurrence that is preordained. Some people suggest even predetermined by a higher power."
Tom stared at him. Baffled. "Yes, I know what fate is."
"Oh, but that's not what I asked. Do you believe in fate?" Rutherford asked slowly.

Tom, now his mind scrambled, struggled to answer.
"I...don't know. I'm not sure what this is to do with me but...Look sir, no disrespect but..."

"None taken, Tom" Rutherford intervened," I appreciate you have got
things on your mind and you need to get up to New Jersey. That's fine, I
understand, " Rutherford paused and turned back to Tom.
"Tom. Before I go. I want you to know. You are special. You have goals
to achieve. You have a purpose. You came here for a reason. And it's my
job to make sure you fulfill your potential and ensure you achieve those
goals. Do you understand?"

Tom suddenly felt nervous and never replied but Rutherford continued.
"If certain things happen that make you feel uneasy or upset then just
remember you need to put them to the back of your mind and carry on.
Look at what you have, Tom. Everything. Great job with a great salary.
All the perks. Beautiful house. Wife. Don't spoil it all by worrying about
the little things."

Tom's stomach felt a wave of heat. He couldn't help but think of what his
Mum had told him and how the two were similar. It was unusual.
"I will always be here for you, Tom. Don't forget that. If certain things
confuse, upset or even anger you. Then come to me. Speak to me. Don't
let things get on top of you. It's my job to keep you tip-top."

There was a silence. Tom felt himself nodding without actually meaning
to do it. Like his mind was subconsciously telling him to just agree
regardless.
"Tom. I also have a responsibility to other people to make sure you
achieve your goals. People that you nor I really understand. But like you, I
have personal goals. And I must ensure I fulfill them. One of those goals
is you, Tom. You are my responsibility. I will do my best for you, but you
have to promise me that *you* will help me to do that"

Tom said nothing.
"You won't let me down will you, Tom?"

Tom didn't know what to say. It was like his mind had been removed and
he had lost the power of speech. He shook his head and eventually he
managed a slow and quiet.
"I promise."
"Good!!" said Rutherford loudly making Tom jump from his confused
state, "that's settled. Now, you go and be with your family. They need
you. Keep me updated and take all the time you need...Obviously within
reason," Rutherford smiled, winked and then got up and walked out, "I
will see myself out. Regards to your family"

Tom sat. He was stunned into shock and silence.

Chapter 17

Everything had run smoothly. The car Rutherford had organised picked Tom up on the dot and swiftly took him to the airport. He had been booked into the private flight lounge and also had VIP check in, and so before he knew it he was sitting in the lounge with an hour to kill before his 9pm flight.

He thought about having a drink but then dismissed it and realised it was it best to keep a clear head. He couldn't trust himself and was worried a whisky or a beer would relax him too much and he would carry on and end up landing at Newark drunk.

He was also conscious of the fact he that was still paranoid after what had happened in the city. Someone had had tried to kill him and, if he hadn't already worked it out himself, it had been confirmed he was in danger. But, like it would be for most ordinary people, Tom was struggling to take it all in. He kept wondering if it was a case of mistaken identity. Did the assailants have the right man? And did Odin have the right man? Tom had tried to think of it all being one big mistake, but it was just too difficult to see how. Odin knew his name and had his phone number. It couldn't be a mistake.

Rutherford's visit was also playing on his mind. It was so unusual. And he couldn't help but keep reflecting on what his Mum told him before she died. But what was most difficult to accept was the similarity of what they both said. Tom tried to tell himself it was coincidence but found it almost impossible to convince himself.

Tom got himself a cold water and then picked up a newspaper from a nearby rack. He sat down and turned to the crossword. All the while he kept a check of the people in the lounge. Nobody appeared to look suspicious. He eventually relaxed, but not completely. He had looked up a couple of times and noticed an old guy staring who looked away when Tom looked up at him. But later Tom noticed him doing it to another couple of people and though he was obviously just nosey.

He had sent his sister a text informing her the flight was due in at 10:40pm and so he should be at hers by midnight. She had insisted that she would pick him up, but again he refused and said he would get a cab. She had replied and said she was looking forward to seeing him.

On the plane Tom had sat next to a very attractive lady who was roughly around mid-twenties. She had introduced herself as Carrie and seemed very keen to get to know him. She had ordered a bottle of wine and asked Tom if he would like a drink. He politely declined. She had explained she was a beauty therapist and was attending a seminar in NJ. Tom had dampened her spirits by telling her why he was flying to New Jersey.

He would've normally kept that to himself. Tom wasn't a player by any stretch and had never cheated on Jenna or anyone for that matter. But , in other circumstances, he would've had a few drinks and enjoyed her company during the flight. No harm in that. But he genuinely wasn't in the mood and he also couldn't help recalling Odin's text about not trusting anybody. It was all probably very innocent, but Tom felt it best just to keep a low profile for now.

He shifted his body and had turned towards the window to get more comfortable, he closed his eyes and soon heard that Carrie had turned her attention to the guy the other side of her, and it seemed he was more than happy to indulge. Tom left them to it and eventually dozed off.

It had taken a little longer than usual to get to Newark due to what the captain called "an intense headwind" and so he never got outside the airport until 11.30pm. He texted Claire to inform her that he had arrived and went to the taxi queue and got into a cab.

The journey to Claire's house in Glen Ridge evoked lots of memories for Tom. Driving up the Garden State Parkway Tom felt a huge sense of nostalgia. A time when his life seemed so simple and enjoyable. He thought about good times with his friends and family and, for some reason, he recalled Claire's 18th birthday party in their garden, where he fell in love with all of her friends. He could almost feel those strong feelings of young lust. He remembered days at South Mountain and the zoo. Trips into the city for meals. He could almost feel those times again; like he could grab them. He wished so much that he could go back and asked himself why this had happened to him.

When Claire opened the door, she just stepped up to him and held him. They stood hugging in the doorway for almost five minutes before anything was said. They both cried and then laughed in embarrassment. It was like they had both realised that they were brother and sister again.

Claire's husband, Paul, was a good man. Tom had always liked him, and it was now that Tom regretted his life had been the way it was. He had never really got to know Paul the way he should have. Paul just stood close by smiling as the had embraced. Claire had then invited Paul to join in. He had. Tom had felt a little unusual with this as it was all new. It was wrong that it was new, and he knew that. Him hugging his brother-in-law and feeling strange was completely his fault. Tom had lived in a bubble and the rest of the world had been a fuzz, off in the distance. He had only focussed on himself. It made him feel sad. But he felt safe and, for the first time in a long time, he felt loved.

Tom had not been able to refuse a whisky from Paul and they had all sat and talked into the early hours. Claire had given Tom an update on their mum first. Then they had spoken about the boys and how well they were doing. She had shown Tom photos of them in various places and doing various activities. Tom felt proud and made a pact with himself that, despite everything, he would make an effort to reconnect with his sister and her family.

They got around to Tom and Jenna and the issue of babies. Tom had laughed it off and said all in good time. Paul had reminded Tom he wasn't getting any younger and Tom had to admit he was right. Claire had asked him straight up what was going on with him and Jenna and Tom had just repeated what he had said on the phone that 'it was a little strained'. He had said work was crazy and she was busy finding new friends and social circles. But he had assured them it was fine, but he wasn't sure if they, or he, believed it.

Eventually around 2.30am Claire had said she needed to get some sleep as she had got up at 5am that day. The whisky had started to seep into their bloodstreams and the thought of bed had been far to enticing to stay up any longer.

Paul had showed Tom to his room and as he was about to leave, he had told Tom to be strong and that Claire loves him dearly. Tom told Paul that he appreciated it and he genuinely did. As he had laid in bed he felt as content, safe and as comfortable as he had felt for a long time and was soon in a deep sleep.

The next morning had been nice. Tom had slept well, and the kids had run in and jumped on the bed and woke him up, which he didn't mind. He loved it, but in the back of his mind wished he had visited a long time ago without his mum's condition being the reason.

They had had breakfast together and soon enough as the morning slipped by Claire had started to get ready and soon the mood changed to a calmer, more solemn one. Claire had told Tom the night before that the boys knew Grandma wasn't well, but she had not explained that it was a matter of time. They were going up to the hospital today not realising that it could be the last time they see their Grandma alive. Claire had said she was going to speak to them before they go to make them a bit more aware of the situation.

Tom had started to get ready. He took a shower and got dressed and as he was coming out of the spare room, he saw the boy's bedroom door open and they came out with Claire; all three of them had red eyes and so Tom realised that she had obviously given them the talk. Tom gave Claire a smile and as they walked past, he stopped her and gave her a hug. This was going to be a tough few days.

It was only a short drive to Mountainside Medical Centre which Tom was thankful for as the mood in the car was very low. Tom held little Paulie's hand in the back of the car as he was sniffling. Trying to understand his first experience of death to a loved one. Someone like your Grandma who, at Paulie's age, you think is indestructible.

They soon arrived and Claire, who had been several times before, led the way. They took the lift up to one of the cancer wards and after speaking to someone at reception they were advised to wait in a family room. Claire was slightly confused as she told them that before when she came, she was told to go straight in. But it soon became apparent that all was not well when one of the senior doctors came in and asked to speak to her. Claire introduced Tom and said she would like him to come and so they left Paul and the boys in the family room.

The doctor explained that their mum had not been good overnight and had since deteriorated further. They had had to increase oxygen and morphine. Her organs were now struggling and were starting to shut down. Claire took the news better than Tom who became very upset. He was desperate to speak to her one last time and he was now worried it may be too late. The doctor explained that a decision had been made a short while ago that it would be best to call the family for them to come up but, as they were now here, there was no need.

Luckily, the doctor told them that she was still speaking at this time but it may not last long, and it may be a good time to go in and speak to her. Claire stayed strong and started organising. She told Paul and the boys to go in and see her. Paul immediately took the boys in and told Claire he won't keep them in there for long. Tom sat down in the family room and noticed a drinks machine. He did fancy a coffee, but he felt anxious and strange and couldn't think of doing anything other than speaking to his mum.

He noticed Claire pacing outside of the room and after a few minutes she went in. Shortly after Paul and the boys came out. Paul looked upset but was smiling. Jake was crying but Paulie looked OK. Jake looked up and said something to Paul and he smiled down at him again. They came in the family room and Tom and Paul smiled at each other. Again, it was a very intimate situation they found themselves in which neither were best prepared for. Tom smiled at the boys and they both awkwardly smiled back.

After several minutes Tom saw Claire open the door and she gestured to him to come. The anxiety hit him, and he knew this was going to be hard. Paul smiled at Tom as he walked out, but Tom was so nervous, he couldn't muster anything in return.

Claire waited at the door for Tom and when he approached, she stopped him and whispered "Tom, she has gone downhill very quickly…Even since a few days ago, her condition and appearance are a lot worse."

She ushered him in and followed slowly behind him. As Tom went in he noticed that his mum's bed was in a sitting up position. She was wearing an oxygen mask and had various tubes going in and out of different parts of her body, with lots of equipment around her, slowly beeping and flashing with numbers, dials and codes.

He looked at her face and but could hardly recognise her. She had lost a lot of weight and looked gaunt and bony. Her little hands, that had once strongly held him, looked frail and damaged. Tom could barely believe they could get a needle in her hands, but she had two in one hand and one in the other.

Tom sat down next to her and Claire stood behind Tom with her hands on his shoulders. A tear ran down his face, but he had not even realised he was crying. His mum smiled and spoke quietly, "It makes me happy to see you two together again…" her voice trailed off. She then continued "Last time was at uncle Joe's funeral".

Tom lent over and held her hand and realised how thin she had become as he could feel every single bone.
"Mom, I am so sorry…"
"Don't apologise, Tom. Cancer sucks. It's not your fault it got me"
Tom smiled and heard Claire laugh behind him, but it was more of a cry.
"I will leave you two alone," she whispered.
Tom turned and hugged her, and she blew a kiss and walked out. As he left the room Tom heard her start crying.

Tom's mum coughed and spluttered, Tom leant over and grabbed a tissue and wiped her mouth. She settled down and smiled at him. He always loved her smile. It radiated a whole room. He would always remember as a boy he only needed her to smile at him and he felt better. She was such a beautiful woman.

"Tom, you have made me so proud. I have loved being your mother. You have achieved so much," as she spoke tears rolled down Tom's face and he grabbed a tissue to wipe his eyes.
"Don't cry, Tom. I have had a good life," she leant up and grabbed his hands. Tom sat down and pulled the chair in close.
"Tom, there's not much time," he leant in as her voice had lowered to that no more than much of a whisper.
"Tom, when you were born I knew you were special. But I found out that you are more special than you could ever imagine."
"Mom, your confusing me, what do you mean?" enquired Tom anxiously.
"Just hear me out. Strange men came to me when you were born. They told me that I was to protect you and that later on in life they have a use for you. I was confused. But as time went on they told me more...."
"Who? What men? Mom you're scaring me," Tom wished he didn't have to waste what could be the last precious time with her talking about this.
"Listen to me," she cut in, "Don't be scared. Everything that has happened to you in the last few months is real. You have to believe me you are not going mad," despite her already low voice she pulled Tom closer, and then spoke even quieter but this time deliberately.
"But Tom, listen very carefully, I won't be around much longer. If you are not coping with it then you are in danger," Tom stared at her, the emotion of losing her suddenly evaporated with his mind trying to calculate what she had just said.
"I have already spoken to some people that can help you. Some people that can get you away and help you move on"
Tom stuttered, "But...Mom...Who? What people?"
"Shhh," she interjected and put her hand over his mouth, "Just trust me. They will be in touch and hopefully they can help."
Tom suddenly realised and he jumped to life.
"In the city a few days ago, I...I...I think they may have already made contact."
"Shhhh," his mum repeated, but this time she coughed and spluttered again. Tom grabbed a tissue and held it against her mouth.

The coughing eventually subsided, and she pointed at a nearby flask of water. Tom poured some into a cup and slowly tipped it into her mouth. He realised how tired and exhausted she looked and wondered if in her own mind she had had enough and wanted to go. Tom felt her body relax and with tears building in his eyes he sat down again and got as close as he could.

His mum turned her head and looked at him.
"I know I have done the right thing. You will be fine," she pointed to her bag and said so quietly it was hardly audible, "Open the side zip."

Tom leant over and opened the side zip. Inside he felt a very small box with a similar design to a ring box which was made of wood and stained black. He took it out and looked at her and she nodded at it. He looked down and opened it and inside he saw what looked like a tiny scroll. He took it out and opened the scroll and it revealed the number 294574 in tiny written script. He turned it over and it had, written in black pen, his date of birth.
"Keep it safe," she whispered. Tom saw her body physically deflate and she let out a sigh. She looked at him and smiled a smile of contentment and he knew she didn't have long. He never asked what the scroll was as he feared there now wasn't much time.
His mum held out her hand and he leant in and took it in his.
"Tom, you are my angel, and I love you so, so much." Tom saw a tear run down her face and her smile slowly dissipated, "Go...get your sister".

Tom sensed it was time. He rushed out and opened the door and looked out; as he did Claire looked up and she must've seen his face as she immediately jumped up and came towards him. They both went back into the room and Claire went the opposite side and they both took one hand each.

"I...love...you two..." their mum whispered and suddenly her face hardened, and her eyes slowly shut. A breath came from her mouth, but no more air was taken back in. She was gone.

Claire started to sob and fell into her mum. Tom went around and just held her. He stayed holding her a good few minutes while they both cried together, as one. One of the doctors quietly came in and moved around to the body. Tom picked Claire up and slowly walked her out, Paul looked up and came and got Claire and ushered her into the family room.

Tom felt numb. He hadn't been sure how we would feel, but now he knew. Like a whole part of his body had been ripped out. He felt empty and soulless.

He was going to go into the family room but realised that Claire, Paul and the boys needed some time alone as a family. His mouth was dry, and he

149

realised how thirsty he was. He looked up to see if he could spot a vending machine and as he did, he noticed a man who appeared to be a doctor, with a white coat over his shirt and trousers. He was at the far end of the corridor, staring straight at him. When the doctor realised Tom had seen him he immediately looked away and started to look at a notice board.

Tom looked in the other direction and spotted a sign 'Refreshments' and an arrow. He started to walk towards the sign and took a deep breath to try and pull himself together. But as he was walking, he looked back and, again, he noticed the same doctor looking at him who, again, looked away. Tom wasn't too concerned but just thought there was something strange about him.

Tom followed the signs for refreshments and after walking down a maze of corridors came to an area with all variety of vending machines. He bought a bottle water and drank it down in virtually one go. His thirst refreshed, he then bought another two bottles waters for the others and got himself a black coffee. Close to the machines was an exit and so Tom went outside and sat on a bench and drank his coffee.

People walked past slowly, it was a nice warm day and Tom realised he must look like someone who has lost a loved one as a couple of people passing smiled at him affectionately. Tom smiled back. He couldn't understand why he wasn't more upset like his sister. But he realised that she had almost certainly been so strong through it all and has now only just let her emotions go.

He reached for his phone and sent a text to Jenna:

'Hi J. She has gone. It was peaceful. Going to stay for a few days to be with Claire. I am ok. Will see you soon xx'

He finished his coffee, got up and went to go back in, hoping that he could find his way back. As he went to go in, he noticed the doctor he had seen before walk quite quickly into the area with the machines. As he did, he stepped back and moved behind the wall with the entrance door. Another man appeared in jeans and a tracksuit top, they both looked up and down the corridor and then spoke to each other. The man in civilian clothes then headed for the exit so Tom quickly slid further behind and into a recess which luckily housed the automatic door operational box. The man came outside looked left and right and then went back in.

As the door slid shut Tom slid out and edged out enough to look round. They both spoke and this time the doctor went through some doors one way and the man in civilian clothes went back the way he had come.

Tom became anxious and annoyed. Was he being paranoid again? Was this anything to even do with him? This wasn't really the best time to start getting all wacky on his sister. He stopped. Took a deep breath and told himself to get a grip.

He went back inside and looked both ways and couldn't see anybody along either corridor. He knew he had to go back the way the doctor had gone and so putting his paranoia aside he went through and started to make his way back along the corridor. As he did a door opened to the left of him and made him jump; two female nurses came out and passed him in discussion.

He made his way to the end and recognised to his left a gallery of patient artwork which he had stopped and looked at on the way to the vending machines. He took that route and kept going, slowly started to recognise the way. As he reached a large set of glass sliding doors, he remembered it was through them and then to the end and right, which would take him up to his mum's ward and the family room.

He went through the doors and quickly walked to the end passing two doctors and a patient in a wheelchair. All of them in discussion and not even noticing Tom. He made it to the end and as he turned right, he saw the doctor walking towards him at the far end close to the family room. He had a beard and tight black curly hair and looked agitated. It was the same doctor. He looked up and saw Tom looking at him but this time he never stopped and never looked away. He stared and walked directly at Tom.

Tom backed away. Something told him it wasn't safe. As he backed around the corner he then turned and ran. As he did two people ahead of him turned and looked at him strangely. Tom apologised as he ran past them and went back through the large sliding doors. As he got through, he looked back and the doctor hadn't made it to the corner yet, so Tom burst through an exit door leading to upper levels. He then bounded up the stairs three at a time and never stopped at the next level but continued onto the next and then went through a door into what looked like the reception area for another ward.

As he went through the nurses at the desk looked up, but Tom smiled and looked around at the signs on the wall pretending he was looking for some location. Noticing the nurses looking down again he slipped back out and looked down the stairwell. To his shock the doctor was coming up them.

He darted back into the ward and saw a sign for lifts with an arrow pointing through some adjacent doors. He made his way past the reception and around the corner to the lifts and pressed both buttons. He moved back to the corner and slowly looked round but the doors from the stair well stayed shut. He moved back in and pressed the buttons again and noticed the number flick from G to 1, but he was on 3.

He took another look and this time noticed the doctor burst through the doors and look both ways. Tom rushed back to the lifts and pressed the buttons frantically. The number flashed from 1 to 2 but Tom pressed the button again. His instinct told him to look back and see where the doctor had gone. A 'bing' sounded and Tom looked round to see the number now on 3. The doors slid open. Tom jumped in and immediately pressed the G button, but the doors didn't close. He pressed it quickly and repetitively, then pressed the 'door close' button, eventually, after what seemed like an eternity, they shut. Tom felt the lift move and he tried to slow his heart by taking huge gulps of air. As the lift slowed, he had visions of the doctor standing there as the doors opened.

But luckily as they did nobody was there. He looked up and saw a sign 'Exit – Car Park' so he immediately made his way towards it. He kept following the signs and eventually he was outside and could see the car park a few hundred yards away. Away from the hospital he felt the sense of claustrophobia lift and he could feel himself calming.

He stopped and phoned Claire. She answered and sounded a little upset.
"Hey, where are you?" she said lovingly.
"Look, Claire, I thought I was OK, but I couldn't cope with being in there. I felt strange. I needed fresh air, so I am making my way back to the car"
"Oh, well, ok. Look don't worry. I have just spoken to the doctor and they are taking mom now and clearing the room. We are just waiting to get her stuff…"
"Look Claire, I'm really sorry, I am not good at this…"
"Tom don't worry. The doctor has given me his card and I have to call him tomorrow to discuss things…"
There was an awkward silence but luckily Claire filled it
"The boys are upset and want to go home anyway so we won't be long. Are you ok?"
"Yeah, I will be at the car. I love you"

Claire hesitated but then replied, "I love you too".

Tom made his way back to the car cursing his situation. He knew he should be in there and helping Claire. Supporting her. Doing things that a brother should do. Be with his sister and nephews. He suddenly felt embarrassed as Paul must think he was a real useless arsehole. It made Tom hurt and angry at how it must be perceived.

But he knew that if that doctor, or not a doctor as Tom was starting to think, was trying to harm him then he needed to be away from Claire and the boys. Just by being with them he was putting them in danger. An image came to his mind of them all at their home eating dinner when two men like the ones in the city turned up. He couldn't take that risk.

The incident back in the hospital could have been nothing. It was so difficult for Tom, it was almost like he was sure that the doctor and the other guy were following him but, then again, he couldn't at all be sure, and it could be paranoia running away with him again.

His mind wasn't in the best state and seeing his mother die had made things much worse. He didn't really know what was real and what wasn't. He cursed again for the situation he was in. Wishing he could just wake up and be at his mum's house with her, Jenna, Claire, Paul and the boys enjoying a nice meal and playing in the garden.

He felt himself starting to get upset. He took a took breath and rode the emotion out. He looked up and got his bearings and calculated roughly where the car was. He made his way over and eventually spotted it a few rows away from his position. As he started to walk towards it his phone rang, and he noticed it was Jenna. He went to answer but stopped himself and let it ring out. He was struggling with his emotions and his instinct was that a conversation with her would cause him more anguish as Jenna would be upset too

He got to the car and Jenna rang again but, once again, he ignored it. It rang out and a few minutes later his phone beeped, and he noticed she had sent him a text, he opened it:

'Tom. I am so sorry. I really wish I could be there with you. I tried to call. I understand you must be dealing with things. Please give Claire and the boys a hug for me. I love you so much. Ring me when you can x-x-x J'

Tom put his phone away. His initial plan of staying with Claire for a few days was now not possible. The two men in the hospital had spooked him badly. Once again, he felt in a situation where he was completely alone and isolated. Although the thought of Odin gave him hope. Tom felt he was his only hope. He needed to get back and his instinct to leave was now suddenly overwhelming.

He would ring Jenna later and let her know what he was doing. Although he knew that once home she would be in the way and he may have to invent something to get away and meet Odin. If Odin was even real. Tom knew he was better off away from Jenna so he could work this all out without any complications, but he also knew he couldn't stay around with Claire and put them all at risk.

He tried to think ahead and work out a plan of action when he heard a shout.
"Tom!".
He looked up and Claire, Paul and the boys were approaching. Paulie and Jake ran towards him and sat down and hugged him. Clare and Paul approached soon after and Tom got up and dusted himself down. They all hugged. Tom never wanted the moment to end.
"Are you ok?" Claire asked
"Yeah, look sorry again, I am just not cut out for this and…"
Paul interrupted, "Tom. Stop. Nobody is cut out for this. Just take it easy and stop beating yourself up," as he spoke he moved in and gave Tom a hug. Tom was a little taken aback but realised that it was an important and kind gesture and the first time they had connected properly.

They made their way along the exit road but as they got closer to the main exit Tom just happened to look up to the main entrance of the hospital. It was there that he saw something that really worried him. Two security guards and a nurse were standing talking to the doctor that he had thought pursued him. The doctor gestured to them but then suddenly one of the guards grabbed his arm and they marched him back inside. Tom's heart sank. Was he not a real doctor? Did it confirm Tom was right to evade him?

They left the hospital grounds and as they did Tom was unaware that the other man, that the doctor had spoken to when pursuing Tom, was stood 100 yards away, watching the vehicle drive out, whilst talking on his mobile phone.

The drive back was quiet, but Tom sensed an air of relief. He realised that for Claire the last months and weeks had been hard caring for their mum and although she must be devastated to have lost her, the weight off her shoulders must have been immense.

Claire had said that they would all go to O'Neill's that night for steak and lobster and a few drinks, just to keep morale up. It would be a treat that they all deserved after such a tough day. Tom knew he had no intention of going but smiled and had said it would be nice. He wished he could go but he knew he couldn't. He had to get back. Something was tugging at him to get back. Niggling away at him. The drive became more uncomfortable as they got nearer home as he knew that what he had to do was approaching.

When they got in Claire said she would get some coffee on. Tom went straight to his room and started to pack. He opened his bedroom door and noticed that he could get to the front door without being seen. He made his way along the hallway and as he did, he could hear the boys shouting and the TV come on. He opened the front door and slid his bag outside.

He went back in and walked through the arch that led into the kitchen and lounge. He could see Claire in the kitchen.
"Claire."
She turned and looked at him and he gestured with his head for her to come to him. She made a confused look on her face but walked over. As he got to him, he took her arm and led her through the front door and out onto the driveway.
"What's wrong" she asked
"Look, Claire. Just let me speak. Don't ask questions and don't try to give me advice" Claire's face turned from confusion to worry
"I know I should be here with you, but I can't be. I have to be somewhere else. I have got into a situation that I need to work out, OK?
Claire interrupted "Tom? What? I can help. What ha…"
Tom held his finger up to her lip, "No! Claire, no. You are amazing, but this is one problem you can't help with. There are some people that want to speak with me, and I need to go to them…"
"Oh my god. What's going on, Tom?"
"Don't panic," Tom pulled her towards him and hugged her and spoke in her ear, "I cannot be here right now. But I promise when it's all done, I will come back."
Tom heard Claire start to cry and she held him tighter.
"Tell me Tom, what is going on…..Are you in trouble?"
"Claire, I will get this all sorted and will get in touch. Just be strong for the boys, OK?"
"Oh Tom, what have you done? Why do you have to go?"
"I'm sorry. I have to get to the airport and get back. Me being here is not helping. I need to go. Give Paul and the boys a hug and tell them I am sorry".

Claire was now quite distressed, and Tom was upset with what he was doing, and how he was making her feel, when she just needed to be calm. He let go of her hand and picked up his bag and walked away. He expected her to call him back but she never. He left her there crying. As he got further from the house he walked faster and was angry at the situation he had left his sister in trying to explain to her family why he had just left.

Tom knew Paul would be angry too; causing his sister this unnecessary distress. Leaving in such a cold and heartless way. But Tom knew things that they never knew and that it was for the best. Him being there endangered them and it wasn't fair. If anything happened, he would never be able to live with himself.

He made his way to the bus station which he knew was a fifteen-minute walk and luckily picked up a connection to Newark. He would get on the next available flight and get as far away from Claire and the family as possible for their own good.

As he approached the airport, he hoped that one day he would be able to explain it all to Claire and Paul properly.

Chapter 18

Tom had slept most of the flight. It had been a very tiring day. The loss of his mum had obviously taken its toll both mentally and physically. But added to that was what she had told him. As the plane had taken off Tom had felt that he knew more now, but he was also more confused than he had ever been.

He had been holding the small box she had given him which held the scroll and thinking what he could do to get out of all this. He wondered how to get his life back on track and pondered whether to involve Jenna, but he just couldn't help but sense that she only paid lip-service to him. Jenna was so keen to get him into counselling or therapy. Perhaps it was just her way of sorting him out and getting back to her perfect life. Tom thought that he couldn't really blame her for that.

He remembered back to that day, just before Frank's death, when he genuinely believed had had her on his side. Tom wondered what would have happened if only he had got Jenna over to Frank's and into that room to see the CCTV. He wondered what her reaction would have been. But since then he felt as though he had lost her support. He genuinely believed now that she simply thought he was a nut-job who just wanted him counselled and medicated.

He asked himself if he should involve work. Or tell his sister. Each time he thought of someone to tell to try and help he dismissed it as they wouldn't believe him. He wanted to believe he wasn't going mad and a lot recently had helped him prove it, but it wouldn't prove it to anyone else.

He knew that perhaps his only hope was Odin. From his brief texts Tom felt that this was the only person that seemed to be completely on his side and could possibly explain what was happening. Tom had realised that he hadn't heard from him and he felt a sick feeling when he wondered what might happen if he never heard from him again. Tom had suddenly realised that Odin was now more important to him that he had ever imagined possible.

As the plane had reached cruising altitude Tom had fallen into a deep sleep. The toll had been too heavy, and it had only been the 'bing-bong' and the voice of the captain that had woken him. He looked out and could see the city off to the right. The skyline off in the distance and, as late afternoon was turning into early evening, a pattern of lights dotting around the suburbs. He yawned and wiped the dribble from the side of his mouth. The man next to him looked and smiled politely and Tom returned the smile. He sat up and took a deep breath. The plane lurched to the right and the wing dipped, Tom looked down and could see the lights of the suburbs below. The city on the horizon suddenly moved to the left and out of sight as the plane set up for its final approach.

As the plane slowly descended and the cabin-crew made their final checks Tom started to plan his next move. He still needed to be vigilant. It was so difficult to constantly be on guard, plus it was physically and mentally draining. But Odin's warning to him about not trusting anybody was in his mind. An attempt at his life had taken place already, and the doctor in the hospital had spooked him. Tom was convinced that had he not stumbled across the exit that when he did it almost certainly would have gone the same way.

He hadn't made any plans with Jenna to be picked up. He thought he would just get a cab and then head home; but he could tell the driver to take a scenic route and keep an eye on any cars potentially following. Rutherford had given him as much time as he needed within reason and so Tom would contact him in the cab and let him know his mum had died. He calculated this would give him a week, or maybe two, without having to worry about work, which Tom thought was a huge relief.

Tom thought about his home. Was it safe? How long could he be there? Was it safe for Jenna? He needed to get home, talk to her and not let her dictate what was happening. He needed to get them both out of there while he waits for Odin's next message, if it ever comes.

The plane had landed smoothly and taxied around to the terminal. Tom looked up and down the plane trying to spot anyone looking suspicious. He mostly saw people tired and hungry who just wanted to get home to their own lives.

He had shuffled his way through security and out into the airport. He stopped and got his phone out of his pocket and turned it on. As he did, he heard it bleep a few times. He looked at his text messages and saw four new messages. One from Davy, one from his sister, one from Jenna and the last from an unknown number. He looked around, picked up his holdall and went over to a coffee shop. It was pretty busy, but he found a table with a stool and nestled in quickly.

He looked around the airport again without trying to look too suspicious. He opened the unknown message first:

'Tom. I have selected a meeting place. I will send you a location tonight at 9pm. Do not reply and delete this message. Odin.'

158

Tom was so relieved it was from Odin and clenched his fist under the table. He immediately deleted it and then opened the message from Jenna:

'Ring me when you land and I will come get you. Hope you are ok. Want you home for hugs. So sorry. I am waiting here for you my darling. I love you more than you know x'

Tom closed his eyes and put his head in his hand. He realised he loved Jenna. He needed to be with her. He opened the text from Davy:

'Hey Tom. I tried to call but no answer. I called your home and Jenna told me about your mom. I am really sorry. Not sure what to say but hope you are ok. Please keep me posted on arrangements. Whatever and whenever I will be there. Please call me when you get back from NJ. Don't feel alone. You have support. Love you pal. Davy and family xx'

Tom smiled. He felt his chest get heavy and his bottom lip quivered. He took a deep breath and wiped a tear from his eye. Davy had never told him he loved him before, and he laughed quietly thinking about them as kids and how weird that would have sounded.

He finally opened the text from his sister:

'I hope you are ok. I am very confused. I was truly hoping you would have stayed up here for a while. It worried me the things you said. I need to talk to you and I just want to make sure you are ok. Please ring me when you land. Promise? I need to know you are ok. We all do. I love you loads. Claire X'

Tom smiled and felt the emotion rising again. Four texts and three of them from people telling him they love him and the other from probably the only person that can help him. Tom smiled and thought that maybe things couldn't be that bad.

He looked up. Scanned the airport again. He then instinctively made his mind up that he would not call Jenna. The taxi plan was the right one. Travel alone as much as possible. It's easier if anything happens and he would not have to worry about the safety of who he was with. He then thought he would reply to them all when in the cab.

He closed the messages and put his phone away. He took another look around the airport and as it appeared that nobody was interested in him he made his way quickly across the main hall to the exit.

The fresh breeze of the early evening was refreshing and made Tom feel more awake and alert. The taxi terminal was just a short walk from the airport exit and he noticed only two other people in the queue as he approached. They were soon quickly picked up and disappeared off to their destinations and so Tom managed to get a cab soon after arriving in the queue.

The driver got out and put his bag in the boot. As Tom got in he took one last look around and didn't see anything suspicious. As the taxi left the airport road he got his phone and sent messages in response to his sister and Davy:

'Hi Claire. Just landed. Do not worry. I am fine. I will be in touch soon. I love you xx'

'Hey Davy. Thanks man. I truly appreciate it. Things are obviously tough at the moment. I will be in touch. Xx'

Tom then started to text Jenna:

'Hi Jen. Change of plan. Just landed and in cab and on way ho'

But his instinct made him stop. He deleted the message and closed his phone. He looked out the window at the traffic passing the other way and couldn't really understand why he never sent the text to Jenna. He just knew it felt right.

He rested his head back on the chair and closed his eyes. He was very tired. As the taxi cruised along his head gently rocked from side to side and with each small bump he slowly descended into a slumber. From time to time he opened his eyes to check progress but part of him wished he could stay in the taxi for a long time. It felt safe and warm.

Eventually the journey came to an end and as the taxi approached Sheridan Road. Tom now hoped that Jenna was out. He just didn't feel like being intimate and talking about things. He just wanted to be alone to try and process his thoughts. He was grieving. It was difficult enough to process that he had just lost his mum. But trying to do that and everything else that was going on was going to be difficult. He needed clarity of thought. He needed to be able to think straight and work out what his plan of action was going to be.

As the taxi slowly turned into Sheridan Place Tom realised that a lot of his next move may be reliant on what Odin was going to tell him and where they were going to meet. It was strange. Tom felt uncomfortable that his life now seemed to be in control of a person he had never met and knew next to nothing about. Tom lent his head back on the headrest and stared at the ceiling of the cab and took a deep breath.

"Where do you want?" said the taxi driver suddenly, and broke Tom out of his temporary slumber. Tom sat up and looked ahead, "Number 1316. About 8 houses up on the left".

The driver never responded but sped up slightly towards the house. As he did so Tom looked ahead anxiously hoping he wouldn't see Jenna's car. The driver slowed and looked at each house as it passed. As he did Tom could now see his driveway and Jenna's Audi was there next to his Merc. But just past the house Tom noted a black SUV, similar to a presidential type vehicle. Instinct told him something wasn't right. The driver started to slow to a halt and as he did Tom tried to get a look at the house but couldn't make out any movement inside. As they approached Tom noticed the SUV was empty.

"Don't stop...I think I have the wrong house," he directed instinctively.

The driver picked up speed and as they got directly outside the house Tom took another look "Faster, just go, it's down the far end" Tom said a little abruptly. The driver rolled his eyes and accelerated past the house and the Sedan. Tom looked the other way and slumped down a little as they passed. He then looked back to confirm the SUV was empty. It still appeared to be so.

"So, where do you want?" the driver asked with no attempt at politeness.

Tom bobbed his head around looking for a good place to stop. He looked back and the SUV slowly disappeared as they cruised along and round the arc of the road then just as the SUV went out of sight, Tom advised the driver that it was OK to stop.

"Which house you want?" the driver asked.

"Oh, no, that's fine. Here will do."

The driver stopped. Tom noted the fare was $56 dollars. He got out looking back towards his house. A fearful thought passed his mind of the SUV suddenly roaring to life, appearing and then driving towards him at speed.

The driver got Tom's holdall out of the back and Tom got his wallet out. He had two 50's so gave them both to the driver and told him to keep the change. The driver's eyes widened, and he offered Tom a genuine thank you. Tom never responded as he stared up the road towards the house and picked up his holdall.

"Oh, can you do me a favour?" Tom asked the driver.

Before the driver could answer Tom continued, "Can you go on towards the end of this road, take a left and then pick up the main road out. Don't go back that way," and gestured with his head towards the way they had come. The driver smiled and shrugged his shoulders and replied with a simple, "Whatever".

Tom was now thinking. He needed to get to the house but had to be careful. If the SUV was owned by the same people who Tom needed to be fearful of then he could be in trouble. He started to slowly walk towards the house suddenly now aware that he could look unusual. He never knew the neighbours too well at this end of the road, but they would know where he lived and may wonder what he was doing. But Tom had to put that aside for now. Keeping up appearances was not his highest priority at this moment in time.

Tom kept his eye on the road ahead, but also now and then looked at his neighbour's houses as he passed hoping to not see anyone. As he slowly walked around the corner the SUV, still parked, started to edge into view as Tom made his way closer to the house. His stomach turned. He realised he needed to be brave and just approach and check it out. What else could do he thought. The Sedan was now in full view and luckily Tom noted still as vacant as he had first seen. He focussed on it and prayed that the doors would not open or the engine would not burst into life. As he approached, his house now came into view and he realised the time had come. He was now only about 30 yards from the SUV and his front drive.

He slowed as he approached. As he got closer, he tried desperately to see inside the main downstairs window to look into the lounge. He couldn't see any movement although noticed a light on upstairs. He was now almost at the SUV. As he got closer, he stopped and put his holdall down. He had some slight cover by a lush cherry red Acer tree on his front garden, just before the driveway. He opened his holdall and put his hands in to appear to show he was looking for something. As he did, he glanced at the house and the windows trying to see Jenna or, in fact, any movement at all. He noted a light on beyond the lounge that led into the kitchen but no movement. He realised that from this vantage point he was not going to see any more than that. He zipped up the holdall and made a move.

Trying not to look like he was acting covertly he walked onto his driveway and brushed the Acer tree as close as he could to avoid walking up the middle of the driveway. He then stayed close to the foliage and bushes that ran along the edge of his fence to his neighbour's house. Realising he was now out of sight to most of his neighbours he crouched down and used Jenna's Audi as cover. It allowed him to get virtually all the way up to the side of the house without being seen. He ducked down at the side pathway which led to the back of the house. He was still a little exposed so without hesitating he made a move towards the side of the house and ducked down in between two large pots containing large palms. He was now only a few yards from the main front window into the lounge.

He suddenly realised that this was probably all way too much stealth. But then thought that people in those cars had tried to kill him. It may just be a coincidence, but could he take the chance? It may not be so far-fetched if what Odin had said was true. He took a deep breath and looked down the side of the house to the rear garden. He then slowly made a move back along the house to the front to get closer to the window. He slipped around the large plant pot to the left of him and suddenly felt very exposed. He had felt a lot safer in the middle of the two pots where he couldn't be seen.

He reached the corner of the house and moved as close to the wall as he could around the corner. Now at the front of the house he was only a few steps from the large bay window. He wondered what Jenna may say if she came out and saw him. He realised she would probably shake her head, roll her eyes and go inside and almost certainly book him in for therapy, if she hadn't already.

With his back to the wall he crept along until he was at the window. He turned and got onto his knees and pushed himself up and got into a position where his eyes were barely above the ledge and peered in. He could still see the light through the lounge into the kitchen. No movement though. He looked around the lounge, which was darker and hard to make out, but nobody was in there. He realised that he may just have to go in the front door. He stopped and thought that perhaps he needed to throw caution to the wind and just and do it. He thought he will probably just find Jenna cooking.

It was now starting to get a darker as the sun had slipped away and shiver went through his body. He turned and looked again. Still nothing. Then suddenly movement in the light and he noticed Jenna walk past and then out of view. She was in. But he realised from the quick appearance she looked upset. He tried to look further into the kitchen and then more sudden movement as a man walked into view. Tom's stomach turned. He then realised it was Phil Carter. He looked like he was shouting, and he appeared angry.

163

Tom turned away and put his back to the wall. He took a deep breath. Why was Phil there? Tom immediately thought he had probably broken up with Carly and was trying to see if Jenna could help. He turned and looked up again. This time Jenna came into view quickly and looked stressed. She then turned, pointed and looked like she shouted to someone who Tom assumed was Phil. Were they arguing?

Tom froze. What should he do? He suddenly realised that he was being stupid. This was his house and he should just go in. He turned away and looked around. He then looked in again but couldn't see neither of them. This time he got up and quickly moved to the front door. He wondered whether to just walk in normally or go in quietly. As he got to the door, he got the key from his pocket and put it in the lock. As he opened it, he realised he had not made his mind up. But he pushed the door open anyway, slowly walked in and suddenly heard shouting.

He stopped and listened and heard Phil shout angrily.
"You were never up to it anyway...I told them to get rid of you ages ago. You fucked it up,"

He heard Jenna try to cut in, but it was inaudible as Phil shouted over her, "You only had to open your fucking legs and keep him happy...Jesus, it's not hard for a slut like you"
Tom heard Jenna cut in, "Fuck you Phil. It's not that simple! You should try living with him...He is going insane!"
"That's because you couldn't keep him keep him happy, you fucking moron. Just suck his cock each day!" Phil shouted.

Tom was shocked to the core. He had the urge to run in and beat the life out of Phil, but he was held back by the confusion of it all. His eyes wide and holding his breath. He listened further. He heard lower volume chat which was pretty much inaudible. Then he heard Phil speak and it chilled him to the core.
"So now I have to clean up the fucking mess," there was a pause then Phil continued, "And you better fucking hope they take pity on you, otherwise you will be in the ground with him."

Tom was paralysed with fear and bewilderment. What was going on? He had the urge to run and contact Odin. But Jenna was in danger.

He slipped inside and put his bag down. He had to be careful. He closed the door quietly and as he did, he could still hear inaudible chatter between Phil and Jenna. He quietly moved across the hallway passed the lounge to the kitchen entrance. He held his position but then realised his

164

plan hadn't been thought out too well. He was hoping to catch a glance of Phil with his back to him and take him out from behind. He was acting on complete instinct and suddenly wondered if he should just slip back outside and call the police.

But just as he did, he spotted Phil across from move to the island. He couldn't see Jenna. Tom figured if he moved quick enough, he could get behind Phil and find out what the fuck was going on.

But, just as he was about to make his move, he felt a hard, cold point in the back of his neck. He froze. A deep voice behind him spoke slowly and calmly.
"One move and you die".

The hard, cold point pushed into him and he had no choice but to stumble forward. As he did, he looked around and noticed a Latino man with a beard, pointing a handgun at him. "Keep moving!" the man shouted and pushed Tom again in the back.

Tom fell forward into the kitchen. He noticed Phil and Jenna look round. When they saw him, they looked utterly shocked and Phil then turned and to Tom's own shock he noticed Phil too was holding a handgun.

Then Tom felt a sickening hard thud on the back of his head. For a split second it just smarted. Then the pain intensified, and he felt dizzy, like he was spinning over on a swing. His stomach turned and the floor came rushing towards him. He recalled a finger pulling his eyelid up. And then nothing.

Chapter 19

Tom felt nauseous. He was aware of movement around him, but everything was black. He could hear talking but was unable to make out who it was and what was being said exactly. It was more just a murmur. He realised he wasn't laying down but felt upright and quite steady. He didn't move but wanted to lift his head up, although the pain was so intense he was worried doing so would cause it to increase.

The talking got louder, and Tom started to hear odd words much more clearly but still unable to make sense of it. A man's voice was speaking "…Rutherford…I don't know!…To go see him."
Then he heard who he thought was Jenna, "…Can you come too?…So fucking unfair…Can you at least back me up?"
Then he heard the man again, "You fucked up, not me…Explain it, Rutherford will be ok. Just get you re-assigned…"

Tom stayed as he was. He was scared to move. He was confused and the pain was making him even more nauseous. He tried to listen in over the ringing in his head. He heard Jenna laugh, then say.
"Ok? You hear that Ortega? Phil says Rutherford will be OK," she laughed again and then continued, "You both know I am dead, just like Tom".

Then silence. Tom tried to think of what he should do. He now felt he was able to lift his head, but he knew when he did things would change. It was calm now, but whatever the hell was going on it was all going to take a new twist as soon as they knew Tom was awake.

But Tom suddenly felt a surge of sick and couldn't hold it down. He tried to swallow but the pressure was too much. Pain fizzed through his nose as the vomit gushed out of his nostrils. He opened his mouth and vomit came out too. He tried to get his breath, but he couldn't. He looked up and saw Phil and Jenna looking at him in surprise. He then felt his hair tug and his head pulled up sharp. More vomit came out and he felt the warmness of it on his lap.
"Leave him, you fucking pig!" Jenna shouted, and Tom saw her lunge forward.

As she did Phil grabbed her arm and forcefully yank her back.
"Leave him. Let him settle," Phil ordered to Jenna and pushed her away.

Tom gathered his breath enough to stop the panic then felt his hair release and his head dropped down. The pain through the back of his head throbbed and he saw flickering lights and colour. He grimaced and let out a grunt of pain. He looked down and saw chunks of vomit on the floor and on his lap. The smell then hit him and made him gag.

"For fuck sake, clean him up," Phil barked.

Tom looked up and Jenna went to the sink and ran a cloth under the tap. She approached him slowly with a look of fear and guilt on her face. She slowly started to wipe his lap and as she did Tom asked.

"Jenna...What the fuck? What is happ..." he then felt a cuff on the back of the head.

Jenna shouted, "Leave him!"

But a deep voice from behind boomed, "No talking!"

Phil then cut in, "Grow the fuck up, Jenna. You want Rutherford to give you a break then cut the fucking lovebird routine."

"Fuck off Phil," Jenna replied indignantly, as she walked to Tom and bent down in front of him and started to clean his lap. She then looked up at Tom and whispered.

"Don't worry. Relax".

Jenna got up and went back to the sink and run the cloth under the tap again. Tom looked at her and she noted the desperation in his face. Pleading for her to explain. She looked at him and then immediately looked away.

Phil went up behind her and put his arm around her waist.

"You best start dealing with things more professionally," Jenna pushed her body back onto his and turned, then used her hands to push him away with force. Tom tried to get up, and as he did, he realised his hands were bound. He pulled on them again and he realised there was a little give, but they wouldn't move. He felt the chair rock forward and then felt a hand grab his shoulder and pull him back.

Phil looked at him in disgust, "Sit down you freak. You've caused me a lot of trouble. Don't make it worse".

Tom's mind cleared slightly. His vision become slightly sharper. Although the pain in his head was still intense and made him wince.

"What the fuck is going on?" he asked.

Phil replied abruptly, "You don't need to know, pal. All you need to do is sit tight and shut the fuck up."

"Jenna!!" Tom shouted, "What the hell is..."

Another cuff hit him around the back of the head. Tom felt anger rising up in him. He tried to get up again and pulled on his hands as hard as he could. He felt some more give as the bind slipped to the base of his thumb. He felt another cuff but harder. But it didn't matter to him anymore. He rocked the seat forward and an angry growl emanated from him. Another cuff struck him, but he hardly felt it this time and then Phil approached and stuck a large handgun directly into his face.

"No!!" screamed Jenna. Tom realised he needed to calm down quickly as he felt the intense fear that having a gun in your face created. The fear that rises up through your stomach and grips you. He turned his head away from it but felt the cold hard steel on the side of his temple.

He held his breath as saliva blew out from his nose and mouth. Phil spoke slowly.
"One more move, and I swear to god I will blow your fucking brains all over this kitchen."

Tom settled. His breathing was still frantic but his body slowly relaxed. He looked up. Jenna was now crying, she put her hand to her mouth and rushed out the kitchen towards the lounge. Phil looked to Ortega and nodded in Jenna's direction.
"Do it," he said calmly, and the large built man walked in the same direction that she had gone.

Tom panicked as he feared the worst. He tried to scream out, but Phil stuffed the gun into his mouth. Tom's voice was muffled, and he realised it was too low for Jenna to hear. Phil then launched a tirade of punches with his other hand down onto Tom's head, one after another, Tom tried to move from side to side but most of them caught him. Tom then felt his nose crack and a warm dull pain followed. He stopped moving and the punches stopped. He looked down and saw blood had started dripping profusely onto his lap. He sniffed hard and spat a mouthful of blood and mucus onto the floor.

Phil took a step back and looked into Tom's eyes.
"I am very angry now. I am waiting for a call. Until that call, I do not want another word from you, or I will kill you."

Jenna had gone through the lounge and into the study. It was the quietest place in the house. She sat down at the desk and couldn't help but start to cry. Emotions suddenly rising up and coming out that she had held back for too long. It was also frustration. Tom deserved to know. She wanted to tell him and explain it all. She had realised some time ago how innocent he was in all of this and she had done her best. But as Phil had said, she had failed. She had failed Tom and failed Rutherford.

As she sobbed, she heard the door click. She looked up. Ortega's head looked in. He then came in and closed the door quietly behind him. Jenna noted he still had his gun. He stood in front of her and smiled.
"Look, these things happen. It's not an exact science. You tried. I have seen situations like this before," Jenna tried to gauge the point of his comments and suddenly realised what his intentions may be.
Ortega then continued, "I've always liked you Jenna. You're cool. I just don't want you to think its personal or anything like that," Jenna wiped her eyes and took a deep breath.
"I like you too Ortega" she said, "You've always been nice to me."

She stood up and took a few steps towards him, noting his hand holding the gun with a silencer down by his side. Ortega smiled genuinely and Jenna continued.
"One of the ones I can trust. Someone I can rely on," Ortega smiled again, "Do you think Rutherford will be ok?" she then asked.
Ortega blew out a deep breath, "Well, about that....." he paused, and as he did he looked down with a hint of sadness. But in that split-second Jenna moved her hand around the back of her jeans and grabbed the handle of the carving knife she had discreetly lifted from the drawer before she left the kitchen.
Ortega went on, "I mean, as I say, it's nothing personal..." and as he rose his gun Jenna knew it was now or never. She lunged the few paces forward and swung the knife round and into the side of his chest. She heard a muffled shot sound out and a sharp blast of air flashed across her head as he fired.

Her hand suddenly felt warm and wet. Ortega let out a quiet shriek and a wheeze and Jenna felt his body stiffen, as she did Jenna pulled the knife out and slammed it back into the same point, but this time even harder. She heard a crunch as the steel blade obliterated Ortega's ribs on its way into his lung. He went limp and Jenna pulled the knife out and slammed it in again and then again for a fourth sickening blow. Blood now exploding out onto her arm and face, and with each removal of the knife blood splatter flickering onto the walls. She twisted the knife with a sickening crunch, and she felt warm air caress her arm as his lung punctured and started to deflate.

Ortega slipped to his knees and Jenna went down with him, still holding the knife in its deadly position. He wheezed as the air slowly left him. She looked at him and he looked into her eyes as the fear of what was happening was now realised. Blood spurted from his nose and a large red bubble blew up and popped. Saliva and blood seeped from his mouth. Jenna heard a thud as the gun fell to the floor.

She pulled the knife out and as she did Ortega winced, and he let out a quiet whimper. He knelt motionless. Jenna stood up, slowly moved around behind him and pushed his back with her foot. He fell like a large oak tree onto the now red soaked carpet. She heard a last gurgle from him and then nothing. His whole body twitched and then went rigid. She looked around and it appeared that everything was now coloured red. She, herself, was dripping in blood.

She suddenly panicked as the reality of what she had done hit her, but she realised now she needed to be calm. From the moment Phil had turned up at her house and told her that the plan was to wait for Tom and then kill him, she had made her mind up. But during that time, she had tried to think of a plan. Maybe a way of warning Tom. Desperately hoping he would not make contact or, even better, just not turn up at all. But when he suddenly appeared without warning in the kitchen, she knew what she had to do.

It had dawned on her then that this had almost certainly been a decision that wrote her own death warrant. But she had got involved, now she had to make amends and face the consequences. It was all her own fault for being too greedy. The time to do the right thing had arrived.

She took a deep breath and bent down and picked up Ortega's gun. As she did, she noticed the amount of blood on the floor. What was once the soft ivory carpet was now mostly dark red, albeit for the areas towards the edges of the small room. She looked at Ortega and blood still gently pulsed from the large hole in the side of his chest. There was now no going back.

She gently opened the study door. All was quiet. She had hoped she would hear Phil speak to Tom, as this would indicate to her roughly his proximity to her. She slipped quietly into the lounge and looked down at the gun in her blood-soaked hand. She took another deep breath and slowly crossed he lounge and, as she did, she suddenly heard low talking and realised it was Phil. She quickly made her way across and close to the kitchen entrance. She heard Phil again but this time louder.
"Jenna is taken care of. She was too far gone. Way too much of a liability," then a pause.

She stiffened her back against the wall and listened again.

"Ok, I will get this done, we will clear up and be back later tonight. Speak soon."

She realised that Phil wasn't talking to Tom. He was obviously onto the masters. Maybe even Rutherford?

She then panicked as she knew Tom was almost out of time. Shen the heard Phil again.

"Ok, sorry Tom, it was a blast…Literally. Oh and, just another thing, that night you treated me like shit with your friends. You were lucky I didn't cut your heart out and stuff it down your throat…"

Jenna heard a click.

Instinctively she twisted her back from the lounge wall and pounced out into the kitchen. Phil was pointing a gun at Tom's head. Phil heard the movement and turned. His eyes widened in shock. As he twisted and lifted his arm Jenna aimed and fired. A silent, muffled shot sounded, and a piece of Phil's shoulder cracked and exploded. He cowered and went to one knee and fired back exactly the same time Jenna fired a second shot. There was a dull thud and Phil's forehead exploded and several pieces of flesh and bone hit Tom's face and body.

Jenna crumpled as the thud of the bullet knocked the wind out of her. Tom screamed, "Jenna!!"

At the same time Phil slumped to the floor into a pool of blood, lifeless.

Tom looked at Jenna and she fell back and dropped the gun. Tom with all his power, rocked and pulled at his bonds. He screamed again and another powerful growl emanated from him and he suddenly found the strength to pull his hands free. As he did the chair slid on the blood that had started pooling onto the marble floor and it slipped over sending Tom tumbling into the blood, now thick and oozing.

He tried to get up to get to Jenna, slipped again and found himself lying face down in a pool of red. He pulled himself across the floor and got to Jenna. As he did, constantly repeating, "No, no, no, no…"

He lifted her head. He looked down to try and locate the wound. She was already covered in blood, so it was hard to tell where she had been hit. Then Tom noticed an oozing pulse from her stomach. He put his hand on the wound to try and stop it, but Jenna screamed in pain. He realised he needed 911 but didn't know where his phone was.

He felt her face which was suddenly gravely cold. Tom, now crying, screamed at her and she opened her eyes. She smiled.

"Jenna?" Tom shouted, "Got to get you to hospital," and he tried to lift her.

"No!!" she screamed, "No, put me down!".

She held his hand and looked at him, "It's too late," she whispered.

"No!!" shouted Tom in anger and frustration.

"Tom" she whispered again. He was panicking, "Tom!" she shouted at him, and as she did, she felt the effort drain the energy from her body.

"Tom, listen carefully," she wheezed, and blood spat from her mouth, "You are in danger. Get help," Tom shook his head, crying, trying to understand.

"Don't trust anyone. Not Rutherford…Stay away," Jenna stopped in pain, as a burning sensation shot through her body and she yelped in agony as the bullet in her stomach slowly claimed its victim.

"I am so sorry…None of this is your fault. You aren't insane…People can help you" she said, now struggling to make full sentences.

A tear ran down her face and Tom wiped it away creating a smudge of red on her face. Suddenly the urge to just close her eyes and sleep hit her. But she fought on for as long as she could. She spoke but was struggling.

"I need you to know…I did really love you…"

Her breathing became laboured. Her blood-soaked hand reached up to Tom and pulled him closer to her. She tried to speak but the words were taken from her by the pain.

"Jenna, no…" cried Tom.

She tried again and pulled him down closer, but her voice was barely audible, so Tom held his ear to her mouth.

"I did…really…love you. I am so sorry I failed…There are people…that can help you"

And with that her head fell back and her eyes closed, and Tom knew she was gone. He held her head in his arms and started to sob uncontrollably.

Chapter 20

Tom eventually stopped crying. He had sat for at least half an hour holding Jenna's limp body in his lap and hoping she would come to but knowing she wouldn't. He had thought about calling 911 but realised that she was gone and all it would do is make a bad situation a lot worse. The police would also turn up and then Tom would have a lot of explaining to do.

He had thought about telling them that he came home to find the two intruders, a struggle ensued and what they find is the result of that. But then he remembered Odin's advice not to involve the police.

There was blood everywhere. Thick and oozing and in places starting to turn almost black. The whole kitchen just appeared to be a dark red pond. As it thickened it became sticky and Tom had shifted a couple of times and felt it squelching underneath him. Blood from him, Jenna and Phil all now mixing into one mass of liquid, pooling on the floor.

He decided then he needed to contact Odin. He got up and looked for his phone then realised it was in his bag by the door. He gently lay Jenna down, her face now contorted unusually. Tom thought that she now only resembled Jenna and didn't actually feel like her anymore. Just a shell.

As he walked across the kitchen, he felt a sticky pressure with each step on the thickening blood. He went to the sink and ran the hot tap and cleaned his arms and hands as best he could. Even with washing up liquid there was a reddened stain that he couldn't shift. As he went to leave the kitchen he hesitated, realising that his blood-soaked socks would leave footprints across the hallway to his bag by the door, but he continued, realising that the mess was unescapable and almost not worth being concerned with.

He got to his bag and opened it. As he felt around for his phone, he looked back at the red trail he had left across the hallway. He felt his phone and took it out. He had one message from an unknown number. He looked at the time. It was 9.44pm. He realised that Odin had sent him the text he had promised. He opened it and read:

'Tom. Head for Pittsburgh. Leave tomorrow at 8am by car. Use hire car. ETA 4.00pm. Sorry its so far but closest I can get. I will explain more then. Do not reply and delete this message. Odin.'

Tom panicked. If he left the scene then it would look like it was him and he was running away as the guilty party. Tom needed to call Odin, then thought that sending a text was the way to start. He realised Odin may not be happy with him contacting him, but this was an emergency.

He selected reply and typed, but found it hard due to shaking:

'Odin. Sorry. Need help. Two men came to my house. I knew one of them. They tried to kill me. They are now dead. My wife is dead. Please help. What do I do?'

He hesitated, realising that the text was incriminating, but he felt he had no choice and so pressed send.

He leant up and slowly opened the front door. He put his head slowly through the gap and peered out. The black SUV remained parked. All was quiet and Tom felt a slight chill as he closed the door. He sat down and as he did, he felt a warm wet sensation which he assumed was his or someone else's blood.

Tom realised now that this had totally consumed him. There was now absolutely no doubt in his mind that he was not going mad and involved in something bad, of which he didn't understand. It also dawned on him that there now seemed to be no way of going back. He started to think what he needed to do get in a position to leave the house and he wondered how much time he had before Phil and Ortega's associates try to check in with them.

Suddenly his phone rang and startled him. He looked at the phone and noted that the number was the same one he had texted. It was Odin. Tom felt a wave of nervousness pass through him. He took a deep breath, pressed answer and held the phone up to his ear.

"Hello" he said quietly.
"Tom?" asked a calm low voice.
"Yes, who is this?"
"Listen carefully," said the voice, "Do not say my name. You know who this is. Are you hurt?"
"Er…No, well yes, but…"
"Can you function normally?" interrupted the voice.
"Yes," replied Tom.
"Listen carefully. We need you alive. Get out of there as quick as you can. Take essential's only. Money and cards. Get out of town and hole up somewhere overnight. Then leave for the meeting point tomorrow," Odin's voice remained calm and constant.
"But…The mess, my wife…I am covered in blood…" Tom's voice started to crack, and he felt himself becoming fearful and anxious.

"Tom!" said the voice forcefully, "Stay calm. Do not say anything else. Breath slowly. Listen. Clean yourself up quickly get the essentials and leave. Do this immediately. We don't know how long you have so move fast. Do not worry about the mess in the house, we will deal with it."
There was a silence and Tom waited for Odin to speak again.
"Listen, before you leave ring your wife's mobile from your house phone"
"What? I mean…Why?" Tom asked, puzzled.
"Just do it. And then ring it again several times from your mobile shortly after you leave. I will explain when we meet."

Having the conversation felt weird. Tom felt like he had known Odin for years but, in reality, he obviously hadn't. He didn't know him at all, apart from the odd texts. The conversation that was taking place felt like it was between two people who were close and had been for a long time. But they weren't. Tom felt like they had so much in common, but they didn't. It felt strange for them to be talking.
"Do not ring or text me again as I will no longer answer. Head towards your stop tonight and then to Pittsburgh tomorrow. I will send you further instructions before you arrive."

The phone then clicked off. Tom slowly moved his phone down from his ear. He just sat. His mind was fuzzy, and he wished everything would disappear and he could just be sitting with Jenna by the pool. A wave of emotion rose up and hit him hard. He let out a scream and burst into tears. His sobbing started to become uncontrollable, but it felt so good.

Like he was exorcising himself and as he cried all the bad was leaving him. He sobbed and then after a few minutes the emotion settled. He wiped his eyes and nose and felt a sting of pain which made him curse.

He looked down and he noticed how much blood he was covered in. He slowly stood up and again opened the door and looked outside again. Nothing had changed except it was a little darker and roosting birds could be heard off towards the lake. A faint orange glow now hung behind the clouds in the distance. He closed the door and rushed upstairs with a sudden feeling of focus and intent.

He ran into the bathroom leaving a trail of red footprints behind him. He quickly got into the shower and turned it on and while waiting for the water to heat up he took his bloodstained clothes off and threw them on the tiled floor. As the water warmed, he waited no longer and got under the strong pressure of the jet spray. He was surprised how good it felt and he rubbed his body all over cleaning the red from his skin. As he did the plug hole became enveloped in a red whirlpool of blood and water.

Eventually the excess blood had been cleaned off, but his hands and arms still had a blushed pink stain on them, and Tom realised he would need a better wash when he had time.

He jumped out of the shower and started to dry himself. As he did, he noticed the shower wall had hundreds of red spots adorning it as he had brushed his hands up and down his body in the water. The house was a complete mess and Tom wondered how on earth Odin would get it sorted.

His mind then flashed to Jenna's parents. Their daughter had been killed and they had no idea. How on earth was he going to tell them? Jenna kept in regular contact with them, especially her mother, and soon she would be trying to contact Jenna to see how she was. As he quickly dried himself, he realised he never had the answer right now and it would need to be something he sorts out another time.

Still damp he ran from the bathroom to his bedroom and opened the wardrobe and just grabbed what he could. He felt lucky as his comfortable jeans came out first and he slid them on. He grabbed a polo shirt, socks and then cursed as he realised he hadn't put underwear on but carried on regardless. He put the socks on and then grabbed his trainers and put them on quickly.

He turned and left the room and ran downstairs avoiding the blood trail so as not to spread it further around the house. He put on his jacket and felt the pockets making sure he could feel his mobile phone, wallet and car keys. All were there.

He thought about door keys. Would he need them again? Would he ever be coming back? A pang of anxiety hit him as he realised that in the garage he had a box of his life's memorabilia. Old schoolbooks, trophies, photos of him growing up, newspaper articles of sports events, photobooth photos of him and old flames.

Then a huge sadness engulfed him as he realised he had a photo album of him and his dad on a fishing trip when he was 12. It had been the best time that he had ever spent with his dad and he had treasured it his whole life. He hesitated. He wondered if he had time to grab any of it. Then he realised that he didn't. Whoever was trying to kill him could soon be here. Phil's associates, whoever they are, could be driving into the street right now.

Tom cleared his mind. He made the decision that he would take door keys as he may be able to come back at some point. He ran to the kitchen to go to the bowl they were kept in and he came face to face with a bloodbath again. The kitchen floor was now a sea of red, sticky and foreboding. He could see the bowl on the other side and so he clambered up onto the worktop that adjoined the entrance from the hallway which, luckily, had remained blood free, except for a few spots.

He made his way to the end and grabbed the keys from the bowl. As he did he took one last look at Jenna's lifeless body. It still hadn't sunk in yet that she was gone for good. He knew he was in shock and that the real grieving was set to come. Her hair was stuck to her face with blood. He wanted to lean down and clean her and move her from that damp, red pool. But he never had time.

Clambering back across the worktops, he suddenly heard a phone ring. He stopped, startled. Eyes wide. He listened intently and realised it was coming from Phil's dead, limp body. Whoever Phil was working with was checking in. He was running out of time.

He jumped down from the worktop with a swing which took him down and round into the hallway, he looked back and took one look back at Jenna's body. He felt guilty for leaving her. It was almost like he was abandoning her to whatever fate lay ahead for the bodies. His instinct was to go grab her and take her with him to keep her safe. Odin had said he would "deal with it" but what did that mean? Tom went cold as he had a vision of Jenna's body being thrown into the back of a van and dumped in a hole in the ground. He felt emotional again "Fuck!!" he shouted as he hit the wall, "Why??" he asked himself.

He was angry and emotional but knew he never had the time to pick it all apart and find the answers. Whatever it was that was happening was getting close and he needed to get away. He looked at his hands and they were trembling.

Tom composed himself. He patted his jacket down again. Phone, car keys, wallet, door keys. He tried to think of anything else he needed and couldn't think. He had transport, credit cards, money and could get back in. If he ever would again. He moved to the door and slowly opened it. He looked out again all was quiet. It was the same peaceful evening that he had seen twice before. The black SUV still sitting idle close to his drive.

As he went outside and shut the door, he trembled in utter disbelief at the carnage he was leaving behind. Quickly, he walked to the Mercedes and opened the door with the fob. It bleeped and he pulled the door open and got in. He started the engine and it growled to life and sat purring awaiting direction. Tom reversed off the driveway being wary to look around for neighbours. Luckily Tom didn't see anyone but was sure that someone must have seen the SUV near his driveway.

He hoped nobody had seen Phil and Ortega go in. Hopefully that afternoon and evening everybody had been, just for once, taking part in their own lives instead of paying attention to other people's. Tom shook his head. Not a chance he thought. And with that he put his foot down and the car sped out of his drive and away from the grisly scene that his house had become.

After a mile or so he pulled off the road and into the car park of a restaurant and checked Odin's text on his phone. In his rush to get out he realised he was heading north so deleted the text and pulled out of the restaurant and picked up the road south back the way he had come. He took the off ramp for Northfield and then picked up the road South.

Tom suddenly felt anxious. They could be following him now. He checked his mirrors and various vehicles were behind him and so he made a mental note of several of the makes and colours and then sped up. He figured if one of them was following him they would also speed up and he may be able to identify them. After a few miles he slowed down again hopefully he wouldn't see any of the vehicles he had noted.

As he drove, he realised he actually had no clue where he was heading. Odin had told him to hole up somewhere overnight. Then suddenly he instinctively decided that he would make Indianapolis his first stop for the night. He had been there before several times and knew of motels and car rental places on the outskirts. It would mean he could find a hotel easily and then grab a rental car in the morning to make his way to Pittsburgh.

He felt physically drained, but his adrenaline was buzzing around his body. His mind was alert and focussed and he settled in for the drive, in complete silence.

Chapter 21

The first leg of the drive to Indianapolis had been smooth and thankfully without incident. Tom had remained focussed all the way and even kept a check on cars behind him until darkness had fallen and all he could see was headlights. To counter this he had taken three off ramps he never wanted and driven away from the freeway to see if any vehicles followed him. Then when he was sure none had, he made his way back to the freeway, picked it up again and got back on his way.

A few times he had wondered what he was doing and why. Logging vehicles and taking note of who was behind him and deliberately diverting from his normal route to check for pursuers. He had laughed to himself at the insanity of it. But, after what had happened back at the house, any denials could no longer be accepted, and he had to start behaving differently to make sure he stayed alive.

As Tom had driven and his focus waned from time to time it had allowed thoughts and questions to flash around his head.

What if someone finds the bodies? Will he ever be able to go back home? What will he tell people? Jenna's parents? His sister? His work? Why had Jenna told him not to trust Rutherford? How was Jenna involved? What did Odin mean by 'we need you alive?'

He desperately tried to think of answers and solutions but each time his mind became fuzzy and all he could do was tell himself he will simply have to wait to meet Odin. Eventually he cruised into Lebanon, on the outskirts of the city and passed a motel and decided he didn't want to go directly into the city tonight, so turned around and went back.

The two-level motel was old and probably the last time it looked welcoming was back in the 50's or 60's. As Tom pulled in he immediately thought it looked exactly like the motels that criminals on the run use in the films. The faded, cracked paint and the empty swimming pool added to its charm.

But, it had vacancies, and Tom had booked a single room with little trouble for virtually next to nothing. It was pretty basic, but it would do. The receptionist had been helpful and had given him directions to a car hire place further in towards the city where he could also leave his own car.

It had been just past midnight when Tom had got into his room and he sat on the bed and put the TV on. He drank the bottle of water he had bought at reception and suddenly realised his eyes stung with tiredness and he was physically drained. He turned the TV off got undressed and got into bed. As he lay down the throbbing in his nose increased and he had to prop his head up a little to reduce it. The blankets were stiff and cold but didn't stop Tom falling almost instantly into a deep sleep.

Soon enough the darkness engulfed him, and the figures started to slowly shuffle around his bed. Tom tried to look up and see them, but his head felt heavy and was aching. He managed to lift his head only just off the pillow and when he looked down the bed he could see shadows and movements. He felt a cold claw touch his foot and he shuddered. He tried to scream at the unknown figure to leave him, but nothing came out.

A damp, musty smell filled the air and the environment became cold and damp. Cold enough for it to penetrate deep inside him. The figure drew closer and Tom saw flashes of its body as the light, from an unknown source, flickered and danced around the room. A wet, scaly dark skin glistened and moved with foreboding intent. As it slithered and shuffled around his bed Tom felt more presences come into form and he realised it wasn't alone.

Cold clawed hands started to push and pressure Tom's arms down into the bed. He screamed, but again silence. He tried to move but the force was too much, and he could only writhe on the bed in the same position. The light from the corner grew larger and it pierced his eyes. He knew it was wrong to look but something made him. He wanted to move his head and avert his eyes, but he was unable to. He felt the grip of scaly hands on his arms and body holding him in a cold and horrifying bondage.

The light grew wider and lighter, then a figure appeared in its radiant glow. The figure moved forward towards Tom in an effortless floating approach. Slowly it crossed the room to eventually stand over him. The figure was black. So black it was like looking into space, but the face emanated a light of its own.

The figure leaned over Tom. As it did the face became slowly clearer. It was Jenna. Tom stopped struggling. He tried to call her name, but nothing came out. She smiled at him. She looked so calm and peaceful almost like in the form of an angel. She reached out a dark hand to him and caressed his chest. Tom felt suddenly warm and comforted and was desperate for her to speak to him. As her hand moved across his chest the other presences and dark figures became excited and Tom heard an unknown, inaudible language, and in a split-second flash of light, a large snakes tongue flicked and dripped ooze.

As the excitement appeared to grow the pressure holding Tom down became stronger. He was helpless but hoped Jenna would intervene. He looked into her eyes and they looked directly into his mind, he felt her trying to communicate a message to him without speaking. Her eyes penetrating deep into his soul and Tom suddenly felt strong and powerful, almost almighty. He now felt the strength to move and to cast off the scaly bonds holding him.

But as he attempted to move Jenna's eyes changed. The calm serenity suddenly stopped. A look of anger became apparent and the strength Tom felt disappeared and the weakness returned. Her hand that was previously caressing his chest started to press. As it did Tom struggled to breath. He tried to release himself, but he was no match for the pressure being bound onto him.

He looked down at her hand and the soft, tanned skin had turned white and an ice cold feeling penetrated and almost took his breath away. The skin on the end of her fingers begin to split and tear, and suddenly dark claws slid out, pushing and splintering her human nails off the end of the fingers.

Tom felt the fear engulf him and the cold, desperate feeling took control. Jenna spread her hand wide across his beating heart. The dark figures were now screaming in an orgy of excitement. The noise they made now almost unbearable, piercing Tom's ears with screeching and howling. They circled the bed as if trying to compete for position closest to Jenna.

Her face was now gripped with anger and contorted, as if she was using all her energy. Then suddenly her claws pierced Tom's skin. Blood spattered across Jenna's face and Tom felt the pain and screamed out in silence. As the skin broke and split, her hand pushed harder and went deeper into his chest. Her hand slowly slipped deeper even more, and Tom tried to catch her attention to beg her to stop.

He struggled to breath as he felt her hand moving and gouging inside his chest until it found its target, and he felt cold fingers slither around his heart. Tom shook his head and screamed out in silence. The excitement around him grew and the dark figures screeching sounded as if what they were witnessing was too much for them to bear.

Then a slow grip around his heart stopped him. He lay motionless as the grip intensified. He looked at Jenna's face and the angry contortion had changed to a vicious smile. He then felt a hard pull and a rip that felt like his soul was being removed. The pain in his chest burned as Jenna's hand started to appear from his chest. Then, as it came out, Tom saw his own heart pumping and dripping in blood.

His whole body was now a mass of red blood and sticky ooze as the heart was lifted away from his body and held up to his assailant's face. Jenna looked at the heart and a forked tongue flicked from her mouth to taste the dripping red muscle.

Tom tried to scream but his whole body was lifeless and limp, and he could not muster the energy to do anything. As he stared at the evil face of the woman he loved, she pulled the heart close and took a large bite at it, sinking her teeth deep into its pumping mass. Blood splattered out and the screeching became so loud Tom felt the insides of his ears burning. Jenna's face became unrecognisable with the red mass.

In Tom's mind he was shouting, "Jenna! Jenna! Jenna!" and then suddenly he heard himself. He realised he could now make noise.

He shouted again, "Jenna, no!!" and this time he heard it very clearly. He also felt lighter and his bonds had been removed. He tried to grab her to get his heart back and as he did he sat up and all around was dark and still.

Tom breathed heavy. Panting hard like he had run a 100-metre sprint. He felt his head and sweat was dripping from him. He looked around and saw a soft light emanating through the curtains. Then a banging behind him and a deep voice booming.
"Hey, keep the fucking noise down in there!"

Tom suddenly felt cold as the coolness of the air-con in the motel room caressed his wet, sweaty body. He calmed himself and spun and sat on the edge of the bed and the sound of passing cars in the distance became more audible. Tom felt his heart pumping and put his hand up to his chest and tried to ease the aching. He put his head in his hands and slowly began to cry.

Tom had noted that in the last few months the nightmares had got worse and much more vivid. He had always suffered with bad dreams. Even as a kid. And they all contained the same dark, foreboding presences and creatures. Tom's mum would often be in his bedroom with him crying after a bad dream. She would hold him tight and rock him back to sleep and tell him he was her, "Special boy."

At the time Tom just thought it to be a mum assuring her young son. Nothing unusual. "Rest now my special one," she would say, and eventually Tom would fall back to sleep.

Tom got up, walked over to the window and moved the curtain aside a little. The sun had not yet risen and there was a dark grey hue blanketing the outside world. He was now desperate to meet Odin, who he hoped would help him understand. But Tom couldn't help but have a nagging anxiety of what would happen if Odin never showed up. He wondered how on earth he would manage this on his own.

Tom sat back down on the end of the bed. His nose and eyes felt even more pain from Phil's punches. He knew he shouldn't have, but he touched his nose gently and it made him shudder. He put his heads in his hands.

He had also had visions of his neighbours ringing the police to say they heard commotion in his house and detectives and scenes of crimes officers analysing the massacre that had occurred. Obviously, the prime suspect would be him, and he wondered what he would tell the police under interview. He kept wondering if it would be best to turn himself in and tell them everything. But if that was the best course of action, Odin would have told him to do it. But he hadn't. So, Tom felt he would just ride it and if Odin didn't show up then it may be his only option.

He also kept wondering about his sister and Jenna's parents. He sister taking care of funeral arrangements. Before he left New Jersey she had said she would let him know and invited him and Jenna to stay with them for a few days before and after the funeral. A deep worry suddenly shot through him when he thought of the funeral, and if he would even be able to go. Hopefully after meeting Odin things would be clearer and he could work something out.

But as for Jenna, what would he tell people as to why she wasn't at the funeral? What would he tell her parents. They would obviously want to come to the funeral too and so things were going to get very complicated.

For all he knew the police had already found the bodies and had contacted them and they may know she was already dead. For all he knew he could now be a fugitive and a major manhunt was underway. He opened his phone and searched national and local news and hoped that his face didn't appear. It didn't.

He focussed. Took a deep breath and had a shower. Wincing each time his hands went close to his face. He got out and dried himself and looked in the mirror. He looked tired and stressed. His nose was swollen and one of his eyes had turned black. The other eye was severely blood-shot, and he had a smaller bruise on his cheek.

He also thought he looked out of shape. He had lost the tone that his regular gym sessions had created. He grabbed his stomach and hips and pulled at the paunch that had appeared. He hadn't shaved for a week and his stubble was starting to resemble more of a patchy beard. But he thought under the circumstances this wasn't a bad thing. He then decided that day he would get some sunglasses and a cap.

He looked at his phone and noted the time was 5:46am. It was going to be an 8-hour drive to Pittsburgh and Tom thought he would stop on the way, perhaps around Columbus. He also had things to do like get a hire car. He had thought against it a few times but had eventually chosen to follow Odin's advice.

He was nervous about meeting Odin. Nervous in case it came to nothing and Odin was a nutcase and Tom would be no nearer the truth. He lay back down and changed the alarm on his phone from 8am to 7am planning that the extra hour would give him time to eat breakfast before he set off.

He lay back down and stared at the ceiling. His phone bleeped. He rolled over and picked it up. He noted it was a text from Davy. He opened it and read:

'Hey Tom. Really hope you are ok and bearing up? I figured another weekend may be the thing to take your mind off things. Please tell me you will come up. You can stay here again. Take care man. D'

Tom was confused as to why Davy would be texting him at this hour and made a mental note to call him on the way to Pittsburgh.

His plan to get breakfast before he left had gone wrong as he had fallen back to sleep and then woke to find his alarm had been sounding for 15 minutes and never woke him. He had had to check out quickly and he noted that the receptionist for the motel had changed and it was now a young, punky looking male, who had been staring at Tom intently as he signed out and paid.

184

He had gone outside and tried to call Davy but got no answer. He also noted the young man staring again. Tom had realised that paranoia may well be something he must come to expect to live with. As he had driven out of the motel, he noted the young man watching him leave and did not appear to hide the fact that was doing so. Tom felt the urge to give him a sarcastic wave goodbye, but then thought better of it.

As Tom's car left the parking lot, bumped onto the main road and away, the young man was already on the phone dialling the number. The number that the strange man who visited the motel earlier that morning had paid him $50 to call him when the guest, matching Tom's description, checked out and left.

Chapter 22

The drive was quite relaxing, although was still a little gruelling. A drive that distance was always going to be. Tom had checked out and made his way to the car rental place just on the edge of the city hired a Toyota Corolla. It was nice and comfortable, but nothing like the Mercedes for performance. But he had got a good deal and, as the receptionist had advised him., he could leave his car with them for the period of his hire; although at extra cost.

He hired it for three days. When he did it, he realised he had not a clue if was too long or too short. He was winging it and without any other detail he just had to use his instinct.

He had been lucky as only a few hundred yards from the hire car place was a department store. He had gone in and was able to buy an Indianapolis Colts cap and a pair of aviator glasses, hoping that with them on, and his rapidly growing beard, any potential pursuer would now not recognise him. The fact he was also now driving a different car may also help. He could only hope.

When had had left Indianapolis he had, every half an hour or so, come off the freeway to check for any pursuers. Each time he did it and then got back on he never noticed any vehicles of note. By the time he got near Columbus he had stopped doing this out of tedium. Although he realised he may curse his lack of focus and organisation if it did turn out he was being followed and he never noticed it.

After eating at on the outskirts of Columbus where, despite his nerves and anxiousness, he devoured lunch, and got back on route 70. Although was now starting to get tired of driving and just wanted to get there so had driven a little faster. Plus, he knew he also needed to make up some time.

Eventually he started seeing the signs for Pittsburgh and he became concerned that he would arrive not know exactly where to go. However, to his surprise, shortly after this as he drove through Wheeling, he heard his phone bleep and a wave of nerves rushed through his body.

He came off the 70 and spotted a piece of waste ground opposite a U-Haul Depot. He stopped and left the engine running and grabbed his phone from a small compartment under the stereo. He noticed a text from an unknow number and opened it:

'Tom. Do not enter Pittsburgh. Too risky. New meeting point. Go to Zip Code 15901. ETA 4pm. Await further instructions. Do not reply and delete this message. Odin.'

Tom entered the zip code into his phone map. It showed him that 15901 was Johnstown, Pennsylvania and that it was a short drive east of Pittsburgh. He had never heard of it before. But he quickly got back on the freeway and followed the Sat-Nav all the way and as he got closer he started hoping to hear from Odin again soon.

The time was now 5:46pm and he checked his phone again to make sure Odin hadn't sent another text, but his message list was clear.

Tom approached Ligonier and stayed on the 271 through Laurel Ridge State Park towards Westmont. It was a beautifully wild, place but the previously blue sky had turned a sullen grey which added to a strange oppressive feeling Tom couldn't shake off. But he knew he was zeroing in on the meeting point and had to keep going.

Getting closer to Johnstown he decided to find somewhere to hole up in Westmont and wait for Odin's contact. He wondered whether to go straight into Johnstown, but something was telling him to hang back until he knew Odin was there.

He pulled off the 271 on the outskirts and parked up in the car park of what looked like a community building of some sort. He pulled in and parked between two other cars and thought to himself it was as good a place to stop as any knowing that he was only a short drive in.

He got out and stretched which felt good and he tingled as it set off his blood flow around his body. He got back in relaxed. Then picked up his phone again to check for contact but found there was none. The thought that this was a wasted journey occurred to him again.

He remembered Davy's text and opened his phone and called him. He held up the phone to his ear and heard the ringing. It continued until it clicked and went to Davy's answerphone. Tom thought he must be on his way home from work and as the bleep sounded he wondered about leaving a message, but he was tired and couldn't be bothered to put on a pretence, so just ended the call. He then went back into Davy's text and selected reply and typed:

'Hey Davy, got your text. I would love to catch up. I have a few issues going on at moment which I am trying to resolve then I can hook up. I am happy to

come to you. I will contact you in a few days. I am ok at moment, bearing up.
But will survive. Thanks. T'

Tom pressed send and put the phone on the passenger seat. He laid back
and closed his eyes. A few cars drifted by slowly and made Tom open his
eyes and look around to get his bearings, just out of curiosity. As he did
his phone bleeped and his heart skipped. Was it Odin? He picked up the
phone and saw it was from Davy. He opened the message and read:

'Tom, really sorry, can't talk right now. Would be so happy to see you. Look
forward to it. Hoping it can be sooner rather than later. I have some problems I
hope you may be able to help me with. Just personal stuff. D'

Tom typed a reply and pressed send:

'OK D. Will come to meet as soon as I can. Is everything ok? Hope nothing too
serious? T'

Within 30 seconds of sending the message his phone bleeped and Tom
opened the reply:

'Thanks, nothing too serious. But just hope you can meet up sooner rather
than later. Or I can come to you if you let me know where you are now or
where you will be in a few days. Thanks again D'

Tom replied:

'Ok, I will be in touch later. Will call you. T'

He put the phone down again and felt concern for Davy. Maybe he hadn't
told him the whole story when they met up a few weeks ago. Maybe Davy
had wanted to tell him but couldn't. Tom made a mental note to call him
later to speak.

He sat back and took a deep breath realising he was thirsty and needed to
find somewhere to get a drink. He looked around again but couldn't see
anywhere that looked like it would sell refreshments. The time was now
6:19pm and he felt concerned that Odin was now over nearly two hours
late in contacting him with further instructions. He thought he would give
it to 6:45pm and if he hadn't heard he would make his way into
Johnstown and find somewhere to grab a drink.
He took a deep breath and laid back and closed his eyes. It was quiet and
very peaceful and the sound of cars drifting by increased the relaxed
feeling. Tom started to doze off, but the bleep of his phone startled him
to life. He picked up the phone and saw he had a message from un
unknow number. He opened it:

'Tom. Sorry for delay. I have selected a meeting place. The Tavern Bar. Far end of Railroad Street. Be there at 7pm. Get a drink at bar and wait. Do not reply and delete this message. Odin.'

Tom made a note of the meeting place and time and deleted the message. He looked the bar up on his phone and advised him it was 12 minutes away. As the grey dusk was slowly throwing an oppressive, sullen blanket across the pink and orange sky, there was a chill in the air. Tom started the engine and drove out of the car park with a heavy feeling of dread and anxiety in his stomach.

Chapter 23

As Tom drove into and along Railroad Street, he realised that this part of town had seen better days. It was getting dark and Tom reminded himself of the old saying never to arrive anywhere at night. But he wondered if it would have been any better arriving in the day.

As he cruised along derelict and boarded up buildings and premises littered the side of the road. In some spots, nature had started to reclaim the concrete and brick and small areas of natural life had sprung up in between buildings and roadways.

A he made his way along he noticed a few dimly lit bars, derelict houses and cars parked away from the main road with occupants inside sitting in the tiny car light. Only those inside the cars knowing exactly what they were doing. He started to wish that Odin could've chosen a better location, but, then again, he thought this could be exactly why he had chosen it.

As he approached the far end, he saw to the left a piece of open waste ground with a bench in the middle and two guys sitting on it with bottles of drink, the two men looked happy. The kings of their own world. Beyond that he spotted a poorly lit neon sign emanating the words 'The Tavern Bar' with the a and v of the word Tavern barely lit at all.

He stopped at a red light adjacent to the waste ground and looked at the guys on the bench. Whatever it was they were discussing it looked very entertaining for one of them who appeared to be holding his stomach in pain from laughter. The light changed and he turned left onto the road that the bar was situated, and slowly approached then drove by. A couple of scantily dressed young girls were talking to an old man outside. Tom drive by looking for somewhere to park but couldn't see anywhere on the premises.

He continued but kept the bar in his rear-view mirror and as he got to another junction, he noted vehicles parking up on the opposite side of the road. Further down he saw space for about 3 vehicles and so quickly indicated right, cruised further down to the empty spaces and parked up. Tom was surprised at how nervous he was and took a huge deep breath which for a few seconds released the heavy anxious feeling, but as he blew out it came back just as quick as it had gone.

He got out, looked around and started to walk back to the bar. As he approached, he could hear the two men on the waste ground shouting and laughing. He looked over and one of them was balancing on the back of the bench on one foot until his wind-milling arms could balance him no longer and he fell into a laughing heap. The other man who was already struggling with laughter screamed and slid off the bench onto the floor also.

Tom looked ahead at the bar and now noticed that the old man was now in an embrace with one of the young girls and had one of his hands up her short skirt. Her friend leaned against the wall looking over at the two drunks on the floor, and as she did she shouted.
"You pair of dumb-fuck's!"
To which a reply came back, "Fuck you, ho!" and the sound of laughter. The girl stuck her finger up and shouted back.
"Fuck me? You ain't got the money, boy!" She then turned and looked in the direction of Tom, anxiously approaching. He looked down, hoping she hadn't seen him staring. He now wished he was anywhere but here. This was an awful place he thought, but he told himself to be bold and focus. Although, if he was given the choice right now to disappear, he would take it.
He looked up at the bar as if to demonstrate he had only just decided to go for a drink, rather than it being planned. He felt this would help him look less conspicuous. As he approached, the young girl who had shouted, pushed herself off the wall with her back and started to approach him.
"Hey, never seen you before."
Tom's mind raced as to what to say, "No, just passing through."
"You want some action sweetheart?" asked the girl, as she grabbed the bottom of her top and pulled it up to reveal a small but pert breast.
"Er, no, not right now," said Tom uncomfortably, "I need to get a few drinks first; maybe later?"

Tom surprised himself with the 'later' part and immediately regretted it. By now he was close to her and only yards from the main door and the muffled sound of music and crowds could be heard from within.
"Ok baby. I will be here. And if I am not then just wait, I never take too long," she said with a smile, which revealed to Tom that she was actually very attractive underneath the obvious toil of her life. Tom smiled and nodded embarrassed, then eased by and went inside.

As he got inside the sound increased and hit him. Heavy rock music blasted out of speakers which couldn't handle the sound and the tinny sound cut into his ears. The smell of beer and detergent hit him harder though. It was dark and musty and took a few seconds for his eyes to adjust which meant he almost bumped into a man mountain stood just the other side of the main door. He towered above Tom and wore a white vest, had a bald head with a handlebar moustache and a small badge emblazoned 'Security'.

He gave Tom an arrogant once over and then nodded. Tom nodded back trying to look as though this was all normal to him, but he couldn't help but feel completely alien. However, he took confidence from the fact that a few people in a booth near the door had seen him and the large man nod at each other.

At first it seemed a small bar but as Tom walked through it opened out into a much bigger place. A large circular bar in the middle and a smaller bar off in the far corner. It was very loud and busy, but Tom noted there were tables and booths available. He looked at the main bar and headed for a space within the people. He stood at the bar and an older lady pulling a drink looked round at him and nodded. She served the drink and them headed over and nodded again. Tom ordered a Bud and with little fuss the lady brought it back and took his money and was gone.

Tom took a few sips of beer and realised how thirsty he had been as it quenched his thirst. He felt the crispness and continued drinking and the urge to keep drinking saw him put the bottle down with only a couple of gulps left. He looked up and the lady, who previously served him, looked round and shouted to him, "Another?"

Tom smiled and held the bottle up. Within 30 seconds he had another cold bottle next to him on the bar. He looked around. The people inside seemed to be having a great time. The music was loud and so were they. Tom realised why Odin chose this place as in the throng and mayhem of people, forgetting their shitty lives, many things would go unnoticed.

Tom looked back ahead of him and took another swig finishing his first bottle. He put it down and, as he did, he felt a presence to his left. He went to look and noted the figure a medium sized man with a beard and swept back, longish hair.
"Just look straight ahead," the man ordered.

Tom was instinctively confused and was about to question what the man had said, but he then realised that this must be Odin. Tom did as he was told and took a huge gulp from his new bottle.
The man then spoke again, "In a moment I will put my arm round you. Just pretend to know me," only just loud enough for Tom to hear.

Tom was confused but had no time to figure it out before the man grabbed him and spun him round with force, "Hey! What the fuck are you doing here!!" the man shouted.

Tom looked bewildered. Through a smiling face and without much lip movement the man ordered sternly but quietly, "Pretend to know me." Tom put his hands on the man's shoulders, "Hey, how are you?" he said uncomfortably. The man grabbed him and pulled him close in a tight embrace, "Hug me," the man said in Tom's ear, "smile. Be friendly". The man then pushed him away, "Look at you!" he said, "It's been too long. Come on, sit down," and the man pointed to an empty booth in the corner.

As they walked to it Tom noticed that as he sat down the man suddenly appeared edgy. He was looking around and appeared to be mentally noting the other people in the bar. They sat down and the man, still looking around the bar, introduced himself.
"I'm Odin. Odin Alstaad. It's good to finally meet you."

Suddenly Tom realised that he was in the moment that he had been imagining for what seemed like an eternity. In an instant a thousand questions came into his head.
"Look, I need to you to tell…"
"Just be cool," Odin interrupted, now looking a bit less edgy and taking a sip from his bottle.
Tom tried to relax, "OK, I'm cool."
"So…" Odin cut in, "your mother called me a couple weeks back…"
"My mom called you. What? How…? How do you know…How did you know my mom?" asked Tom a little frantic.
"No. Not here. Haven't got time to explain all that. I have to get to the important stuff," replied Odin still clocking the bar.
Odin leaned into Tom, "There's a guy behind you…" Tom went to turn and look, "Don't look!!" hissed Odin and Tom looked back at him.
Tom stayed looking at Odin, "That guy at the bar? Just take a quick look when I say and only when I say…Guy with shaved head, stubble and grey suit…Ok look."

Tom slowly turned his head as if to pretend he was just relaxing and looking around. He saw the guy who was stood a short distance from where they both were a minute ago and looked back at Odin, "Yeah, I see him."
"Don't look at him anymore. He's unusual for this bar. He came in fifteen minutes before me and five minutes before you. He hasn't clocked the joint yet so he either knows his target or is not involved and so not a

concern. He's drinking orange juice, and this is generally a beer and whisky bar. His car is too good for this area, I saw it earlier. If he moves towards us, I will tell you and we will go at him, subdue him and get the fuck out of here, OK?"

"What? Oh, fuck off, man," complained Tom, "Look, I'm going to…"

"You are in danger. Just sit tight and look relaxed. I will keep my eye on him," Odin confirmed as he nodded his head in the direction of the suited man.

Tom wondered what the hell he was doing in this place with this strange guy. He let out a huge sigh, shook his head and put his head in his hands. "That is not looking relaxed," said Odin.

"Look," said Tom interrupting, "Can we please get to the point? And what about Jenna, my house. You said you would sort it"

"It's done," Odin interrupted, "Don't worry. There's not a speck of dust left in the place."

"How? I mean, it was a bloodbath…"

"Keep your voice down," scalded Odin, "Don't worry. I know people. That's of no concern now."

"What! No concern," snapped Tom, "There are three dead bod…."

"Shut up!" Odin ordered under his breath and looked around, "Just be fucking cool or I am leaving"

Tom noted from Odin's glare that he was serious, he slowly lifted his bottle and downed his beer.

"You want another?" Odin asked.

Tom shook his head, "No!" he said getting frustrated.

"OK. I am going to get another. Just try to fit in. Look like a regular. Then we can talk".

Odin went to the bar. Tom looked him up and down. He was scruffy and unkept. Both he and his clothes looked like they could do with a good wash. He fitted in well. Suddenly Tom felt out of place. He tried to relax. He suddenly had an urge to look at the guy in the grey suit. He turned his head as if to scratch the side of his head and quickly glanced and noticed the man still at the bar. Could he be dangerous? Tom suddenly wondered.

Suddenly there was an increase in volume from the other side of the bar and raised voices were followed by two guys squaring off and a woman, who looked like she was probably quite attractive in her younger days, tried to get in between them. They pushed and shoved and eventually two other guys calmed it all down. Both men sat down, and the woman sat on one of their laps and caressed the man's face. Tom looked at Odin who was being given his change and he walked back over and sat down.

"This place is a time bomb," Odin said, "I don't like it here. Too many opportunities for The Order to get close."

He said the last part under his breath and as he was looking around. Tom thought he had heard him but couldn't be sure, "What did you just say?"

"Don't worry," Odin said tensely, "Look. The best thing to do is just not say a word. This is not a conversation. I am simply here to tell you what the hell is going on with you." He took a large swig from the new bottle. "This is where it gets wacky. But just hear me out. Your mom contacted me to try to help you. I am Odin Alstaad and I am an agent for an organisation called The Network. We protect people like you, Tom...Or at least we try".
Tom shook his head and went to talk, "No. Not a conversation. No time," interrupted Odin with a raised finger.
"There is a power that has been written about and spoken about. But nobody truly knows of its true extent. I don't expect you to believe this right now, nor understand it. But there is a power...And it is real. You have been chosen to be a portal for that power."

Tom suddenly felt all the noise around him fade out and all he could hear was Odin's words.
"Now, you have heard the phrase 'God moves in mysterious ways' haven't you? Well, I can confirm he does..."
"What?" interrupted Tom and he got up, "Thanks, but I don't..."

Odin got up and suddenly looked very serious and very agitated.
"Sit the fuck down. If you leave here without hearing me out, you will die."

Tom looked around. He noted among others the man in the suit had taken interest in them. Odin looked nervous and acted out a cover and he spoke louder than required.
"Look, sorry man, I promise, I'll pay you next week...You know I'm good for it."

Tom realised what he was doing and played along by nodding and sitting down. Odin slowly sat down and when they realised nobody was interested anymore he continued.
"You do that again and I will walk away. I am risking my own life by coming here to speak to you, so don't fuck about. Just let me finish. Then if you don't believe me then walk away."

Tom took a large swig from his beer and then suddenly felt the urge to down it which he promptly did, "Another?" he asked Odin who smiled.

Tom returned to the table with two beers and two shots of whisky. Simultaneously they downed the whisky, and each pulled a beer to their chest as they hunched in.

Odin then continued, "Look, this is not easy for me to explain and it's going to be hard to believe. It is impossible for me to give too much detail now, but, when you were born you were chosen and marked. Once marked you were then used to transmit a power. A power that is way beyond them realms of our understanding. Even beyond our imagination. It's all predestined. Your life has been carefully planned, and a chosen path set over time to create coincidental meetings and occurrences at certain times. To allow you to be a portal to transmit that power onto earth."

Tom sat stunned, hearing the words, but not digesting them properly. Odin continued, "Look, I know this is hard, but you are used as a portal for God to come directly into contact with human-beings who have sinned."

Tom's hands were clasped together, he was rocking backwards and forwards and shaking his head.
"Be cool," said Odin, "I know this is difficult but please be cool. This power is controlled by The Order who are there to make sure portals stay on the right path to harness that power at the right time," Tom could see Odin becoming more comfortable the more he spoke.
"But…" Odin continued as he looked around the bar nervously, "what we are talking about here is an almighty power that has the ability to cut short a human's preordained timeline, as punishment for a crime or an act that has gone unpunished. A sin. That's where you come in. Your life was already set. And your body and soul are a key which opens a gateway. A gateway from the ultimate and almighty god to enter this world to deliver his wrath…"

Tom woke from his trance like state.
"No disrespect. But you are fucking nuts…I'm getting outta here," Tom finished his beer and went to get up.
"Oh, I'm nuts, am I?" said Odin and taking a swig of beer, "So why the hell did your mom ring me to help you?"

Tom stopped. He looked around. Then slowly sat back down.

Odin continued, "I know your mom died recently and she told you a few things that confused you before she died didn't she? She rang me and told me it was getting too much for you. She told me about the bad dreams and the strange feelings. That you need to be protected from The Order. She told me…"

"What the fuck is The Order?" said Tom with a sarcastic tone.

"What? Oh…" replied Odin, "They are the people that create the platform on earth for god to do his work. They will contact the parents of marked babies. Nurture those babies into kids, teenagers and adults. Make sure they stay on the right path so that when the time comes they can be in the right place to do what they have to do" Tom shook his head nut Odin continued.

"Look, we are getting too deep into this now. When or if we get time, I will explain it in detail to you, but not here, not now. It's not safe."

"Why? Why is it not safe?" asked Tom

Odin laughed, "Look around. This place isn't safe for anyone full stop."

He took another swig of beer.

"The Order and The Network are enemies. The Network, that's my people, try to save portals from The Order's control...But T=they have eyes and ears everywhere…"

"Portals?" quizzed Tom

" Portals. Portals are humans who are used to transmit the power…Or, the old-fashioned term is 'Angels'."

"Oh, fuck off," Tom put his head in his hands and looked down at the beer stained table.

Odin realised how crazy he sounded and gave him time. Tom looked up. He didn't know what to do or what to say. He felt like leaving. But something was stopping him. Then he realised, it was the connection to his mum. What else did Odin know about his mum?

"So, you say my mom contacted you? What did she say?" Tom was struggling to believe he was entertaining this weirdo.

"Ok, listen. We can trace portals and their families, and we try to infiltrate them. Try to get them to see what is happening and get them away. One of our agents has got to your mom and given her my contact. She would've known when you were born what the truth was. The Order had already traced her and made contact. It would've been explained to her, but also made clear that if she does anything to prevent the destined line from being completed then you would both be in grave danger. But she has obviously, for some reason, felt inclined to try to help you now. By contacting The Network she has potentially created an alternative timeline…Because if I protect you and get you somewhere that you can't be traced then you obviously cannot fulfill your rightful duties to The Order...You can't be used as they need you to be."

Odin stopped. He took a deep breath and calmed himself from the excitement and tension that had risen as he spoke.
"Tom. We really cannot be here for much longer. By contacting us your mom has tried to free you from this, but she has also put you in danger...Well, for the short term. Long term I hope to be able to free you for good. But for now, are you with me or not?"

Tom just stared at Odin. Trying to collect his thoughts and analyse if this guy was mad or whether it was true. If he was really caught up in something he doesn't understand and can't control. His mind was racing. He thought of Jenna, his work...How was this going to affect them. What happens now?
"Look Odin...I just...Why are people trying to kill me?"
Odin interrupted, "Look, I know how you feel. I was once in your position. Long story. And you aren't the first person I have has this conversation with and hopefully you won't be the last. I know your mind is frazzled. You have thought you were going mad in the last couple of months and ow I tell you all this. I know how that feels. But you are in serious danger. If The Order believe you are compromising them they will liquidate you quickly. They have already tried!"

Tom sensed the sudden increase in urgency in Odin's voice.
"So, you must decide now. Even if you get up and walk away now they may still feel you are too far gone anyway as they cannot afford to have rogue portals. Even if you still have work to do for them. Your mom believed this whole thing was breaking you and you needed to get away. The Order need portals who comply and can cope with the sudden change in their lives and the strange feelings and dreams. Any who are not coping are seen as too dangerous to them and must be snuffed out. It's too risky for them. Look, I can..."
Tom interrupted, "Dreams. You mentioned dreams...And strange feelings...What do you...."

Odin's finger raised again, "This is the last time. I have already said far too much to you at this stage. If you want to walk away then get up and walk away. But remember..."

Odin paused, before continuing, which gave Tom a sense of foreboding.
"You can choose to ignore me and get on with your life. That is your choice. But you will either always be used and manipulated by The Order or you will be killed. And even if you do you complete their final work

then your lifeline also expires. That is the end. Portals do not live on past whatever missions of death The Order has for them. Your life ends when you have done their bidding. Once they have no further use for you they will snuff you out in an instant. These people are fanatical, but they professional and brutal killers. It could be tomorrow, a week, a year...You will be liquidated once your work is done."

Tom noted Odin's eyes becoming more intense with each word he spoke. "Nobody knows the path and timeline that has been set for them. But let me warn you...Our intelligence suggest that portals are generally brought to certain locations, maybe twice or three times, so that their ability to be a portal can be maximised to as many sinners all located in one place and at one time in history. Your mom told me you feel you have been linked to 'some' deaths. And I can now confirm you definitely have. You may have more to complete, but, it could only be one more, two more.... Maybe three. And then boom, the end."

Tom stared at Odin. His stomach knotted and he realised he was shaking his head but had been for a few minutes without realizing. Was this all real?

Odin cut into Tom's thoughts, "Tom, we need to go now. I have a safe place arranged".

Tom suddenly felt fear. He was still not sure if he accepted any of this. But what choice did he have? If Odin was right and the so-called Order had already realised he was rogue he couldn't just carry on with his life anyway. Basically, he was screwed whichever way he went. Tom suddenly realised that he had to give himself more time to figure things out. Tom slowly nodded, "Ok, let's go."
"Wait," Odin interjected, "I need you to do something. Slowly get up and walk to the toilet and go in and take a pee."
Just as Odin said it Tom felt the urge to go. The drinks in quick succession had taken their toll and, now his mind was taken away from what Odin had told him, he was, in fact, desperate to go.
"OK, but why?" said Tom as he slowly rose from his seat.
"Just do it." Odin replied with a smile and a laugh which was then proceeded with him standing up and patting Tom the shoulder.
"Laugh," he ordered Tom under his breath.

Tom hated the acting but he realised why it needed to be done. Tom patted Odin back and then moved out of the booth and away towards the toilets which were in the far corner. As Tom approached the toilets a small crowd of people standing around the door stopped and looked up at him. He maintained his composure and did not look anyone in the eye.

He went through the door which opened into a long corridor with three doors adjoining it. At the end of the corridor against a black door sat a man looking very drunk, dazed and in need of help. Tom looked along and realised none of the doors had signs but luckily a man came out of the door at the far end and gave Tom the sign he needed. The man brushed past Tom as if he wasn't there and never acknowledged as Tom's shoulder was jarred slightly as he went by. Tom never looked back or said anything and went inside the door the man had come from.

Inside the smell of urine almost made Tom gag. It stung his eyes. There were no windows or ventilation. The urinal ran the whole length of the toilet and at the end, closest to the door, a pool of vomit blocked the hole and it had started to back up. Tom walked to the far end and started to go. It felt good and he took a deep breath.

He then heard a door outside bang. He looked up but nobody came in. He looked back down and then up at the rotting wet ceiling. He then heard another bang of a door and this time the huge security man, who had been at the bar entrance, walked in. He looked straight into Tom's eyes and walked to the urinal; Tom looked back up at the ceiling.

The man stepped up the step to the urinal but carried on walking and stopped only a few feet from Tom; which Tom thought was way too close when the whole urinal was available. Tom looked round politely, and the man looked at him, Tom blew out in relief and spoke.
"I needed that," and the man grunted but never looked at him.

As Tom finished, he suddenly felt a rapid movement close to him. His instinct made him look and he noticed the man twist to face him and swiftly raise what looked like an iron bar above his head. Fear hit and Tom instinctively held his arm up waiting for the impact but all he heard was another grunt and a snap.

He looked up again and saw Odin holding the man's arm which was now in a very peculiar position up his back with the wrist bent almost around the man's head. The bar fell to the floor with a loud clang. Odin then brought his elbow down onto the man's shoulder and he made another grunt. The giant man fell to his knees and Odin brought an elbow smashing down directly onto the man's head. With the impact Tom heard a crunch and the man stared straight at him with wide frightened eyes. Eyes of a man that knew his skull had been cracked. Then finally Odin

200

grabbed the man's head with one hand and smashed it with so much force into the urinal Tom barely saw it move.

The man crumpled and hung limply until Odin released his arm and he bundled onto the floor face down in a giant 20 stone heap. Tom looked at the urinal which was cracked and had blood and flesh particles spattered across it. Blood oozed from the man's head and quickly started to infiltrate the urine and spit that was backing up.
"They were one step ahead. They knew. Did you delete all your messages?" asked Odin authoritatively.

Tom looked up from the man's lifeless body and stared at Odin but said nothing.
"Did you delete the messages!?" he asked again
"Yes," replied Tom quietly.
"Fuck, they had the jump on me. Fuck!" exclaimed Odin angrily, "We need to go now. Out the back, move!"

Odin turned and quickly darted for the door and Tom followed now in panic mode. He had no time to think or analyse. It was time to just follow and do. Odin never moved to go back to the bar but went the other end towards the black door. He shifted the drunk out the way with his leg and pushed the bar which opened the door into the cool, dark night. He turned and put his arm out to Tom who moved towards the door. As he did the bang of another door was heard the other end.

Both Tom and Odin looked and the man in the suit, they had noted at the bar earlier, stood there staring directly at them. All three paused for a second. Then the man turned and darted back into the bar. Odin pushed Tom through the door and out and then followed, the door closing on its own with a bang. They looked round and found themselves to be in a rear courtyard with an alleyway leading from it.

Odin ran towards the alley way and Tom followed. Odin stopped at the end of the alley and held his hand out to Tom to do the same. He looked around beyond the alley and into the night, his head darting left and right in quick succession. Tom looked back from where they had come hoping to see the door remain closed.
"How far did you park from the bar?" Odin whispered. Tom hesitated, his mind flashing with what he had just seen.
"Er….A few hundred yards."
"Ok, they have obviously trailed me. So, we go in your car. Where is it from here?"
Tom hesitated again, "Think. Quickly!" blurted Odin.

"Right ok. As I passed the bar was on the right. I turned right and parked…So…"

In Tom's mind the car should have been just ahead and to left, but he didn't want to commit as he wasn't sure.

"Where from here. Lead the way," barked Odin and as he did, he grabbed Tom and shuffled him to the front.

Ahead of Tom was what looked like two derelict houses and he thought that running between those would bring him out onto the road he had parked. He set off checking Odin was with him and looked back as they jogged from the alleyway. He then noticed Odin was now holding a handgun. They reached the back of one of the houses. Tom pointed through the houses and then to the left.

"I think it's up this way?". Odin nudged him forward and Tom started off again making his way slowly up the edge of the house with Odin following. They reached the front of the house and Tom looked left and was pleased to see the car about 50 yards up on the right-hand side. He pointed ahead and turned to Odin, "Silver Toyota".

Odin nodded, "Give me the keys".

As Tom handed them to him, he nudged Tom out of the way, Odin now took the lead. He looked up and down the road and couldn't see anyone, although the sound of commotion and shouting could now be heard coming from the alleyway. Someone had obviously found the security guy with his head smashed in laying in the urinal.

"Follow me!" Odin ordered, and with that he sprinted across the main road to the same side of the road the car was parked on. Tom ran as fast as he could making sure he followed in every footstep Odin took. As they got to the other side they ducked down behind a beat-up old Dodge. Tom looked ahead and saw several cars parked on the same side before his. He was grateful that they may get some cover while making their way to the car.

Odin started to move slowly along, keeping his head down as low as he could whilst intermittently popping his head up to scout for pursuers. "Check behind," he instructed Tom.

Tom took a look back and across at the houses and saw a guy in jeans and leather jacket pop out from in between them, frantically looking up and down the street as he did. Tom nudged Odin and pointed. Odin stopped and looked up through the windows of the car that was hiding them. The man started to run across the road. Odin grabbed Tom and dragged him down in between two cars and held his finger to his mouth.

As he did he reached into his pocket and pulled out a cylinder which he fitted to the end of the handgun to silence it. He cocked the hammer and waited. They heard footsteps approaching which then stopped, then a scuff and more footsteps, but this time going away from them. As the footsteps got further away they heard a shout, "Nobody this way!"

"Are they The Order?" asked Tom.
"Not sure," said Odin "They may just be the big guys pals, but we can't risk it".

As things quietened down again Odin shuffled out back onto the footway. The hire car was now only 3 car lengths away. Tom looked at him and he nodded in the car direction. They shuffled along again Tom now constantly checking behind them. Eventually they reached the Toyota and used it as a barricade.

Tom heard the car beep as Odin pressed the fob to unlock it and it seemed to be the loudest beep he had ever heard. The lights flashed twice. Odin grimaced as if to say to Tom that it could alert their pursuers. They waited, frozen, awaiting any shouts or commotion, but none came.

Odin slowly opened the driver door and nodded his head towards the inside looking at Tom. Tom shuffled forward and slid into the car and across to the passenger seat trying to stay as low as possible. He looked over his shoulder at the corner that led to the bar and then back towards the houses which led from the alley. No movement. Odin slipped inside and put the keys in the ignition. He started the engine and put it in reverse.

The car jolted back slightly and then Odin quickly turned the wheel and edged forward slowly to maneuver out of the parking space. As he cleared the car in front, he put his foot down and the car leapt to life pushing Tom's head back. As it picked up speed Tom noticed the man in the suit suddenly appear ahead from in between the houses. He then ran out into the road and looked one way up the street and then back down in the direction that Tom and Odin were now quickly driving from.

Tom felt the car quickly jolt across the road and the acceleration make his stomach turn. The man squinted at first as the headlights blinded him, but as they got closer his face turned to shock. He saw the man put his hand around his back and pull out what looked like a gun.

The engine roared as Tom realised Odin was heading straight for him, Tom's body pushed back into the seat even harder. The man got closer in a flash and, as he aimed his gun at the car, Tom could see the whites of his eyes, and then a sudden bang and a crunch. It was then, for a split second, he saw the man's face smash and spread awkwardly across the windscreen. Tom put his hand up to protect himself from the impact, but then looked up and the man wasn't there.

He felt the car jolt the other way to straighten up and turned and looked behind. He saw a body lying in the road and then another man appeared from the houses and run to the body and bend down next to it.

Tom looked across at Odin who was focused on the road ahead. Tom looked ahead without any thoughts or words able to register in his head. The car sped away from the scene but eventually, after a mile or so, slowly dropped from a roar to a gentle hum. Tom had no idea where Odin was going, but he never asked.

Chapter 24

They had driven to a motel approximately three miles from the bar near Ferndale. Tom had a lot of questions but felt that now wasn't the right time. Odin appeared unflinchingly focused and Tom realised that he would communicate when he was ready to.

As Tom's mind flickered with flashbacks of the death he had seen in the last 48 hours, Odin pulled him out of his grisly trance by suddenly informing him that his colleague was waiting at the motel and they were going to collect him. When they arrived, Odin had first suggested Tom wait in the car, but Tom felt safer going with him; although soon wished he hadn't.

Finding Odin's colleague in the motel room, laying on the bed with his throat cut so deep that his head was barely still connected, was not exactly what Tom had hoped for. Tom had seen so much blood in the last few days he was beginning to find it unbearable.

It hadn't seemed to bother Odin who simply focused on getting his belongings and getting out. Odin had told Tom to keep a look out as he collected a large holdall, some folders and various documents, all from under the bed. As they had walked back to the car, Odin had said to Tom that he thinks The Order may have got their whereabouts from Connor; who Tom assumed was the guy in the room that had almost been decapitated.

Additionally un-nerving, was that when Odin had gone to reception to check out, he couldn't find the girl who had been working the desk. Upon closer inspection she had been found stuffed under the desk with her throat cut and hands bound. Tom was starting to understand what Odin meant by The Order being brutal killers. Tom had caught a glimpse of her, and she couldn't have been more than 18. Just working a late shift at the motel for some extra cash and found herself caught up in a deadly situation that snuffed out her innocent life in the blink of an eye. Tom had briefly thought of her parents when they find out, he shuddered.

Odin had finally ordered, "We must move now; The Order send cleaners very quickly."
Tom had look puzzled at this and Odin confirmed it to mean the people they send to get evidence of the bodies removed.

Odin had taken the driver's seat and started to drive. Tom had noted they were heading West in the direction from which he had travelled, but he asked no questions as to where exactly they were going, although, he was finding it hard to care about it at this time. They had travelled in silence for about 25 minutes when Tom suddenly asked.

"Why did you ask me to go to the toilet back in the bar?"

Odin looked round, "I'd seen the man in the suit go up to the big guy and put something in his pocket. I guessed it was money. Possibly as payment to take you out. I noticed the big guy kept watching us after that," Tom realised how oblivious he was to all of this.

"So you used me as bait?" replied Tom a little indignantly.

Odin looked around again, "I suppose so," and then diverted his eyes back onto the road.

After a short pause Odin finally looked back at Tom.

"So, I suppose you have a lot of questions?"

Tom laughed out loud, surprising himself by the outburst, but also because of the fact that the laughter was truly genuine. He wondered how he could laugh at a time like this, but he found it genuinely funny.

"You suppose right...But where do I start? I mean..." Tom laughed again and looked out the window.

"I know this is hard, I speak from experience," said Odin calmly, "You just need to be patient and eventually try to understand. In time you will understand."

"Understand what?" interrupted Tom.

"What you are."

"What I am? What the fuck does that mean?"

"Understanding what you are and learning to live with it. The only wat to truly understand what you are is in time. It's my intention to give you that time."

Tom shook his head and looked out the window at nothing but black passing trees and forest. He thought that Odin was talking in riddles and didn't have the capacity to make sense of it. Instead his mind flashed to Jenna.

"What happened to Jenna's body?" asked Tom sharply. Odin gave no response and looked ahead at the road.

"I said, what happened to Jenna's body," asked Tom again directly.

"It's not import..."

"What? Not important!" Tom swung his head round quickly to face Odin, "Not important? What happened to my wife's fucking body?"

Odin sighed and looked at Tom and then looked back at the road, reluctantly he then answered.

"We have people that we work with, mafia connections, underground organisations. They provide cleaners. If something nasty goes down they go in and make it look like nothing happened. The Order use their own. We are very secret organisations and its vital we maintain a covert existence. It can't be like a wild west showdown."

"What happened to Jenna?" Tom said slowly and sternly.

"A cleaning team was dispatched and spent the night cleaning. Bodies removed, blood cleaned, mess cleaned."

"You are not answering my question," said Tom.

"Come on, Tom. Do you want me to spell it out?"

"Vat of acid? Buried in woods? Thrown into the sea?"

Tom looked at Odin, who was aware of this, but he never diverted his eyes from the road. Tom looked ahead and saw that they were leaving Westmont. Nothing else was said for another 15 minutes until Odin broke the silence again.

"Do you want to ask me questions or do you just want me to tell you?"

Tom laughed sarcastically and looked out if his side window, again at nothing in particular, as there was nothing to see in the dark. His mind raced with questions, but he genuinely did not know where to start.

"By the way," said Odin, "I have a letter for you. It's a forged letter from Jenna telling you she has met someone else and she has left you. Did you ring her mobile from your house and then again several times from your mobile?"

"What? A forged letter?" quizzed Tom.

"Yes, we have professionals that do stuff like that. When they cleaned up they got some documents with her writing on. Pretty easy stuff. You needed an alibi. Now you've got one. Did you ring her mobile like I instructed?"

"Er...Yeah, I was confused as to why but I..."

"Good, so listen. This is important. Your version is that you and Jenna had been having relationship issues and you believe she was having an affair. You came home and saw the letter and she has left you. You tried to call her but no answer. Tried again. Then went to Pittsburgh, as you believed the person she was having an affair with was from that area. Just say she had been going there for work reasons. You then rang her parents and asked if she had been in touch with them, which you can do tomorrow. Explain to them what's happened and say you can't find her. They will probably ring the cops and report her missing, but you will also do that. Cops will probably see it for what it is and tell you to move on. They may visit the house, but they won't find anything. Our cleaners left clothes strewn across the place and drawers open. Looks like someone packed in a rush. And now you have the letter as proof."

Odin leant across into the back seat and picked up one of the files. He put it on Tom's lap. Inside was an envelope with the word, 'Tom' written on it exactly in Jenna's writing.

He slipped it open and started to read and then stopped after a few sentences. He took a deep breath and shook his head. There was nothing he could say. It looked exactly like her writing and he felt the hairs on his body stand up.
"Keep it safe," said Odin sternly.
Do you know if she was part of them?" asked Tom
"We were never really sure?" replied Odin, "After she contacted us, she was the first one we tracked but she never showed any signs of being a 'foster'"
"A what?" quizzed Tom.
"A foster. It's the term The Order use for the person closest to the portal. Usually a mother, father, sibling, husband or wife, depends on the circumstances. It's not that uncommon for a husband or wife foster to be organised by The Order. A set up. Someone within that can infiltrate the portals life and manipulate them on behalf of The Order, like an arranged marriage, but just one of the parties is unaware."
"You mean Jenna could've married me for them?" Tom asked, shocked.
"Yeah, we aren't sure, but it can happen. Although it needs to be well organised. It's an old-fashioned technique but still used. Today though they normally infiltrate by threat or bribe. They are much more direct these days...And brutal"

Tom suddenly wondered if his marriage to Jenna been fake. A sham marriage for her to do their work. He remembered back to Vegas and how keen she was to get married and that she had pushed him into it. It was so hard to take in. He thought back to countless conversations they had had, trying to make sense of it or if they gave him any clues.

A few minutes passed and Tom's thoughts prompted him to continue.
"She kept saying I was going mad", staring straight ahead, "She said I needed to see someone."
Odin cut in quickly, "May have been her way of trying to get you to be more accepting and co-operative for The Order? It's the foster that will try and keep the portal on the straight and narrow and in a lot of cases move them physically from place to place as required."
"That makes sense," Tom interjected pragmatically, "She was desperate for me to take the job in Chicago, almost demanded I take it," Odin nodded and Tom continued.
"Before she died she told me not to trust Rutherford," Tom turned to Odin, "That's my boss."

"I know. And one person you want to stay well clear of. Our agents have been tracking him for some time. He seems to be way up within the structure and moves in high places. Known for his brutality and complete and utter devotion to The Order. A very dangerous man."

Tom shook his head. He had been so close to Rutherford, "He was in my house with me before I went to see my nom. Telling me how important I was and how he would look after me."

"Exactly," said Odin excitedly, "He is the man you were assigned to. You are his portal. His angel. And him and his little minions will do everything they can to keep you care free and in line so you can carry out their work. He will have people all around, pulling strings and making sure you are looked after. Any sign of unwilling or not coping then they will pounce to resolve. Any portals that can't take it or, as you did, start to realise all is not right, they will eliminate. And take out the foster too," Odin stopped with a confused look on his face, "The only confusing thing is they tried to kill you on your way to work when we first intervened; but you say he spoke to you at your home?"

"Er…Yeah, that was after I was nearly killed in the city," said Tom.

"Unusual," interrupted Odin pragmatically, "The decision to terminate a portal comes from up high, way above Rutherford… Well as far as our intelligence tells us. It seems he really does have a thing for you. There's a lot of intelligence on you, Tom. Our agents have picked up a lot of activity within The Order related to you."

Tom couldn't believe what he was hearing but he had to admit a lot of what was being said did make sense.

"I never trusted Jenna towards the end. I had heard her on the phone, and she was being very secretive. When I told her Rutherford was coming to see me at home, she seemed suddenly worried and got out quickly"

Odin blew out his cheeks and shook his head, "She knew. As soon as he got involved directly she knew she had messed up. She also knew what they do to fosters that fail. Rutherford would be pulling the strings from afar and doing his bit at work, but ultimately it's down to her."

Tom looked at Odin, "But why? What was she getting out of it?" he asked with a hint of desperation in his voice.

Odin shrugged his shoulders, "If she was approached and worked alone then probably a threat to her life. But if working with others then money. On the payroll. And lots of money. Normally a huge lump sum."

"She must've been on the payroll," said Tom, deflated, "Another guy we knew, Phil, he was there, and they were talking. The things they said to each other. When I got with Jenna he was, as far as I knew, the boyfriend of one of her friends," Tom shook his head and sighed heavily.

"Probably both on The Orders payroll," interjected Odin, "Jenna was the foster and he would've been what we call a 'guide'. Someone inside The Order who can influence and help the foster from afar. It's often a very intricate network of people in place for one portal."

"So they knew each other personally" said Tom, "but…From the things they said they were also working together. That was until Phil gave the order to have her killed."

Tom looked down at his lap trying to quell the emotion that suddenly started to arise within him.

"She came back just as I was about to die. Saved my life." Tom paused and then in a broken voice said, "I just can't believe she's gone," and a tear ran down his face.

Odin never spoke and continued to drive into the night through the deep forests. He decided not to tell Tom anymore; nor prompt him to ask any more questions. He felt that Tom had seen and heard enough for now.

The drove for a few hours until Odin announced he had decided to lay low and get off the main route. He took a few local roads for a mile or so and then drove along a dirt track into some deeper forest where he found a clearing and pulled off, turned off the engine and the headlights.

He reached into his holdall and got out a handgun which alarmed Tom. Odin assured him it was just a precaution and then Odin's only instruction to Tom was, "Get some sleep."

Tom never questioned what they were doing and what the hell was going on. He was too exhausted to question anything right now, so he just retracted his chair and lay there. Cold, scared and confused.

Chapter 25

He wasn't sure how long he'd been asleep when a jolt rocked Tom awake. He looked up and could see what looked like a diner directly in front of him.

"Sorry," said Odin, "I need coffee."

"That's fine," said Tom, as he sat up and stretched his back realising his seat was still inclined and he realised he hadn't woken up when Odin had decided to leave the forest where they had laid low for the night.

He rubbed his eyes and noticed it had got lighter. They both got out and started to walk to the entrance across the empty car park. Tom noticed Odin was carrying his holdall. The diner and the parking area didn't appear busy and only contained two other cars and, across the far side, two parked trucks with the drivers talking.

"Where are we?" asked Tom.

"On the outskirts of Lancaster" replied Odin, looking round as he held the door open for Tom.

"Where are we headed?" asked Tom, still rubbing his eyes and face.

Odin smiled, "Don't worry about that now. Let's get inside."

As they walked in the old lady who was waitressing looked up and smiled sincerely at them, grabbed two menus and followed them down to a booth at the far end. Tom noticed Odin looking around as he went. The waitress introduced herself as Maggie as they sat down, and she asked what she could get them. Odin ordered two coffees. As Maggie was away fetching the coffee Odin scoured the menu. Tom thought he'd best do the same but wasn't particularly hungry.

Maggie returned with the coffee and Odin ordered eggs, bacon and waffles, whilst Tom settled for pancakes. Maggie smiled and left them alone. The only other diner was sat at the breakfast bar and was an old, unkept guy who hadn't even acknowledged them come in.

Tom sipped his coffee and immediately felt a rush of life go through him.

"You wanna talk?" asked Odin, looking up at Tom from the special's menu.

"I suppose so," replied Tom, not sure if he was or not.

"Well, I know I told you some stuff in the bar and some more since then, but I realise it was a lot to take in. So I suppose I may as well explain a bit more...if you feel...."

Tom nodded, "I'm ok... Just continue"

Odin sipped his coffee, "Ok, just hear me out. It's difficult but just let me speak."

Tom took another sip of coffee and then a deep breath.

"You are an angel, Tom. You were born and chosen to act as a portal, to help God move on earth..." Tom went to speak but Odin raised his finger and shook his head then continued. "Look, we don't know yet how they do it. How you are chosen and what sets you apart. But, you are what is traditionally referred to as a 'Dark Angel'. A helper of God. A conduit. You help deliver wrath in, what The Order say is 'In the name of God'."

Tom sipped his coffee and wondered if it was ever going to reach a point where he believed any of what he was being told.

Odin continued, "I asked you before have heard the phrase "God moves in mysterious ways"; well he does. Through humans. Or more specifically through dark angels, or now more commonly termed as portals. Portals allow his work to be done through them."
Tom couldn't speak. He had lots to ask and say but he just couldn't speak. He felt as though this was all a joke or a cruel prank and soon enough someone with a microphone would burst in with a cameraman behind them.

"Your mother told me about strange circumstances in which you felt you'd affected other people. Well, you have. I can absolutely assure you that you have."
Tom sipped his coffee and then spoke, "It was weird. I did things that I know I had done. But then it...Well, to me I had done them, but to anyone else I hadn't. In some cases, not even a big deal. One of them was a work report. Then I got my brake light fixed and..."
Tom's voice started to break. He looked out of the window and took a deep breath.
"One afternoon I painted the fence at front of my house and when Jenna came home...It wasn't done. I just...I don't know"
"Don't worry," interrupted Odin, "You aren't going mad."
"But why was it the people that knew I did those things then died?!" Tom said, starting to get anxious, "A guy at work.... I phoned to say I wouldn't be in and spoke to him. But work never get the message and then before I could ask him, he's gone!!
"Whoa...Calm down," Odin said, as he looked around and noticed Maggie had looked up at them. Odin smiled at her and she smiled back and carried on what she was doing.

"Tom, just calm down. Those circumstances were not coincidences. They were a planned connection. You were moved close enough to those people for it to happen. Those coincidences were the link. The key to open the door. We are talking about an almighty power only a few humans on earth truly understand. That only a few have learnt to control. It's like opening a channel to god. But, it is not an exact science and there can be problems with time shifts." Odin noted the confused look on Tom's face.

"OK, look. The portal must be close enough to be symbiotic with gods power which comes through a quantum realm. Most portals won't even notice it, and if they do it's minimal, and can be shrugged off as odd, or even in a lot of cases 'déjà vu'. But it can sometimes go wrong and a physical paradox is caused. It was obvious to you as your own time has obviously shifted too much. Those incidents were paranormal imbalances that occurred when creating the circumstances or scenario for contact between the angel and the sinner. The science is out there but the true understanding of the exact details is sketchy and not properly understood. But we have some real brains within The Network. They suggest that present time is filtered and then overlaid to create the link, but the physical paradox creates an overlap in time. It shouldn't be noticed but obviously something with you wasn't quite right and it's all been too obvious. What we call a 'time lapse'."

Tom smiled, to him they were just words which he didn't understand, but he felt, despite this all being too unbelievable and confusing, he should, at least, ask some questions.
"So, things I thought I had done, I actually hadn't done them? Or had I?"
"To you, yes, to others, no. The physical paradox created two timelines, one which you thought was correct and another which everyone else thought was correct. It's technical."

Tom still never really understood it and it showed.
Odin continued, "Forget it now. Each time it happened it's like a blink of an eye on the history of life itself. It's gone. And in time you can do research, and we will provide you with heaps of stuff on it. But that's not really important right now."
Tom interrupted, "So, go back. You said 'Angel'. What do you mean?"
"Well, an angel. Exactly what it means. A celestial being, an intermediary between God and humanity, carrying out Gods tasks. But, in your case, a dark angel. It's an old-fashioned term and, as I said, now they more commonly known as portals. But, technically, you are an angel".

Tom laughed and shook his head then took a large gulp of coffee as it cooled. Despite everything he still never fully knew if Odin was mad and talking rubbish or whether to believe him, "So I suppose this is not a good time to tell you I am an atheist?"

Odin's shoulders sagged; making it clear to Tom he was hoping he would take it more seriously.

Suddenly then Tom remembered the scroll his mum had given him, "Oh, look, my mom gave me this before she died," and he reached inside his jacket pocket. He pulled out the small black box and handed it to Odin.

Odin smiled and nodded and as he opened the box and took out the scroll he spoke.
"Your birth scroll. It's got your number on it."
"Number?" asked Tom.
"Yes, the number you are given by The Order. Each angel or portal is assigned a number and its used as a reference. I will take this and dispose of it."
"What?" interrupted Tom angrily, "My mom gave me that!"
"No, Tom, believe me you don't want this. It ties you to them. Your mother may have given it to you, but they gave it to her. The day you were born, or maybe a day or two after. They would've written your date of birth on it and given it to her as a reminder that you are there property. By disposing of this you break a bond and separate yourself from them."

Tom couldn't help but feel sad. He had never really known what it was or what it meant but he just knew it was something his mother had given him, and so had held it dear. He now felt like a part of her had been taken away but, if Odin was right, then he realised that he never wanted it.

Odin then continued, "When angels are born, The Order somehow know and then make contact...Look, we don't yet understand how they know when angels are born. We are trying to develop our intelligence on this. But from that point your life has been manipulated at each stage for you to be in certain places at certain times. Then the incidents are paranormal imbalances in order to create circumstances or scenario for contact between angel and sinner."
"But, why are they sinners? I mean, I had known H for years, he wouldn't hurt a fly."
Odin interjected sternly, "Stop. Do not even think about that. All people have a past. People do things they shouldn't; it's not for us to judge or question why."

Tom sighed, he felt tired and physically and mentally drained. He was struggling to take it all in and looked out if the diner window at nothing much in particular.

Odin leant in towards him to get his attention back.

"Look, I told you, I was the same as you...I am the same as you. Things started going very weird for me a long time ago. When I was a young boy. It's a long story but it's similar to yours and it happened to me. Dreams, weird time shifts, people around me dying. But I knew, I knew it wasn't right. I lost everything. My family and friends. I was betrayed by people I loved. But someone never gave up on me and gave my details to The Network. That person paid with their life, but I was helped. Contacted and pulled out just before The Order got to me. But later, things settled, and I finally accepted my situation, but I was still confused and needed to know for sure. So, I did some research on the people that had died, and I wish I hadn't. I found out things I should never have known."

As Odin finished speaking, he realised Maggie was approaching with a coffee pot to top them up. He smiled as she approached and nodded to Tom. Tom looked round and sat up and tried his best to not look like someone who had been told what he just had been. He smiled. Maggie topped them up and told them their food was just being plated up.

Tom didn't add milk and just drunk the coffee black. He thought about Red, Frank, Mrs McGeedy and Conway. What could they have done that was so bad? It made Tom not want to believe Odin. But Odin knew too much and everything he said had a point and made sense. Tom sat back and took a deep breath.

Tom and Odin sat in silence for a few minutes before Maggie appeared with their food, delivering it to the table with her usual charm. Tom still wasn't hungry, but he ate the pancakes reluctantly. They both ate in silence. As they were eating several different people came in and Tom noticed that Odin checked every one of them out. As soon as he returned to his food, Tom relaxed again. Tom finished before Odin but never spoke to him, he just stared out of the window onto the road cutting through the forest that had now started to take on its usual shades of greens as the sun slowly started to pop from the horizon.

Odin eventually finished and took a large swig from his coffee. He leant over and grabbed his holdall, reached in and pulled out some documents. He looked around the diner and then back at Tom.

"I know how you feel. It's all way out there and it will take some time to sink in. But you are part of a war that has been going on for centuries. Through all the ages. There are scripts, images and evidence that prove this is real. Look..."

Tom picked up the documents, the first three colour copies, one of a religious renaissance painting with a note in the bottom corner

'Michelangelo – The Last Judgement'. The next, which Tom recognised again as being a renaissance painting, with a scribbled note 'Raphael – Transfiguration'. The third what appeared to be angel with a sword and looked to be slaying a devil, the written 'Guido Reni's St Michael'.

Underneath were more documents, but in black and white copy. One with a scribbled note 'Giving of the 7 bowls' and another with a note 'Guido Reni – Massacre of innocents' to which Tom starred at more than the others.
"That's an important indicator." Said Odin pointing at it, "Theorists argue this could indicate angels or persons being manipulated to carry out the extermination of sinners…Although some argue otherwise."

Tom looked underneath at the final documents which appeared to be religious and scientific conspiracy and theory articles from the internet. One titled 'Are angels real? The other 'Can science prove god exists?' The final document titled 'Proof angels exist'.

Each were a few pages long and Tom scanned them he realised there wasn't a lot of evidence, just theory and conspiracy. He laughed quietly and shook his head.
"What do you want me to say," he asked Odin.

Odin sensed Tom's attitude was a little sarcastic and knew what he was implying.
"Look, I am not saying this is evidence. I don't expect you to look at these and believe me. It's just a starting point. Indicators from history and current writing on all of this."
Tom paused, stared back down at the documents and shuffled them as if to inspect them again but without much concentration. Odin continued.
"Just put them in your bag and use them when you get time to do some research. It's important to understand the enormity of all this. But you have to start somewhere. As time goes by you will get more detailed information to help you understand. It's the best I can for now."

Tom shook his head, gathered the documents together and gently tapped them on the table to get them neat and straight. As he put them in his bag he asked another question.
"What did my mom say when she called you?" asked Tom
Odin wiped his face with a napkin and then threw it on his plate.
"She told me that she needs my help. That her son is marked and is under control of The Order. She said his wife rang her and told her about dreams, weird stuff, thinking you are going mad. That your wife wanted her to call you to get you to see a therapist. But your mother knew exactly

what it was. She has known all along. From the moment you were born. And in her bid to help you she contacted us."

"How though? How did she get in contact with you?" asked Tom.

"Agents. Double Agents. It's a very intricate system. The Network are an underground resistance. But we operate in a world of secrecy, deceit and betrayal. We had a guy on the inside of The Order. He got to your mother and gave her my contact. She told me that it was her only way of helping you. She probably realised she had nothing to lose. I still am not sure why Jenna rang her though, but I think Jenna was slowly turning from The Order. She saved you after all, which I think was the moment she truly turned."

Tom looked down. He thought of his mum and Jenna and wished they were here so he could speak to them. Odin broke him from his thoughts. "Your mother protected you. She knew how dangerous The Order were and tried to create a life for you where, what you are and what you are capable of, wouldn't affect you. She may have known Jenna was part of them, I don't know. She wanted you to have a good life. She said she was heartbroken when she found out you wasn't coping…"

Odin noticed Tom's eyes filling with tears. It stopped him. He took a sip of coffee and gave Tom time to steady himself.

"Look Tom, she couldn't explain it to you. It would've been too hard to. And if she had then she would've put you all in danger. The Order had her tied up too tight. Then when the time came, they manipulated you into the job at New York, then the job in Chicago, and the rest is history."

Tom scoffed, "And there was me thinking I got those jobs out of merit."

Odin laughed. It was the first time Tom had seen any real emotion from him.

"So, were none of my friends or associates real?" asked Tom

"Of course!" said Odin emphatically, "Many people would've had no clue, and would've been with you for who you are. But…" Odin deliberately paused

"What??" asked Tom sternly

Odin sat back and took a deep breath.

"But, you also don't know if any of them were guides. Family or friends. Could have been genuine or could have been working for, or threatened by, The Order. People around, just to keep you grounded and in place ready for The Order to do what they want you to do."

"So basically, my whole life has been staged?" said Tom angrily and Odin sensed Tom was getting frustrated.

"Tom, stop thinking about that. Over time it will settle, and you will come to terms wi…."

Tom rose abruptly from the table and walked towards the toilets. Odin knew how hard this was. He slowly started to put the documents away in his holdall and waited for Tom to return. A
short while later Tom came out and Odin noticed his hair was swept back as he had obviously thrown water over his face. Tom came back and sat down. Odin waited for him to speak.

They looked at each other.
"I know when the people die," Tom said, very matter of fact.

Odin never said anything, Tom continued, "I go cold. And a feeling comes up from my toes and hits my stomach. It's like a feeling I cannot describe apart from the sense that a person would get at the exact second they knew they were going to die. It hurts. It's crippling. It's a deep, primal despair that I don't think many humans ever experience," Tom stopped as he noted Odin was nodding
"I know," said Odin, "I know. I had similar. Part of the reason why they tried to kill me. And still want to. But, I know…" Odin's voice trailed off and Tom believed him to be sincere.

Odin's mind started racing and memories that he had put to the back of his mind a long time ago started to surface. He hated this part of what he did. Each time he pulled a person from the grasp of The Order and had to explain what was going on it took him back. Back to that dark, foreboding place. Odin then looked up and took a deep breath and smiled at Tom. Neither of them spoke for a couple of minutes.

Eventually Tom broke the silence.
"I just can't believe all of this. I am just, well, it just doesn't make sense. I just can't see how I am truly connected."
Odin interrupted, "Ok. Think of how you may have been part of their death. Where were they? Where were you before-hand? I guarantee you will find that you moved closer to them just prior to them dying."

Tom thought of H. He had worked with him for years in New York. The strange occurrence with the file, and his death happened just prior to moving to Chicago. But it was shortly after moving to Chicago that Red, Frank, McGeedy and Conway died. Tom made sense of the last three, if he believed what Odin was saying, it was very clear that Tom was moved to Chicago to be in that place at that time.

"How many were there?" asked Odin, getting a pen and blank piece of paper from his holdall and handing them to Tom, "Write their names and where they died."

Tom took the pen and paper and exhaled, trying to think, trying to sort all of the confused mass inside his head.

"Five in all. One in New York, Harold Tweddle, a good friend of mine. That was before I moved, and then three in Chicago; Frank Harrison, a lady I only know as Mrs McGeedy and Conway Harrison two where I lived and one at work." Tom scribbled the names and places as Odin had asked as he spoke.

"But..." Tom paused

"What?" asked Odin anxiously

"Another. A man called Red. His real name was? Oh, damn, what was it?" Tom thought hard and then it came to him, "Charlie Redmond!" and scribbled the name on the list. "But...I drove a long way to Indianapolis to see him and it was..." Tom stopped

Odin looked at Tom, "Did you see your friend?"

"Yes, Davy. A childhood friend..."

"What happened?" asked Odin, then taking a large sip of his fresh coffee.

"He contacted me. Out of the blue. He said he had found my name on Facebook and so sent me a message. I went there to see him. We had a night out and fishing and...It was just a weekend thing. But, it was on my way home, my taillight was out, and the police sent me to get it fixed. A local man, Red, he did it at his garage, I saw it with my own eyes. But then it wasn't fixed, the police sent me back but...." Tom started to panic.

"Whoa!" Odin put his arm on Tom's shoulder, "Easy. Just stay calm. Don't worry too much about that now..."

Tom jumped back in, "But you said I had been manipulated. You talked about fosters and guides. I moved to Chicago through work. Rutherford was involved. Jenna, Phil. I get that. But Davy...This was Indianapolis, it's nothing to do with Chicago..."

Odin raised his finger and interrupted but lowered the volume of his voice.

"Look I get where you are going. But think about it. Chicago is closer to Indianapolis than New York. It's quite clearly a move closer. Who is your friend? Davy?" Tom nodded anxiously, "He could be involved. He could have been used to get you there. Or he could be one of them. You don't know. I don't know."

Odin took the pen and paper from Tom and wrote Indianapolis next to Charlie Redmond. As he did, Tom got his phone from his pocket and showed Davy's text about meeting up to Odin. Tom watched Odin's eyes scan the texts. He gave the phone back to Tom. Tom realised exactly what Odin was thinking and Odin did not have to tell Tom what he was thinking. He knew that they both realised.

Odin finished his coffee and took out money from his holdall and laid it on a small plate on their table. Tom was going to argue about going halves but realised it seemed a slightly trivial matter under the circumstances. "Let's go," said Odin, but as he went to get up Tom grabbed his arm and he slowly sat back down.

Tom stared at him for a moment and then spoke.
"Why do you do this? What do you get?" asked Tom.
Odin smiled, "What choice do I have? I lost everything. I am on the run. I am wanted by The Order. I wouldn't last a week on my own. The Network supported me and then gave me a worth, a focus. I recall how lost and alone I was, and I want to stop other people feeling that. I want to stop The Order ruining innocent lives. It's the least I can do."
"So, what happens to me now?" asked Tom forlornly
Odin smiled, "All will come to pass," replied Odin, "Don't worry now. But it's the reason why I told you we need you alive."

Tom never really understood what that meant or even if it answered his question, but he never pushed for a clearer answer.

As they got outside, they both realised what a beautiful day was emerging. A chilly breeze that had been cutting through was starting to lift and a gentle warm haze was starting to evolve. Odin took a big deep breath and exhaled and then smiled at Tom. Tom smiled back.

Odin took several glances around as they walked to the car and bleeped the car open as they approached, then threw the holdall in the boot. Tom walked to the passenger side and went to grab the car door.
"You need to ring Jenna's parents. To create the alibi." Odin ordered and, as he spoke, Tom's stomach felt a pang of nerves hit.
Odin continued, "Tell them what I said. You think she had been having an affair you came home to the note. You came to this area on a hunch but can't find her. Ask if she has been in touch. The rest will fall into place," the last part of what Odin said was almost inaudible as he was getting into the car.

Tom hated it when he was so pragmatic when discussing things that normal people find so gut-wrenchingly difficult to talk about or do. Tom opened the passenger door and leant in, "But what if she gets suspicious? What if she asks questions?"
"She won't," replied Odin, "And just tell her what you know. Stick to the facts. You've asked about but nobody has seen her. Tell her what's in the note, just do it."

Tom shook his head and got into the car, "Outside!" barked Odin. "It's personal. I don't want to hear."

Tom sighed and got back out, as he did, he uttered, "It's going to break their hearts," and slammed the door. As he said it he thought that the comment won't even register with Odin.

It had been an awful call. Jenna's mum, Cindy, could hardly speak due to crying. Not only had she been told her daughter was an adulterer, but also that she was missing. As Tom spoke, he couldn't get the image of Jenna's dead body out of his mind. That image plus the despair in Cindy's voice made him cry and, for at least two minutes, no words were spoken from either person. Tom could also hear Jenna's father, Bob, in the background asking questions. At one point he came on and asked Tom what the hell was going on, but Cindy had obviously taken back control of the phone and told Bob not to worry.

Eventually the crying stopped, and the conversation resumed. Tom has asked if Jenna had been in touch already knowing the answer and, obviously, Cindy confirmed she hadn't.

Tom had promised Cindy that he would keep looking and if she contacted him, he would let her know. She had said the same and told him she would immediately report it to the police. Tom said to her to tell them that he has a note telling him she has left him. He said it to ensure things were clarified, but he also hoped that if she told the police that, then the case won't get the attention it deserves, and they will leave him alone.

Tom finally gave Cindy a boost when he told her that he was sure Jenna will contact them to tell them herself, and that Jenna is obviously confused at the moment and not thinking straight. He felt her react positively to that. She told him she had wished they would've told them they were having difficulties, but Tom said they were too proud and had thought things would straighten out.

At the end Cindy had simply said, "I'm so sorry, Tom"
Tom replied, "So am I, Cindy, so am I."

As they drove out of the parking lot and away Tom noticed a small traditional white beamed church on the opposite side of the road. The message board adjacent to the road simply read, "God is among us - Always."

Normally, Tom would not have taken any notice of it but, under the circumstances, it resonated with him, and suddenly took on a whole new level of relevance. He wondered if he would ever really believe and understand what Odin was telling him. If he would ever believe what he was and what he was now involved in.

In the distance Tom noticed dark grey storm clouds gathering which suddenly flashed as the sheet lighting exploded across the sky behind them. They made him nervous. A storm was approaching. But Tom suddenly wondered how on earth he was going to navigate his own storm. A chill ran through him as he realised his future was suddenly out of his control.

Chapter 26

They cruised along through varying environments of dense lush forest, vast open farmland and small towns that were there and then gone again. The beautiful weather made Tom wish he was just on his way to work. That this was just all a nightmare that he would wake up from.

Odin had decided to head towards Cincinnati and then, before they reached the city, head back out North West to Indianapolis. It would take longer but it was to try and keep their route more random to avoid any locations which The Order may have pre-empted as their arrival point.

About 15 minutes after they had set off Tom's phone had rung, it was Jenna's mum, Cindy. She had informed him that she had called the police and explained what had happened and they had asked for a current photo to be sent to by e-mail address to the missing persons bureau. Cindy had said that Bob had already taken their most recent photo off of her down to the shops to get it scanned. She had said the lady was very nice and the case would be assigned to an officer who will start to make some enquiries. Although the lady had also said the fact that there was a note meant that it may not be a top priority. Exactly what Tom had wanted to hear.

She had finished by saying that she was sure Jenna would contact her soon enough when she gets her head in the right place. Tom had agreed with her, but it was difficult to sound genuine as the guilt ran through him. which was almost unbearable. Knowing that, despite her optimism and them sending the e-mail to the police, Cindy and Bob would never see their daughter ever again.

The thought had flashed across his mind that it would be better to tell them the truth. But then Tom immediately realised that this was ridiculous as he was struggling to believe it all himself. He started to think of Davy. Was he involved? Had his contact with Tom been simply to get him to Minneapolis for the purposes of The Order? Or was it genuine? Odin had said that not everyone in his life was involved. But Davy's recent message to Tom that he needed help did seem unusual and coincidental in its timing.

Tom was still not sure if he believed Odin about The Order anyway, but he did know that someone was after him. And Davy's text fell directly into the suspicious category and needed to be dealt with carefully.

His thoughts instinctively prompted him to seek advice from Odin.

"So, what should I do about Davy?"

Odin looked round at Tom, "Forget him."

Once again Tom felt frustration at Odin's pragmatism.

"But he's my oldest and best friend," replied Tom sharply, "He could be in genuine trouble?"

"But it's too dangerous to find out. He already contacted you out of the blue once before, now he's done it again. It's too risky."

"What? I can't even see my friends now?" Tom noticed a look of frustration on Odin's face.

"You don't get it do you, Tom?"

"Get what?" he asked.

Odin sighed and shook his head. He never said another word but Tom realised that he had obviously missed something quite monumental. "What?" asked Tom again frustrated.

Odin clicked the indicator down up and Tom noticed a lay-by ahead roughly 200 yards away. The car slowed and Odin pulled in, parked up, switched the engine off and turned to him.

"Look, Tom…I am not sure what your take on all this is and, well, I suppose I could've been clearer before now. But, your life, as you know it, is finished. There is no going back to the life you had. It has gone. And you now have two choices. You are either with The Network or you are not. Your life now is on the run, laying low, moving in the shadows. Going from place to place, trying to stay one step ahead of The Order, who are hunting you with the intention of killing you and anyone that helps you."

Tom suddenly realised that deep down he knew this but had just not yet not allowed himself to accept it.

Odin continued, "Tom, The Order have people working for them who are professional killers. Highly trained, slick and organised. Utterly focused and insanely dedicated to their cause. They simply do not stop, and they do not discriminate. They have no thought for collateral damage and who gets caught up. You are now their target and they will not stop until you are dead. You can run, but you have to stop sometime. Evading them in the long term is almost impossible. Now, you can try do that with me and The Network or you can try it on your own. But your odds of staying alive are much higher if you join The Network. The fact that you are sitting in front of me now is testament to that. So, you can either go it alone, take a gamble and see how long you last, or you can become one of us. You will still be on the run, moving, staying out of sight; but you will have our help. We can support you with contacts, information, tip offs, finance. We have a network of agents and support. I already have a contact lined up for you."

The sudden realisation of exactly what was happening was now hitting home. It was like Tom's life flashed in front of his eyes. Images of him at home with his mum, dad and sister. Days out, beaches, boats, trips, holidays, Christmas', birthdays. All flashing through his head. All of it gone. Even though he still had those memories, and that was all they were, they somehow suddenly felt very distant. More distant than they had ever been. Tom suddenly felt like everything up to this point was no longer real, he felt like he had lived someone else's life.

Odin broke the silence, "There is nothing else for you now. All your ties with the past are broken. And the ones that you still have will have to be broken..."
This comment startled Tom back to the car in the present.
"What do you mean?" he asked, suddenly feeling anxious.

Odin took a deep breath, "Well, The Order controlled your past, growing up, people you met, places you visited, jobs you had. You don't know if any of those people were or are still connected to The Order or not. You can't just go back home, carry on and go back to work. It's all controlled. That's why I said to forget Davy. It's too risky. And other old friends, do not contact them or respond if they contact you. And your sister..."
Tom jumped in "What? Cut her out completely too?"

Odin looked back ahead staring at the woods in front of them, he never spoke. Tom stared at him but realised his silence said everything it needed to.

Odin spoke but stayed looking ahead.
"It's time to make a decision, Tom."
Tom suddenly felt hot and his mouth became dry, "So you are asking me to give up everything?"
Odin Looked back at Tom, "No," he answered, very sternly, startling Tom a little, "I am not asking you to give up everything. That has been done. There was no choice. Your 'everything' has already been taken, it's gone, and you need to accept that."
Odin paused and looked straight into Tom's eyes "I am asking you to decide which path you take now, the one with me or the one without me"

Tom sat back and felt his body slump onto the chair. What choice did he have? If he took his own path he knew he wouldn't last 24 hours. But he was suddenly intrigued as to why Odin cared so much.

"Does it matter to you what I decide?"

"Of course," answered Odin immediately, "Because all of this would have been in vain! And because we lose a good man. Your mother risked everything coming to us. She knew by doing so The Order would have you killed. But she hoped and prayed that we could get you out and you could live your life with a little sense of freedom. Not being manipulated and used to bring death on others. Or be controlled or end up like your father…"

Odin suddenly stopped. He looked away from Tom as if he was going to change the subject, but Tom felt that if he held on Odin would continue. But Odin remained silent.

"What?" asked Tom with a sense of frustration.

Odin sighed, "I hoped I wouldn't have to tell you this but, she told me that your father was very proud, and he loved you very much….." Tom felt unsettled. He squirmed in his seat.

"And?" he interjected.

"Well, she explained to me that your father found out somehow, when you were a teenager. The Order contacted him at some point to try and get him on board, as another guide. But he responded badly, threatened to report them to the police, which your she knew was futile. They have police connections…Connections throughout authority and establishment…"

"What are you getting at?," asked Tom, now getting very frustrated.

Odin continued "They told him to sell his business and move to New York. They had asked your mother to persuade him, but she couldn't, he loved New Jersey too much, so they stepped in. But your father wasn't receptive. He kept making threats and said you wouldn't be their pawn and he would go to the police and…." Odin cut off and turned his heads to look out of his side window.

Tom suddenly felt panic. He wasn't sure if he understood but instinctively he somehow realised what Odin was going to say, "Tom, your father's boat accident. I am really sorry. Your mother told me it wasn't an accident"

He felt like he had been hit with a hammer. He froze. He felt emotion inside him rising, wanting to scream, start to throw punches and kicks, but that same emotion immobilised him. He was trembling with anger and could feel his teeth grinding.

"They told her if your father doesn't start complying, they would kill him. She desperately tried to persuade him, but he wouldn't listen. But they told her if she warned him, they would kill you and your sister too. She felt she had no choice. They made it look like an accident. She knew all along and she had to hold that secret inside her whole life until…Well, until she told me"

Tears streamed down Tom's face. He shook with anger and then let out a wail of anguish.

Odin had had this type conversation with many people before, but he couldn't recall one being this hard. He had hoped Tom would've realised himself, but some people, in all of the confusion, just don't see the wood for the trees.
Tom began to sob uncontrollably. Odin leant forward and grabbed him. He pulled him close and let Tom cry out on his shoulder. He stayed holding him until Tom had no tears left in his body.

Chapter 27

As they slowly cruised back west it had been quiet. Tom had been struggling with the concept that his father had been murdered and there is nothing he, nor anyone else, could do about it. The accident had been investigated and a steering fault had been judged as the cause, and this was all now so long ago. Tom felt frustration that he lived his life thinking it had been an accident. But there was nothing he could do now.

Tom had thought about forgetting all this and just going to the police and telling them everything. But he realised how ridiculous he would sound and would probably end up being framed for Jenna's murder and put in a lunatic asylum.

This was almost certainly one of the many weapons that The Order used to maintain their existence and power; the fact that any person reporting them to the police would simply be ushered out and labelled a crackpot. Plus, as Odin had already alluded to, The Order had connections within authority. Tom would just have to accept it all and move on as best he could.

After sitting in silence with his mind racing and thinking about different situations and scenarios, thinking about his past and his future; he had started to feel a little more focused.

Finding out his father had been murdered by The Order was hard to take, but it also acted as a cleanser. He had started to feel much sharper of mind and more alert. Tom realised that somehow, with little more to lose, he had started to accept the situation and that his best option is just to go along with Odin and see where it takes him. He had nothing left anyway, no wife, no kids, no job and no family ties. It was a now case of just accepting everything Odin told him and going with it; even if he was still struggling to believe it. He had suddenly realised he had no other choice.

The hours and miles passed then when they started to get close to Indianapolis Odin asked Tom if he was OK. It had been the kick that Tom had needed. He had smiled and turned to Odin and nodded, "So, where do we go from here?"

It had been the answer that Odin had been hoping for. He had known Tom's mind had been racing with questions and the battle to accept what, in normal circumstances, would be completely unacceptable and impossible to believe. Tom's response had given Odin some confirmation that Tom had started to accept it and was ready for the next part of the plan.

Odin had taken the next junction off the freeway. They eventually found a small rest stop close to Greenfield, that had a motel, fuel stop and a diner. It was mid-afternoon and Odin had not slept since the day before and both of them needed a wash, food and a good sleep. Odin had also mentioned that, from time to time, its best to get off the road and lay low for a while.

Odin had gone in and booked a room for the night while Tom filled the car with gas. They ate a meal in the diner nearby and went to the room to clean up. The shower felt so good Tom didn't want to get out. The water hitting his head seemed to dull his thoughts and he zoned out from all of the madness.

Tom sat down on the bed and Odin got paperwork and documents from his holdall. He shuffled through the documents, picking them up, scanning them and then putting them down. After about ten minutes Odin gave Tom a pen and piece of blank paper and told him to make notes, as he was going to only say this one.

It was then that Tom's first real briefing had begun.

Odin had started by telling Tom that he needs to contact his sister and tell her that things are going to be different from now on and it may well be that he never sees her again. To explain that he had got involved in something which means he can't settle anywhere.

Tom was obviously very upset at this and his reaction had been negative at first, but Odin had explained clearly that Tom does not know her involvement. She may well be a guide for The Order. Tom's mum had never said if his sister knew about it. She could simply organise a visit and The Order would be waiting. Tom knew this not to be true, but he had now found himself in such a surreal world that he could not be sure of literally anything.

But, as Odin explained, and more importantly, if she isn't aware, nor involved, then she will be the next target that The Order may use to try and lure Tom in. Getting his sister and her family involved is the last thing they would want and so Tom staying away from her was for the best.

Despite Tom's upset and anger at this he knew deep down that Odin was right. And Odin had said to Tom that maybe one day things may be different, and he could see her again, but definitely not now or for the foreseeable future, at least.

The next thing that Odin said made Tom feel even worse. And this was that he cannot go to his mum's funeral. The anger Tom felt was palpable, but again, Odin explained that The Order will be waiting. And, if Tom goes, he simply endangers himself and others. Again, Tom knew that, in reality, this was right but he realised that he would find this hard to accept and it would take a long time to get over.

Odin had then reminded Tom that although he had agreed to be part of The Network, Odin, nor anyone else, can stop him doing what he wants. The Network was not a cult and they don't imprison people - they help people. But only if those people want that help.

Odin said to Tom he could only advise him, but he could guarantee, almost one hundred percent, that agents from The Order will be close to the funeral - it would be suicide to go. Tom had suddenly wondered if suicide was an option for some and had even asked Odin the question and his reply had been short and frank, "Sadly, for many, it is. But you are stronger than that".

Odin had then quickly moved the conversation back and explained to Tom that he must think of others. His sister and family will be there, and The Order are there to get him, so it creates danger and anguish for everyone. He must tell his sister that he won't be seeing her for again for a long, long time and he won't be going to the funeral. Tom realised that it would be a tough conversation.

Odin then told him he must ring missing persons and make an enquiry as to Jenna's search. Ask if the police had any leads or lines of enquiry. This was just to keep his alibi up and to make sure he doesn't become a suspect. Tom had been expecting a call from the police by now, but it had not yet come. He wondered if this was a good or bad sign.

They then had to get the hire car back to where Tom had picked it up. Tom had said to Odin that he can then pick the Mercedes up, but Odin told Tom it would not be going anywhere. The car and Tom's home are the two main assets he has that The Order know he owns. They will have a trace on the car and, almost certainly, eyes on the house, so the car will be left and a new car, which already been arranged, will be collected.

Odin advised that he has arranged a fixer to attend to repair the damaged lease car they were in. It would be done later that night under cover of darkness. The windscreen will be replaced, any dents be ironed out and, more importantly, blood cleaned off. If it leaves a few scuffs, then they will be paid for when the car goes back.

Odin then told Tom that The Network have contacts and they will organise the sale of his house and the money will be put into an account for him. Odin quickly ended this part by saying, "Financials are not important now. I will give you more info on that later."

Tom already feeling like he had very little, now suddenly realised he now had even less.

The next thing they needed to do was to go to Tom's home. Odin had warned that this will be very dangerous, and it will be an 'in and out' job taking no longer than 15 minutes. This is to get a small number of items, clothes, passport and any other cards or money. Also, if time allows, a few personal belongings. Tom immediately thought of his box in the garage and all the old photos and memorabilia he had. In his mind he knew exactly what photo's he was going to grab. He just wished that he could spend a day there going through them. He knew it was going to be a rush, but he would get what he could. Odin reiterated the danger of this; but it is vital he get his passport more than anything, as if there is a need to leave the country then he can.

Odin had then advised Tom that he now listen very carefully but to not make notes. He told Tom that a contact had been set up. It was a Mafia connection who would take Tom in, settle him and direct him from there. A man called Tony Vitola. Odin explained he would be going there with Tom and introducing them and then leaving for New York City to pick up a new assignment. He said Tony was a key contact for The Network and has taken in several portals for them. He has a lot of contacts and will set up Tom's next move in a few months' time, but for the short term he will be Tom's main contact.

Odin explained that Tom must now keep moving, generally every few months, or sooner if intelligence tells them that The Order are moving in and around that location. He had reminded Tom that The Network intelligence has picked up a lot of activity around his location and his movements, and so it is obvious there is something The Order need him for. But Tom's life now was one of a nomadic existence, keeping on the road and changing locations as often as possible to prevent The Order from pinning down their target.

Odin advised, that as time goes by, he will be kept fully briefed with information and data, new contacts, safe houses, motels, helpers, people who can be trusted. He will be given updates on Order movements and which areas are safest to be. That over time he will create his own contacts and recruit his own help. People that he can trust who can eventually be integrated themselves and used by all members of The Network.

Odin emphasised how vital it is to keep the network evolving and growing and not just to keep it strong but make it stronger. And how The Network is modelled on the French Resistance of World War 2 in its secrecy and intricacy.

Tom would be given details of The Network hierarchy, how it works, how he fits into it. To keep The Network secret the hierarchy changes, and so will his reporting contacts, but this will all be filtered to him. Information would be made available briefly in phone texts, but more detailed information will be left at special pick up areas like storage premises, bank deposits, public lockers at train stations and bus garages. Drop offs will be arranged via courier where information and documents can be handed to him.

Over time scripture, writings and reading information will be sent to him explaining in detail the religious and scientific understanding of what he is. Huge amounts of intelligence and writings have been taken from The Order and can be made available. Odin warned Tom that the scientific and medical data is a hard read but it will give him a much deeper understanding of it all.

Eventually Odin finished by saying as time passes the hope is that Tom will eventually become an agent and have cases assigned to him. This surprised Tom. He had asked Odin to explain but he had told Tom he did not have enough time and simply said "Basically, you will be like me". But Odin reminded that this was a long time ahead and to make sure agents are sufficiently tasked and able to cope the selected members are taken to a secret location for full training. As Odin continued Tom couldn't help but interrupt and had asked Odin what he meant by "training".

"The Network has military and mafia connections and contacts. We don't just send agents out into the field untrained. The Order are a force with specially trained agents whose job it is to kill targets. We have to match that. The training is high level, physical training, firearms, driving skills, martial arts, espionage. Six months intense. You will be tested. Interrogation techniques, code-breaking, survival skills. It's the only way that we know we have people capable of matching The Order. Do you think I just walked into that bar and did what I did instinctively? I was trained. And you were my 17th case. I am good at what I do now. You will be the same"

Tom was struggling to take it all in, "I don't remember signing up to be an agent?"

Odin started at him.

"What?" asked Tom innocently.

Odin shook his head, "Have you understood anything I said?" Tom didn't know what to say.

He was confused. He couldn't work out why Odin had automatically thought Tom had signed up for all of this. Tom just wanted to get going on the run, away from it all.

Odin explained, "They killed your father. They manipulated and threatened your mother her whole life. They took Jenna from you. They took away your life. And now they want to kill you. Don't you see? If you don't fight them, who will? If I didn't fight them, who would? All of our agents across the world. If we all just gave up and ran away who would fight them? We all have a cause. This thing has brought us together. You, me and all the other agents and portals on the run, we all have one thing in common. The Network. Together we are stronger. If you just run away now and hide, we are weaker."

Tom stared at Odin but wasn't sure what he was supposed to say. He knew Odin was right. What had happened to Tom was heart-breaking. His whole life was a manipulated scheme. Regardless of what he supposedly was, nobody deserved to be used the way he had. Nobody should have to have that happen to them.

Odin walked towards the door, "I need a drink. And there's stuff to organise. Carry out your tasks," and he opened the door and left. But as he walked out of the room he sent a final order, "Then smash that phone to pieces," and slammed the door.

Tom sat at the table. His scribbled notes in front of him. Suddenly the room was very quiet, and all Tom could hear was birdsong and the odd car drifting past. He realised what he was now into, but it had all happened so quickly. He hadn't had time to think. Tom knew Odin was right - there wasn't a choice. This wasn't like joining the military. There are no recruitment offices. Tom realised that this was it. It was this or go it alone. And after seeing what The Order were capable of Tom did not think the latter was the best option.

He picked up his phone and dialed his sister's number. He took a deep breath and after a few rings she answered, "Tom? Oh, I have been desperate to speak to you. I am really worried. Look, I hope you don't mind, I told Paul and he..."

"Claire!" barked Tom forcefully, "Don't speak, just listen."

Claire tried to speak some more but Tom cut her off again.

"Claire. Listen. First of all, I am truly sorry for the way I have handled mum's death. I know I should've been there much more before she died to help and support you. And I am also truly sorry for leaving you the day she died..."

Claire tried to speak again. "Oh Tom, please don't worry..."

"Claire! Please just let me speak." Tom heard Claire start to cry but he carried on speaking. "I am involved in a situation that I cannot control and cannot get out of, but I have some people who can help me. But in dealing with this situation I cannot see you or communicate with you."

Claire interrupted and this time sounded much more forceful, "Tom, you need to go the police for god sake!! Paul said he can...."

"The police and Paul cannot help, Claire!" Tom shouted, "The only people that can help me are already doing that. I have to do it this way. I pray that one day I will see you again and can explain it all. But until then you need to understand that you won't see or hear from me," Tom could now hear Claire crying loudly, "I am sorry," he added.

Tom felt that he had no more to say but suddenly heard Paul's voice, "Tom, it's Paul, please tell us what is going on, we can help you."

Tom cut him off instantly, "Paul. Please tell Claire I cannot come to mum's funeral. Please look after her. You are a really good man and you should be proud."

"Tom, please let us help....."

"Paul, it's too dangerous. I don't want you involved. Look after Claire and the boys."

Tom ended the call. As he did he could hear Paul speaking, but didn't hear exactly what he said.

Tom realised that they will almost certainly call him back, so he switched the phone off. He wiped a tear from his face and went to the window. The late afternoon sun glowed in and warmed his face and body. He knew it was right. Claire, Paul and the boys did not deserve to be involved in all of this. He sat down and took a deep breath. He went through his notes for a short while, reading and then re-reading them, trying to digest them and the situation.

He then turned his phone back on, and as he did he noticed three missed calls from Claire. His intuition that she would call back was right. He then looked up the non-emergency missing persons hotline and called the number. The lady at the end of the line had asked him for some details, missing person, his name, address, date of birth, the date Jenna went missing. He got put through to different departments twice before eventually landing at the correct office on the third attempt. He had to give the young girl all of the same information he had given out before; but didn't mind too much.

After being put on hold an older sounding man came on and informed Tom that no trace of Jenna had yet been found. A couple of odd enquiries had been checked but had not turned up anything. The man confirmed that Jenna's mum had told them that she may be in Pennsylvania, around the vicinity of Pittsburgh, but enquiries and missing person links had also not turned up anything. The man advised him that there is a note on the file that there was a 'Dear John' letter. Tom confirmed this to be the case and so the man told him that they would need a copy of it, and to take it into his local station. Tom confirmed that he would as soon as possible.

The man then told Tom that unfortunately 'Dear John' cases did not receive as high a priority as others. Tom confirmed that he understood. The man also confirmed that there was a note on the file that a lady named Cindy who is logged as Jenna's mum had called each day since Jenna went missing. Tom confirmed that was his mother-in-law and that if they could let her know of any updates, she would pass them on.

The man ended by saying he would log Tom's enquiry and ended by saying, "I hope she turns up, sir," but Tom knew that hope was the only thing that there ever would be for Cindy and Bob.

As he sat thinking about Jenna and the life they had, he wondered if she had been with The Order when they got together or if they had got to her afterwards. He assumed he would never find out. But as he sat there, he looked down at his phone thinking that when he disposes of it a lot of his contacts in life will be gone for good.

That night they had both laid on their beds but were too tired to talk. Although Odin had told Tom that a contact had set up the repair of the windscreen and bodywork on the hire car and they would be arriving later tonight. Tom had thought how organised Odin was as he probably would've dropped the hire car off with cracked windscreen, dents and blood, obvious to the world what had happened.

Tom couldn't remember falling to sleep but he was awoken by a gentle nudging of his shoulder. He opened his eyes to see Odin sat on his bed.

"Tom?" he asked quietly. Tom went to sit up.
"No, it's OK" advised Odin, "Our guy is here. I will be outside. Stay there."

Tom looked at his phone and noted it was 3.36am. He laid back down and gently drifted back off to sleep again.

Chapter 28

The light pierced Tom's eyes. It was intense, bright and very welcoming. From the light floated a figure. A figure that Tom was desperate to get close to. The urge to get as close as possible and hold the figure was over-whelming.

As the figure got closer Tom felt happier and with each second, the closer it got, his happiness increased, almost to an ecstasy. As it got close enough for Tom to touch he suddenly made out the nun's habit the figure was wearing. It's hands gently clasped together on its bosom holding a wooden crucifix.

Tom looked into the dark face of the figure and slowly his mum's face appeared. Tom felt emotion like never before and knew his mum had returned to help him, support him and hold him. She smiled that serene, beautiful smile and Tom felt the love that transmitted from her lift him. She was the most beautiful person he had ever seen, and he knew that in just one step, he could reach out and feel her everlasting love again. He wanted her love to flow through him.

He stepped forward and reached out with both hands to embrace her, but each time she pushed him away. Frustrated Tom tried again but she pushed him away harder. Tom shouted at her, "Mom! Mom! It's me, Tom!".

She floated just an arms-length away and Tom reached again with all his might desperate to feel her physical touch but, again, she opposed him and pushed him away harder. But this time an apparent anger came across her face. She shook her head and moved closer to Tom. But now he no longer wanted to embrace her, he suddenly felt cold and that this was not his Mum but another being.

Tom moved back but now she moved forward faster. As she did the skin on her face started to slowly peel away and Tom was caught in two minds as to whether to help her or run. He shouted again, "Mom! No!"

But the skin peeled away to reveal a bloody skull with blood oozing from its sockets and holes onto the black and white habit and crucifix. It suddenly grabbed Tom and he quickly felt bound and could no longer move. The thing moved closer to him and its bloody jaw opened, and a leathery forked tongue flicked across Tom's face, smelling the blood and flesh under his skin. Tom screamed at the creature to stop but it's mouth, slowly opened wide and then wider still until Tom could see nothing but black.

From the black a dark lizard jumped at him and bit his face. Tom felt the sharp fangs penetrate and tried to raise his arms to get it off, but his arms were still being held by his mum's hands. The creature shook him and kept shaking until Tom thought his head would be bitten clean off…

"Tom! Tom!" he suddenly heard. He screamed and awoke to find Odin shaking him gently. Tom sat up and Odin stepped back.
"Take it easy, Tom"

Tom then realised what had happened and became aware of his surroundings. The panic faded and fear quickly faded. He took a deep breath and the tension in his muscles ease and he relaxed.
"Bad dream, huh?" asked Odin.
"Something like that," he replied as he laid back down and tried to calm his breathing and trying to get the image of his mum out of his head. He hated the dreams and how they involved the people he loved. He took another deep breath and realised he was sweating.
"You were screaming." Confirmed Odin.

Tom shook his head. But wasn't embarrassed. He felt he now trusted Odin enough to not have to be due to his understanding.
"It's just before 7." Odin advised him, "No rush to get going so we will just chill for a little while, grab some breakfast then move out. We aren't too far from the city. We need to get there to hook up with the car being left for us but it's not being dropped until later."

Tom nodded and yawned. He sat up and stretched. Odin had already put the kettle on and had two mugs out on the side. Tom lent over and picked up his phone and noticed an unread text from Davy, so he opened it:

'Tom. Is there any way we could meet? I know you have loads going on right now. Are you still in Jersey? I can come to you there. Or if you are back in Chicago I can come there. I just need some help and need to see you face to face. Sorry for all this. Let me know what suits you. It's urgent and needs to be asap. Thanks and sorry. Reply soon. Davy.'

As they sat and drank their coffee Tom had shown the text to Odin. His response had been to look at the text, shake his head, then look at Tom with a resigned look.
"They have got to him, it's obvious," he said in his usual matter of fact way.

"But he may actually be in trouble and really need some help," replied Tom anxiously.

Odin smiled and shook his head again and spoke as if he was thinking aloud.
"They somehow got one up on me, and knew we were meeting. How? I don't know, but we dodged them and got away. Now they are desperate, using any connection or lead they can get. But I don't believe they have just got to Davy. He dragged you over to Minneapolis once before and look what happened. The old man at the garage died, Charlie Redmond...Or Red, whatever his name was. They very likely used Davy to get you there. He was working for them then and he still is now. I am sure of it."

Tom knew Odin was almost certainly right. Davy had been in financial trouble with his failed business, and so a big pay out would have been very enticing for him. But Tom still couldn't quite believe it.
"But we went out drinking and went fishing, I would've known," said Tom, realising that his argument was weak.

Odin responded straight away.
"Look, Tom, we still don't really know exactly how they do it. How they harness the energy and make the connection. We are talking about thousands of years of this symbiotic link. It seems that they just need to you to be close and in the localised area of their target. We don't know the exact radius, but intelligence gathered shows us it can be quite wide. Once before he got you where they wanted you to be around an approximate time. But now they have lost your mother, Jenna and Phil. Plus Rutherford no longer has you on a leash, and so they are trying to reel you in using Davy again. But this time it's not for the deliverance of wrath. It's to kill you. You have gone rogue and you are with me, they know that. You can deny it all you like but I have seen it so many times, this is not an uncommon scenario."

Once again Tom thought about it and no matter how hard he tried he couldn't see past Odin's explanation. He knew, deep down, it was too risky to meet Davy. Odin continued.
"You have to ignore the message. It's simple. I told you, destroy the phone and its gone."
Tom interjected, "But they won't know I have done that, they will keep harassing him. He has a young family. What if...Well, you know" Tom's voice trailed off and Odin knew what he was inferring.

"Well then, text back and make it clear it's a no. At least then The Order have no need for him and may leave him alone, but I can't guarantee they will,"

Tom sighed, "There has to be some way..."

"Tom!!" growled Odin emphatically and put his hands on his head in frustration, "You need to adjust your thinking. You cannot be the person you were. If you show weakness, they will find you and kill you. And probably me at the same time. You cannot control what The Order do. And you can't manipulate them. Text Davy and tell him you can't meet. Tell him he must not contact you again. Just do it," with that Odin turned to his bed and started loading up documents into his holdall, preparing to get on the road again.

Tom sighed. This was the end of a lifetime of friendship. Over in the press of a button. Tom shook his head, opened Davy's message, pressed reply and started typing:

'Davy. Really sorry. I can't meet you. Please do not try and contact me again. Tom.'

Tom read and re-read the message, wondering if he should at least give some explanation. But Odin was right, the more information he gave, the more reason The Order had to hold onto Davy. He needed to end it. He pressed send.

His heart sank and a wave of anguish swept over him. If The Order had Davy working for them, then Tom's message would hopefully mean that they see Davy as a no hope and leave him alone. But Tom couldn't help wondering if Davy wasn't involved and genuinely needed help. If that was the case, then reading that message would confuse and shock him.

Tom heard the shower start and noticed Odin in the bathroom stripping off. He noted that Odin did not appear big in stature, but with his clothes off he was very muscular and wiry. Tom also couldn't help but notice huge scars running down his back and across his shoulders.

Tom laid down on the bed and closed his eyes. It was peaceful. The sound of the shower, the smell of coffee and the odd car cruising past was all very relaxing. Tom felt like laying there forever. His body ached but felt as comfortable as he had for a while. Suddenly his phone rung, and he jumped out of his slumber. His first thought was that Odin had told him to destroy the phone, so he was lucky that Odin was in the shower and didn't hear it.

He quickly leant over and grabbed the phone and noticed it was Jenna's mum, Cindy and he quickly answered it.

"Hello, Cindy?"

"Oh, hello Tom. Sorry to disturb you, I know its early. Were you sleeping?"

"Oh, no, I was awake. Are you ok?"

"Well, not really, we just want out little girl back."

"Yeah, me too. I just wish she would've spoken to me."

There was an awkward silence and Tom realised he may have inadvertently intimated that Jenna was to blame. He quickly wished he could retract it but decided not to say anymore or try to rectify the comment.

Cindy continued, "Look, Tom. Chicago Police have been on and asked me for your number. They need to contact you. They say they want to speak to you," Tom sensed a hint of embarrassment in her voice, "They need to ask some questions too, well, you know. Rule you out."

Tom interjected "Oh yes, that's fine, I was fully expecting that. This is a difficult situation and…"

"They want to see the house too," Cindy interrupted, "I am not sure why but…"

"I understand. I am sure it's all just procedure. I am on my way back home so will do it then," Tom tried to sound as innocent as he could as he spoke but wasn't sure if it came across as guilty.

There was another silence, which Cindy eventually ended.

"How did you get on?"

"Oh, I had no luck. It was just a hunch. But, well, I didn't know what else to do…And you would've been the first person I spoke to had I found her"

"Oh Tom, you're such a good man. I keep crying. It's just all such a shock that she would just leave you like that. We still can't quite believe it…And, well, even so, we just want to know she's safe."

Tom never spoke. He didn't know what to say. Cindy continued.

"I am so sorry, Tom. Sorry for all this damn mess!" As she spoke her voice became angry, then Tom heard her start to cry at the end of the phone.

"Cindy, please don't cry…"

Tom heard a muffling sound and then Bob's voice.

"Tom. We are both really sorry. If we get any news we will be sure to call you"

Tom noticed that, as ever, Bob was an image of calm and pragmatism. He thought that he would get on well with Odin.

"Thanks, I will do the same. I am really sorry."

There was slight pause and then Tom heard then a click and then call end. Tom shook his head and thought what a mess this all was.

He was about to put the phone down but then noticed an unread text that must have arrived while he was talking. He opened it and noticed it was from Davy:

'Tom. I hope you get this. Get the fuck out. They know where you are. They are coming. I am so sorry. D'

Chapter 29

Odin was driving fast. Tom had shown him the text and all he had said when he read it was, "Move!"

In the car, some fifteen minutes after leaving the motel, Odin had not said anything about it. Tom was expecting, "I told you so," and a bit of a knuckle wrap for not really believing him, but Tom knew Odin wasn't like that. He also realised that this was all a learning curve for him, and Odin knew that.

As Odin sped through the traffic, switching lanes and receiving the off horn, Tom thought about Davy. Now they knew for sure he had been in contact with The Order, and he must have been very close to them to know that they knew where Tom and Odin were. This was bad for Davy though and Tom hoped that they would not find out he had betrayed them. He pictured him sending the text with them there and hoped that he had time to delete it and they would never know.

But, ultimately, Tom just couldn't believe Davy was helping them, although thinking more into it, it was all so obvious. But now, like Jenna, Davy had appeared to have betrayed The Order in a bid to help him. Friends to the end. Davy may well have saved Tom's life, but Tom hoped that Davy would not pay with his own.

Without warning Odin had suddenly burst into life and given Tom a verbal briefing. The plan was still the same. They would drop the hire car back in Indianapolis and pick up the car that had been left by The Network. They would go to Tom's home for a quick pit stop so he can get the items and belongings and then back to Pittsburgh to meet Vitola. From there Odin would then leave for another assignment. Vitola would take Tom in, continue with his resettlement and provide information going forward to help him get integrated into The Network.

The last several days had been completely insane. Tom had not properly had time to grieve the loss of his mum, he was worried about his sister and on top of that Odin was now talking about resettlement and integration. It was all so confusing and stressful, and Tom was finding it hard to take it all in and think straight.

Tom was also a little frustrated at the prospect of having to travel all the way back to Pennsylvania to meet someone in Pittsburgh. He questioned this with Odin.

"Look Tom, it just happens that way sometimes. When I was in Pittsburgh I set up a safe place for you with one of our best network members. Tony Vitola." Odin had responded.

"But you said it was too risky in Pittsburgh. That is was a code red," stated Tom.

"Yes, it was then. I had some intelligence The Order had agents in the city, so I got out. It's just precaution. We have to keep on our toes, or they get ahead of us."

Tom sighed heavily and Odin snapped.

"Look, Tom, I don't have time to set up another safe place for you now! It's just a day's drive back. Shut the fuck up!"

Tom looked at Odin, shocked, and then looked back ahead at the road ahead. He was annoyed with himself for angering Odin. He was going to a lot of trouble and without him Tom knew he would already be dead. In reality it didn't matter where they had to go as long as he had Odin to protect him. He realised that Odin was obviously a little stressed and was working things out and didn't need to be questioned.

And much more worrying than a boring days drive back to Pittsburgh, Tom had also learned that, although almost certainly procedural, the police now needed to speak to him and, according to Cindy, wanted to check the house. Although it wasn't a surprise to him.

In most missing cases the police talk to the persons loved ones. But the fact that Tom had the forged letter was a godsend, but it still caused major unrest in his mind.

"The house is clear right?" he suddenly asked Odin.

He looked at Tom, confused, "Our cleaners went in, and I am informed the job was completed. And if I am informed it was completed then I can assure it was. You won't find a speck of blood with a magnifying glass"

Odin questioned why he had asked, and so Tom told him about the call from Cindy. Odin had sworn out loud and berated him for not telling him sooner. But Tom explained that with Davy's text and the sudden exit he had forgotten. He noted Odin's temperament cool down and assured him not to worry. Tom realised that Odin had felt he was too stern on him.

Odin calmly explained that the house would be clean. And he reminded Tom the cleaners had also left it to look like someone had quickly packed. He then assured Tom that he was not the first-person Odin had been assigned to and all manner of scenarios and problems arise. It was nothing new.

Tom felt more confident, but he then asked a question that he could see threw Odin.

"But, we are going back to get my passport and a few other items, and you said a quick pit-stop."

Odin looked at him a little frustrated that this wasn't clear, so Tom continued.

"But, if we get in and out and then back to Pittsburgh then it looks like I am running. I mean, if Jenna was really missing then surely I would be waiting there for her to make contact. I wouldn't just leave...It doesn't make sense".

Odin never replied. He just looked ahead as he drove. Tom could see him digesting the information but continued.

"I am going to have to meet the police there at some point, but I don't want to wait around at the house. I will be a sitting duck!" Odin never turned to look at Tom, nor did he speak.

They drove on and something told Tom not to ask Odin again. He felt that if he did it would simply create more frustration. He knew Odin was thinking and he was sure, if the last few days were to go by, Odin would get it sorted.

A short time later as they started to drive through Cumberland Odin pulled over at a small rest stop. He told Tom that if he wanted to pee, he should go now. Tom got out and stretched and walked past a small cafe towards the toilets that were situated away from the pull in, tucked into where the forest loomed over it. He noted that there were not a lot of people and other vehicles about. As he walked into the toilet he looked back and saw Odin standing at the car talking on his phone.

He went inside and as he stood at the urinal, he realised how tired he was. Physically and mentally drained through the constant running, thinking and lack of proper rest. Recalling his past and thinking how, what Odin had told him seemed so far-fetched yet also checked out. The events of the last few months had been difficult to understand and accept. The events of the last few days had been impossible.

He wondered how this was going to work out and if it was going to be as straight forward as Odin made it sound. Being on the move and going from place to place didn't sound too bad, but Tom was a creature of habit and knew that it would start to become difficult. But if he was going to stay alive and be of any use to Odin, he needed to adapt.

He thought of his mum. Her face had been flashing across his mind randomly at different times since her death. A small wave of emotion turned his stomach, but he managed to hold it together. Her face was beautiful, and he remembered his dad always saying that only Doris Day had a better smile.

He then thought of his sister back in New Jersey arranging the funeral and wondering what the hell was happening with him. Each time he thought of her he felt a sense of frustration and anger that he wasn't with her. Paul was a good man and looked after her, but she was very matriarchal, and deep-down Tom knew that nobody was there for her. Claire was always there for everyone else. She always had been. Tom wanted to be with her and tell her to relax, take things on himself to give her a break. He felt that he had let her down but was comforted by the fact that, little did she know, by not being there for her he was actually doing her the biggest thing he could ever do for her. Keeping her and her family safe.

He wanted to speak to her to just assure her he was OK. But he realised that this would have to be authorised by Odin. Tom would speak to him later and hope, by some chance, Odin says contact can be made. But Tom doubted it. It seemed that Odin didn't have time for sentiment and would rule out any opportunity to give The Order an advantage. Tom wondered if Odin had any emotion or sentiment left. Or had his time battling The Order drained him of it completely.

Tom washed his hands and pressed the button on the dryer. The air that came out was so soft it resembled a baby breathing. Tom shook his head and wiped his hands on his jeans. He looked in the mirror and noticed the bruising around his eyes was now fully black. The cut across his nose has started to scab but the area wasn't as painful to the touch.

As he left the toilet he looked up and saw Odin standing at the car now looking at his phone. He noted a stern appearance on his face and wondered if all was OK. He walked back across the open space towards Odin and noticed him shake his head and put his phone away.

As Tom got close to the car, he asked Odin if he was OK. Odin looked up and nodded his head in the direction of the car as if to order Tom to get in.

Tom walked round and got in and looked at Odin. Odin took a deep breath. He looked at Tom.
"Ok, first things first. I have spoken to one of my superiors. They have said you need to get the police off your back, so it is imperative that you

make contact and get them to your house. The quicker the police can rule you out then the better. Until they rule you out it leaves you in limbo. You can't travel about. You have already been to Pennsylvania to meet me and your excuse for doing that was to look for Jenna. But it's going to get harder to be on the move as the police may see that as trying to avoid them."

Odin spoke quickly and directly, Tom nodded intently.
"The new plan is that you go to Evanston Police and tell them that Cindy has informed you they want to speak to you. You tell them that you are struggling with Jenna leaving, and you want to just sell the house and move on as being there is affecting your mental health. Say it brings back too many memories. They will understand. The idea is to get them to interview you and look at the house as soon as possible. If this drags on, then you will have to remain in one place too long and it could give The Order a chance to pinpoint you."

Odin stopped. Tom held his breath and waited.
"Are you taking this all in?" Odin asked
Tom snapped out of his concentration, "Yes! Of course."
"OK. My people are going to do another forged letter and get it dropped at the house tomorrow. It will contain an apology from Jenna to you and tell you that she is moving far away; something along those lines. But the most important thing is that it will confirm that she is alive and well. It should be enough for the police to just put it down as her leaving you and then take her off the missing list."
Tom interrupted "But what if they say they can't interview me or that I have to wait…"
"You tell them that you are planning to travel around to get over it. You are selling the house. You need to get away and can't wait. Say it's killing you. They will understand."

Odin paused again, waiting for any questions. But Tom was silent, so he continued.
"Look, I am sure this isn't high priority, so you don't have anything to worry about from the police. Your problem is being tied to one spot waiting for the police to do what they need to do. It's frustrating. But something we have to deal with."

Odin paused and look in the rear-view mirror.
"The most important thing is trying to get the police to act quickly, and if you say you are going away, they may just move on it," as Odin said the final part he shrugged his shoulders, "If they don't then…Well…Let's just worry about that if it happens."

247

Tom nodded and noticed Odin take in a deep breath and thought he looked uncomfortable about something. He never asked why but, before he could, Odin turned and looked at him and then shuffled his body around in the chair to face Tom.

"Look Tom. One of my agents has also been in touch. It's about Davy" Tom felt his stomach turn, "What? What about Davy? Is he ok?"

Odin got his phone out of his pocket and clicked the screen with his thumb. Tom felt a wave of anxiousness pass though his body. Odin turned the phone to show Tom.

"I just got sent this."

Tom looked at the phone and at first saw two men standing with each other. One he recognised. It was Rutherford. He was holding his hand out and smiling to another man, standing at an angle and slightly more difficult to recognise immediately. Tom took the phone and held it closer and studied it. He suddenly realised that he did recognise the other man. It was Davy. He was also holding his hand out to Rutherford and from the side you could see he was smiling too. Tom's heart sank and an almost uncontrollable feeling of desperation and anger hit him like a lightning bolt.

"I am really sorry," Odin said.

Chapter 30

They sat in the car at the rest stop. Tom was stunned. Odin explained that once Tom had made him aware of Davy's involvement, he had passed this information onto a contact in The Network. It had been passed to intelligence and they had sifted through everything they currently held on Rutherford. As a key player in The Order Rutherford had a lot of intelligence on him including movements and meetings, much of which were recorded by photograph.

The photograph he had shown Tom was taken roughly a week ago, and intimated that Rutherford and Davy already knew each other and that this was not a first meeting. Odin suggested they probably met before to get Davy to contact Tom get him to Indianapolis. It was only an assumption, although Tom realised that it was a very strong one and was almost certainly correct.

Odin said that Rutherford had been difficult to trail since Tom went rogue. His position at the bank would have been a ruse for his work within The Order. But intelligence had suggested that Rutherford had hardly been seen at the bank in Chicago. It seemed that getting to Tom was more important, and his position within The Order now took priority.

Odin had given Tom a lot of information in his usual pragmatic way. Some of it went in and some of it never. Tom felt numb and he was finding it hard to believe that Davy was involved. He was also, again, very concerned that, even though Davy had tried to lure Tom in, he was now in serious trouble. Davy had taken a huge chance warning Tom.
"Do you think Davy was ever really my friend?" asked Tom, as he watched a truck pull in and drive slowly across to the parking bays.
Odin turned to him, "I don't know. I would guess he was. I am sure when you were both younger he was. But at some point, in later life, The Order got to him and used him to move you around. It would be very unlikely they put him in place all those years ago and then brought him out until you went to visit him more recently. I mean, The Order are very good at what they do, but not that good."

Tom took some assurance from Odin's words.
"Look, Tom" Odin continued, "don't be too hard on Davy. The Order are relentless. Once they get a person connected they don't let go. Davy had money problems and a young family. They probably offered him more money than he could refuse. He probably felt he had no choice."

Tom looked at Odin but stayed silent. Odin took a deep breath and continued.

"Plus, he came through for you in the end. Your friendship is stronger than The Order. That's a big deal. No money is more than true friendship."

Tom smiled.

"Will he be ok?"

Odin looked around at another truck coming through into the stop and he watched it trundle past them.

"I will be honest," he turned to look at Tom, "I doubt it. But you never know."

Tom looked away. He had seen briefly what The Order were capable of and despite everything, he desperately hoped Davy would be ok.

He thought back to them as boys riding their bikes through the woods, fishing at the lake, going down to the diner and daring each other to speak to girls. Tom truly believed it was genuine. It had to be. He would hold onto that belief as comfort.

"Anyway…" Odin cut in, and pulled Tom out of his daydream, "We have important things to do. We are only an hour or so from Indianapolis. We have to get this car back and pick up the new one. It's now been left for us. As planned we go straight to Evanston Police Department and you go in and register to give a statement. The objective is to get them back to the house to check it. Not only will this remove you from their enquiries but will also be some protection while you are there. I will be close by, but not in sight. Do you understand?"

Tom nodded. Odin reversed out of the bay and back onto the highway that headed into Indianapolis. A short while later they reached the outskirts of the city and Tom directed Odin to the car hire place. The traffic was not heavy and so they cruised easily to it and, as they approached, Odin advised Tom they would stop close by, he would get out and Tom would take the wheel. Tom was to go in and drop off the keys. Odin told him implicitly to immediately pay any extra charges without hesitation.

Odin then advised that he would go and pick up the car that had been left for them by The Network and come back and collect him. Tom was to get a coffee at the car hire place and wait. Just look calm and don't act edgy. Tom didn't like this idea as he knew he would be isolated if anything happens, but he chose not to express his concerns and, as usual, just nodded.

Eventually they pulled up just outside and Odin immediately jumped out, as he did he told Tom to hold on. Tom heard the trunk open, looked in the rear-view mirror and then saw it slam shut and Odin walk away with the bags. He looked across to the car hire premises and couldn't see any sign of his own car, he thought that it was probably in a lock up around the back. Tom slowly drove into the car hire premises and parked up in the vehicle return bays, went inside and was relieved to find he was the only person there. He approached the desk and a young man greeted him with a name badge that said 'Clark'.

A lot had happened in the last few days, but Tom had to tell himself he was just returning a hire car. It was no big deal. But he couldn't help feeling like a criminal on the run. He grabbed a coffee while Clark went outside to inspect it. Tom sat sipping his coffee trying to look inconspicuous hoping that whoever Odin got to repair the car did a good job.

After a few minutes Clark came back in and smiled and went back behind the desk whilst uttering the words, "It's fine".

Tom felt a wave of relief. It wasn't the fact that he couldn't pay for any damage Clark may have found, he just didn't want any additional aggravation or questions as to how the damage was caused. Odin obviously used a good repair service.

Clark completed some paperwork and entered some data onto the system. He informed Tom there would be no additional charges and once Tom had signed the returns form it was all sorted. He would go and get Tom's car, and have it brought round the front.

Tom thanked him and sat down hoping that Odin would turn up soon as he realised that if Clark brings the car quickly he will have to leave which was contrary to Odin's instructions. Although he then thought he could just sit in the car and wait. No big deal.

After ten minutes Tom started to get anxious. His car had not been brought round yet which he wasn't sure was a good or bad thing. He had a thought that Clark had probably been informed to ring the police when the owner returned. Plus, as Odin hadn't returned either, Tom was getting nervous he may not see him again.

Most people sit and check their phones but Tom's was turned off for obvious reasons and so he had to just sit tight, and hope Odin would return. Tom scanned up and down the road desperately hoping for a sign of Odin. Tom's hopes were soon repaid as he noticed an Audi slowly drive into the parking lot, as it approached he saw the driver wave a hand and made out Odin's face in the driver's seat.

A wave of relief hit him, and he quickly got up but as he did he noticed Clark return through a side door behind the reception. He was holding a set of keys and some paperwork.
"I just need you to sign to say you got your car back, we can do an inspection before…"

Tom had heard no more as he left out of the man door. He walked quickly to the car and opened the door. As he got in heard a shout.
"Sir, your keys…"

He closed the door and the second it shut Odin had engaged the power and quickly sped off the forecourt. As they got onto the main road Tom wondered what conversation would take place between the staff at the hire shop as to why he had left without his Mercedes.

Odin soon made his way out of the city and picked up the road north towards Chicago. When they met the freeway Odin put his foot down and Tom felt a surge of power.

He suddenly realised that he admired Odin greatly. No problem or challenge seemed to phase him, and Tom wished he was more like that. He also liked the fact that, like him, Odin was not concerned about silences. They had had many since they met. Tom usually using the silence to work out in his head what the hell was going on. But Odin was like a machine, thinking, calculating, pre-empting. He was always in control. Everything he did was fluid and efficient which Tom thought the complete opposite to him in the last few months. His life had been a complete mess.

Tom remembered back when his life was under control, structured and organised. When he used to manage business and pleasure perfectly and be outstanding at everything he did. A pang of sadness then hit him as he realised that a lot of that was almost certainly down to The Order. He looked across at Odin. Flashes of light flickering across his aviator glasses as he drove.
"Do you ever see or hear from your family?"

There was a silence and then Odin came in sharply.
"No, they are all dead. The Order killed them. I saw things that nobody should see. I lost everyone and everything. My only living relative is a

great-uncle who still lives in Norway. Up North in the mountains. I have no way of contacting him, so I don't know if he is OK. He managed to stay out of it and The Order never got to him...Well, not that I know of. The Network moved me to America twelve years ago and the rest is history," Odin then turned to Tom, "and if it's ok, I prefer not to talk about it."

"Sorry," replied Tom hesitantly.

"Don't apologise," replied Odin, looking back at the road.

Tom was frustrated that he had created an air of negativity and wished he hadn't asked. But thought about it more and he was sure Odin didn't mind nor was he upset. Tom wondered if Odin ever did get upset. Maybe after what he had been through and seen, nothing could ever make him upset. Maybe he was now just an emotional shell. Tom wondered if he may ever end up like that.

Tom sat back and closed his eyes. But as he started to settle Odin's phone rang. Odin checked in his mirrors and then picked it up. He answered with, "Yeah," and during the short conversation he mustered only an, "Ok, Yep," and then a, "Thanks," before putting the phone down. As he did, he turned to Tom.

"The new forged letter has been delivered to your house. If the police see it when you go there it should be the evidence you need for them to get off your back." He then looked back at the road.

Tom nodded. Again a reminder of Odin's efficiency and his attention to detail. Tom wondered what he would've done had Odin not come into his life. Tom then wondered about The Network and its operation.

"So, how many people work for The Network?"

Odin took a deep breath and Tom thought he may not be in the mood for talking. Tom looked away expecting nothing in return but then Odin spoke.

"Not able to tell you exactly, but The Networks last update showed we have approximately 32 operational agents working in the States. Many more across the world. No agent will know the identity of many others; only probably just a handful of contacts. The ones you need to know for joint operations. The Network's recruitment is key. It's all managed by the ID; that's the Internal Department. They send out the updates, data, info, briefings. They organise everyone and everything. It's like a spider's web. I mean, Tony Vitola in Pittsburgh. That was fed to me by ID a few years ago and I have worked with him ever since. He will also probably know several other agents and so on and so forth," as Odin spoke Tom could sense his enthusiasm lifting.

"The Order work in very much a similar way as far as we can make out. As I said before we have people on the inside who feed ID info which we act on or use to get an advantage. The Order is huge. Much bigger than us. They are a global secret society made up of religious fanatics and extremists. Nobody really knows the full scale and extent of their operation but, more and more these days, we are finding it harder to operate without being caught out by them. They seem to have people everywhere".

Tom looked straight ahead. He realised he was not yet fully aware of the magnitude of what he had fallen into. Odin continued, "As time goes by you will receive more and more information to try and keep you updated and a step ahead each time."

Tom nodded, then asked.
"You say a secret society of religious fanatics and extremists," he shrugged his shoulders, "I mean, how high does this thing go?"
Odin smiled and turned to look at him.
"I asked that question once. I was told to imagine ants scurrying around at the bottom of a skyscraper," Tom looked confused, until Odin spoke again.
"Well, we are the ants."

Chapter 31

The drive back to Chicago had been long and tedious. Tom felt exhausted and still had so many questions, but just did not have the energy to discuss them. But as Odin had said previously 'All in good time.'

Odin had told Tom to call Evanston Police station and try to book an appointment to see someone as it may save time. Tom had tried this but was put on hold and re-directed three times eventually returning to the person he had first spoken to. They advised him that it may be better to keep it local and go to the station to book it.

Tom called them and spoke to a very polite lady who said she cannot make an appointment but if he comes in at his earliest convenience she will see if she can assign somebody. It was obviously the best that Tom could hope for.

When Tom finished the call, he noticed that Odin was constantly checking his rear-view mirror. As Odin continued doing this Tom realised that something may be going on and asked if everything was OK.

Odin never replied and just kept eyeing the mirror. They were on the 65 and had just passed through Roselawn. Odin had intended to pick up the 53 North and head into east Chicago to pick up the coast Road, it was then Odin calmly said.
"We are being tailed." Tom's heart froze.

Odin then explained that he had thought this when they had passed Lafayette and he had been doing some speed tests and, sure enough, the vehicle he suspected had slowed and sped up to replicate them.

"It's a black 4 x 4. I don't know make as yet as they are keeping just far enough away,"
"Are you sure?" asked Tom nervously, but Odin never replied.

Tom took the silence to be confirmation that he was sure. Odin never spoke more than necessary. No more was said until at East 81st Avenue until Odin filtered left and picked up the 30 heading towards Schererville. "Let's do a real test," he said confidently.

Tom just sat nervously not moving just staring straight ahead hoping and praying that Odin would tell him that the vehicle is not trailing them. They joined the traffic and headed west. The traffic was busy, and they could only travel at medium speed.

"Are they still there?" quizzed Tom.

Odin looked ahead and then eyes flashed to the rear-view mirror. Then back again to the road and back again to the mirror. Tom knew he was concentrating. Odin suddenly changed and became focussed and alert. "Ok, they are four cars behind. I think it's a BMW, looks like windshield is darkened," Tom's stomach turned. He readied himself as best he could and felt his hands clench.

Odin continued along East Lincoln Highway and then suddenly as he reached the crossroads at the 41, he filtered right and headed north to Hartsdale. Tom never spoke. Then suddenly Odin burst to life. "Ok, listen. We are definitely being tailed. It all checks out. They are about six cars back. I have tested them several times, but I am sure they don't know. To make sure we don't spook them I am just going to head North through Wolf Lake and pick up Shore Drive along the beach to Evanston. I am going to drop you off at the police station as planned. That should throw them off. When I drop you off just walk straight into the police station and do not look back. I will keep a check and make sure that if anything goes down, I will be there to help."

Tom never replied and just nodded. He desperately wanted to know what Tom meant by 'go down' but he never asked. He found himself not asking Odin a lot of questions as he worried it would annoy him. He felt it was just better not to analyse the detail.

Odin asked Tom to pass the holdall on the back seat. Tom grabbed it and Odin put it on his lap. He reached inside and pulled out a handgun and Tom watched as he emptied the chamber and checked it. He then put the magazine back in, cocked it, put the safety on and slid the gun into his door cavity. Tom felt his stomach turn as the nerves start to increase. He looked in his wing mirror but could not see the pursuers vehicle.

Odin then reached inside and pulled out what looked like a thick silver pen, but it appeared too long to be a pen. Again, he never asked what it was as Odin also slipped it into his door cavity next to the gun. Tom could now feel the focus and tension that emanated from Odin.

Odin put the bag back and put both hands on the wheel and Tom felt a steady surge of power as Odin deliberately, but without being too obvious, opened up the power and started to pass other vehicles. Tom realised that he was still testing the pursuers.

After a short while Tom started to see signs for Wolf Lake Memorial Park and as he did he felt a sudden decrease in the power as Odin slowed. Tom noticed Odin's eyes flashing back and forth from road to mirror. He desperately wanted Odin to say they had gone and was about to ask but felt it just better to leave it to him.

However, without thinking, Tom spoke his thoughts.
"How do you think they got onto us?"
"Who knows?" replied Odin quickly, "Could be one of their contacts has spotted us along the way and notified them? Anything. But that's not important now."

Odin now kept a constant speed as the cruised past East Side and then up past South heading along the coast to South Shore. Tom knew they were getting close as Odin cruised onto Lake Street and headed in.
"Are you ready?" he suddenly asked Tom

Tom never replied. He was very nervous. Odin noticed this and reassured him, "Tom, you can't go into the police station nervous, OK? Don't worry about what's happening with the guys behind, I will deal with them. You go in, ask to see someone urgently. Explain you have been told by Cindy they want to speak to you. You tell them that you are moving away as you can't live there through emotional and mental pain. You need time away and are going travelling so you want to get this done. Really ham it up. Cry if you have to. Put on a show. Whatever you do make sure they take your statement and send someone over to your place. If they say they are busy then just tell them you are leaving to go travelling soon. If they say you can't leave then cry. Make them feel awkward. Make them feel bad. Just get it done."

As usual Tom nodded the whole way through. Taking it in and trying to get himself focussed. Odin continued.
"And get your story straight. You had been to the gym and got back and found the note. You had a feeling she was having an affair and she had been to Pennsylvania a few times. Things were rough between you and it was on the cards that you would split but you had hoped she would stay. Keep emphasising her leaving and the affair. Have you got the letter?"

Tom patted himself down and felt it in his jacket pocket. He nodded and Odin then added, "You can do this Tom. Once this is done and they have been to your house you are free. We can get to Pittsburgh and you can start to move on. It's important, OK?"

257

Tom nodded and took a deep breath as the police station came into sight. He noticed Odin look in the rear-view mirror. He indicated to go right to stop in the drop off bay which had one space.

"They have dropped back. They are watching what's happening," updated Odin, but Tom never heard as his mind was racing with what he had to do. Before he had a chance to think anymore Odin had stopped and Tom knew it was time.
"Don't look back at them," ordered Odin. Tom got out and shut the door. The urge to look back was immense, but he resisted and slowly jogged up the stairs into the police station.

Odin slowly drove away. He noted that it was quite busy around at the time with a high volume of traffic and pedestrians. This played into his hands and as he pulled away, he kept a close eye on the pursuers. They had now edged further up and sat in traffic close to the police station. Odin desperately hoped that nobody would get out and run into the police station. If they did, he knew that it was Tom they were after, and he would have to act quickly.

Luckily for Odin up ahead a red light came on. He sat in the queue of traffic and had a clear sight of the 4x4 and could see all the windows were darkened and it was definitely a BMW. It pulled into the same space that he had used, and the door opened. A large man with a beard and short dark hair got out. He was wearing black jeans and a black leather jacket. Odin held the car door and grabbed his gun, but the man hesitated and never went into the police station. As the traffic light went green Odin needed to decide.

In his mind were two scenarios, he gets out and takes them both out now and then leaves the scene. Tt would leave Tom alone, but he had the protection of the police station. Or does he wait and see if it could be ended less dramatically. He always liked the last option but sometimes it just wasn't possible.

Odin heard a horn from the car behind and knew he had to decide. He put the gun down and slowly drove on. As he did, he noticed the man start to slowly walk up the stairs to the police station and the 4x4 move off and join the traffic. As it did Odin noticed it then switched lanes quickly and parked up across the street from the station about 200 yards away.

Odin was expecting the BMW to follow him, but it was now obvious that the pursuers target was only Tom. Odin knew what he had to do.

Inside the police station Tom was waiting at a sign just in front of the reception which advised people to 'wait until called'. He looked around in the waiting room and there was an elderly lady who he noticed looked like she had been crying. She looked up at Tom and he looked away, but not fast enough for her to not notice him looking at her. Tom wondered what she was here for and wondered it may be a lost cat or dog, but realised it could be something much worse, although he hoped not.

As Tom had entered there was already a young man at the reception booth, dressed in torn denim and a bandana. Tom had not worked out what he was reporting as the receptionist was talking calmly and quietly and all the young man kept saying was, "Yes, that's right…. I am very worried". After a couple of minutes the young man said thank you and, after telling the receptionist he was very worried for a final time, he eventually walked out with some paperwork.

The receptionist never looked up to acknowledge Tom and she typed some data on a computer. She pulled her glasses down to the end of her nose to read the screen and then pushed them back up and started typing again "Be with you in a moment" she uttered without looking up. Tom smiled, but the receptionist never noticed as she had pulled her glasses down and was looking at the screen again.

Tom looked around again. The old lady was wiping her eyes and never noticed him looking this time. Outside he saw a man on the stairs down to the street. He was dressed in black leather jacket and jeans and had a face that looked like it had taken a lot of knocks down the years. With bold prominent eye sockets and a flat nose it looked like the man had had a boxing career of 46 fights and 46 losses.

Tom wasn't sure if it was one of the pursuers. Odin had strictly told him not to look round. He hoped it wasn't, and if it was, he hoped that being in a police station may protect him, "Okay, sorry about the wait," the receptionist said, bringing Tom out of his thoughts. Tom moved forward to the desk. She looked up and smiled with her glasses on the end of her nose again.

Tom explained who he was and why he was there. He didn't give a lot of detail but was immediately frustrated at the receptionists confused look. Tom gave her the missing persons reference number and told her he was here to give a statement. With a confused look still on her face the receptionist typed some data into the computer and after a short while smiled and gave a nod.

"Right OK, makes sense now. Yes, they will want to interview you and make a house visit, just procedure. But we are busy so they will call you when they can do it. Okay thank you, sir."

Tom shook his head, "No. Look, I'm sorry but that's not good enough." Tom looked around at the waiting area and then back at the receptionist leaning into the window which separated them.

"You don't understand...I need to do this today. I can't go back there. Too much has happened," Tom reduced his voice to a whisper, "She may have left me and, well, it's difficult y' know...Just being there". Tom realised that the last line was a little cheesy, but it had just come out.

Tom raised his voice back to normal level again.

"I am moving on to get away from it all, I am going to visit friends, and I plan to go straight away..."

"But you will just have to wait, Sir they will..."

"No!" Tom said louder to which he noted an element of surprise on the ladies face, "I can't...I just can't...It's all too painful and..." Tom felt himself getting upset and although he was acting, in some way he had managed to make himself genuinely emotional, and he felt his eyes water up. He put his head on his arms which were folded on the reception desktop and tried to make himself cry and to his surprise he felt himself start to get upset.

He looked up and the noticed the lady showed a hint of distress and discomfort.

"Please" pleaded Tom, "Please, can this be done today?"

The lady got up from her seat, genuinely very concerned.

"Right, OK wait here...Be calm, don't worry," she handed him a tissue from a box on her desk and then went out through a door behind her. Tom looked around and the old lady was staring at him and this time she looked away as Tom caught her eye, but she didn't do it quick enough either.

A few blocks away Odin had found a place to park. He knew he had limited time. His hunch was that The Order wanted Tom alive, and he had thought this for a while, without telling Tom. He hoped he was right because if they truly wanted him dead and the pursuers were as fanatical as Odin knew they could be, then the man may have already walked straight into the police station and popped a bullet straight in between his eyes by now.

Odin looked around trying to see if the 4x4 had followed him. He couldn't see it so ascertained that it hadn't. He leant forward put his gun down the back of his belt. He opened his holdall and took out a hunter's knife, pulled up his jeans and slid into a leather sheaf that was strapped to his calf. He then grabbed his most efficient weapon, the tube knife.

It was a six-inch copper tube. Odin pulled it in half, and it revealed a steel tube which gradually drew to a very sharp, deadly point. Odin had used it before with great affect and knew it was a good choice of weapon for discreet, efficient kills. Odin hoped he would not have to use any of them but deep down knew, under the circumstances, the chances of that were now very low.

He pulled out a pair of surgical gloves, stretched them and slid them onto his hands. He checked around him once more and then got out and closed the door. As he walked back towards the police station the car locked with a bleep and he pulled his cap down and his hood from his training top over the top.

After a minute or so he got to the junction. He looked up and noticed the police station a few hundred yards away on the right-hand side but, more importantly, he noticed the BMW was still parked. He slowly crossed the road to the same side as the BMW and when he got to the other side felt much more hidden by the row of parked cars. He took his phone out of his pocket and stopped walking, pretending to answer his phone. The ruse gave him time to analyse and check the situation. He laughed and spoke about a meeting time and place and as he did, he saw the other man who had got out already, at the top of the stairs also on a phone. He assessed the situation and thought they were waiting for Tom to come out and they would either attempt to kill him or kidnap him. He had to act fast and take control.

Inside Tom was still waiting, but through a glass pane that was slightly faded he could see the receptionist talking to a police officer. He was pleased to see the police officer looked concerned and was nodding his head. Hopefully it would work, and they can get back to his, take a statement, look around and he can get the hell out of Evanston.

Outside, Odin put his phone away and started to slowly walk along the sidewalk up towards the BMW, which was now only about 150-yards away. Odin realised that there was only one way to gain control, but he had to take a huge risk. When he was trained, he was always told to keep all doors locked when waiting; until you know it's safe to open them. He hoped that the driver of the 4x4 was not as well trained. Odin had to get in and suppress the driver without the guy on the steps seeing. He realised that if he tries to open the door and it's locked, he gives himself away, which will result in a less discreet resolution.

Before he knew it he was only 30 yards from the 4x4. He stayed on the far side of the sidewalk not making it too obvious what his target was. Luckily, he noticed another 4x4 and a van behind the target vehicle which should give him the protection from the guy on the stairs. He noticed up ahead that the traffic lights had gone red and so the traffic that was passing was now slowing and forming a queue, more protection and distraction he thought. This was the moment. He reached into his pocket and pulled out the tube knife and un-sheaved the thick sharp deadly point, now set to find its target. He looked back and noticed nobody behind him, and up ahead, 30 yards away, a couple walking towards him. It was now he had to move.

In the blink of an eye as the couple ahead turned and looked at each other Odin moved swiftly across the sidewalk to the rear of the car and in one movement pulled the handle up and as he felt the it click, he pulled the door open, slid in and closed it.

"What the fu…" the driver shouted in a thick New York accent, as Odin slammed the tube knife into the side of his neck. Odin felt the muscle puncture and the sharp tube slide in like a deadly, steel snake.

The driver made a gargling noise and tried to speak but only jumbled nonsense came out. The rear windows were blacked out and the driver windows dimmed slightly which gave Odin more protection. He turned the steel knife, so the drivers head looked away from the passing couple and as he did, he felt a warm ooze trickle down onto his wrist.

The driver started to breath frantically and his body started to convulse and shake. Blood spurted from his nose and covered his chest and lap with red. Odin lent forward and looked at the police station and noticed the other man looking back inside.
"Who are you working for!?" said Odin aggressively in the man's ear.

The man was unable to communicate properly.
"Fucking tell me who you are working for!" Odin now shouted sending saliva into the man's ear. The driver panicked and screamed in fear and started to cry. Odin lent forward in front of the driver and delivered a brutal elbow back hard to the drivers face. As he did, he felt the man's nose smash and collapse, he stopped convulsing although his eyes remained wide open and his breathing frantic.

"Last time, who are you working for?" Odin said more slowly and clearer just to ensure the guy heard.

"Fuck you," came the response with a spray of blood hitting the dashboard.

With that, Odin shuffled across to directly behind the seat and put his hands around the headrest. He grabbed the top of the man's head with one hand and his chin with the other, and delivered a fast, vicious snap. The driver went limp.

Odin looked up and down the street and noticed people coming from both directions towards the BMW, so he quickly reached around and lowered the seat, so it was flat, and the body slumped down as it retracted. He moved across and with all his might heaved the dead body into the back. He lifted the legs and folded them up to the bodies chest and then lifted the front seat back to its normal position.

Now he had the full protection of the blacked-out windows and so, with difficulty, he got the body in a sitting position in the back. Once done, he sat back himself, breathing hard and sweating trying to get his composure and breath back, his arms and back aching from the exertion.

He looked up and saw the other guy still waiting outside still looking into the police station. But it was then he noticed the man look around and then walk inside. Odin hoped it was not to kill Tom and, if it was, there was enough police around to deter him. Odin jumped across into the driver's side and kept a close eye on the entrance hoping that if the man comes back out, he won't notice Odin.

The receptionist had since been back to Tom and told him someone would see him with a concerned look on her face. A minute or so later a police officer had opened a door off to the right and asked Tom to come though and so he had gone into a small but bustling office and sat at a desk with the officer. The officer smiled at Tom and typed some information into a computer and then looked up to Tom.

"What happened to your nose?" he asked politely, pointing at his own nose.

Tom felt the tense heat shoot through him. Was this a genuine question or a test? He realised he needed to stay calm and sagged his shoulders. He then smiled.

"Ah, this?" he asked pointing at his face, "the result of my nose meeting the end of a football."

The officer smiled and Tom added, "It was a good pass but...Just took my off it for a split second."

The officer had nodded, and Tom wasn't sure if he had done enough to pass the test, if it was one. They had then proceeded to Tom's statement and he had told the officer the story as briefly as he could, realising that time was against Odin, who would be hanging around to find out what was going on. As Tom spoke, he was thinking about how this was going to play out, but it all added to the confused and desperate state he was trying to portray.

Tom had focussed on his mental health and just wanting to get away. As a final desperate act he had even told the officer he was having bad thoughts and being in the house is making him question his worth and that things may be better if he takes the easy way out. The officer looked concerned and a bit uncomfortable but in a very friendly response had said "You need to be positive, sir. Try and remain upbeat, I am sure you can cope with this."

It was exactly what Tom had wanted to hear, and it had pleased him that the officer had said, that to help him cope, he could he get this done today. The officer had smiled and looked at his computer screen. He spoke without looking away.
"This isn't high priority as according to the case file there was a note. Your wife, she left you, is that right?"
Tom interjected, "Yes, that's right," and got the letter out and handed it to the officer. Tom continued as he read it, "But she is still missing. We don't know where she is. It's still a missing case. Her parents are desperate. We all are," Tom tried to make himself sound close to breaking point, "I need to get away from it all...I am visiting friends in Pittsburgh."

The officer sat back in his chair and looked at his watch, "Look, ok, I have an hour before my shift ends. I suppose it makes sense to do this now, seeing as you are here," and shrugged his shoulders. The officer took a deep breath, "Okay, sit tight, I will bring my car round and I will give you a shout you when I am ready".

Tom smiled and sat back in the chair. The officer got up and walked across the office to a key press and grabbed a set of car keys. He opened another door that had a section of frosted glass. Tom heard the officer, "Sir, just heading over to North Shore to tie up some missing persons enquiry."

The officer closed the door and looked at Tom and smiled,

"Won't be a minute," he told him and, with relief, Tom smiled again.

Odin waited and watched. The man had not yet come out. He looked round at the body and noticed a small trickle of blood coming from the tube knife. One of the advantages of using it was that it was relatively clean. Odin realised how lucky he was that the car had blacked out windows in the rear, as this would have been a lot more complicated. Odin sat back in the chair. He focussed and waited, and whilst watching got his gun to hand and started fitting a silencer.

Inside the officer had called for Tom and they had walked out through the reception. It was then that Tom noticed the man he saw outside sitting in the reception area talking to the old lady although Tom was unable to hear what they were saying. As they walked through the reception to the patrol car bays at the side the man looked up and looked into Tom's eyes.
Tom looked back and knew that something was wrong. He knew enough already about The Order to know this was one of the pursuers. He could feel it.

The officer led him through another and as he did, he said to the receptionist.
"Ok Betty, just taking this guy home to do the necessary," to which he got a "Uh-huh" for a reply, as she looked over her glasses at the computer screen. As they walked through the door Tom looked back and saw the guy get up and leave walk towards the exit.

Odin saw the guy come out and as he did Odin saw him hold his finger in the air with a spinning motion, which Odin took as, "We are leaving."

Odin was confident the man hadn't noticed him driving and not his colleague. He started the engine and started to reverse out of the space. He noticed the guy looking up and down the street trying to find a place to cross. Tom edged out of the parking bay and waited as the man crossed the street, jogging as he saw another car approaching. Before Odin knew it the door was open, and the man started to get in saying.
"Looks like he is going home with the cops…" as the man slid in and looked round Odin noticed the look of shock on his face, but before the man could react Odin pumped two silent bullets into his stomach.

The man grunted as each bullet penetrated his insides. Odin lent across the man to try and shut the door but as he did the man came to life and grabbed his throat and screamed.
"You mother fucker!!"

Odin felt hands like clamps suddenly stop oxygen getting to his lungs. He was in an awkward position with his head on the man's lap whilst being throttled. He somehow managed to move his arm round and pump two more bullets into the man's stomach and as he did blood splattered across his own face. The man grunted again and after a few seconds, Odin felt the pressure release and was able to sit up.

The man wheezed and let out a cry. Odin sat back and looked up and in the rear-view mirrors and suddenly heard the horn from the car behind, waiting for him to move. He composed himself and wiped the blood from his face and reversed back into the parking bay. He checked for passers-by and when a gap in the pedestrian traffic came, he slid into the back.

He took a deep breath and performed the same manoeuvre to get the next body into the rear seats. Luckily this guy was not as big as the first and so, although still difficult and awkward, it wasn't quite as hard. Whilst in the back with the dead bodies he leant over and pulled the coat sleeve up of one of the men. It revealed what Tom had already known. A crude tattoo on the underside of the man's wrist of a small circle representing an 'O' with a capital 'T' in the centre. It was 'The Order's symbol which all of their agents were marked. Just for confirmation he leant further over and did the same with the other man but this time had to unbutton his shirt sleeve collar. Again, the crude tattoo was on the underside of his wrist.

He got back into the front seat and looked in the mirror. His face was smeared with blood and sweat so he tried to clean it some more, pulled his hood around his face and sat back and took a deep breath. Now all he needed was for Tom to come out to let him know what was happening.

As Tom walked across the car park, he suddenly remembered he need to tell Odin. He stopped.
"Oh no, I forgot," he said and put his hand on his forehead. The officer stopped and turned. Tom continued, "my friend dropped me here, they said they will wait until I know what's happening…I need to let them know"

The officer shrugged his shoulders, "Well OK, go tell them and I will meet you out front."

Tom smiled and quickly jogged back across the lot. He went back to the door to the reception, but it was locked. He looked up and saw a buzzer which he pressed. 20 seconds later the door opened, and Betty's head popped round looking as confused as before.

"I just need to let my friend know I am going" said Tom.

Without the enthusiasm to ask any more questions Betty allowed him through, and Tom jogged towards the reception, desperately hoping not to see the man that had raised suspicion. But suddenly thought to himself what he would do if he did see him. Tom slowed when he reached the reception and tried to peer out to see who was inside. Luckily, he did not see the man, so he continued out to the exit to the main stairs. He stood at the top looking around but couldn't see Odin or the car. He then heard a horn and looked and saw a black BMW parked opposite. He didn't recognise it but then heard the horn again.

He looked closer and the window came down and he saw Odin in the driver's seat. Confused he made his way down the steps and, as he did, the BMW came to life and drove out of the bay and made a circle to come around to where he was standing. As it did a car that almost collided with it beeped its horn as it passed.

As the car pulled up the driver side window came down, and Tom saw Odin, looking angry with red smears on his face.
"What the fuck is happening?" Odin asked abruptly.
Tom leant in and was about to speak when he noticed the two men in the back, "Woah! What the fuck?!"
"Shut up," said Odin calmly but sternly, "Forget them. What's happening? Quickly!"
"Er, shit," stuttered Tom, "An officer is taking me back to mine to…"
"Holy shit, is this him?" interrupted Odin, looking up ahead, and as Tom turned, he saw a cruiser slowly drive out of a side exit.
"Yeah, I suppose…"
Odin cut in again abruptly, "Ok, go home, do the necessary. I will be there in half an hour." As he finished talking Tom felt the 4x4 spring to life and leap from its position and screech off past the cruiser slowly approaching.

Tom stood and waited for the cruiser to pull up. He got into the rear and as he did the officer spoke, "You tell your friend they keep driving like that they will get pulled over and issued a ticket for reckless".
Tom laughed nervously and replied, "Sorry, he is in a rush, I have made him late. It's my fault."

Odin looked in the rear-view mirror in between the two dead men's heads and watched the cruiser pull away. He was relieved that the plan appeared to be working and hoped that Tom would keep his nerve and be convincing enough to cut off any police involvement.

In the meantime Odin was now driving the 4x4 used by The Order that had two of their dead agents in the back. He had a few options. One was to just leave the vehicle at the side of the road and wait for the bodies to eventually be found. If they weren't found by a member of the public, or the police, then it would be by agents from The Order scouting the area for the vehicle and their agents.

This was the best option he thought. The Order would clear up as they wouldn't want any unnecessary involvement from the authorities. But if it was a public or police find then it may well be regarded as a 'hit' and with little evidence the police would report it and file it off as 'gang related'. Odin's only problem was that if they did check CCTV, they may get a lead on him.

The other option was to erase the vehicle and make it disappear. But Odin wasn't aware of any contacts close by that could organise this. Plus, time was against him, as The Order send scouts very efficiently. The agents he had killed would have a deadline to check in and, when they didn't, the place will be swarming. It was how The Order operated.

As he drove, he looked up and down looking for a spot to dump the vehicle now realising he was getting further away from his own car. Eventually Odin decided that it would be best just to park up at the side of the road and leave the car out in the open. There was less chance of being picked up on CCTV, plus, the blacked-out windows should hide the bodies from pedestrians, and they would either be found by the police if its towed, or if it was found by The Order.

Odin found a spot in between a long row of cars and manoeuvred in. He looked around to check for pedestrians and both ways appeared clear. He leant round and pulled the tube knife from the neck of the dead agent. As he did the body slumped to the side and blood started to pour from the wound. Odin pushed the body back away from the window and as he did its head fell the other way, almost as if it was leaning on his dead colleague's shoulder. Odin wiped the knife on the man's jeans and re-sheaved it into its brass tube holder.

Odin took his gun and also wiped the blood from the end of it on the dead man's jeans. Odin knew that when he had time, he would have to get the weapons deep cleaned. He took off the surgical gloves, both smeared and covered in blood, folded them inside out and stuffed them in his pocket. He would dispose of them further away from the scene. He pulled up his hood, checked it was clear of pedestrians again, and got out.

He locked the car and walked away briskly heading back to his own car. On the way he nonchalantly threw the BMW keys in a litter bin.

Chapter 32

As Officer Bolton pulled up to the house, Tom suddenly felt a feeling of nervousness. The neighbours would be watching, and in this neighbourhood, you would sometimes see a patrol car cruise past from time to time, but the fact that Tom was getting out of one would be unusual. None of the neighbours would have seen him or Jenna for several days and so would have probably just thought they were away. But seeing Tom walking to the house with a police officer would get tongues wagging.

Officer Bolton stopped the car directly outside and Tom immediately took a look round to see which houses were visible from their position and calculated that it was several; including the Harrison's, Anderson's and the Wrigley's, plus a few others of people he didn't know. As Tom got out he imagined telling one of the neighbours that Jenna had left him and what their reaction would be. But, then again, with any luck Tom would soon be out of Evanston for good, and would never see any of these people again, so it didn't matter. In the grand scheme of things neighbours gossiping were actually very low on Tom's list of worries.

Officer Bolton smiled and held a hand out for Tom to lead the way which he did. As Tom approached the front door, he couldn't help but imagine him opening it and the smell of rotting flesh hitting him and a swarm of flies buzzing around the house having their feast on the three dead bodies he had left behind. He felt mostly confident by now that Odin was true to his word and would have, as he had told him several times, had the house 'cleaned'. But the nagging feeling Tom had was hard to control. A knot in his stomach that had started when he first got into the patrol car had now tightened to an almost unbearable tautness.

He felt sick, but there was no going back now. Advised by Odin to do this to clear his name and any suspicion the police may have over Jenna's disappearance; he knew deep down the plan of action was correct. He just wished he had checked the house first before returning with the police. He should've insisted on it with Odin and suddenly he questioned if his trust of Odin had been naïve. His life and future relied on Odin and as he turned the key in the lock, he realised that he now relied on him more than ever. If the house still contained the bodies, he could very well spend the rest of his life in prison.

The lock clicked and the door released. Tom pushed the door and it felt stiff and he realised there was an obstruction. His heart stopped. But he pushed harder and felt the obstruction give way and the sound of shuffling papers. He realised that the doorway was jammed with mail. He opened the door wide enough to slip his leg round and push the mail out of the way with his foot and as he did, he felt a warm, musty sensation, but luckily, also a fresh clean smell. He went inside and looked through the main access into the kitchen and saw no bodies and no blood. His stomach knot released, and a wave relief washed over him.

"I need to open some windows. It's been warm," Tom said, as he opened the door wider to allow Bolton access to the house.

Officer Bolton smiled gratefully and walked in nodding in appreciation of Tom's invitation. He turned to Tom politely waiting for the invitation to go any further as Tom bent down and picked up the envelopes, brochures, leaflets and other junk mail, and then advised Officer Bolton to follow him through. As he followed Officer Bolton spoke.
"Look, I appreciate this is difficult for you so I won't keep you long. It's just some procedural questions and I will have a quick look around, if that's OK?"

Tom nodded and they walked through the spacious access into the kitchen.
"That's fine," he replied, "Coffee? Tea?"
Bolton declined. But Tom needed a coffee so put the kettle on and started going through the mail flicking through the formal looking items and junk until he got to a small white envelope with his name written in what looked startlingly like Jenna's writing.

As he opened it Bolton spoke again, "So, where do you want to do the statement?"

Tom never replied. He slipped the letter out and unfolded it and started to read Jenna's forged writing:

Tom my dearest Tom,

I felt compelled to write to you again.

I am so sorry. It was not my intention for this to happen and to hurt you. Any hurt I have caused I truly apologise for.

As you know things were not right between us and hadn't been for some time. I know you suspected I was having an affair, but I wasn't brave enough to tell you face to face. I at least owned you that. I am sorry and ashamed. I wish things could have been different between us. Now is not the time to explain my feelings and what pushed me to leave you. But what has happened has happened, and there is now no going back.

I am in love with another person and I have been with him. We were at his house for a short while, but we have now left to start our new life together. It will be far away and possibly even abroad. I need to tell you this so you don't hold any hope I will return to you. I know that sounds harsh, but for your own benefit, you need to move on. There can't be any reconciliation. My mind is made up.

I am too ashamed to tell my parents. I know they will be worried about me. And I realise that, in view of all this mess, asking you for a favour is completely inappropriate. But I wonder if you could contact them and let them know I am safe. In time I hope that I will be get over my shame and be able to contact them. I would be truly grateful if you could do that for me.

If it's any consolation I want you to know I did love you and I was happy for a long time. Our life together was special, and I am truly sorry this happened. I hope one day you can understand my position and why I had to do this.

I hope you find love again and live a healthy, happy life.

With love and regret,

Jenna xx

As Tom finished the letter a genuine tear rolled down his face. He realised immediately that the letter almost completely and utterly eradicated him from any suspicion. And it would be exactly what he needs to get the police out of his hair and allow him to get away. But, as he was reading, the true impact of what had happened hit him like a juggernaut. The brutality of the situation was too much to bear and unable to resist, he started to cry.

The woman he loved had betrayed him and was dead, gone forever. Her parents would spend the rest of their lives clinging to a lie that one day they will see her again. As Tom cried Officer Bolton came over and put a hand on his shoulder and took the letter. He quickly read it, folded the letter and put it on the side.

Tom quietly sobbed, "Come on, sit down," Bolton said as he led Tom out of the kitchen and into the lounge. Tom sat down on the couch and tried to compose himself, Bolton continued, "Look, I will give you a minute and I will take a look around and, well, if you are OK we will do a quick statement and I will be on my way," Tom nodded and wiped his eyes. As Bolton walked out of the lounge Tom realised he was in the clear. The letter had been perfect. But Tom had been surprised at how emotional he had got. He felt like the letter was real and that Jenna had actually left him. He hadn't had to act or put on a show. It was genuine.

Tom got up and took a deep breath. He heard Officer Bolton walking up stairs and walked back into the kitchen and he looked around. Odin had been right. The place looked spotless; as clean and tidy as it had ever been. But not too clean and tidy that it looked completely sanitised. There were still every-day items dotted around and the place still had a lived-in look. Magazines, the remote controls, two cups in the sink; various items. It was perfect. As Tom imagined the fake story of Jenna leaving him, he realised that the house played perfectly into that scenario. Once again, Tom had a lot to thank Odin for.

Tom left the kitchen and went upstairs. As he got to the top, he saw Bolton come out of the bedroom with a notepad and open in his hand. "Look, sorry about that," Tom said.
"Whoa!" interjected Bolton, "You have nothing to apologise for. Please, I appreciate this is difficult," he put an arm on Tom's shoulder, "I think I am done here. Shall we do your statement? Then I can leave you alone?"

Tom nodded and smiled, and as Bolton started to descend the stairs Tom quickly popped his head around the bedroom door and looked inside. The wardrobe doors were open, and a small suitcase was open on the floor. Clothes were strewn across the floor and bed. Drawers were open and some paperwork lay on the bed. At a glance it fitted perfectly into the scenario of a person rushing to pack and get out.

As Tom got downstairs Bolton stood in the kitchen with his notepad and pen to hand. Tom noticed the kettle had boiled and set about making a coffee, as he did Bolton asked the first question, "So, what time was it when you got back and realised she was gone?"

Tom answered and then did the same for all the questions and gave very honest and detailed answers. At no point did he feel under suspicion. In fact, he felt that Bolton was only asking the absolute necessary questions, and never once pushed for Tom to elaborate. Tom realised that Bolton already believed Jenna had simply upped and left and that was it.

Bolton only asked him several questions. The most difficult question was why Tom felt Jenna had gone to the state of Pennsylvania. It initially

273

threw Tom and he realised that he had not planned for this question. He tried desperately not to make it look obvious we was searching his mind for a plausible answer. But thinking quickly he said that she had got involved with a mail order business her friend ran in a small town near Pittsburgh. Jenna had told him the head sales office was there.

He then stated, "Which I now find was a lie and it was obviously where the affair was taking place. I checked for the business and It doesn't exist."

Bolton had written it all down and given Tom a sympathetic look. He eventually told Tom he had all he needed and first thing tomorrow he would update the missing persons case with the information. He also took two photos on his mobile phone of the letter and told Tom to keep the original. As they walked to the front door Tom asked.
"So, as far as this being a missing person case goes, what happens now?" Bolton stopped and turned to him.
"Look, Tom, I'll be honest, this is now about as far as a missing persons case as it can get. Jenna has made contact and I will find it hard to keep this one alive. It will remain open but a very low priority. I mean, I know how..."
"No, please don't explain. I realise that. I mean, it was her mother's idea to report her missing which is understandable,". Bolton nodded as Tom spoke and put his notepad and pen away into his pocket.

Tom continued, "I suppose she is technically missing, but I am sure there are thousands of people who just vanish with nothing to go on."
Bolton nodded again. "Yep, too many to even comprehend. At least you and her parents have the knowledge that she has told you she is safe. Many people would be desperate for that at least," Tom nodded and they walked towards the door.
"So," continued Bolton "What's your plans? You mentioned friends in Pittsburgh?"
"Er, yeah. Just old friends who have offered me a lifeline."
"That's nice. Good luck with everything,"

Tom smiled. He was genuinely touched by the officers sincerity.
"Look, Officer Bolton, I want to thank you for your time and appreciate you coming out at short notice...I am sure you understand I need to get away..."
"Don't explain, Tom. It's been good to meet you and I hope you get some news soon. But, I think moving on is the best option for you."

Tom held out his hand and Bolton returned his and they shook a firm handshake.

"If we hear anything I will be the first to let you know," said Bolton, opening the door, he smiled, walked out and closed the door quietly behind him.

As the door closed Tom took a deep breath. The biggest and deepest breath he had ever taken.

Chapter 33

Odin had collected the car that had been organised and had slowly made his way to Tom's house. He guessed it had been roughly an hour since Tom left the police station. He hoped that this had been long enough.

As he had driven to a few streets from Tom's house he parked up and seen the police cruiser pass him. He just looked straight ahead and watched in his wing mirror as it made its way onto the main road and away. He hoped that Tom would not be much longer.

Inside the house, as soon as Tom had seen Officer Bolton pull away, he had gone into overdrive. The house was almost certainly the most dangerous place for him right now. It was, in fact, so dangerous, that Tom wondered if The Order would even check there, as it would be so stupid of him to go there in the first place. But he could not take that chance, and knew his time was limited. Odin would not allow him to take his time.

He had already packed a sports bag of clothes and essentials. He had retrieved his passport and the bundle of emergency cash that he always kept in a wooden box behind the cereal boxes in the kitchen cupboard. At a glance he calculated roughly $600.

He had left everything by the door and then quickly headed to the garage. Inside he opened the unit he had fitted when they moved in which contained his personal items. In between the trophies and pictures of him receiving them there was a large box. He took out the box and laid it down and, as he did, he felt a wave of sadness engulf him. He had a vague idea in his head of some of the photo's he wanted to take but couldn't be sure exactly where they were.

He knew his mum had lots of photos of him growing up, that Claire would now take ownership of those when the house is cleared. But he had some special ones and wanted to find them. He pulled out various packs and started quickly to flick through the contents. As he did, he smiled without realising it. Photos of him at college, proms, nights out, camping, on the beach. But he realised he couldn't take them all. Most of the ones he looked at, he discarded with anger and resentment; wishing that he didn't have to toss away his memories.

Eventually he found one he wanted. It was 1994 in Mexico on a family vacation. His mum, dad, Tom and Claire were sat on a beach in Cancun and the genuine happiness on all their faces was clearly evident. It was a moment that Tom had always wished he could go back to, stop time and then stay there forever.

Another photo he kept was him and his dad on their first fishing trip in 1992, upstate New York. He smiled as he looked at it and thought that his dad looked so vibrant, funny and strong. It was the photo that epitomised his dad. Another of him and Claire on a boat with their Mum around 1989. It was the photo that completely emulated the beauty and dignity of his mum. She looked utterly stunning in her swimwear, with the sun beaming down onto her tanned face. Tom and Claire stood side by side holding her with obvious pride in their faces.

Various strewn packets and photos built up around him. Emotion rose within him, but he subdued it, although couldn't prevent a tear rolling down his face. Knowing that Odin would soon arrive he pulled more photos out. More holidays, more days out, more memories. He flicked through them as quickly as he could and over the next five minutes pulled out another fifteen to twenty photos.

Some of them made him laugh out loud. In one; Claire and his mum had sat to have a photo on the beach, but the tide had come in rapidly without warning and the look of horror on their faces as the cold Atlantic sea soaked them was priceless.

He also found a great photo of him and his friends from New York at his wedding party. Another of him and H on his first day at work. He laughed when he saw H had one arm on his shoulder and the other doing a V sign above his head.

There were lots of him and Jenna on holiday and various events, but one photo in particular stuck out. It was Tom and Jenna on a skiing trip in Catskills. Tom remembered his friend taking it and he can still recall how in love he felt with her at that time. It was taken around lunchtime and they sat on a bench with the mountains behind them covered by a clear, bright blue sky. The table in front of them contained beer, wine and food. They both had suntans and rosy cheeks from the cold mountain air.

Their faces exuded love, joy and happiness. Tom remembered that it had been a wonderful day. One that he would never forget. And, despite everything and what she had done, he couldn't deny how he felt at that time, and so he put it with his small collection and smiled to himself.

Tom could've sat there all day. And wished that he had looked at them more when he had time to reminisce and enjoy them. Grabbing his bundle of photo's he stood up and exhaled a large emotional breath. It wasn't perfect but he felt as happy as he could under the circumstances with the photo's he had picked. A small snippet of his best memories, hopefully now safe.

But as he looked down, he noticed another packet he wasn't sure if he had looked in. He quickly bent down and picked it up and opened it. Inside he noticed several photo's bundled together and pulled them out.

The first was him and Davy around 1988 on their BMX bikes. Another they were sitting in Tom's room making screwed up faces. One that normally made Tom laugh was one of around mid-90's with Davy running naked across a friend's garden after he had got into the hot-tub and they had stolen his clothes. But this time Tom didn't smile. He felt no emotion. Just a numbness. He dropped the photos on the floor with all the other discarded memories.

Just as they hit the floor Tom heard a horn from outside. It was time to go.

Chapter 34

They had driven for about ten minutes but had not spoken. Then Odin had asked Tom if he was OK and Tom had simply nodded. Odin realised it had been difficult for Tom to go back home. A few minutes later Odin asked him if the police officer had seen the letter. Tom nodded again. Then he realised that Odin wanted, and deserved, more information. "Yeah, it was fine. The letter was perfect. Jenna is fine and living with her new man. I have to supposedly just move on and forget about her."

Odin never replied. He didn't need to say much more, although he reminded Tom that it may be best to call Jenna's parents to update them. Tom had questioned this, but Odin reminded him that very soon he will be uncontactable, and so it would be a good opportunity for him to tell her about the second letter and reassure her. Tom realised he was right as usual, "It will also give you an opportunity to cut them off," Odin had also said, following on from his original advice.

Tom took his phone out and found the contact 'Jenna Ma & Pa'. Odin looked across.
"Do you want me to pull over and give you some privacy?"
Tom shook his head and pressed the call button.

The phone rang a few times until Tom heard a click and Cindy quietly say. "Hello?"
"Hi Cindy. It's Tom"
"Oh Tom! How are you? I am so happy to hear from you."
Tom knew she was genuinely happy to hear from him, but he couldn't help noticing in her voice it may have been more to do with the desperate hope he had some news.
"Er, Cindy. Just to let you know I have spoken to the police and they came to the house."
"Oh. Everything OK?" Tom sensed genuine concern in her voice.
"It was all fine. Just procedure. They weren't there long. They took my statement and said they would be in touch."
"Oh, that's fine," he sensed a hint of disappointment in her voice as she couldn't hide the fact that she had been hoping for Tom to tell her they had found Jenna.
"But there is something else. When I arrived back home there was another letter. From Jenna."
"Oh!" her voice suddenly animated with a sense of excitement. Tom heard her shout away from the phone, "Tom got a letter from Jenna!" realising that she was now talking to Bob.
"Go on, Tom," she requested.

"It's…Well, it basically said that she is really sorry. She did go to Pennsylvania and now she is going away with her new lover. She said she never wanted to hurt me, and she never planned it to be like this…"
Tom paused waiting for a response but all he could hear was quiet breathing as Cindy listened intently.
He continued, "She is going away. Far away. She said she is very sorry for not being in touch, but she is ashamed and…"
Tom then heard her break down and a sickening moan come from the other end of the line followed by uncontrollable crying and, knowing the actual truth, Tom felt unbearable guilt.
"Cindy, are you ok?"
"Tom? What's going on?" came Bob's voice, who had obviously now taken the phone, but Tom didn't feel he had it in him to tell the same lie again.
"Bob, look, just tell Cindy she can get a copy of the letter from the missing persons file."
"What? Cindy, calm down. Tom? What's going on?" Bob asked, now sounding a little desperate himself.
Tom interjected, "Bob. Jenna has written to me. It's over. She is moving away with another man. She hopes to be in touch with you soon. She has told me to move on. I have to go."
"Wait! Tom…I don't understand!"
"Bob, I have to go. I am sorry. Jenna is safe and she will be in touch," and with that Tom terminated the call and turned his phone off.

He felt sick with guilt and angry with himself for ending it that way. Cindy and Bob were good people and deserved to know the truth but telling them the truth was impossible. It would complicate the whole thing more than he could ever actually realise. Tom relaxed his body back into the seat and stared out of the window.

After several minutes Odin looked at Tom.
"Don't feel bad. At least you have given them some hope to live with".
Tom felt like shouting at Odin that they deserved more but, as usual, he knew that in the grand scheme of things he was right. That little bit of hope may prevent them from going insane.

They set in for another long drive but this time it would be easier as they would basically take the most direct route from Lake Michigan to Lake Eerie, skirt around Cleveland and then zero in south-east to Pittsburgh.

At the same time, back in Chicago, a black van was parked on waste ground close to Indian Harbour. In the back, Officer Bolton was confused and hurting from indescribable pain. The tape across his mouth was preventing him from shouting for help, although the beating he had taken had crippled him to the point where he couldn't speak anyway.

When the men in masks had started the interrogation, they had used a blow torch to burn his fingers individually. They had asked him about a man called 'Tom'. The man that he had been with. After burning three fingers down the bone; the pain reached such a level, he had told them that all he knew was Tom had mentioned he was going to Pittsburgh. They had then stopped burning the fingers, as Bolton had given them the information they wanted, but also one of the men had to get out and be sick, due to the intense smell. The pain had made Bolton scream in pain so loud and so they had taped his mouth.

Then the beating had started. As the blows rained down Bolton had wished he hadn't stopped the van for cutting across him at a stop sign. He should've realised it was a set up. With his hands bound all he could do was move his head to avoid the blows, but he had reached a point where he had stopped as it was futile. His head throbbed to the point of feeling as though it was going to explode but, from a point, he almost became numb to the subsequent blows. All he could see was the men standing above him bringing their feet down on him. He tried to open his eyes but couldn't see and was struggling to breath properly as blood chocked his airways.

When the beating stopped Bolton lay there. Drifting in and out of consciousness and seeing his family running towards him through a hazy field of long grass, smiling and laughing. He felt the warmth of the sun and a sense of contentment and happiness like he had never felt before, but each time his beautiful wife and two young girls reached him they snapped back to the other side of the field and started to run towards him again.

Finally, as they reached him for the last time a metallic clang snapped him from his dream. He felt a sensation of being dragged and suddenly felt cold and isolated. He looked up and saw a masked man above him and a crane beyond him overhead. He also heard the sound of seagulls and the deep horn of a ship close by.

They were the last sounds he heard. As with one last drag he felt his stomach turn like he was on a rollercoaster. His body flipped and his last memory was dark water rushing towards him, then a crash and a sudden frozen, deathly feeling. He screamed in fear and immediately felt a rush of cold water enter his nostrils with a burn. Then everything went black.

281

Chapter 35

Eventually Tom started to feel his eyes get heavy and, realising Odin wasn't in the mood to speak, he relaxed and soon became very sleepy. After seeing a sign for West Unity he realised they still had a long way to go, so eventually gave in to his tiredness, and fell into a deep sleep. It wasn't until a few hours later he felt himself being gently roused with a hand on his shoulder. He opened his eyes and looked around and saw Odin looking at him.
"Coffee time," he said with a smile.

They walked across the parking lot and Tom yawned, "Good sleep?" Odin asked with a smile. Tom nodded and smiled.
"No nightmares?" Odin enquired, this time with a different tone, intimating it was a genuine question.
Tom shook his head, "Not a thing," appreciating Odin's concern.

It was late afternoon and the sky was clear blue with not a cloud to be seen and Tom felt the sun warm his body and could almost feel it penetrate his bones. It vitalised him and a warm, fuzzy feeling flowed around his body. As they crossed the road Tom looked around to get his bearings, which Odin noticed.
"We're in Ambridge. Quiet little town I use to hole up sometimes," he notified.

Tom noticed they were heading towards a coffee shop overlooking what he calculated as being the Ohio river. As they approached Tom noticed the people, couples, friends and families all dotted around outside on the grass, benches and tables. He looked at them, happy and content. People with their children, brothers and sisters, aunts and uncles, cousins. Lovers, friends and families that were together and were there for each other.

People who took days like this for granted.

He felt a sadness. A sadness that he could not be the one sitting there with his mum and sister, having a hot Americano and a slice of cake. Planning what to do later that evening, whether to go to the cinema or out for a meal, or whether just to all go home and relax together, talking, laughing and just enjoying each other's company. Things that normal people take for granted that Tom could never experience again.

A sudden wave of emotion engulfed him, and he desperately wished his mum was still alive. He wished he could just sit and talk once more with her. To tell her how grateful he was for all she had done for him and the sacrifices she had made. The sacrifices that her and his father had made. To thank them for the life that they built to provide such a comfortable and loving home for Tom and Claire. He missed them both terribly and he looked away from Odin as he battled to hold his emotion in.

He knew he would never have days like this again. A day with his family without worrying what the time was or about deadlines or appointments. Where the only decision was what cake to have with your coffee.
He had experienced the perfect family unit that as a young child, into his early teens and then onto being a young man, ready for the world. Adult life and the responsibilities that came with it had slowly eroded that over time. But that was a natural evolution for a lot of people. He accepted that. But what was so hard to accept was how it had been ripped from away him by The Order and by who and what he actually was.

The enormity of the situation suddenly hit him. Here he was walking into a coffee shop and he was an angel. It was absurd. If only these people knew.

But, then again, was he really an angel? He only had Odin's word for it and was yet to receive any real evidence, just coincidental stuff. It couldn't be true. But at some point he intended to try and find out for certain.

His thoughts were broken as they entered the coffee shop. As they queued, Odin told Tom that they weren't staying long and had to be back on the road to make the drop off time. They picked up two coffees to go and walked back to the car. After a few sips Tom felt more awake and had his focus. He realised he had obviously needed the sleep.

As they got into the car Odin asked Tom if he had managed to get any photo's or personal belongings. Tom had smiled and retrieved his holdall from the back and got the photo's out. He showed them to Odin and explained when and where they were taken. Odin was genuinely happy for Tom. He had been in the same position before and knew how important it was to maintain some of the memories from your old life. He saw the happiness in Tom when describing the holiday they were on or the circumstances of the photo.

Once Tom had finished showing Odin, he asked him if he had any old photos. Odin looked away and took a sip of coffee. He sighed.
"Afraid not. My situation didn't allow for it," Odin paused, and Tom wasn't sure if he was going to continue. Tom thought he wasn't and was about to speak when Odin spoke, stopping Tom, "I was whisked away in the dead of night before The Order burnt my house down with

everything in it…" Odin hesitated. Tom sensed that Odin had deliberately stopped the story at that point and although Tom wanted to push for details, he did not.

"I am sorry," was all he said.

Odin never spoke. He stared straight ahead, and Tom noticed that he was looking into a dream. Re-living a moment in his mind. To his surprise Odin continued.

"They burnt everything. But also everyone."

Odin paused and Tom froze, suddenly realising the true extent of Odin's story.

"All that was dear to me burned in that house. I was saved by The Network. Dragged from my bed. As I got put into the back of the car, I could hear their screams. I was driven away through the forest, the orange light from the fire was so vivid. I remember staring at it for miles until it was a dot in the night like a star…"

Tom held his breath. He couldn't move. It was the first time Odin had ever demonstrated any emotion. Tom now knew why Odin was so against The Order. Why his life was now dedicated to The Network. Tom also now understood why Odin was so unemotive and pragmatic.

"I hear those screams each night before I go to sleep. And the same screams wake me up in the middle of the night."

Tom didn't say a word. He didn't know what to say. Was there anything he could say at that time? Odin continued and broke the silence.

"A twelve-year-old boy, dragged from his bed and never seeing his family again. Taken to live with strangers. It was traumatic but…"

Odin put his coffee into the drinks holder and snapped out of his trance. He turned the engine on, revved the engine and sped out of the parking lot heading back to the main route into Pittsburgh. Tom wondered why Odin had told him. He wondered if he had to tell someone every now and then, just to help to cope.

Tom never asked him any more about it and Odin never said anymore. Tom knew there was no need for any further questions or discussions.

Odin had told him enough.

Chapter 36

Interstate 279 was busy, but the traffic was at least flowing well enough to make progress. As they neared, the city appeared off in the background and started to grow taller and bolder with each mile they completed. The nicer suburbs were slowly left behind and the streets around them became greyer and harder. Tom suddenly felt a gritty edge to the environment.

They crossed the Allegheny river over Veterans Bridge with the UPMC and Fifth Avenue Place buildings dominating the city skyline off to the right. They traversed the main freeway dissecting the city, crossed the Liberty bridge and then back out eventually driving into Allentown.

Tom had been deep in thought on the approach in from Ambridge and hadn't noticed up to now the change in the weather and the sky that roughly an hour ago was clear blue had darkened, and it had started to drizzle. The area looked destitute, run down and unforgiving and gave Tom a nervous, uneasy feeling. It was a place that did not welcome outsiders and where only the tough, street smart and strong willed survive. His immediate thought was that he hoped he wouldn't be staying here too long and he wondered if Odin sensed what he was feeling.

Eventually, at the end of a main street, they came to a fork in the road. Heading right led up a hill to what looked like some rundown two-level apartments. Heading left led to a piece of waste ground which, across the far side, were some old industrial buildings and lock up's. Beyond that stood what looked like more apartments. They looked so dilapidated, Tom wondered if they were disused and vacant.

Odin took a left and drove slowly across the waste ground and bumped back down onto an access road which led up through the industrial buildings towards the apartments. He drove around the back and pulled up onto the kerb. Tom looked at the apartment block and the area that it was situated in and wondered if it was safe for anyone to live here, let alone even him in his current situation.

Odin told Tom to wait in the car and then got out, walked to one of the front doors at the ground level of the apartment block where he rang the bell. He looked inside one of the windows to his right and then moved back to the door and the door opened. An elderly lady stepped out and her and Odin embraced. She then went back inside, and Odin followed her.

After a few minutes Odin came back out and gestured to Tom to go to him. Tom grabbed his holdall from the back seat and went over noticing that Odin was now holding an envelope.

They walked through a door underneath an arch that led to a garbage disposal area where a sweet, sickly smell filled the air. Odin led him through another door and inside was a communal entrance which was cold, damp and very uninviting. Odin led Tom up the stairs to the first floor and they walked along the corridor to door no.7 where he turned to Tom.
"The keys to your new pad," he said with a smile.

Tom rolled his eyes, shook his head and took the keys. He opened the door and inside was surprisingly pleasant. Unlike the rest of the building it was warm, cosy and looked relatively, clean. It was just a single room with a large window. Tom moved over to the window and looked out and could see the car, the waste-ground and beyond in the distance the tall buildings downtown. All in front of him appeared grey and brutal. In the distance a large freight train could be heard slowly lurching along the track with its deep clickety-clack and bell ringing continuously; which slowly started to fade as it made its way out of the city.

The apartment had a bed, a small kitchenette, an armchair, coffee table, small TV and another door that led to a bathroom. Tom looked in and again noticed it looked and smelt pretty clean.
"It's a bit of a come down I know but, hey, it's the best we can do at the moment", said Odin as he opened a few kitchen cupboards to reveal a few plates and bowls.

Tom was silent. Odin continued.
"Look, it's just for a week. Until your first more permanent place can be sorted."
Tom realised he may be coming across as ungrateful, "Odin, it's fine. Thank you."
"Well, it's cosy. And Marie downstairs, bless her, she is one hell of a landlady. Very caring and attentive. She's been working with us for years. She worked hard to get it like this for you"

Tom smiled. He walked over to his bed and sat down. It felt surprisingly comfortable, although he was very tired and probably could've slept anywhere. He laid back, crossed his ankles and put his hands behind his head. He looked up at Odin who smiled.
"Make yourself at home, why don't you?"
Tom smiled.

Odin sat down on a stall at the kitchenette.

"We have an hour or so before the meet. Look, I had our intelligence put together some information on the people you had been connected to. The people who died." Tom sat up and slid his feet off the bed so was sitting on the edge as Odin continued.

"It was all mailed to Marie. Here you go," and he held the envelope out.

Tom got up and walked over and grabbed the envelope. Odin walked to the door.

"I am going outside to make come calls. We leave in an hour. Check the documents and freshen up," he ordered and left the room and closed the door quietly.

Tom first walked over and opened the window slightly to let some fresh air into the stuffy room and the sound of traffic and police sirens suddenly drifted into the room. He went back over to the stall and sat down, opening the envelope. He pulled out a handful of documents which appeared to be made up of photocopies of newspaper headlines, written statements, lists and photographs. They were all clipped together in what appeared to be three separate individual sets.

He picked up the first set and removed the paper clip to reveal several separate pages. The first page was a photocopy of a front-page newspaper headline from the 'The Plain Dealer' dated Thursday November 29, 1969. Tom looked through the documents and found two other copies of front-page newspaper headlines from 'The Washington Post' and 'Chicago Tribune' both of which were dated around end of November 1969.

All three showed very graphic images of dead bodies strewn along a dirt track and were reporting a massacre of unarmed civilians by American soldiers in the village of 'My Lai' in Vietnam.

Tom had some recollection of this from school but had never read up on it in any real detail. But, from the reports and photo's, he found that the victims included men, women, children and even babies, and that the massacre was perpetrated by soldiers of C Company. Tom found the images very disturbing but was confused as to why he had been given the information.

He put the headline copies down and picked up another document which was a newspaper report on the investigation that notified 14 soldiers were charged, but all charges were later dropped. And only one high ranking officer eventually stood trial but was acquitted. Although later investigations saw two officers sent to prison but were both given early release through a pardon by President Nixon.

Tom sifted through and looked at the final document which was a two-page list of around 30 names split into what appeared to be officers and soldiers. As he studied it he soon realised it was the list of participants or people that were there that day and each entry had a rank, name, duty and a brief description of what they were charged with, plus their comments made under oath.

He didn't recognise any of the names and was, again, confused as to why he had been given this. But then Tom turned to the next page and within the list two were highlighted in yellow. He looked at both which read:

```
Lieutenant Corp. Frank Harrison - C Company
Charged with killing of unarmed civilians, dereliction of
duty and failure to report misconduct
Testified his section were not involved even though
witnesses testified he was seen shooting people at the ditch
site - Pleaded not guilty
Charges dropped

Private First-Class Charlie Redmond - Rifleman - C Company
Charged with the killing of unarmed civilians
Testified that he was told the civilians were V.C. and he
was threatened with being shot if he did not participate -
Pleaded not guilty
Charges dropped
```

The last document was a copy of a photograph that showed around 35 soldiers all smiling and joking, taken in what looked like an army base in Vietnam. Written on the copy was the date Nov 26, 1969. Two of the soldier's faces were circled with marker pen and Tom immediately recognised one as Frank Harrison, as he had seen photos of him from his Vietnam days in his house.

The other person Tom didn't recognise but assumed it was Red. He looked carefully and tried to remember Red's face and somehow he found a likeness. The photo was taken 46 years ago, and so it was difficult, but based on what this information gave him and the likeness he could just about get, he knew it was Red.

Tom was stunned. His eyes widened and he put his head in his hand. He realised now what this meant. Was this their sin which they were never punished for? Tom shook his head as the reality of what Odin had told him suddenly found new life and substance. But now, fully engrossed, he grouped the documents together and put them aside then picked up the second set.

Again, the first page was a newspaper headline, 'The Washington Times', dated Monday 26th May 1987. Tom looked at the photograph of a man entering court named David McDonald Rankin and went on to read that the story was related to an investigation which uncovered a huge number of sexual abuse cases within the Boy Scouts of America. The photograph also had a lady, unknown to Tom, circled in red marker and she was walking closely behind Rankin into the court. The headline was on the day that Rankin was being sentenced after pleading guilty to fifteen counts of child abuse and sexual abuse.

Again, Tom was confused. He had not known David McDonald Rankin, nor had he come into contact with him. He wondered if he had without knowing or inadvertently done so, but then Tom turned the page over to find a typed statement from the court hearing which had the name 'Eva Jane McGeedy' highlighted. Tom froze. He took a deep breath and carried on reading and the statement notified that 'Eva Jane McGeedy, 50', was a Troop Leader Assistant working with Rankin from 1979 to 1986 and was also charged with six counts of child abuse due to several witnesses testifying to her involvement.

McGeedy had pleaded not guilty all the way through the case and in his final address Rankin clearly stated that he worked alone, with no accomplices and with nobody else's knowledge. The judge stated that although the testimonies and evidence against McGeedy were overwhelming, Rankins statement that he worked alone had to supersede this and McGeedy was acquitted.

Tom now realised that the lady in the photo was a younger Mrs McGeedy. Eva McGeedy. He exhaled a large breath and suddenly felt sick. He stood up from the stall and noticed the light in the room suddenly darken. He shook his head in disbelief. Did this make everything Odin had said true or was this just coincidence. These people did bad things, but how did Odin know this was what they died for? He wondered if it was just coincidence. It could still be that Odin was stringing Tom along. He desperately wanted to believe that to be the case but, then when he thought some more, he realised that actually this was exactly what he needed right now. Some evidence to prove his connection to all of this was real.

Tom sat back down and set aside the documents and picked up the last one. Just a single document with a photo clipped to it. He immediately recognised the man in the photo as Arthur Conway, his trading floor boss. The document looked like details taken from a police record and, again, Tom wondered what the relevance of this was.

Then he started to take in the detail, and it notified of two sexual assault charges against Conway in 2004 and 2006, both of which he was acquitted due to lack of evidence. Tom turned the document over and found a photocopy of a small story from The New York Times dated Thursday 15th June 2006 reporting the mysterious death of a young girl who worked for a law firm. Her name was Sherry Langford and she was, at the time of her death, giving evidence in a trial where she had accused her boss at the time, Arthur Conway, of raping her. She had been found dead at her apartment after being stabbed several times.

Tom sat and stared at Conway's photo. He had always hated him, and he hated him even more now. It sent Tom's mind back to the night he found Conway and the secretary in the office and he had always known it wasn't right. Tom had questioned himself for a long time as to whether it was innocent or not. This evidence now seems to suggest it was not innocent and Conway had not learned from his two previous brushes with the law for rape charges. Tom realised that this never categorically meant he was guilty, but someone obviously thought he was.

Tom got up and stared out of the window. The sky was dark grey, and the sun was trying to pierce through the clouds above the city skyline. All of these documents, photos and evidence were absolute concrete evidence that these people had done very bad things and that Tom had, at some point, known or met them and had a connection to them.

However, in Tom's mind, it did not provide any evidence that he was an angel. This was way out of his thought process and Odin would need to come up with a lot more to convince him of that. Or it may just be something he eventually accepts himself. Tom laughed out loud at the absurdity of his thoughts and at this whole situation. He smiled and shook his head, unable to believe it.

As he did he noticed Odin walking across the parking lot on the phone. It was then that he suddenly wondered why there was nothing here for H. As far as Tom could work out the situation with H was no different to Red, Frank, McGeedy and Conway, so why was there no evidence showing him what H had supposedly done?

The thought of it made Tom's stomach turn. A feeling of sadness overcame his body to know that H was capable of something. Something on par with what he had seen the others had done. Then another thought crossed his mind.

Tom then heard the door click and Odin entered the room. Tom turned from the window and he noticed Odin look at the documents on the table. He looked at Tom and smiled.
"You OK?" Odin asked.
"Great." quipped Tom sarcastically.

Tom sat on the edge of the bed and Odin went to the kitchenette side and started to put all of the documents back inside the envelope.
"What did you think?" Odin asked.
Tom shrugged his shoulders, "How can I argue with it? I mean, it's all there in black and white..."
"Look Tom," Odin interrupted, "I just got intelligence to do some digging on the names you gave me and, well, this is what they found. I am not saying it's absolute evidence, but it certainly proves..."
"Where was the stuff for H?" Tom cut in sternly.
"Who?"
"H. Harold, Harold Tweddle. My best friend at work for 5 years."
"Oh, nothing came through, they couldn't find anything...This is why I say..."
Tom laughed, "Yeah, right. Look I don't need your protection from the truth...I can handle it."
Odin laughed "Really? Can you?"
Tom never replied and just shook his head.
"Nothing came through for him," repeated Odin.
"Look, I know there is something..."
"Nothing fucking came through, OK!" shouted Odin, startling Tom and making him jump, "Just don't push it, Tom. Don't make things harder than they are."

Tom realised that Odin was right. He knew he had removed the documents relating to H for Tom's own good. He wondered then if he would ever know and, in fact, even he wanted to. Odin was, as usual, right and that should be the end of it. There was enough evidence to suggest to Tom he was linked to the people and the deaths. He didn't need anymore. He had loved H and he didn't want to know what he had done.

Tom heard a police siren close by and noticed that the drizzle had now turned to rain, which then very quickly became a downpour that clattered heavily on the roof and window. He closed the window and suddenly hoped he would not have to spend too long in this place.

Chapter 37

A short time later Odin advised that they needed to go, "I need to get you to your drop off with Tony's man. You'll get acquainted with them and they will organise your next move."

Tom sat up, put his holdall down, slid it under the bed and they both headed for the door. But Odin stopped Tom halfway.
"Here, take this," and he handed him a small plastic fob the size of dollar coin, "it's a GPS tracker. Keep it on you. It's something that we have recently started giving to portals. Just for added security."

Tom nodded and smiled and put it in his pocket. During the drive Odin had told Tom they were meeting at one of the usual drop off points, which was an underground car park downtown. As they crossed Liberty Bridge heading back into the city the skyscrapers just to the left of them had started glowing like stars. The rain had eased but it was still very wet and there was a chill in the air.

Odin took lefts and rights making his way through the city and eventually they came to the underground car park. It was not very busy, with just a few vehicles dotted about here and there. Odin drove down to the basement level, which had even less cars, and as they got to the bottom of the ramp Tom noticed only three vehicles on that level; one of which was a red BMW which had a stout, well-built man leaning on the front wing smoking.

They slowly cruised over to its position and Odin flashed the lights a couple of times to indicate to the man who it was.
"This is Gianni. A good man. Solid. Works for Tony. He will take you to meet him tonight."

Tom smiled and nodded but nervousness hit him inside. He couldn't understand why, but then realised it felt like the nervousness as a child when going off to first summer camp or school trip away from home. He realised that he was suddenly now about to lose the protection of Odin. He knew this moment had been coming but it hadn't really affected him, nor had he thought about it too much. Without Odin he would've been dead weeks ago. Tom suddenly felt vulnerable. Everything Odin had done was for him and to now lose that comfort and support was obviously going to be hard.

Tom realised that he would now have to rely on himself and The Network. It would be a tough adjustment. But it was also a new chapter.

Tom's life since Odin had come into it had been crazy. It had been a physically exhausting, tiring, stressful and emotional rollercoaster. But Tom had adapted to it and now, even though he was at the start of what should be a more settled period, a small part of him felt sad it was over. He would miss Odin. He wouldn't miss being hunted and Odin having to continuously save his life, but he would miss him.

As the car stopped, he saw Gianni offer a big, broad Italian smile. Tom smiled back but actually wished Odin would keep driving, turn around, drive out the car park and away to anywhere else. Just as long as he stayed by Tom's side protecting him. Tom snapped out of his thoughts. He needed to be strong. He needed to take control and stop relying on Odin. This was his time to take matters into his own hands and get his life back on track as best as he could.

The car stopped.
"Let's go" ordered Odin, "I need to get going."

Tom smiled as he opened the door and got out thinking that this was obviously not going to be as difficult a goodbye for Odin as it will be for him. It wasn't the first time Odin's lack of emotion or empathy had made Tom smile.
"Yo, Odin you old pro. How you doin'?" boomed Gianni as he moved towards Odin, grabbed him and gave him a big hug. Odin laughed and patted Gianni on the back.
"I'm good, Gianni. Well, as good as can be expected,"

Gianni smiled and took another puff on his large cigar. Odin gestured towards Tom with his hand.
"This is Tom. Tony has all the info."

Gianni moved towards Tom and held out a large hand with sausage like fingers. Tom shook his hand and was surprised at the crushing intensity of the handshake.
"Good to meet you, Tom".
Odin continued, "It's the usual. The warehouse to meet Tony and then back to Marie's"
"Yeah, yeah" Gianni cut in, "I spoke to Tony. We got it under control. I mean, how many we done now? Five or Six?"
Odin shrugged, "Must be," answering as he moved to the back of the car and took Tom's holdall out and brought it round to him.

293

Tom smiled as he took the holdall which held all of his worldly belongings. Tom felt uncomfortable and that this moment had come all too soon.

"Look, Odin...I don't know what to say..."

Odin smiled and shook his head, "Don't say anything."

"No, I mean, everything you've done...Thank you."

"It's fine. It's what I do. Just take care of yourself, OK?"

Tom nodded and smiled as Odin patted him on his arm.

"Remember Tom, you're not alone. The Network will protect you and guide you. People like Gianni, Tony, your next contact and then your contact after that. The Network will provide you with updates and information. You won't be left to fend for yourself. All of our members are cared for and supported, OK?"

As Odin spoke Tom smiled and nodded. Odin paused and looked straight at him.

"Keep your memories alive. Look at those photo's every day. And remember The Order may have fucked with your life but there are still parts of it that are genuine. The love that you had as a family was genuine and cannot be tainted. Remember that, OK?" Tom nodded and had to hold down a sudden wave of emotion.

"Will I see you again?" asked Tom.

Odin smiled, "I don't know. Maybe? Remember we are both wanted by The Order so being together endangers us both. But who knows? I am sure there will be a time."

Tom wasn't sure if he liked the answer. He wondered if he would have preferred if Odin had lied and told him he would see him soon. It would have been some comfort. But Tom realised by now that Odin wasn't one for bullshit. It's always straight down the line and you deal with it or you don't.

Tom, slowly at first, moved forward. But knowing that he may never see Odin again made him realise this wasn't a time to be hesitant. He moved forward and grabbed Odin and hugged him. He eventually felt Odin's arms reach and up on his back and felt several pats.

Tom pushed Odin away and they stared at each other. Odin put his hand on Tom's shoulder.

"The Network will be in touch. And don't forget, eventually we want you out there helping. But, for now, just settle down and let things even out."

As ever Tom was assured by Odin's words.

Odin smiled and looked at Gianni.

"See you round, big guy".

Gianni waved as he grabbed Tom's holdall and put it in the back of the car. Odin then walked to his car, got in and reversed around. He started to drive away and after only ten yards the brake lights flashed on and the car abruptly stopped. The driver door swung open and Odin got out and looked at Tom.

"And get rid of that goddamn phone!" he shouted and with that he got back in. The engine revved and with a screech of the wheels the car sped away up the ramp and out. Tom smiled and realised that; whoever Odin was headed to now was very lucky.

Tom took his phone from his pocket. It was strange. Once his whole life was on it. Numbers, contacts, messages, data. From family, friends, work, associates, clubs, groups. But now, all that had changed. He knew his sister's number off by heart and so, as it stood, what else did he need?

He lifted his arm into the air and threw the phone forcefully down onto the concrete floor. It smashed and bounced and ended up a few yards away in a twisted mess. Tom walked over to it and smashed the heel of his boot down onto it several times until the phone resembled nothing but a mangled, crushed mass of glass and alloy.

They both got into the car and Gianni started to drive them up the levels to streets above. "Odin is a good man. Solid," Gianni told Tom.

"Yeah, he helped me out of a few situations."

Gianni laughed, "I bet," and his laugh evolved into a crackly and wheezy cough. As the coughing eased Gianni opened the window and spat a large phlegm out.

They got to street level and Gianni turned out onto the main road. The road was pretty quiet and rain from the downpour previously was starting to evaporate but left wet stains and puddles dotted around the roads.

"You like Italian food?" asked Gianni

"Oh yeah," replied Tom

"Good… Good. Tony has got some meatballs on with his special sauce. So tasty. Homemade pasta and bread to go with it."

"I love meatballs!" exclaimed Tom with a smile.

"The sauce he makes has been passed down through generations of his family. He won't tell a soul what the recipe is but, boy, is it good. You can meet him over a huge bowl of that and a glass of red. Tony will do a briefing and then we will take you back to Marie's. A good night's sleep will do you good."

"Sounds good to me," said Tom as he felt his nervousness subside and his body relax a little.

He closed his eyes. Gianni drove on for a further five minutes or so taking various lefts and rights through the South of the city. There weren't a lot of people about and the streets looked rough. Gianni told Tom that it wasn't too further to go as they approached a red light and stopped. Tom opened his eyes and took a deep breath as he felt himself get more comfortable.
"So, where you from?" asked Gianni.

Tom was about to answer when he suddenly felt a powerful light shine directly into his eyes. He squinted and turned and saw two headlights heading directly towards them from Gianni's side, "Holy shit!!" Gianni shouted before the ferocious impact caused both of their bodies to smash together.

The sound of the crash was sickening. Steel and metal banging, grinding and crunching, glass smashing and bodies thudding. Tom had a sense of movement and sound, but he felt completely out of control. His arms lifted and as his body raised out of the seat as the car was pushed violently across the road, he felt several brutal cracks to his head and body. Then it suddenly stopped.

Tom wasn't sure if he was awake or not. He felt the sensation of movement around him and some shouting which was mostly inaudible due to the ringing in his ears. He tried to open his eyes, but the dizziness and pain prevented him from doing so. He tried to lift his head but just felt it flop back down so his chin was resting on his chest.

He then heard talking and felt a sensation of being lifted and then dragged across something hard. He tried so hard to open his eyes and look up. He managed it and saw the black night sky at first, stars and clouds. But then noticed a masked man pulling his arms and the cold wet sensation from the road.

He tried to get up, but his body was non-responsive and numb from the trauma of the impact. He then felt a strange pricking sensation in his arm and tried to speak but couldn't get any words out. Suddenly a dizzy and tired feeling washed over him and a strong urge to sleep set in.

Then everything went black and silent.

Chapter 38

Tom hadn't felt the sharp jab in his arm from the injection. The first he knew of coming around from the strong sedation was a woozy feeling that made his stomach turn. He inhaled a large breath and felt his senses return. He then suddenly became aware of his environment. Cold and damp. He then heard shuffling, voices and echoing. It was quiet and calm, in what he felt was a vast, open space.

Pain in his right leg, ribs and neck started to increase, which brought his consciousness back rapidly and suddenly the fear of the unknown hit him. He lifted his head and opened his eyes but could only make out darkness with odd hints of light coming from various points. His eyes stung and were full of tears, so he pulled his hand up to wipe them but found himself bound. He tried to move his arms again with more force but the pain from his right side prevented him from trying any harder.

He blinked and squinted, eventually making out where he was. It appeared to be an old disused warehouse. Dark, cold and ominous. The sound of dripping and running water could be heard off in the distance. He suddenly felt isolated, as he realised, he was sat on a chair, in the middle of the space. He tried to look behind and the pain in his neck caused him to wince.

Figures became visible. All in dark attire. Tom's vision started to quickly return, and he made out one figure in a dark suit. Next to him were two figures holding large machine guns dressed in full 'stormtrooper' type military attire. One of them had a face mask with a skeleton, they all stared straight at Tom in silence.

Tom looked to the left slightly and saw another soldier and behind that one another. As his vision returned fully, he noticed several others all in full combat gear, carrying what looked to be very large powerful machine guns, all in different locations around him, all staring directly at him.

The man in the suit started to step forward and as he got closer Tom immediately recognised him. It was Rutherford.

"Hello Tom. Or should I say portal 294754. Such a shame we find ourselves in this situation. Such a shame indeed".
Rutherford stepped closer to Tom and went to walk past him but bent down close to Tom's ear as he passed and spoke into it.
"Things could've been so different. Had you had only just accepted what you are."

Tom tried to turn to look at him but as he did Rutherford stood up and walked behind him and put his hands om his shoulders.
"You could have lived a very exclusive and comfortable life. Let me take care of things in the background. The Order working behind the scenes, while you just happily cruise through life enjoying yourself".

Rutherford came full circle of Tom, moved back around to the front and stood directly in front of him. Tom was trembling with fear and pain and could feel anger brewing inside him. His breathing became erratic.
"I told you that I would look after you, didn't I? I told you that you had nothing to worry about. To forget the stress. But that wasn't good enough for you was it, Tom?" Rutherford shook his head and wagged his finger condescendingly.

He then turned away from Tom and put his hands behind his back. Tom noticed he was wearing black leather gloves, "I like you, Tom".

Rutherford turned to face him again, "In fact, I love you. Very much. I was there the night you were born, Tom. It was so hot. The early hours on 16th June back in '83. A young man then myself. Desperately ambitious and wanting to prove my worth to The Order. You were my first angel, Tom. I waited excitedly for you too. Just like your father was waiting. So, in some ways, I love you like a son. And I have seen you grow from a baby into a boy and then into a man. I love all the angels that I am responsible for but…Well…I love you more, Tom. So much more."

Tom wasn't sure if he was hearing it right. He wasn't sure the fear he felt was playing tricks on him. Rutherford was there when he was born. How? Why? It didn't register and his mind was unable to calculate what he was hearing.

Rutherford continued, "And it seems others clearly love you too. I mean, just think, Jenna. The gorgeous Jenna…She would still be around had she not been weak and allowed her feelings for you to make her act the way she did."

Tom started to realise the gravity of the situation and suddenly that things looked very bleak. A feeling of despair hit him, and he started to think that Rutherford's talking was a prologue for a scenario that was, almost certainly, going to end badly for him.

"Phil Carter, a good man, carrying out his duties for The Order, and sadly taken in his prime."

Rutherford, once again, walked slowly past Tom and behind him and, again, put his hands on his shoulders, but this time with much more force. Tom's injury sent a shock wave of pain through his neck, he yelped and recoiled.

"Davy's family. Oh, they would also still be here, had he not been so weak,"

Tom shook his head hoping to not hear anymore. He prayed to be transported to anywhere but here and to have to listen to this. Rutherford continued but this time his voice became louder and more aggressive. "He was warned! Warned that trying to help you would have consequences. And now his little family lay at the bottom of the sea, feeding the fish. Such a shame. Oh, how the youngest one screamed as he saw his mother tied up and thrown overboard."

Tom was stunned into shock. Was this really happening? He felt sick. What was Rutherford capable of? Sickening images flashed across his mind but were suddenly broken with a shout from Tom's tormentor. "Bring him out!" Rutherford then gestured with his finger in the air. Tom noticed a door open off to the left and a shaft of light emanate through. He watched as a figure appear who seemed to be pushing something. As it got closer Tom realised that the 'something' was, in fact, a 'someone' in a wheelchair.

The wheelchair was slowly pushed over and stopped a few metres in front of Tom. He looked at the figure slumped in the wheelchair, but it was hard to make out the face and their head was down. But they were bedraggled with torn, dirty clothes and covered in blood. Rutherford moved to the figure and violently tugged its hair to lift the head up. Tom then knew instantly it was Davy.

He felt a surge of emotion and wanted to scream. Davy's face was swollen almost to the point of unrecognition. Battered, mangled and distorted. Dry and wet blood covered his face, neck and chest. One of his hands was bent at an unusual angle and Tom noticed that several of his fingers were missing. Blood and discharge ran from his nose. His body covered in bruises and cuts. Davy looked broken to an inch of his life and Tom knew if he could see into his eyes, they would already be dead.

To stop himself screaming in anguish Tom looked away, now breathing frantically, saliva dripping down his chin. To control his breathing Tom breathed through his nose and out through his mouth in huge bursts. He felt his heartbeat increase and began to feel panic.
Suddenly Rutherford burst back into life.

"Davy! The man of the moment!" Tom looked up and felt an urge to try and break his binds, but the pain was too immense.

Rutherford walked around Davy still holding his hair.
"A weak and pathetic human! If he had just complied he would also still be alive!"

And as he said the word 'alive' Tom saw Rutherford pull a knife from behind his back, put it under Davy's chin and slowly cut into his neck, and slash it across, with the sound of blood splashing out and onto the wet concrete.
"No!" screamed Tom, "No! No! No!"

He didn't want to look but something made him. Davy's head had fallen to the side and Tom was stunned at the amount of blood pulsing from his neck. It was like water from a tap. Rutherford then grabbed the wheelchair, turned it and just pushed Davy away off into the darkness leaving a trail of blood as he went.

Tom went into shock. He started to cry and couldn't stop repeating the word 'No'. He shook his head and looked down at his lap hoping to get away, hoping it was a nightmare. He tried to wake up but knew that no dream was this vivid. Tears and saliva ran from his face as he knew what he had just seen would haunt him forever. He then felt his hair being tugged and his head lift, as he looked up he saw Rutherford with his arm in the air and before he knew it he had delivered a sickening back hand to Tom's face. His head twisted and the pain of the slap and his neck injury made him scream. He slumped in agony frantically trying to get his breathing under control.
"Pull yourself together!" shouted Rutherford, "You bring shame on your kind."

Tom kept his head down. Quietly sobbing. His plight now taking control and a feeling engulfing him that this was the end.
"And your father. Such a stubborn man. Very genuine, I may add. But just too stubborn for his own good. We offered him everything to keep quiet and comply. But we couldn't pay off a man that had everything. So, we were forced to offer him another choice. Comply or die. Simple."

Tom could hear every word. But he never looked up. He didn't want to give Rutherford the satisfaction.
"The fact that he chose to die is not our fault. His stubbornness and love for you over-ruled his logical thought."

Rutherford sighed and Tom sensed he had moved around the back of him again, circling him like a shark.

"He loved you so much and wanted us to leave you alone, but we couldn't let one man get in the way of gods divine work, could we? Such a waste though. He paid with his life and we carried on regardless, we always do. The Order always carry on, and we get the job done."

Tom managed to get his breathing under control and blinked and squinted the tears from his eyes.

"But we had the help of your mother, who always did as she was told and kept you on the straight and narrow. She loved you, Tom. She loved you very much. And do you remember Mr. Carlisle, Tom? Your old college tutor. He looked after you, didn't he? Went out of his way to make sure you were in the right circle of people and got good grades. To help you with your transition into the workplace and get you into the right company."

Tom had always remembered Mr. Carlisle. He was always so helpful. Always there for Tom. So much so he often wondered if he went too far out of his way to help him. Now he knew why.

"Didn't he eventually become good friends with your father? Very good friends, as I recall."

Rutherford had now slowly made his way to the front of Tom again. "And sadly…he also died in that boating accident". Rutherford approached Tom and bent down next to him and put a hand on his knee. "A good man was Mr. Carlisle. Did his service for The Order. He was the one driving the boat that day wasn't he Tom? The man that rigged the steering, so your father's boat went head-on full speed into the harbour wall."

Tom looked down and started to feel the anger build. He prayed so desperately for his hands to be free and for him to find himself in a room with Rutherford. He pictured himself punching his face until it became a mass of red and pink flesh.

"I can remember the explosion, I was watching from the viewing platform," Rutherford turned to Tom and made an explosion noise, his eyes wide and crazy.

"A good man was Carlisle", as he spoke Carlisle's name Rutherford made the sign of the cross over his chest and head.

"Two good men taken; but both trying to help you in their own different ways". Rutherford stopped and sighed, "So, you see, Tom, lots of people dead because. Of. You!"

Tom heard Rutherford approach and looked up and before he could see he had delivered another sickening slap to his face. Tom's face jerked to the side but this time it just felt numb.

"No doubt that bastard from The Network has filled your head with rubbish and lies. Told you what you are and how you came to be. Such a shame that you had to be involved with scum like that. They don't have your best interests at heart, Tom. They just want to use you to fight their petty war against us. For them you are just a disposable foot soldier".

Rutherford quickly bent down and pulled Tom's hair, so he was facing him.

"But, for The Order, you would be a glorious and special being. Treated as an idol with adulation and respect. Treated in the way that you deserved," Rutherford stood over Tom and pulled his chin up to face him.

"Such a wonderful creation you are. Even more special than any other angel. An angel with the ultimate power. A leader of angels,"

As he spoke, he stroked Tom's face and Tom lurched his head away from the touch and shouted, without thought and not sure where it had even come from.

"You would've just used me and killed me once my work was done!"

Rutherford looked down in shock.

"Lies! All lies! Fed to you by that parasite. Himself once a beautiful creation. Now just a backward, unholy creature lurking in the world's underbelly, scavenging and begging for people like you to join their pathetic group." Rutherford turned his back on Tom and laughed a deep, satanic laugh. A laugh that sent fear through Tom's mind and body.

But, now ignoring that fear Tom shouted again.

"You are a fucking murderer!" the anger within him starting to overflow with the confession from Rutherford that his father had been killed.

Rutherford turned slowly.

"Murderer? Murderer?" Rutherford smiled, "Oh Tom, such a shame. That word is...well...It's just so human. You think what The Order does is 'murder'. It is so much more divine than that, Tom. People that are removed are done so for god's holy work. They are sinners and they die as part of the divine sacrilege, allowing god to cleanse the human race."

Rutherford stepped forward to Tom and now, in defiance, Tom looked up straight into his eyes. Rutherford spoke slowly and quietly and without blinking stared back into Tom's eyes, "The Eternal War rages. It has for a thousand years. In previous centuries the opponent to The Order has been strong and organised. Once a true match for us. But now, a rag-tag population of weirdo's, strays and hobo's pretending they have a purpose. Thinking that they are strong enough to stop us," Rutherford then bent down close to Tom and whispered, "And you fell for it. You believed him,"

He stood and laughed the booming satanic laugh again which startled Tom.

"You chose a pathetic group of cretins over The Order. Your sole purpose in life was to serve The Order as one of its truly beautiful creations, in sync with gods power, a symbiotic divinity," as Rutherford spoke he closed his eyes and looked up.

"A divine and holy key inside your body, allowing us to harness gods power from heaven unto earth to deliver sinners from evil and take their soul to hell for retribution."

Rutherford's voice increased in volume and he was now almost at shouting level.

"Just as people are destined to die once, and after that to face judgement, so Christ sacrificed once to take away the sins of many, and he will appear a second time, not to bear sin, but to bring salvation to those who are waiting for him."

Rutherford now moved his arms straight out either side of him, and as he shouted saliva jumped from his mouth.

"All of us have become like one who is so unclean, and all our righteous acts are like filthy rags! We all shrivel like leaves and the wind sweep us away with our sins!"

Rutherford opened his eyes wide and walked towards Tom, so he stood directly over him. "Show me, Tom. Show me you are the one. Show me!"

With that Rutherford launched a tirade of slaps to Tom's face. Again, again and again.

"Show me the power!" he shouted at Tom showering him in spittle.

Tom tried to duck and move to avoid the thuds but then Rutherford grabbed his face and squeezed it so tight Tom felt like it was being crushed. Then he felt two hands slip around his neck and squeeze and suddenly found it difficult to breathe.

"Show me Tom! Please, show me!"

Tom suddenly felt panic. He exhaled and tried to inhale but his airway was closed. He felt a sudden burn in his lungs and tried to move his head side to side but Rutherford's grip was too intense. As Rutherford squeezed, he shouted frantically.

"Gods wrath is to be feared for those have sinned and fallen short of gods glory! Gods wrath is to be feared as we are justly condemned sinners. Gods wrath is to be feared because he is powerful enough to do what he promises! Gods wrath is to be feared as he promised punishment on all apart from Christ!!"

Tom looked up at Rutherford whose face was contorted in rage, saliva hung from his mouth. Tom's vision blurred and he felt his face and lips tightening. He started to experience a feeling of floating, and his vision was blackening out. Rutherford looked up to the ceiling of the warehouse and closed his eyes.
"Behold the Storm of the Lord! Wrath has gone forth! A whirling tempest; it will burst upon the head of the wicked!"

Just then Tom suddenly felt free. He felt his body lift. A light blinded him, but it felt warm and comforting. His body felt energized and he felt he could stand. The warm sensation suddenly became hot and the energy within him was like nothing he had experienced. He wondered if he had died. Everything he felt was like slow-motion but the commotion around him moved at normal speed. As he stood he felt himself float up and suddenly found himself looking over Rutherford. Rutherford looked up at him, crouched on the ground, his face, now showing both fear and sheer amazement. Tom then heard shots and noticed Rutherford look around and scream.
"No! No!" Hold your fire!"

The hot sensation started to burn. Although Tom felt he was in control, and that the feeling was not be feared. The heat increased and Tom saw Rutherford's eyes widen but this time there seemed to be no amazement in his face. It was all fear. Anger then rose from within. Tom felt like his body was about to explode. He couldn't control it. He felt his arms rise up and although he was not controlling his movements they felt completely natural. His hand reached out to Rutherford and his fingers opened and with a deafening clatter, a ball of light flashed from his hand as he felt the heat transmit through is body like fire. Rutherford's body was suddenly lifted and thrown in an explosion of fire and lightening.

Then Tom felt the cold suddenly return and he fell to the concrete with a thud that took his breath away and sent pain rattling through his body. He couldn't open his eyes, nor could he move. He was just aware of the silence, dark and cold.

Suddenly he heard gun fire and the crackle of machine guns. He looked up and saw one of Rutherford's soldiers fall to the floor like he had been snapped in the middle like a twig. Then more crackling and shots, loud intense and confusing. He raised his head and looked up. He saw the rest of the soldiers fleeing for cover, firing as they went. But not at Tom, at something behind him.

As he lay on the floor, he looked around and saw bursts of light and the sound of rattling and crackling from guns. He felt the bullets whizzing over his head and the wind brush him as they went to their targets. Tom then realised he was in the middle of a gun fight.

He put his head down and covered his head with his arms hoping to stay low enough to ride it out. Through his arms and hands, he noticed the figures from behind him moving closer. With each burst of fire, they moved forward, and he noticed that they, too, were in black military attire and looked like a special forces team. Then suddenly from nowhere he felt a presence. Then a hand pushing down on his own hands that covered his head. He looked up and saw a black figure lying next to him. They pulled up their mask. It was Odin.
"We need to go!" he shouted, "Keep your head down!"

Tom realised that The Network had come back for him and a sudden glimmer of hope he may get out of this alive. However, bullets cracked and zipped across their isolated position and Tom felt debris spit and fizz into him. Odin kept his arm across Tom's head in protection and shifted his body to raise his rifle up and rest it on the arm. He fired several bursts and the sound stung Tom's ears. Concrete sprayed up close to them as a bullet ricochet snapped into the floor sending dust and debris flying around them. Tom pulled his arms tighter down onto his head and curled his body into a ball.
"We go! We go now!" shouted Odin and Tom felt a tug on his body.

Without thinking he got up and started running, holding onto Odin's body-armour, just hoping and praying that he didn't feel the punch of a bullet. They were heading towards a huge stack of crates and Tom could see a figure waving at them with one arm whilst firing a handgun with the other. Concrete burst and exploded and the snap and whizz of bullets could be heard all around them. They made a final lunge across the last few yards to the rear of the crates. Tom saw Odin dive onto the floor towards the wall and followed and they both ended up in a twisted heap against the wall.

Tom looked up. His ears were ringing. The man they had run towards had his back to the crates now facing them. Every few seconds he turned and fired a shot into the darkness on other side of the warehouse. Tom looked right and could see others dotted about in various positions in the darkness all firing into the same direction.

He felt another tug on his jacket. He looked to his immediate right and saw Odin smiling at him, who shouted.
"Tom, I don't know what the fuck you just did back there, but it was…It was…Beautiful! Just unbelievable!" Odin followed with a shake of the head laughing to himself. Tom was confused. He knew something had happened, but he couldn't be sure what.

The soldier in front of the crate stopped firing, turned and bent down in front of them. He pulled his mask up and revealed a tough, grizzled face.
"Odin, we need to get out now!"
Odin nodded, "Tom, let's go."

And with that Odin got up and tugged Tom's jacket up. Tom got up and grunted in pain from his ribs. The other soldier followed behind walking backwards with his gun aimed towards the area that they vacated. They burst through a door and into a corridor. It was dimply lit, and Tom couldn't see properly but just held Odin's arm. He could still hear shots being fired but now quieter, as they moved further away from the central warehouse unit.

They barged through another door and then down some stairs. Tom noticed the soldier was close to them but still moving backwards ready to fire towards any movement that followed them.

Odin led them through a door at the bottom of the stairway and they smashed out into a courtyard. The rain hit Tom and immediately sent a chill running through him. Within a few seconds the deluge had started to soak him and the lightning that crashed over their head made them cower.
"Where the fuck are they?" shouted Odin to himself.

Then within seconds Tom heard a screech and a black van appeared and bounced up the kerb towards them. The following soldier smashed through the door they had come from and turned.
"Let's go!" he shouted. The van screeched to a halt close to them and the side door slid open. A black figure jumped out.
"Come on!" he shouted and Tom, Odin and the other solider quickly jumped in.

Before the side door was slammed shut the van was reversing back with a screech. It smashed down the kerb onto the road and all the passengers bounced up and down, their heads being forced in different directions. Tom held the seat in front of him. There were already two masked soldiers in the van who just started ahead and never acknowledged them get in.

"Are we all accounted for?" shouted Odin.

"No. One more to get!" another man responded immediately.

Tom felt the power of the van surge as it sped along the side of the warehouse to the main gate. As the engine roared, he suddenly felt the brakes crunch against the wheels and the passenger's heads all lurched forward. The engine idled. A gun shot was heard. Then to their left, roughly 50 yards away, a door burst open and a masked soldier appeared, he started sprinting towards the van, dropping his rifle halfway so he could run faster.

He got to within twenty yards of the van and one of the other soldiers slid across and opened the sliding door. Within ten yards Tom noticed the warehouse door open again and another black figure appeared, but this time he set himself and took aim with his rifle. Just as the soldier running towards the van dived in a shot was fired and a sickening thud sent a blast of blood flying up from the soldier. He screamed. The others dragged him in and shut the door. As they did a crash of another bullet hit the van door.

The van surged away with its passengers holding on to avoid being thrown from side to side. The sound of police sirens now filled the air and after a few blocks the driver slowed to an easy cruise. As he did several police cars sped past them on the way to the warehouse. Tom was in shock. He wasn't sure if he could take anymore. He shivered and trembled unable to breath normally.

The soldier who had been shot sat up.

"It's my leg. I think I will be OK," and another patted him on the shoulder, "We will fix you up, don't worry".

Tom then felt a hand on his shoulder. He looked round and Odin was looking at him.

"Just relax Tom. You are safe. Just breathe easy."

Chapter 39

The lock up that the van was driven to was only several miles away on the outskirts of the city. As Tom sat with a blanket around him and a black coffee, all around him it was a hive of activity.

Each soldier that had been in the van quickly stripped off. All of their military clothes, equipment and weapons were put into a large wheeled container and put into the back of another van. A man that had already been in the lock up when they arrived got in the van and drove it out and away.

Two other men, in the lock up when they arrived, who appeared to have medical training, had immediately seen to the guy that had been shot. He was now sitting up on a stretcher with his leg being cleaned and bound. According to the medic it, "wasn't too serious."
The bullet had only luckily only inflicted a flesh wound and it had not gone in. He would be OK.

Tom had then been checked over by the other man. A short, portly guy with glasses and a happy demeanour, despite the seriousness of what was occurring. He had told Tom there was trauma from the car crash, but nothing too serious. Tom's ribs had taken the main impact and so the guy had bound them and then given him strong painkillers. His clothes were torn and burnt, and the guy checked him for burns, but he was fine. Tom noticed the man tell Odin that no burns had been found on his body.

A TV that was mounted on the wall had been turned on. The images on the news showed footage on rotation of police marksman, uniformed police, SOCO's in white boiler suits to a helicopter flying with its light shining down, a large crowd of the public being held back by cordon and images of the warehouse. Along the bottom in large bold text rolled across the screen 'Mass gun fight at industrial site' with further statements along the bottom describing it to be believed to be 'gang related'. Every now and then the men would stop for a short while and watch the TV.

As each man got into their civilian clothes, they went around to each other and said goodbye. As each man got to Odin he simply said "I will be in touch" they nodded and started to leave one by one. None of them said goodbye to Tom nor acknowledged him. He never took it personally, as he now understood how The Network operated, and to them he was just another assigned person to protect.

Soon the buzzing activity in the lock up had slowed and it had started to empty. Eventually the only people left were Tom, Odin, the injured solider and the two medics, who were now cleaning and tidying.

Odin had changed into his civilian clothes and had grabbed a coffee and sat with Tom. He had explained that Tom had been very lucky. The team he had assembled for the New York assignment were meeting at this lock up, as they knew Odin would be in Pittsburgh, so it had been the location chosen where they would meet. They were packed and ready to go when Odin got a call from Tony Vitola to say Gianni and Tom hadn't arrived and the deadline had passed.

In another stroke of luck, Odin checked the GPS tracker and they were able to get to Tom's location. They had sent a scout who confirmed they had seen activity in that location and Rutherford had been spotted. Had the team already left for New York and the GPS trackers were not being used then Tom would almost certainly be dead.

Sadly another scout had been sent to the scene of the crash and reported back that Gianni hadn't made it and his body was removed from the car. He had taken the full brunt of the impact. He had no chance.

Tom shook his head. Another meaningless death in this so- called war. It was surreal. As this whole situation unfolded, from the first strange occurrence involving H's death and the file at work, right up to now. With every turn he saw things and was involved in incidents that he would never have believed he ever would. Even now after everything that had happened, he still found it hard to believe he was involved in all of this.

Odin had told Tom he requested authorisation from ID to deploy and they gave it straight away. The team kitted up and went. When they arrived, they formed an attacking plan, spread out and went into the building. They had to take out a few guards to gain access and took up positions and, as they did, Odin stated that it was just as Davy was wheeled out. Odin had wanted to make his move then, but they had not had the message that each unit was in its position.

It was then that Odin had described that, as he gave the message to attack, he saw a bright light start to glow from Tom. It had made him stop in his tracks. The light grew in ferocity and turned to a bright orange and gold, and that Tom had floated at least fifteen feet into the air. It had been almost too bright to look at and as the agents covered their eyes Odin had heard gunfire. He then realised that the agents from The Order were shooting at Tom, so he gave the message to attack, and as they went Tom had turned into a fireball and a bolt of fire and lightening shot from his body down to the ground. He had said Rutherford flew six foot through the air and almost twenty foot away, and then Tom dropped to the floor in darkness. It was then that he had made a dash to Tom under cover of fire.

Due to the intensity of the firefight the team had to leave without accounting for the enemy. After being hit by whatever power came from Tom, Rutherford was assumed dead along with the majority of the other agents.

"Do you feel ok?" asked Odin. Tom laughed and then winced with the pain from his ribs.

"Well, in honesty, I feel like shit, but I will live."

"No," interjected Odin, "I mean, from the light? The fire?"

Tom shook his head, "I don't know? I feel fine, I suppose. Just completely drained. I recall feeling like I was going to burn to death but then it felt...well...It felt like the most wonderful, amazing and powerful feeling I have ever felt. Almost like as if I was..." Tom hesitated.

Odin looked at him and waited. He wanted to hear what he would say.

"Like what?" he asked, intrigued.

"Well, I felt all powerful, like a God I suppose."

Tom shook his head and laughed; uncomfortable at realising how stupid it sounded.

Odin cut in, "Tom, it was mesmerising. I was captivated by it. I still can't believe what I saw. Like watching a dream. And it explains a lot."

Tom looked at him inquisitively, so Odin continued.

"It seems that you do have something that other portals don't have. It also explains my suspicions as I always wondered whether The Order wanted you dead, but Rutherford wanted you alive. Whether he knew something. The Order could have had you killed weeks ago but I wondered whether Rutherford was protecting you," Odin stopped and breathed a huge sigh.

"I don't know. I suppose we will never know."

Odin's phone rang. He got up and answered it and walked to the lock up entrance door and pressed a button. The door cranked and slid upwards. As it got to about halfway up a Ford Mustang drove in and stopped. Odin walked over leant into the passenger window. He then turned to Tom.

"Your ride is here."

Tom was a little shocked. Was this it? He hadn't been sure what to expect after what had happened but wasn't expecting to be going so soon. Tom stood up and started to walk over while Odin leant back into the car. As Tom got to the car Odin turned to him.

"You're going to get your bag from Marie's and then onto another place. None of us can stay here now. Especially you. It's too dangerous. This is Marcus. He will drive you overnight and set you up with your new contact and accommodation. Hopefully this time there will be no snags."

Tom wasn't sure what to say. After a few seconds he decided to say thank you anyway but as he went to Odin cut in.

"No. We have done this once. Get the fuck out of here." Odin smiled and opened the door.

Tom got in and sat back. He looked at Marcus. He was young, clean cut and had aviator glasses on and driving gloves. He looked at Tom and just said.

"Buckle up."

Marcus revved the engine and slammed the powerful Ford into reverse. As they surged backwards Tom put his hand out and waved to Odin. The car screeched to a halt and Tom's body slid back into the leather seat. Marcus put it into forward drive and revved the engine. Tom saw Odin wave and as the car powered out of the courtyard with a deep growl.

As the car bumped onto the main road Tom looked back to see lock-up door close.

Chapter 40

6 weeks later – 8pm local time

High in the Pyrenees, the town of Bagneres-de-Luchon was in the grip of winter. The snowstorm that had raged for the last two days had made accessing the town difficult. Snowdrifts had built up, blocking many routes, and the cold biting wind made conditions outside very inhospitable.

The weather had delayed the gathering but, eventually, the last Overlord had arrived, and Council was now in session. On the steep mountainside, accessible only by a rocky path, stood The Chapel of St Etienne. It had stood for over 800 years and had been the place of religious worship its whole time. But it hid a dark secret. An underground chamber, accessed via a spiral staircase that dropped 150 feet into the granite rock below. The cold, wet, stone corridors which led to the chamber were dark and foreboding and only lit by large candles that flickered as the wind ghosted its way into the depths.

The ominous sound from the mountainous winds above the chamber provided a constant deep moan. The chilling chanting from the choir chamber could also be heard above the wind and it created an eerie, unworldly atmosphere. A place not created for ordinary people. A place that, for a thousand years, had not been accessible by ordinary people. A place that held a power that ordinary people would never understand. A place that only Overlords of The Order had ever visited.

As the echo of religious chanting mesmerised its way through the corridors, a huge wooden staff banged three times onto the stone floor. It was the sign for the introduction of Ganlar, High Overlord of The Order's European Sect. A stone door scraped open and Ganlar, shrouded in dark robes and hood, slowly made his way into the chamber sided by two Holy Guards, both in full black robe with two sabres crossing their chests.

Ganlar took his place at the round stone table and stood silently, joining the other nine Overlords also standing at their places, whilst a priest slowly walked around the chamber lighting the tallow candles, held in the ancient wall mounted wrought iron holders. It created an eerie, orange glow allowing for light and for vision to be improved, but not enough for any of the Lord's to see each other's faces clearly.

Ganlar raised his hands and in unison all ten spoke.

"Irae ad em potestate clavis," to which Ganlar lowered his hands and sat in the ancient oak throne behind him. This prompted all the others to do the same and soon, once again, only the moaning of the wind could be heard.

"Much has been discussed and I have been listening intently. I am pleased with your progress on the matters we were called here for. However, the last matter is now to be discussed of which I will lead on. What is the news of Portal 294574?"

Another robed figure rose from his chair.

"Lord Ganlar, we have intelligence to tell us it is true."

"That he is not just an ordinary portal?" Ganlar questioned.

"Yes, he has the power my Lord. He has it within him"

"You are sure?"

"My intelligence is from a solid agent, my Lord. He paid with his life to get the information to me"

"But we are no nearer finding the portal?"

"The Network are growing again, my Lord. They grow strong and in greater numbers. More members are being recruited...."

"And we are no nearer finding him!?" Ganlar asked in a direct, intimidating tone.

"No, my Lord. Not yet, but we will."

Ganlar rose to stand, " I suggest you all contact your lead agents and ask them to try harder. Please understand, if this power is harnessed by the wrong hands then it could bring The Order down," he paused, "The Pope becomes impatient."

There was a silence in the chamber until another robed figure spoke from a corner of the darkness.

."Should we not be seeking to harness this power ourselves, my Lord?"

"No!" shouted Ganlar, raising quickly from his seat and banging his fist down onto the stone table, "I have already commanded the death of Portal 294574! The risk is too great. The power must be eliminated."

All figures now sat, and silence followed, the wind and chanting echoed again through the chamber.

"And what of Agent Rutherford?" Ganlar asked quietly

"I am afraid that our intelligence tells us that he is now rogue. Working outside of our command," replied the figure next to him.

Another robed figure stood from the far side of the large table.

"Are you sure? Agent Rutherford is a powerful agent for The Order. He is loyal. Can it really be true?"

"Yes. Rutherford has continued to try to use the portal after Lord Ganlar gave the command for elimination. It is obvious what his intentions are," came the reply from another corner of darkness.
"If Agent Rutherford's intentions are against us and he harnesses the power then it would be catastrophic."

The wind moaned eerily from above and the candle lights danced, creating unusual shapes and shadows around the chamber.
"What is thy bidding Lord Ganlar?" asked a robed figure close to him. Ganlar stood slowly. "Rutherford must be eliminated, along with the portal. See it done!"

As the gathering ended, and the dark robed figures slowly left the chamber, 2500 miles away, in Misaki Port, two-hours' drive from Tokyo, stood an old boathouse.

From the outside it looked derelict, closed and dis-used, but inside, for the first time in years, activity was underway. It was just after 4am and so not too long before the fishing boats would start to return with their catch, and the hustle and noise of the dockside sales would begin.

The soft sound of the ebbing tide could be heard above the silence and darkness. Through the black early hours a shadowy figure made its way through the alleyways and units towards the boat house. The figure, now struggling with pain from injuries previously sustained, desperately urging himself on through fear of being late and upsetting his suitor.

As he approached the boat house he stopped. Checking that the way across the courtyard was clear. At the boarded entrance to the boathouse he noticed a large, ominous figure waiting.

A quiet squeaking sound could be heard above from a light that swung slowly in the soft breeze moving the light back and forth across the courtyard. As the light slowly moved away from the courtyard, engulfing it in darkness, the figure moved and made its way across to the entrance.

As he approached, he noticed the large figure at the door hold up a gun and point it at him. Safe in the knowledge that this was normal protocol he continued. As he got closer, he realised that he recognised the large Japanese man from previous encounters; but had never spoken to him. Knowing that access to the boathouse relied upon him fulfilling his own requirements he pulled his jacket sleeve up and turned his arm over to reveal his wrist. The Japanese man shone a powerful torch onto the arm to reveal a tattoo showing the symbol of The Order.

Then, in a deep, stark Japanese accent the huge doorman uttered the words.

"Ikari wa chikara e no kagidesu".

The dark figure vying for access then spoke back.

"Wrath is the key to power".

With this, the large man banged the door behind him and moved aside. In a few seconds a lock could be heard twisting and clanking, and the door slowly opened. The dark figure taking no invitation slipped inside. As he got inside the close and musty atmosphere hit him. For a few seconds while his eyes adjusted, he stood in complete darkness.

He felt an arm grab his but again, was not alarmed. He was led to a small door which was lit by a small lantern on a table next to it. A small Japanese man quickly but assertively frisked him. Knowing he had no weapons he was not concerned and the man then slid an adjacent door open and the figure entered the small room beyond.

"You are late, Master Rutherford. I am very busy. It is during these small hours that most of my work is done."

Rutherford looked up to see the man he was meeting sat in a small chair next to a table with a lamp. Smoke from the man's cigarette hung in the air and two dark figures stood at each side.

"I am sorry Oyabun. This was a hard place to find...And my flight was delay..."

The seated man interrupted.

"Do not use Yakuza language. Do not call me Oyabun. You are not Yakuza. Don't pretend you are. I am 'Boss' to you. Now, explain why we do not have portal 294574 in our possession."

"Do not worry. It's in hand. I have managed to secure the services of some of the best agents in The Order. With the help of your financial gifts they are now ready to be deployed."

"Are they trustworthy?" snapped the Oyabun.

"Yes, they are on our side now. I give you my assurance," assured Rutherford.

"It pains me when I have to pay for things that were not planned, Rutherford. I am starting to wonder if your assurances hold any value. You assured me that the portal would be in our possession by now. So far you have failed. And now I have had to use my hard-earned money to rectify your failure".

Rutherford felt tense and the pressure started to hit him. He never spoke but was glad that the darkness of the room masked the fear on his face.. The man continued.

"But you didn't explain to me why portal 294574 is not yet in our possession."

"The Network is no longer as weak as it was," Rutherford pleaded, "They have recruited well. They have many agents now from military and special forces backgrounds…"

"I do not care for their recruitment. Between the Yakuza and The Order we should be able to take possession of one portal…"

"The man they have protecting the portal is….Well, he is diligent. And very dangerous."

"One man? One man!?" snapped the Oyabun who suddenly stood up, "One man has prevented us from achieving our…"

"They are powerful now" Rutherford interjected, allowing his frustration to loosen his tongue, "They have grown much more powerful and better equipped. We have lost many good agents in the last year…"

"Do not interrupt me!!" The two men at the side stepped forward to stand side by side by the Oyabun, who was small in stature, but very threatening.

Rutherford felt the urge to move back, but he held his ground. The Oyabun moved closer, "You have failed. Your interruption is rude and holds no substance. You assured me. But your assurances are like rainwater in a storm. Draining away with no relevance."

There was an eerie silence. Rutherford bowed his head.
"Again, I am sorry".

The Oyabun then slowly moved even closer to Rutherford with a grunt, and Rutherford sensed it was not easy for him. The Oyabun spoke quietly but with intent.
"I am beginning to wonder if The Yakuza need you at all, Rutherford. You are suddenly becoming more of a hindrance than a help. A very expensive hindrance."

The anger in Rutherford grew quickly from his stomach to his head. He felt the urge to strangle the old man. But he knew to raise a finger would mean instant death. He knew that The Yakuza needed him. He was their only way to infiltrate and get inside The Order. Without him The Yakuza had no access whatsoever. He knew that the old Oyabun knew that too and was just playing with his emotions. It was bravado and mind games.

Rutherford knew it was best to not respond. But he lifted his head to face the old boss and the soft light flickered across his face showing substantial scarring and skin damage.

"I see your injuries are serious. I assume this is the evidence of the portal's power?"

Rutherford replied quietly, "You assume correct."

The old man leant forward and touched Rutherford's scarring. Rutherford moved his head back to avoid the touch and the old man shook his head. Rutherford slowly moved his head back to its original position and the old man softly touched his face caressing the hard, gristly scarring.

"These injuries are nothing compared to what will happen to you if portal 294574 is not in my possession soon"

Rutherford stayed silent. Resisting the urge to get out of the boathouse as quickly as possible.

"You have three months. If I do not have him safely delivered to me within that time then our contract will be terminated. And so will you."

Rutherford felt his hands start to tremble. He knew that when he entered into this secret agreement and started to operate outside of The Order that it would be dangerous. It was like cosying up with two great white sharks. The stakes were as high as they could be. One wrong move and he would be snubbed out by either side.

The fact that he had, so far, failed to get Tom on side and aligned to the Yakuza was wasting time and causing problems. The longer this went on the more chance The Order had of finding out Rutherford's intentions. They had agents everywhere and a person of Rutherford's status within The Order, although generally left to work using their own initiative, was watched very closely, and their actions scrutinised by the higher echelons and The Overlords.

But Okamoto, the Yakuza Oyabun standing in front of him, also had limited time. He was also playing a high stakes game. The other Oyabun were sceptical of the plan. They had not given it their full approval and some of the bosses were now openly requesting that the Yakuza's involvement be withdrawn. Okamoto had one chance, the current Kumicho still had some belief in it, despite the time it was taking.

His agreement and relationship with Rutherford was dangerous. If the Yakuza found out he had been operating the way he had so far, then the call for his head to be removed would be given instantly. Just like The Order, Yakuza bosses were also given freedom to operate but they were scrutinised and watched; so any wrong move for Okamoto would be his last move.

That was why the deadline was given. He could not play this game indefinitely and if the plan did not come to fruition soon then he would fold and walk away. He had too much to risk. But, for Rutherford, Okamoto and The Yakuza, the result of the plan working was still too important for them to give up just yet.

As the old man returned to his seat, a door behind him opened and Rutherford looked up, "In order to assist you achieving our aim I would like to provide some assistance. Nokota, come!".

From the doorway a dark figure emerged slowly, the size of whom stunned Rutherford. As the figure moved forward Rutherford saw his face come into the light and he could see a dark, twisted and hard face that showed a sense of cruelty and evil. At 6' 5" with a powerful physique, Nokota towered over the two bodyguards at the side of the old man.

Rutherford now realised that the stakes had been raised. His immediate thought was for his own safety. Having Yakuza members directly involved would make Rutherford's plan harder to keep secret from The Overlords. He would need to think carefully on how integrate Nokota into The Order. It will make things more difficult, but he knew he had no choice.

The Oyabun introduced the man.
"Nokota is my personal body-guard and soldier. I am sure you will find his services of use"
"Look, thank you, but I think operating with my own agents..."
"I insist, Master Rutherford. I insist. I will send details of when he will arrive in the States. I trust he will be treated well".

Rutherford lowered his head in acceptance of the offering.

Soon after, he slipped out of the old musty boathouse and into the dark, wet night. A storm could be heard growling overhead and lightning flashed. In the distance the first lights of the returning boats could now be seen bobbing up and down in the distance.

Rutherford hoped that by the time they docked he would be as far away from this place as possible.

Chapter 41

17 months later

Tom felt good. As good as he had felt in his entire life. Mentally he was in a sound, balanced place. Time had healed some wounds and given him time to reflect on what and why it had happened. He was now also better able to understand what and who he was. Time had allowed him to accept his situation and he had now started to make the very best of it. In some respects, he felt that he wasn't just making the best of it, he was thriving and had, in some strange way, started to enjoy his life.

Physically he was in great condition. His body was lean and defined. In all his years of attending the gym and playing sports he had never been as fit or looked as healthy.

A lot had happened since that night when Marcus had picked Tom up from the lock-up. They had driven all night directly West towards Kansas and eventually around late afternoon the next day they had cruised into the city. Tom was delivered to his contact, a Kansas mobster, and set up in a bed sit. Then, after a few days, he was eventually moved to a bigger, more inhabitable apartment, where he had stayed for four months.

His only contact from that point had been a lady called Sandra. She had settled him in and given him some initial basic advice. She was what The Network term as his 'parent'. The main point of contact if he had any problems or questions.

The first thing he had to do was get a pay as you go phone and give her the number. She then registered it with The Network so they could contact him when necessary. He was advised that each time he moved on he was to destroy the phone, get another one and give the new number to his new contact. This was to keep contacts data fresh and try and keep The Order off track.

Sandra had given him a debit card which he was to use for groceries, clothes, travel and any other goods or services he needed. She initially bought him some groceries to get him going and then it had been down to him.

After a few days of getting his new phone he had received a text:

"Tom. Do not reply to this text and do not call the number. We hope you are settling in. This number has been registered and will be used for us to contact you. Ensure you have your phone and tracker with you at all times. If you need anything speak to your parent. More information will follow. Internal Department."

Tom then heard no more and had found it difficult to adjust. For the first two months he felt lonely. Very lonely. He even wondered at the time if he had been depressed.

He wasn't used to a solitary life. He had thought of his old life and the fact that he had always had people around him. He had never really ever been alone. He had slowly become anxious and stressed and suddenly his paranoia became a bug problem. His mental state then inflicted negativity on his physical state and he became unwell. He wasn't eating properly, and his fitness had started suffering. He had very little energy and so did nothing physical and even struggled to do anything mental.

In those first two months he felt like he was drowning in his own loneliness and despair. The isolation weighed heavily upon him and he rarely went out. Only for short trips to the grocery store and then straight back. The thought of going out made him desperately paranoid and he was petrified that as soon as he ventured out The Order would be waiting.

He had also started to have very bad nightmares. Very vivid and scary. At that point at least two a night which was meaning he was having little sleep. One recurring nightmare which was particularly vivid whereby he could see Davy rising from the wheelchair, blood pulsing from his neck and he would walk to Tom and start to strangle him. Each time Tom felt like he was about to pass out he would wake up in a sweat. He also had other various dreams of the creatures surrounding him, the claws and cold scaly skin brushing across him.

His normal day would comprise of three meals per day and watching TV in between. Every now and then Sandra would pop by with a newspaper which had been about as exciting as things had got for him at that time. Tom had desperately wanted her to stay, just for some company, but each time she came by he never had the confidence to open up a conversation. Plus, he through that she had better things to do than to keep him company.

Tom was grieving for his mum, missing his sister, his old life and completely and utterly failing to come to terms with everything.

It was one day around 2pm that Sandra had popped. Tom had been on the settee, unshaven, unkept and in his dressing gown. She had dropped a paper and a magazine into him and had asked him if he was OK. He had been unable to hold the emotion in and had just started to cry.

Sandra had sat and held him. Eventually she had asked if The Network had been in touch since their first message and Tom confirmed they hadn't. She informed him it would not be much longer before they do. She told him to shower, shave and start to look after himself, before leaving. It was soon after that day that things started happening and his life had started to slowly turn around.

Three days later Sandra popped in holding a box. She had smiled and told Tom she had received a delivery from a mailer that morning and handed it to him. She told him to take his time and go through it carefully and slowly. It was important. It was Tom's first proper communication from The Network. Sandra explained that, hopefully, this would be the first of many. As she had left, she told him to ask her any questions on anything he didn't understand once he has read it.

The documents were very pragmatic. Much like Odin. And Tom realised that it was one of the reasons why he was like he was. He had become part of The Network as young boy and it was the only way he knew.

Inside were what appeared to be guidance and advice notes. A list of synonyms, jargon, Network protocol, security advice, things to do, things not to do. Like keep your tracker charged and with you at all times, keep your phone charged and with you at all times, only contact family if authorised. Don't discuss The Network, don't leave the city or town of your accommodation without authorisation, don't maintain long term relationships; the lists were substantial. There were pages and pages. And over the next few days Tom did nothing more than read and digest it all. It gave him a focus.

There was also lots of information and guidance on mental and physical wellbeing. It was obvious The Network understood the difficulties for portals, especially early on. There life as they knew it had been taken and they were suddenly alone and isolated. There was information on exercise and physical activity. Links to websites and online videos of intense training sessions that can be done indoors. Resistance training without the need for weights. Advice to get out and go jogging, swimming, hiking, cycling. The Network advised portals that their new life did not mean a life shut away. They promoted the outdoors.

Not only did this keep portals fit and healthy but it also maintained a healthy mind. But to also do this, portals were urged to take up hobbies, past-times, activities and anything that required you to use your brain.

Eventually Tom had started to see a focus to each day. It was hard at first, but he did start to go out more to go jogging and walking. Some days he just walked, for miles and miles, it was exercise but it also gave him time to think and put things into perspective. He also started to do crosswords and buy puzzle books which was something he had never done before. They passed a lot of time and kept his mind alert.

By the time he came to leave Kansas City he had started to turn the corner. Sandra had commented that he was a different man to the one that had first arrived. His mental and physical state had improved, and he even noticed that the bad dreams had subsided. Just before his move he had even visited a Museum and had a meal out. On his way home he had laughed to himself. Something that previously felt as natural as eating out had felt like a major achievement.

It was sad to say goodbye to Sandra. In her own way she had been there for him. She was very unassuming, but Tom always knew if he had a problem she would have been there. She was very caring but never showed it overtly. Tom realised that hello and goodbye were now going to be a major part of his life.

His next stop had been Shreveport in Louisiana. He hadn't liked it much at first, but he wondered if it was just to do with the fact that he had eventually got used to Kansas City and had then been moved. Plus, it was hot and very humid. Some days it the heat was stifling. But he realised that he would have to give each new place time.

He settled into a comfortable bedsit that had been organised for him near Lake View, and his contact, an old grizzly man called Joe, met him there and went through a few protocols. Tom destroyed his phone that he had and was told to go into town and get a new one. He did that and gave Joe the new number. The next day Joe had brought him the keys to an old pick up which he could use for his duration. He had been told the plan was to stay there for five months, so he knew he would have to get used to the heat.

As time passed Tom became a lot more active physically and mentally. He had now added yoga to his daily routine as well as his intense training sessions. Despite the humidity he jogged in the evenings and had become addicted to Sudoku. And for the first time in his adult life bought a puzzle. A huge 2000-piece puzzle of New York city skyline. It would be an ongoing project which he enjoyed doing in the evening with a coffee.

As he had the car, he also decided to visit a few places. He went to an art gallery, another museum and even went to the cinema which, again, he used to love doing; but it felt very rewarding for him and made him feel like he was integrating back into society again.

One day Joe brought some books to his motel room; they included some historical books on world war 2 and Vietnam and a book about astrology. He had suddenly found an interest. Tom would read for four to five hours at a time. Finishing books within days. Exercising, yoga, reading, eating, Sudoku, jogging, cinema. His days started to find a pattern. He had even started to cook and found a website that offered healthy recipes. He was now mostly cooking his own meals and eating as healthily as he had ever done.

Tom found that with so much spare time on his hands his quest for knowledge became insatiable. He was like a sponge and found interest in all sorts of topics and surprised himself at how much information he could take in. Joe would bring him books on economics, politics, crime, psychology and all manner of subjects.

Joe had, one day, even brought him a bible amongst other books. Tom had never read the bible. And now, knowing what he was, it found fresh relevance and once he started he found fresh impetus and ended up reading it in only a few days. He found a connection and hope from it and then realised that it held an important part in his new life. Tom found solace in the bible and all other books, quenching his new found interest for knowledge. He had never had the time to do this before and found it a pleasure.

In Kansas City Tom was starting to shrivel into nothing. His days empty and soulless. But, in Louisiana, he would wake at 6am and go to sleep at Midnight. With eighteen hours to fill every day, suddenly he found that he had more than enough to do that. By the time he came to leave Shreveport he had felt that his new life had given him freedom. He had no responsibilities, no deadlines, no meetings and nothing to prepare for.

He knew his life was obviously bound by The Network guidance. Although he knew if he wanted, he could bail out at any time. He wasn't being held by them. He was being guided. There were limits to his freedom, he knew that, but they there to keep him alive. But he had suddenly found such a positive state of mind, when he looked back at his old life he wondered what freedom he had actually had back then. Tied to work, tied to relationships, tied to living in one place. He realised that he suddenly felt happy with his lot.

Time slowly passed and then one day he received a text:

"Tom. Do not reply to this text and do not call the number. You have a package. A key will be delivered for the locker at Shreveport bus garage. Number 297. Collect as soon as you have key. Internal Department."

That night after returning from jogging he had seen a small envelope on the floor. He picked it up and it contained a locker key with a blue band. He had left immediately and drove to the bus garage and went to the public lockers, making sure nobody was looking, and went to locker 297. Inside, a thick envelope sat, which he grabbed and left to get back as quickly as he could to his accommodation.

When he opened it he saw it contained hundreds of documents and photocopies. Extracts from religious and scientific books, written notes, research, calculations, scripture, images – some from the bible, some from other sources, all with written notes and statements connecting the documents together. He realised that this was The Networks attempt at trying to explain the scientific and religious thinking behind how he came to be and how angels function on earth.

But it was all very overwhelming and he knew that this was going to take time. Not only to read and digest it but even longer to understand it. As to how long it would take for him to accept it he never knew. He didn't actually know if he ever would accept it.

But, this package contained all of his reading for the foreseeable future. He wouldn't rush. He knew it was important to digest it slowly and carefully to give himself the best chance of understanding it. It would be his goal to understand it. And over the following weeks and months it was all he read. Eventually realising that the theorists, academics, conspiracists, scientists and religious contributors to all that he had read; were actually not far off that actual truth. If only they knew how close they truly were.

As the weeks passed, Tom also found himself thinking more about his sister, Claire. He wasn't sure why but put it down to her being the only relative he had a link to. He soon found himself desperate to talk to her and hear her voice. So one day when Joe had visited to bring him more books, Tom asked him he could contact his sister. Joe told him he would get back to him.

The next day Joe told him that ID have confirmed this was not authorised due to the potential risk and danger to him and her family. Those were some of the freedoms he had lost. Tom had understood why. The Network were responsible for him and it could give his position away. But he also had to be responsible for Claire and her family and couldn't risk getting them involved. He had tried to put her out of his mind as best he could.

Towards the end of his time in Shreveport he felt like he was in a good place. He felt so good, in fact, that his confidence had returned, and he had a couple of nights out socially. He had spotted a bar downtown called 'Mack's and had noticed it looked busy on Friday and Saturday, so decided to venture down there. He had enjoyed himself, although he had been alone, so went back the week after.

The Network gave advice on socialising and did not advise against it although Tom had read, 'Maintain low frequency of visits to one particular establishment'. He realised that he was, at that point, soon to be leaving Shreveport and so had thought one more visit would be OK.

He had ended up talking to a lady that appeared to be older than him but very attractive. She seemed friendly and they had got talking, she had said that she had seen him the week before on his own. He explained he was a travelling salesman and so that was why he was alone. They had spoken for an hour or so, had a lot to drink and had started flirting. Until the lady had directly asked him if he wanted some company that night. At first he had felt nervous. The thought of spending the night with another lady had not really occurred to him up to that point.

He realised he was a little too drunk so went to the toilet to pull himself together and make his mind up what he wanted to do. In the toilet the alcohol got the better of him and he threw caution to the wind and decided to take the lady up on her offer. When he came out of the toilet, he had noticed the lady wasn't at the bar stool so had looked around, wondering if she had gone to the toilet or had thought better of it and left.

It was then that he had seen her at the far end of the bar through a crowd, talking a tall guy with dark hair. He moved behind a pillar and stared and noticed their faces looked serious. At first he had thought it may be the guy she was letting down to spend the night with Tom. But the risk was too great. He got out of there fast and ran back to his car. He knew had been too drunk to drive but had just started it up and left downtown rapidly.

When he had got home, he cursed himself for being so stupid. It had shaken him up. He knew it could have been innocent, and probably was, but it brought a lot of things back home to him. Things that in the last few months had started to be pushed to the back of his mind. He had let his guard slip. He had grown comfortable and the incident, innocent or not, was a timely reminder that he couldn't relax completely, ever.

He had, in many ways, enjoyed his time at Shreveport, but the incident had made him a little nervous and so he welcomed the visit a few days later when Joe told him he was moving on. Joe had handed him a wallet and inside had been a bus ticket to Albuquerque. The wallet had also included the name of the person and the number to call when he arrives. There was also the word 'Astro' which he must say when the person answered, and they would collect him and take him to his accommodation.

He travelled overnight and like clockwork when he arrived he called the number, said the word and within 15 minutes a car had come to collect him. His resettlement in Albuquerque had been, up to that point, very smooth.

He completed his usual protocols. New phone, log in with ID. He also made enquiries about where to find local libraries, pop up gym's, swimming pools, good restaurants. His new life was about keeping himself as busy as possible and he had started to cherish his new-found freedom; even if it was still within strict boundaries.

When he arrived at a new place, he never waited for things to happen. He went out and settled in as quickly as possible. His accommodation was modest and up in the north east of the city close to the national forest with lots of things to do. He found solace in doing lots of hiking through the forests and outdoor areas close to him.

But after a few days after arriving he got a surprise when he received a text:

"Tom. Do not reply to this text and do not call the number. I hope you are well. You have been chosen. You will soon be deployed for training. Await further details. Odin."

Tom had been shocked but also pleasantly surprised. He had not heard from Odin for a long time and he had thought that he would never hear from him again. Lots of memories came shooting back into his mind from his time with him and he realised again how much he owed him.

But the text was unusual. He recalled Odin alluding to the fact previously that The Network had a plan for Tom, but he never really got any more details. This was obviously it. But he could only assume and hoped that the details would be forthcoming.

He had then heard nothing for the next few days but had busied himself with his training regime, hiking, reading and numerous hobbies he had on the go at that time. Then one evening he returned to his apartment and just sat down to read when he had received a text:

"Tom. Do not reply to this text and do not call the number. I will knock at your door in 10 minutes. Open the door and take the envelope. Michael."

He had put his book down and waited. He looked out the window but saw no activity. Then, exactly ten minutes later, he heard had a knock at the door. He looked through the view hole and saw his current parent, Michael. He opened the door and Michael passed him an envelope and walked away briskly without acknowledging Tom.

Tom closed the door and upon opening the envelope he found some documents. One, a one-way overnight bus ticket to Seattle. The other a letter with the following information typed from an old typewriter:

```
Chosen for training
Leave 20th July
Text contact will be made upon your arrival
Memorise and destroy this note immediately
```

Tom had realised that the 20th July was three days and so suddenly knew he had needed to be ready. Not that he had a lot of baggage, but he needed to be ready mentally. He felt nervous and excited. This was now serious, and he needed to be focussed.

On the morning of the 20th he had left his apartment and headed downtown to the bus garage and found his terminal. He had purchased a tablet the day before so he could listen to music and watch films and TV shows. He also had a copy of the bible which he thought he would read and analyse again. It was a long journey, so he had prepared lots of things to keep him occupied. He had become very adept at passing time positively and constructively and so the long journey didn't bother him.

As he headed northwards even when he wasn't reading or using his tablet his mind was always working. He often remembered his past life, but it did not upset him anymore as he had been able to put everything into

327

perspective and balance. But as he remembered he often looked through the photographs he salvaged from the house in Evanston.

The bus had stopped at various points along the way for people to disembark, whilst remaining passengers stretch and got refreshed. And he soon started to notice the landscape changing and becoming greener and more mountainous. At one-point Tom fell into a deep sleep and when he woke, he noticed the bus was travelling through thick, lush forest and he saw a road sign for Tacoma, and so he knew they were not too far from Seattle.

The bus trundled north along the 99 and through Sea Tac heading to the bus terminal downtown. Tom saw the city skyline and the Space Needle off in the distance peering above the tree-tops, and as he started to prepare his things and get them packed away, as he did he heard his phone bleep and he notice he had a text:

"Tom. When you arrive in Seattle bus terminal text the word 'arrived' to this number and wait"

Tom followed his instructions and sent the text upon his arrival in Seattle under a grey blanket of gloomy cloud. And as was usual with the slick efficiency of The Network, no later than five minutes after sending the text, Tom's transport had arrived, and contact was made. Before Tom knew it he was heading north out of Seattle in a an old beat up yellow Chevy Blazer, being driven by an elderly Puerta Rican man called Jose.

The journey onwards north had been very tough going through winding forest roads with little conversation due to Jose's limited English. After a few hours Tom started seeing signs for Vancouver and had hoped that this may be their destination. But on the outskirts of Vancouver Jose stopped at a small café and went inside and came out with coffee and donuts, which Tom welcomed.

Their next direction skirted around Vancouver and when Tom asked Jose how further north they were headed Jose simply pointed upwards. That was the best that Tom could get from him. After two more hours they cut off the main roads and started using off-road tracks.

Tom was adamant that some of the tracks they had been down had not had vehicles pass over them for months. Eventually at around 4pm in the afternoon they had gone as far as they could go by vehicle and Jose simply stopped the truck and said.
"We walk".

Tom had tried to recall his geographical knowledge as to what could be a few hour's drive north of Vancouver, but he had no idea. All he knew was that it was pure wilderness and they were now in a place where, if you did not tread carefully or got lost, then it may be the last thing you do.

They slowly made their way through dense forest and at one-point Tom started to feel a little creeped out, and also frustrated at how long it had taken. Each time he asked Jose how much further the old man simply pointed in the direction they were heading. But eventually after an hour or so they came to a clearing and Jose pointed down the valley to another smaller clearing which contained several log cabins.

"You go," urged Jose, and so Tom reluctantly followed the instructions and started to make his way down the steep hill to the clearing. When he looked back Jose was gone.

As Tom had walked down the valley towards the cabins, he noticed a man come from outside and look up at him. Soon after several others came out from the cabins until a small group of nine or ten people waited. As Tom got closer, he started to recognise the first man that had come out; it was Odin. Tom had felt a wave of emotion crash over him and as he got even closer, he could see Odin smile and then wave. Tom had waved back and before he knew it the two men were embracing.

After the emotional meeting, Tom had been allocated a cabin and a bed and Odin asked all the people to join him outside. They sat down around a fire pit, and Odin explained that they had all been chosen to be agents for the Network, and this was their secret training camp. They had all gone through their own experiences that had brought them to this point.

The training would be over the next three months and they will live there on the camp unless specified. Training would be given by special forces trainers and would be gruelling and intense to the point where it is designed to grind a person down and break them. Not all the people in the group would make it and they are free to leave at any time. Nobody was being held there and that if the wanted to leave before the training started, they could. Nobody left at that point.

But before that, as the evening had started creating a pink and orange glow across the dense green mountainside, Odin lit the fire and over food and strong coffee it was their turn to tell their stories. Odin asked them to tell the group their name and their story, with as much or as little detail as possible. It had then suddenly occurred to Tom that these people were angels. Just like him. And they were all here for the exact same reason as him. He wasn't alone. Now it was palpable, now Tom understood more clearly than ever.

He had obviously been in contact with the people who acted as his 'parent'; like Sandra and Joe and Michael. And people who had delivered stuff to him and driven him from place to place. But to be sitting in a group of people that were angels. Portals that The Order had used. People just like him who had experienced the same as him. It made him feel the most clarity that he had ever felt in his life. The Network suddenly felt very real.

As each person had introduced themselves and started their story Tom felt more and more comfortable. As details came out Tom realised that during his worst periods, when he was drinking heavily and questioning his sanity others were doing the same. The weird coincidences, the paranoia, the dreams, it was the same for everyone with varying degrees of detail. Some members of the group were less confident than others and Odin had to prompt them on details where he had been involved. Others at some points broke down and had to consoled and supported by the group. Some of the group, like Tom, had seen violence and loved ones hurt or killed. Some hadn't seen anyone in their family for years.

When it got to Tom, he took a deep breath and decided to tell every tiny detail. Odin had told them that they had no time limit and to take as long as they want, so Tom did. As he spoke, he could feel the group getting closer and hanging on his words. He felt they understood his feelings and emotions and as he continued, he could feel himself being liberated and healed in some way. He spoke for about an hour and as he said the final words of the story about his journey with Jose from Portland to this point, he broke down. The group, some of them in tears, came to him and held him and supported him. It was exactly what Tom needed and he suddenly felt the strongest infinity to a group of people that he had ever felt in his life.

By the end of the night the group, who four hours previously were just strangers, were now a close knit and strongly bonded family. The whole process of telling their stories had been the help they all needed. That night Tom went to his cabin bed and had the best sleep he had had in for as long as he could remember.

The next morning they ate breakfast and Odin, in his usual way, made his exit with little fanfare. He simply said to the group he was leaving, and they would be under the supervision of the trainers who had arrived at the camp that morning. As Odin walked up the hill away from the camp Tom felt sad and, once again, as though he wanted to go with Odin. Tom felt others in the group whose stories had involved Odin almost feeling the same way. As Odin left Tom felt another hole appear in his life.

But he had had no time for lingering emotion. No sooner had Odin left, the trainers had made it clear that the honeymoon was over and the next 13-14 weeks will be the worst of their life. It was their intention to see that nobody made it through. It had been a harsh introduction, but the group realised that the trainers were not there to make friends. They had a job to do and it was clear to Tom that becoming an agent for The Network was not going to be easy. And the trainers kept to their word. Out in that harsh wilderness day by day they put the group through hell.

At first the training involved physical exertion. Hiking for miles each day, climbing, swimming, abseiling. Sleeping rough in the thick forest in the cold and dark and then awoken with a 10-mile hike. After a week Tom could feel the strain and he knew others were struggling. They had little rest back at camp and some nights, just when the group had started to fall to sleep, they were awoken with a shout and torches and taken outside into the cold for a physical punishment designed to break a person into submission.

Much of what they were doing at that time was purely fitness and land navigation. Conducted day and night with heavy equipment, in varied weather conditions, in rough, hilly and mountainous terrain. Some sessions had time limits and they were either individual or split into teams. They had to complete obstacle course runs, team events including log pulls and transferring heavy loads.

After the first week, one morning, Tom had noticed two of the group, Alex and Lucy, were no longer there. It had obviously been too much for them and they had given in. Nothing was announced formally, but one of the group had asked a trainer where they had gone. only to be told, "Don't worry about them. Don't think about failure".
Tom did not think any less of them as he felt the same. He was low in mood and physical energy. He looked and felt gaunt and was starting to question what he was doing in that place. But he had known this was what the training was designed to do. He also remembered what he had already come through. The mental exertion of his ordeal with The Order made him realise he must have what it takes. And as week three morphed into week four he felt a change. He felt a stark focus suddenly hit him that whilst the physical exertion of the training didn't become easier, he was doing things without thinking of the physical toll it was taking on him.

5am and out for a two-mile hike followed by a mile swim. He would just do it. Woken at 2am and outside for an hour of high intensity training in freezing conditions. He would just do it. No thought and no consequences to mind. He felt almost robotic in his approach and it was then he realised that he did have what it takes.

After six weeks there were only five of the original nine left. Four had not been able to take it. But the smaller group had grown close and Tom had grown especially close to Laura, whose story was a heart-breaking tale that resulted in her seeing her mum and dad killed by The Order. Her story had really resonated with Tom as it was possibly the saddest and most violent and had really hit home to him of the brutality of The Order.

As the weeks progressed the training became more technical. They were introduced to firearms, small handguns at first, and they would sit for hours opening the weapon, loading it, understanding the make-up of the weapon, the chamber, the ammunition and how to keep the weapon working efficiently. Then firing the guns. At first close range and then further away. Suddenly Tom felt competent holding and using a handgun. Then larger automatic rifles were introduced. Eventually each day they held and used a variety of firearms and Tom saw himself and the rest of the group becoming more confident and efficient each day.

The training then progressed further into knife and blade skills, hunting, orienteering and map reading, survival field craft, techniques of evasion, resistance to interrogation, resolution skills, recovery planning and tactics. Hand to hand combat and driving skills. They were taken to various points, tens of miles away from camp and just left. Using all they had learned and their basic survival instincts they had to get back on their own.

After 10 weeks at the training camp Tom felt like a completely different person. His personality was still Tom, but he felt as though the old Tom was no longer a person and a new Tom had been created. His inner toughness was almost unbreakable. He knew that whatever the trainers put in his way he would get through it. His emotions were in check and he felt a calm assurance in everything he did. His outer toughness was obvious. His body had taken on a new physicality. Lean and wired, Tom felt like he was made of granite. He had altered mentally and physically and realised then that the training had created an agent for The Network. All of them had gone through a metamorphosis and when Tom looked at himself and the remaining 4 group members, he saw people that were barely recognisable to the ones that arrived at the camp so long ago.

As the training had moved into its fourth month the weather became too cold and harsh to bear. October came to an end and November sent a freezing, brutal wind into the valley and the trainers had notified them the training would soon be completed and they would be away from this place.

The forest had slowly started going into hibernation and in a matter of days the crisp, bright oranges and yellows were replaced with sleek silvers and whites, and each morning was met with biting cold. The training was difficult in these conditions and, again, Tom had to dig deep and use all of his physical and mental toughness to get through. Then eventually after 13 weeks the trainers had told them they were ready.

The group were taken out of the forest and to a cabin nearer to civilisation. From there they were told they had half an hour to prepare for their onward journey to their respective new settlement locations.

Tom was told he would be taken down the west coast to San Francisco. He was handed a bag which contained his clothes, from the day he took them off. He got into his civilian clothes and sat and waited for his ride. As the other group members prepared and were given their instructions, Tom wondered if he would ever see any of them again. Without even thinking he stood up and had said.
"Well, I guess this is it?".

With that, the same thing suddenly dawned on the other members and they all looked at each other. It had been an emotional farewell, Tom was especially emotional at saying goodbye to Laura who, he had realised weeks before that day, he had feelings for. But, as was always the case with The Network, the slick efficiency got in the way of emotion, and Tom heard his name called and was quickly ushered outside, where he saw Jose in his old yellow Chevy waiting for him.

Chapter 42

Tom looked out of his apartment window at the Golden Gate Bridge, off in the distance. A haze of light cloud drifted slowly as it brushed one of the red towers. It was a calm, warm summer evening and he breathed in the fresh sea air from outside that was gently blowing across the bay.

A cool gust flowed through his window and the curtains fluttered, giving temporary relief from the warm end to the day. Boats of all different type and size filled the bay and the smell of freshly cooked sea food was drifting through the neighbourhood, carried by the gentle breeze. San Francisco was a wonderful place and he felt comfortable and happy.

The journey in Jose's old yellow Chevy from the wilderness of the North to San Francisco was now 3 weeks ago. Tom had settled well and was very much enjoying being here. He had always wanted to visit San Francisco and, whilst he admitted to himself that the circumstances in doing so were a little extreme, he was making the most of it and had found the few weeks since the training finished the most settled and enjoyable of his new life.

Tom took another sip of coffee and opened a slim folder on his desk. Inside were documents which had been delivered by a mailer two days ago. Tom had read all of the information countless times. He then slipped out, from within the documents, a photograph of a young girl. Her name was Debbie and she was 18 years old. She was very pretty and looked innocent and as though she had not a care in the world. That she had a wonderful future ahead of her. Tom had been advised that her brother had contacted The Network and wanted her removed and hid away from The Order.

Tom knew that what he was about to do meant there would be no going back. He realised how important he now was to the young girl in the photograph. He remembered how confused he felt. The paranoia and the feelings of being alone. The fear and loss of trust for people who he had close to him. The fighting with his own mind, wondering if he was going insane.

He knew, therefore, that once this first contact was made that was it. He was in and, once you were in, that was it. You could not walk away, and Tom was determined not to let anyone down. He had taken this responsibility on and he knew that he would not shirk it and would give his all in fulfilling it. He not only needed to get her away but also to be there for her when she finds out that any future or plans she had would now no longer be.

On the corner of the photo was a small piece of paper clipped to it which had a phone number written on it. Tom slowly entered the number into his phone and created a new message:

'Debbie. Do not reply to this text and do not call the number. You are in danger. I can help you. Remain calm. Get to a safe place. We must meet soon. I will text again at 9pm tonight. Do not trust anybody. Tom'

He took a deep breath and then pressed send.

Printed in Great Britain
by Amazon

41500796R00199